Praise for MACHO SLUTS

"Califia seeks to buil[d] ... feminist utopia that offers, at ... [possib]le erotic exploration." —*San Francisco Sentinel*

■■

"Intriguing, erotic, exhilarating, and unnerving. The sheer power of Califia's work is undeniable." —*Bay Area Reporter*

■■

"*Macho Sluts* will make you re-think what you thought you knew about lesbian sex or the lesbian life-style. *Macho Sluts* is ground-breaking." —*Windy City Times*

■■

"Now here's something entirely different. Masterful. Controversial." —*Edge* (Los Angeles)

■■

"Decadent, sexy, and very, very thrilling." —*Seattle Gay News*

■■

"Intense and unrelenting. Califia is a bad girl on a joy ride through taboo territory." —*Coming Up*

■■

"Califia's characters are vivid and penetratingly alive." —*The Advocate*

■■

"*Macho Sluts* is a walk on the wild side, a springboard into dizzying sexual taboos." —*Gay Community News*

MELTING POINT

by

PAT CALIFIA

Boston ▪ Alyson Publications, Inc.

Typeset and printed in the United States of America.

This is a paperback original from Alyson Publications, Inc.,
P.O. Box 4371, Los Angeles, CA 90078.

Distributed in England by Central Books, Ltd.,
99 Wallis Road, London E9 5LN, England.

Distributed in Australia by Bulldog Books,
P.O. Box 155, Broadway, N.S.W. 2007, Australia.

First edition: June 1993

2 4 5 3

ISBN 1-55583-162-1

CONTENTS

ACKNOWLEDGMENTS

I'd like to thank those who read earlier versions of some of these stories and gave me valuable comments — Dorothy Allison, Beth Brown, Jan Brown, Peter Cole, J.C. Collins, "Doctor D," Jesse Merril, Carol Queen, Rachael, Sky Renfro, Wendell Ricketts, and Amy Scholder. For those who were patient enough to read the entire manuscript, many, many thanks to Bryn Austin, Wendy Chapkis, Mike Hernandez, Michael Shively, Wickie Stamps, Robin Sweeney, and Abby Tallmer. If I've forgotten anybody, I apologize. None of the people mentioned here necessarily approve of my attitude or this book — all shortcomings and transgressions are most emphatically my own.

I also want to thank all the owners of gay and feminist bookstores who choose to carry my work and other controversial sexually explicit literature. Such a decision can be costly, but it enriches our culture and keeps our politics lively and our bedrooms busy. Without the venue you so courageously provide, there would be no reason for me to write (or for Alyson to publish) this book.

This book is for Rob—
Whose melting point
Is just high enough.

B*i*g *G*ir**L**s

■■

Once there was a bar called Jax. If the drag queens haven't taken it over or the vice squad hasn't closed it down, it's probably still there, giving decent lesbians a bad name.

Jax was in a strange part of town. The neighborhood wasn't bad, exactly. When middle-class white people call a neighborhood "bad," they mean poor black people live there, and Jax was not situated in a residential neighborhood. It was in the middle of an industrial zone full of warehouses, produce wholesalers, sheet metal shops, places where you could rent forklifts or buy several tons of green coffee beans, a recycling center, some union halls, a marina, and a couple of freeway on-ramps. There were also a few oddball shops whose owners couldn't find affordable space elsewhere and whose customers wanted their unique merchandise enough to make the trek — an art gallery that was so progressive, the vice squad attended its openings; a store that sold bones (animal and human) and lizards, turtles, and tropical snakes; a tattoo parlor; and an excellent Italian restaurant.

This location was part of what made it possible for Jax to be a cross between a seventies gay male leather-bar-with-back-room and a fifties working-class dive for dykes. Jax could never have stayed open in the thin strip of the barrio that white dykes were busy gentrifying because those women didn't drink enough (in public, anyway) to keep up payments on the lease. If Jax had been located closer to downtown, where the gay bikers and other butch thangs in black cowhide tried to keep eros alive despite AIDS and the Alcoholic Beverage Commission, the men would have squeezed out the women. Anywhere else in town, the owner would have catered to a straight clientele and made a hell of a lot more money. But here, he was content to have any customers at all, even if they didn't look anything like the Lusty Ladies of Lesbos who almost let their tongues touch on the cover of his favorite X-rated video.

This part of town was, however, surrounded by bad neighborhoods, so cabdrivers didn't like to go there. A gypsy cab company called Black Pearl serviced the area. Black Pearl hired mostly Rastamen and an occasional dreadlocked sister. The dented, crippled cabs were redolent with ropy green smoke, and the drivers didn't care what the oddly dressed women in the backseat got up to as long as they didn't bitch about how long it took to get them home. A city bus came within four blocks of Jax, but it stopped only every two hours or so.

From the row of Hondas, Nortons, Yamahas, Beamers, Kawasakis, and the rare Harley parked outside, you'd think everybody got to Jax on a motorcycle. But on any Friday or Saturday night, the place was too jammed for that to be possible. When the image-conscious drove a car to Jax, they parked it a block away and evaded questions about their mode of transportation. Four-wheelers and pickup trucks were the only things with steering wheels that were butch enough to get parked within sight of the bar's front door.

A few skinny, tattooed punk girls — artists, strippers, welfare mothers, musicians, dealers — who had lofts in the neighborhood just walked to the bar. Black dykes from the shell-shocked parts of town around Jax also turned up regularly, and they formed their own coterie within the rest of the bar's kinky, mostly white clientele. They appreciated the intense sexuality of the white girls, recognized it as a valid reason for being there, but envied the excesses some of them committed with their appearance and disapproved of the thoughtless way they squandered their resources. Many of the white girls who frequented Jax lived on the edge, but if their survival was really threatened, they had somebody to call for a plane ticket home to Orange County or Long Island. They did not know what it means to live without that safety net.

The black women at Jax were mostly into fifties-style butch-femme, but a few of them were there because they were interested in leather or white girls or both. And not all of the butch-femme couples were necessarily vanilla. They just didn't put their stuff out where everybody could take a look. Even in a dyke bar, some things remain your private business.

The sex workers — strippers, phone sex operators, professional dominants and submissives, call girls, and hookers — held the whole mix together. They were the sharpest dressers, the ones who spent the most money, and the white ones were the only Caucasian women who didn't hesitate to cross the color line when they wanted to buy somebody a drink or find a dancing partner. They did this partly because their work rewarded them for being bold and aggressive hussies, and partly because black dykes gave you less shit about being a whore. In their capacity as outcasts and go-betweens, they were the first ones to greet newcomers, loan people money, or perform at benefits, and they knew everybody's secrets. They stopped at least as many fights as they started and reunited as many estranged couples as they blew apart.

The regulars — women who showed up every weekend and at least once during the week — were another important social caste at Jax. The regulars had certain privileges — playing dice with Kat or Lolly, the bartenders, occasionally getting to stash a coat or a purse behind the bar, a free drink when business was slow, running a bit of a tab. One of them might be drafted to fill in behind the bar if Kat or Lolly called in sick, or get screamed at to please clean off some tables and bring the empties up front when there was an insane, crushing crowd. Kat and Lolly looked the other way if they saw one of the regulars slipping little white paper envelopes under the tables in return for a few folded bills. What the fuck, the State Liquor Authority never came here anyway. (The owner had a Sicilian surname.) In addition, the regulars got first crack at interesting newcomers. The bartenders usually didn't trick with anybody the regulars hadn't screened first.

Other women besides Kat and Lolly sometimes used the soda gun or shoved swizzle sticks into mixed drinks, but they came and went faster than the pretzels. Kat and Lolly seemed as much a part of Jax as the scratches on the floor or the scorched wallpaper in the men's room. They were big girls, picked for their popularity and their ability to run roughshod over a crowd that got rowdy even for a bunch of drunk and horny lesbians. The pay wasn't great, but the tips could be good. When push came to shove, Kat and Lolly knew they were lucky to have a job that let them look the way the Goddess made them. It would have taken more than a make-over from *Cosmopolitan* to turn either of them into anything other than bulldaggers. So if the tips didn't stretch their wages enough to make ends meet, the bartenders concentrated on tail. Sex is never free, but at Jax, women didn't have to pay cash.

Lolly was at that stage in a slightly older bar dyke's life when she forgets exactly how many anorexic, pink-haired girls with eight earrings she's slept with. She was kind of afraid to admit, even to herself, that she couldn't even remember exactly how many of them she'd lived with. Did it really matter? Every single time, it was true love. Lolly had short black hair she kept in a DA and a few crude tattoos done in india ink at juvenile hall. She couldn't hold her liquor, so she let customers who insisted buy her a drink out of her own bottle, specially labeled, which Kat filled with iced tea just before they opened.

When Lolly fell off the wagon, she fell hard. She cleaned out the till, picked the best-looking woman in the place, hollered, "Somebody ought to treat you right, sweet thing," carried her out bodily, perched her on the back of her bike, and laid scratch out of there to go on a binge that didn't end until the money had all been spent on bad booze and sleazy lingerie, and Lolly's new mama could hardly walk to the bathroom.

In her younger days, Lolly had extended these benders by shooting up speed. She would supplement her cash flow by soliciting contributions with a .38 from gas stations and convenience stores. But she found out that prison time goes even more slowly than juvie, and the thrill of having a crude design etched into her body with a sewing needle had disappeared with adolescence. Being held in the daddy tank with the other diesels was not her idea of a good time.

Now she puts the brakes on before that can happen. She picks a fight with the "sweet thing," tosses her out, throws all the ripped and soiled lingerie she can lay her hands on after her, and comes crawling back to Jax just before it's time to open, bitching about her hangover and ready to lick Kat's boots in public ("Shit, I'll even kiss your butthole, buddy!") for covering up for her. Occasionally, the sweet thing puts her pretty finger to the wind and splits first, usually after hacking up her erstwhile daddy's dick.

Lolly had been doing pretty much the same thing for (ahem) years, but she was still convinced that someday the love of one good woman was going to save, redeem, and reform her. "Too bad you can't sing," Kat jeered at her. "You're just a country-western singer who missed her calling, girl. You better come to Jesus or just admit you're nothing but a run-around tramp with a military haircut. Too bad you can't sell all those thirty-day chips back to the AA store, honey. You'd have enough money to retire."

Kat, a six-foot-tall, broad-shouldered woman with big hands, feet, hips, and heart, and blonde hair she shaved herself with poodle clippers, was more complicated. She was too young to be a straightforward bar butch. Oh, every now and then, she got an itch for some wildcat in a leather miniskirt and spandex leotard and handed Lolly her bar towel so she could take Miss Lucky out the back way. There was a sort of patio out there, a fenced-in place with a locked gate where Kat and Lolly left their bikes. She liked to stick her tongue down the drunk girl's throat, pull her top down and push her skirt up, and destroy as much underwear as necessary to get access to her cunt. Kat wasn't much good at foreplay. If being dragged outside with Kat's big paws around her throat wasn't enough to make a girl's pussy overflow, she was liable to find herself slinking back inside, unscathed and unsatisfied. The clientele at Jax kept track of such things.

Kat fucked hard when these frenzies took her. She wanted all the way in, right fucking now. And she wanted them to stand up for it, no matter how tall their heels were. Those pretty girls shimmied on Kat's fist and screamed loud enough to be heard inside over the jukebox and the pinball machines and the video games, the crack of pool balls and the beehive hum of a hundred women jammed in denim-crotch-to-leather-clad-butt, satin-cleavage-to-leather-jacket-lapel, talking about everything but their jones and usually drinking too much to do anything about it anyway.

One of these prize felines, an unusually slender dancer by the name of Sage, who floated around the bar on heels high enough to be illegal, had long hair bleached to white and a meaner attitude than most. Once spirited outside, she took the intentionally quick and brutal fist without complaint, and proceeded to walk up Kat's thighs, fucking herself while she stuck her tongue out at the big woman whose quads were being tenderized by her steel-tipped heels. "Show me everything you got," she panted. "Show me something I haven't had before. Do you think you can do anything to me I haven't done to myself already? Damage is my middle name." And she showed Kat the scars on her arms. "Lick them," she demanded. "See if you can lick them off me, big girl."

That bitch got laid out on the seat of Kat's bike and fucked proper, at leisure, until the bartender was completely wrung out and hoarse, and both of her hands were as wrinkled as prunes. The mighty sounds of impact and thankful flesh awed the whole bar into silence. Kat's forearms were so sore from satisfying the white-haired, sharp-hipped dancer that she let people pour their own beers the rest of the night.

After that, she was Lady Sage as far as Kat was concerned. She wouldn't mind having at that fierce little witch again sometime, if she ever showed up wearing the right outfit and the moon was full. But the rest of them she forgot as soon as she let them fall to the concrete. The ones who tried to sit on her boot and suck on her 501s got kicked aside. The last thing Kat wanted after messing somebody up and making her come a hundred times was to get messed up herself. "Gotta get back to work," she would grumble, if she said anything at all.

These quasi-consensual episodes gave her a sort of high, made her feel big and mean and good-looking, and confirmed her position at the top of the fuck circuit in Jax. But it also left the taste of something missing in the back of her throat, and it was such a lonely and bitter flavor, she couldn't imagine making a whole meal of it by taking one of these fancy sluts home to leave her hair in Kat's sink, her nylons under the bed, and the dirty dishes from her attempt to prove she was a good cook piled up in the sink for Guess Who to wash.

Time was when Kat had lived with girls who were a bit like her fuck-bunnies, although a little less wild. She took lovers who were legal secretaries or cocktail waitresses, while she had a dirty job someplace working with men who were usually shorter than she was and never as good at keeping the machines running. If it had an engine, Kat had an immediate, intuitive understanding of how it worked. Broken machines seemed to tell her what was the matter, like old ladies complaining to their doctor, and her capable hands always made it right.

When Kat went home, whichever of these girls she was currently living with would immediately tell her to wash up. The bathroom was always full of nail brushes and Lava soap, and there was a can of mineral spirits or kerosene underneath the sink. One of them had even said to her, over the dinner which Kat had cooked, "For heaven's sake, you never get clean. Can't you wear gloves at work?"

Kat had helped her move out a week later. The bitch (by then, Kat had taken to calling them bitches when they weren't around) wound up with an ambitious and successful feminist attorney who never came home in time for dinner and had beautifully kept hands with long, pearl pink nails. Every time Kat thought of those sexually disabling claws, she smiled and figured there was a little justice in this world.

These straitlaced femmes loved Kat for what she did to them in bed, and for what they hoped she would become after they got her to go back to school. Most of them thought she was not as bright as they were — overlooking the pile of technical journals on her side of the bed, the books by women authors she was always reading, and her subscription to the Sunday *New York Times*. It wasn't hard, usually, for Kat to find out how to make a woman's toes curl and her face get red. She liked seeing her prim lovers rip up the sheets. But they never seemed to be able to perform the same kind of divination for her. Usually they rolled over between her legs and expected ten minutes of mouth-work to send her to the moon. She wouldn't stand for that. So they would roll away and express some sympathy about her being a stone butch, voice some hope that she would "work on it," and fall asleep.

None of these girls was bad-looking. Kat liked fine, presentable women with good legs and pretty faces. When she went out to dinner with them or took them shopping, they made an obvious couple and a striking one. She would look impassively at the men who noticed her partner and feel grim satisfaction when they dropped their eyes and took their prick energy elsewhere. Being big had its advantages.

She had an aptitude for violence, but she wasn't addicted to it. Fighting hadn't been much fun for Kat since she got shot. She was just minding her own business, walking down to the corner store, when the barrel of a gun came out of the window of a passing car, and her shoulder stung. It didn't hurt at all. Passersby had to force her to lie down on the grass and wait for an ambulance. At the hospital, they told her she was lucky — the bullet barely missed an artery.

Having a chunk of lead put in you for no good reason certainly reminded you of your own mortality. After that, Kat lost her patience with two-faced foxes who got themselves hot by setting up two butches to fight over them. If you got killed by hitting your head on a table or having a broken bottle rammed into your throat, you'd be just as dead as a crumpled body in some neo-Nazi's crosshairs. Why should she assault another butch, another woman who was humiliated and frustrated by the simple desire she felt for her own kind, unless the woman was out for her blood or didn't want to pay for her drugs?

When she left her last femme behind, Kat found herself making this speech: "I never let you doubt the fact that I love you. I always held you and defended you. But how do I know that I am loved? Who holds me? Who defends me?" Her ex said impatiently, "How am I supposed to get to work every day if you keep the car?"

Kat couldn't imagine having to make that speech to another butch. She became what she called "a faggot" — a butch who was interested in other butches. She figured there weren't too many vantage points for spotting rough trade better than her post behind the bar at Jax. While she mixed drinks and measured out shots, she kept one eye open for women who rolled their own cigarettes, women who worked out or had a belt in karate, women who rebuilt their own carburetors and put in their own transmissions, women cops or truck drivers, women who carried knives and shot straight, women who had been in the service, women who had bulging arms and calloused hands and stood tall.

It was a preference that a lot of people — including Lolly — didn't understand. "You're some queer kind of queer," Lolly once said to her best, maybe only, friend. "Those kinda girls aren't gonna be interested in you. Whatchoo gonna do anyway, bump pussies?"

"You think that doesn't work?" Kat said, smiling, and put her cigarette out on Lolly's left hand. Lolly yelped and jumped around like she'd been napalmed. "Shit," Kat swore, "I'm sorry, good buddy. I'm gettin' old and blind. Gotta quit drinkin' that sterno. I was aiming for your twat."

It was none of Lolly's business what she did with other big girls. Not that Lolly wouldn't understand, in her gut, what Kat's kinks were all about. Lolly was just down on sex in general these days. The last joyride baby had left deep, angry red scratches on Lolly's cheek, cut her leather jacket into fabric-sample swatches, and broken her heart so completely that Lolly was probably going to be able to stay sober till spring while she nursed on the pain of it. Kat thought the pain of it was the whole point. But Lolly saw her own suffering as an act of God, a Greek tragedy, not as a self-inflicted ritual. Kat thought simple sexual masochism had a lot more dignity. And she honestly didn't think she could listen to a sermon about the healing power of true love without punching Lolly out. So she kept quiet and let it alone.

A baby butch or two sometimes came into Jax, looking for a daddy. If Kat was in the mood, she might oblige. If you had muscles, she liked to see them under stress, in restraint, and covered with the kind of sweat you break out in when you're scared you can't take it and don't really have a choice. The young studs who weren't stupid or resentful sometimes got a little of their own back. Making them satisfy her was another kind of workout Kat liked to put them through. But receiving sexual service — even honest, enthusiastic homage from the fist and shoulder of a delighted and respectful "boy" — wasn't what she really wanted.

When you are a big girl, you have to prove yourself over and over again. You go out to buy groceries and some asshole has to challenge your right to exist. You try to order a beer and another asshole won't let you drink it before you take his face off. Try and get back to your beer, and you have a whole house to clean. Men are the worst, but women are often not much better. You go to somebody's house for dinner, and she wants you to move the refrigerator, fix the washing machine, and insulate the attic. If you spend the night, you better mow the lawn in the morning. If there's something dangerous, exhausting, or dirty to do, you are supposed to volunteer. And the little women seem to think those jobs don't scare you, hurt you, or wear you out if you're big. If you can't handle it, that just goes to show you aren't as bad as you look.

Given how angry that made her, Kat would be damned if she could understand why she had an erotic appetite for being put to work, terrorized, tortured, and fucked until her ears bled. *But if we wait for things to make sense,* she told herself, *the closest we'll come to having sex is standing around with our thumbs up our asses.* Every now and then some big, bad, mean woman would come along who would look her up and down, like what she saw, and take it. When that happened, Kat didn't care if there were cameras rolling and every eye in the place was trained on her ass. She would have crawled over broken glass to follow a tall, authoritative woman out the door, and if some fool didn't recognize good luck and guts when she saw them, well, life's a bitch and then you die.

None of this prepared her for meeting somebody who was extremely mean, imperious enough to be the Empress of the Amazon Nation, and ... short.

Granted, it had been a while since a superwoman had stalked up to the bar and slapped Kat with her gloves or poured beer all over her. So, Kat told herself, appetite, denial, and the blazing scream of the full moon's wide-open mouth were surely responsible for the weakness in her knees and the buzzing puddle in her leather pants when she heard a slap and identified the party who was responsible.

She was playing liar's dice with a misspent youth named Mick who put too much grease in her hair and made jokes about sucking dick in the boys' bars to keep gas in her bike at the end of the month. It was a Saturday, but it was pretty early, so it wasn't too crowded to see everybody who was there and what they were doing. Mick drank too much, and Kat told herself that penny-ante gambling with the child wasn't going to make her get sober. Right now she was swilling tequila because she was crushed out on Kat, and Kat wouldn't take her home again.

Should she, Kat wondered, give Mick another chance? Fuck, no! The last time she'd broken one of Kat's leather bondage cuffs, and in the morning she'd sneaked out and removed her own distributor cap so she'd have an excuse not to leave. She wouldn't say "sir," she couldn't take a decent beating, and she wore cheap men's cologne that gave Kat a migraine. Still, she was awful young to be after her own liver in such a serious way. What if she spun out on the way home? Mick never wore a helmet. Kat sucked in her cheeks and thought, *Sometimes I'd rather work at the SPCA.*

She was on the brink of taking the chain off her boot and dropping it between them to see if Mick could come up with an interesting, or at least a respectful, response when that slap rang through the bar, and somebody started choking and apologizing. There are a few noises that get you instantly hot if you're a perv — the roar of a Harley that's just been stomped into life, a beer bottle breaking on the brick corner of a building, a .45 Magnum going off like a cannon, the deceptively soft thud of a slim arrow hitting the bull's-eye, metal striking sparks off of metal as a barbell hits its stand, a cold switchblade sliding open, ready to do more evil than a woman's sharp tongue, a bullwhip cracking from the stress of going faster than the speed of sound, a kicked-over table loaded with glassware, and a face getting slapped. You have about as much control over your whole body's response — goosebumps, sweaty palms, dry throat, and hard clit — to a moment like this as a piece of steel has over its own melting point.

Kat slammed her dice down on the bar and panned the crowd. She couldn't tell who had done it. Nobody looked the part. Then this four-eyed, redheaded pipsqueak in leather put one hand on her hip and drawled, "Who told you to sit down, snot-face?"

This kid was talking to somebody Kat recognized but couldn't put a name on — a brown-haired, brown-eyed, sweet-faced jock who moved slow and smiled whenever she was confused, which must have been most of the time because she always looked happy. Wasn't she on the softball team for one of the other women's bars, the largest one, the one in the barrio that played nothing but disco and salsa? She hadn't been in here before, but then, neither had that myopic dwarf dressed up in dead cow. Kat snorted. She wasn't partial to redheaded women.

"I'm a winner! I beat you!" Mick was crowing.

"Not on the best day of your life," Kat said under her breath, and shoved all the pennies on the bar into her opponent's lap. "Go play on the freeway, Mick," she said in a normal tone of voice, and used one hand to move the bad boy out of her line of sight. This needed keeping track of. There might be a fight. It'd be difficult to keep Lolly from breaking it up before the impudent squirt got her epaulets twisted off.

But there wasn't a fight. The woman who had gotten slapped was pulling out a chair. For her trouble, she got slapped again. "Don't try to buy your way out of this by making meaningless gestures," the diminutive domme sneered. "Apologize!"

When Artie — yeah, that was her name, Artie — went down on both knees, went down on her *face*, and told the floor she was sorry, Kat's jaw dropped so hard she almost hurt herself. Artie was wearing tight, very faded jeans, and Kat wished with all her heart the seam down the middle of that muscular butt would split wide open. By the time she yanked herself out of this vision, the tiny redhead was putting her hand in Artie's mouth — all of it — and Artie's eyes were closed in bliss. My God, how could a whole hand — well, if you had hands that small, they probably fit just about anywhere.

Kat blushed. So what? You probably couldn't hardly feel a paw that tiny anyway. (But a whole hand that's put inside an orifice, say, up the ass, just for example — not that Kat knew anybody who fantasized about such a thing — even if it was a small hand, would probably feel much more intense than a big hand that couldn't get all the way in. Hmm? Shit, no!)

In the back of the bar, where the green oasis of the pool table floated under a fake Tiffany lamp, one of the reigning mocha divas rocked herself out of her latest conquest's lap. Her name was

Chambray, and she was wearing a knee-length dress made out of long red fringe. She now proceeded to shake those fringes out, a maneuver that created a small fan club which wistfully maintained a respectful distance because of Chambray's proximity to the Shark. You don't try to steal somebody's woman if she's recently walked out of the bar with half your paycheck in her pocket. You think about it, of course, but then you bend over the table and work on your game.

Shark had successfully defended her place at the pool table against a string of seven challengers before Chambray's scarlet dress and slim hips lured her away. "If I knew you were going to take off so fast, I wouldn't have thrown the game," she grumbled. "Not that it's any pleasure to kick her ass around the table," she added, and grimaced at Mick.

That worthy youth was using too much elbow to chalk up her cue and grinning idiotically at a plump blonde girl in a leopardskin Lycra dress who had brought her own cue, which broke down into three parts so it could be carried around in a zippered canvas bag that bore the Uzi logo. This zaftig wench was about to take exactly as many shots as there were balls to clear the table, and then teach Mick the meaning of good sportsmanship. As usual, Mick was too busy perfecting her 'do with a pocket comb to see the sucker punch coming. If you want to grow up to be a wise old stone butch, you got to beware of femmes who tilt their adorable little hats to the left.

Chambray ran her fingertips over Shark's high Cherokee cheekbones. "Gotta make my rounds," she sighed. "Make myself some money, take you out to an all-night diner where you can sate your ap-pe-tite." She leaned forward until her breasts were almost entirely visible, and Shark's hands came up to greet them. Chambray had anticipated this, and caught her by the wrists. She pushed the bold, brown hands down and away. "Keep it warm for me," she said, and briefly cupped Shark's crotch, then stalked off, throwing one molten parting glance over her shoulder.

The touch and the look went through Shark like a burning spear, and she resolved to keep nothing but her own hands in her lap until that fine, hard, round ass got planted there again. My Lord, that girl knew how to shake her — well! It was enough to make your clit poke a hole in your acid-washed jeans, and it was plenty good enough to wait for, yes it was!

Chambray took her time working her way to the bar, where she ordered a Remy Martin three times from Kat before she got it — in the wrong kind of glass — with a twist! "I'm gonna report you to the tavern guild," she laughed. "We ought to take up a collection and send you to one of those bartendin' schools I see advertised on matchbooks. What kind of brandy snifter is this supposed to be?"

Then she saw that Kat's eyes were glazed over, and if she'd had a sleeve, she would have laughed up it. Like the little shit-disturber she was, Chambray picked up the quarters in her change and headed for the jukebox. Kat had three favorite songs, and she punched up every one of them twice. It was music to be subverted by. Let that iceberg woman melt down both of her legs and fill her boots. She was pretty with her mouth open.

Somebody else had her mouth open, too. Artie was still on the floor, and the woman standing over her was twisting her fist slowly, working it just behind Artie's lips. Spit and mucus were dribbling out of Artie's mouth, and she was wringing her hands behind her back, where she'd been told to keep them. Every now and then she mewed a little when her nose got blocked up and made it hard for her to breathe. The redhead was hissing something at her, close up and private, and whatever she said made Artie rub her thighs together like she was trying to start a fire.

And me without my Polaroid camera, Chambray thought. *What a show! Go for it, girl, punch your fist right down that throat.* An itch spread from her fingers up to her elbow, an urge to feel wet flesh close around as much of her hand and arm as she could coax down over it. *How'm I going to go back to Shark in this kind of mood?* she scolded herself. *This is not at all what I been promisin' that champion. I wanted to kick my heels at the ceiling tonight, until five minutes ago. Well, shit, I am a first-place trophy myself and I better not forget it. Everybody wants to take Chambray home. On the top or on the bottom, I always win my race. If the Shark can't deal with it I always got my cab fare tucked in my garter.*

She sailed back to the pool table, dispensing enough merchandise along the way to keep her promise to take Shark out to dinner. Much as she liked seeing Kat's wide-stretched mouth tremble and one hand struggle with the other beneath the bar, she had fish of her own to fry.

Now the redhead had Artie up over one of the silly round tables and was taking off her belt. It was a long piece of leather made weighty with chrome studs. She didn't pull Artie's pants down. There was no need. The belt came down with enough impact to render a mere layer of denim quite meaningless.

Lolly pushed by Kat to help some women who had been waving money at her for so long they'd forgotten their orders. "Caught many flies?" she hissed, and trod on Kat's toes. Her coworker gave her a dazed look. Lolly sighed irritably. "Thought you swore off Quaaludes," she said, and drew a deep breath in preparation for preaching at length from her diaphragm about the evils of artificial stimulants.

Kat lurched into action before the sermon could be delivered. She came out from behind the bar, stumbled over to where the redhead had pinned Artie down on the table with a hand on the back of her neck and was still strapping the daylights out of her. She put a hand on the sleeve of the woman's jacket and said, "Hey—"

The small woman turned and threw off her hand — no, Kat corrected herself, she repelled it. It felt a little like grabbing an electrified cattle fence. Her eyes were gray, the color of fog, the color of ... steel? Her tongue had been sticking out, but it slid back into her mouth behind a pair of very pink lips, lips that tightened now into a thin line of disapproval. Kat almost blurted out an apology for touching her, then remembered that apologizing was what had gotten Artie into so much trouble.

"You gotta knock that off," she said instead, speaking too loudly and without taking counsel with her wiser self. "We don't allow that kinda stuff in here."

Reid looked around the crowded bar, taking her time, inviting Kat to look at the other patrons with her. Artie, confused by the absence of pain, said, "Reid?" Her voice was muffled, and the other women both ignored her, although Reid briefly squeezed the back of her neck.

Shark and Chambray were locked in a hard-core carnal embrace on the dance floor. Two of the other dancers, big women with enormous tits, had taken their shirts off. At one of the tables, a woman in a three-piece suit was getting a shotgun hit off a blimp-shaped joint from her date, who was wearing a sequined cocktail frock. At another table, three hookers in Cher wigs, halter-tops, miniskirts, fishnet hose, and high-heeled boots sat close together, kissing and fondling each other's breasts, while a fourth woman, on her knees under the table, went down on one of them. Her hands were busy underneath the other two women's skirts. Somebody in a baseball jacket was studiously cutting up coke on the jukebox. She lifted her head to protest when the two topless giantesses, who had stopped dancing and started struggling, bumped into the machine. She grabbed her mirror just in time to keep its contents from being scattered all over the floor as the giggling combatants crashed into the jukebox so hard they jarred the electrical connection loose.

Chambray shimmied over to the wall, pulling her dress down, and kicked the plug back in. The sudden return of the music was deafening. Flashing colored lights illuminated the loser's face as the victorious Sumo wrestler turned her over the glass and smacked her ass with a fist the size of a small ham. Meanwhile, the door of the ladies' room was shuddering as if somebody was taking a battering ram to it.

The lock broke, and it became clear that the battering ram was Mick, who flew through the abruptly opened door and sprawled on the floor, a sodden, sniveling mess. Her face was slathered up with lipstick, and she reeked of piss. "You can't do that to me!" she blubbered. The leopard-girl leaned on the splintered door frame, posing like a plump Jean Harlow. Then she pounced on Mick, took her under the shoulders, and threw her back into the bathroom. "If anybody has to take a leak for the next little while, you'd best use the alley," she smirked before she slammed the door shut again, and Mick began to wail in earnest.

"Oh?" Reid said, turning back to Kat. "Really? Exactly what is it that you don't allow here?"

The bartender barely heard her. Kat was lost in those eyes. The thick lenses distorted them, made them seem deep and enormous, all out of proportion to the other woman's face, like the huge, compound eyes of a bee. They were the color of the ocean in winter, an ocean that was brewing up a storm. Kat felt like somebody had arrested her mind and was patting it down. If she let this kid hold her gaze for one more second, Reid was going to know what she had eaten for breakfast and when she last changed her underwear.

"Well, uh—" *Jesus*, Kat thought, *I sound like some dumb buck private getting chewed out for calling his sergeant "sir."*

Reid shook her head and started to laugh. The laugh put goosebumps on the backs of Kat's hands and made her blush red as a baboon's behind. Nobody laughed at her. *Nobody.* Then the redhead put her little white hand in the middle of Kat's chest, right on the heart chakra, and pushed her away. "If you don't want to help me, get out of my way," she said, turned her back, and resumed taking care of business.

The push sent Kat onto the dance floor, into the arms of Chambray, who was grinding her butt back into the Shark's hungry pelvis. "You tryin' to join the space program?" the girl teased, wrapping her arms around the embarrassed bartender. "What's your hurry, sugar, don't I look good enough to spread on your sandwich?"

Kat let Chambray rock her and tug her around, and tried to regain her composure. That wasn't easy with Shark and Lolly both throwing lethal looks at her. When her breathing calmed down a bit, she made her excuses and got back to work. Things had gotten real busy — frantic, even. But damn, it was hard to make change and remember how to make a Bloody Mary when the crack of that belt kept wiping her mind clean.

She was about to announce that for the rest of the night, mixed drinks would be sold only by the pitcher when Reid dragged Artie off the table, pushed her onto all fours, and climbed atop her broad, bent back. She had wrapped her belt around Artie's head, and was using the two free ends like reins. "Crawl," she must have said, because that is what Artie did, through the entire crowd, toward the patio that Kat considered her personal fucking precinct.

Reid did have the courtesy to give Kat a mock salute as they passed. Then she gouged at Artie with her boots, and Kat saw the wicked flash of spurs. Maybe it was the belt that was stretching her lips wide, maybe it was endorphins, but Artie didn't make a sound of protest. She didn't balk or try to dislodge her rider. She just took Reid where she wanted to go, carrying her carefully — maybe even with pride.

At least out there Kat couldn't hear or see what went on. But some of the less-hung-up patrons were already clustering around the back door, which they kept open with a chair. "She's got a knife!" somebody yelped. Shark and Chambray looked at each other and laughed.

"Who let the tourist in?" Shark said contemptuously.

"You run a magnet through this place, it'll come out with more blades than a Swiss army knife," Chambray chuckled.

"One of my women don't need to carry her own protection," Shark scowled.

"Then you better stop messin' with black girls, honey. Ain't you heard we all carry razors in our shoes?"

"I hear you got a razor in your panties," Shark grinned.

"Is that what's keepin' you from getting your hand in there, you afraid I'll bite?"

Shark got both of Chambray's hands behind her back, and the lithe dancer twisted up against her as she peeled a triangle of wet red satin off her hips and rolled it down her long, muscular thighs. "Bite down, maybe," Shark said, her free hand doing teasing things under the fringed dress. "Talk back, definitely."

"You keep doing that, and I'm going to stop talking to you at all."

Shark laughed and kept on stroking her. Then Chambray said, dead serious, "Take me someplace where I can spread myself out for you," and she stopped laughing. It took her ten seconds to find their coats.

They left together and didn't come back. Kat didn't even see them leave. But she did notice that Reid and Artie didn't return. They must have gone over the fence and home — if the alley fish hadn't chewed them up into little pieces. By the time Jax closed, Kat had a headache that made her stagger. The neon beer signs behind the bar had been making her wince with pain. She had a nasty fight with Lolly about dividing their tips, which meant Lolly left without washing the rest of the glassware or telling her that the toilet had backed up. By the time she got the place locked up and was outside pulling on her gloves, Kat was snorting fire and brimstone.

There was a note on her bike, tucked between the seat and the gas tank. It was a phone number, written in large, shaky letters. She harrumphed, then folded it carefully and tucked it into her breast pocket. It wasn't until she got home and retrieved it for another look that she realized it had been written with a finger ... or with a knife, in blood. Ha ha. Some joke.

■■

Kat woke up in the middle of the night with a pounding headache, a throbbing bladder, and a telephone in one hand. In her other hand was the bloody number. What the fuck — what time was it? She couldn't call somebody now! Kat slammed down the receiver. She needed some aspirin and a catheter with a long tube. She tucked the note carefully under one of the phone's rubber feet, then headed for the bathroom, shuffling so she wouldn't accidentally step on one of Jezebel's kittens.

The next morning, she had a sore throat, a stuffy head, and felt as bad as the other guy usually looked. She picked up Jezebel, who had come up onto the bed to avoid the kittens she was weaning, and demanded, "What did you do, beat me up all night long?"

The tortoiseshell cat made an indignant noise that Kat interpreted as meaning, "I hope the fact that you are ill does not mean you intend to neglect my very important feeding schedule."

"I'm not sick!" Kat roared, and carefully put the mama cat down. It took forever to get Jezebel fed (the babies kept trying to help) and longer to get coffee on. Once she'd dumped some food outside for the differently abled marmalade tomcat who lived under the back porch, the three black-and-white cats from the gas station, and the one-eared Persian from the park who always dropped around for breakfast, she staggered back inside and propped herself up against the counter to watch Mr. Coffee take a tinkle.

When the coffee was finally ready and Kat sat down with a cup of it, she realized it looked and smelled terrible. What she really wanted was a nice cup of English breakfast tea with milk in it. *Bleecch.* That did it. If she actually wanted to drink a cup of tea, she was sick, and she didn't just have a cold, she had the flu.

She called Lolly and gave her the good news. "Okay," her buddy said curtly. "Means more work for me. Doesn't matter. Get more than my share of the tips anyway."

"Aw, Lolly, don't snarl. My head hurts. I know I was a horse's butt last night. I must have been coming down with this bug."

Then Lolly turned into the Lesbian Crisis Center and wanted to come over and make her some soup. "I hate soup," Kat snarled. "That kinda slop is for puppies and old people. Besides, you can't cook. That's why you keep falling in love. If it wasn't for those worthless wenches you keep draggin' home, you'd never get fed."

That made Lolly laugh. Kat's head was feeling worse and worse. She had to lie down. How was she going to get off the phone and keep Lolly in a good mood so she would definitely remember to show up at Jax on time, do two people's work, and not get both of them fired? "Hey honey," she shouted into the phone, hoping the old, reliable gag would work, "why d'they call you Lollypop?"

"Because I got me a big sucker," Lolly shouted back, and laughed like a hyena.

Kat hung up. *Glad I'm not a Catholic,* she thought, *or I'd have to go to church and say a novena to St. Jude. That woman's a hopeless cause if I ever met one.*

She had some tea and dry toast and a handful of aspirin (fuck the ulcer; fuck the bills that are going to come in today's mail; fuck your mother if she gets in my way), and went back to bed. Jezebel was already there, taking a nap on her pillow. She eased into the other side of the bed, but the orange-and-black beauty woke up anyway and padded over to knead bread on her. Her claws were nice and healthy, and stuck decent-sized holes in Kat's chest through her pajamas. Kat lifted her up, pulled a blanket between them to buffer her tits from Jezebel's sharp toes, and fell asleep petting her, tracing the vibrations her purr made across her silky flank.

Kat jolted into wakefulness hours later, covered with sweat. The blinds were dark. It must be late afternoon, almost evening. Her heart was pounding. She had been having horrible dreams about being smothered by bears. Her mouth had been — was! — full of fur. She pried Jezebel off her neck, said, "Be grateful my gloves don't need relining," and levered herself up to go answer the door, which was banging and ringing and just generally having a party all to itself. Most annoying for an inanimate object to get busy like that.

On the stoop was Chambray, still wearing her red-fringed finery from the night before. Kat's head was thick with sleep, and she assumed that the usual thing had brought this dark and lovely woman to her door. "You picked one hell of a time to get amorous, darlin'. I'm sick," she said. Then she realized that Chambray had a black eye. Oh-oh. Better duck and cover.

"I didn't come here to crawl into bed with you," Chambray said contemptuously, kicking the door open. The veneer panels obeyed her pointy-toed shoe like a john from Walnut Creek being urged across the floor. "This place is a mess," she added, strolling over dirty laundry like a queen walking to her throne. "You live in a hovel, big girl, and you gonna be raisin' livestock soon, the kind you can't see with the naked eye."

Sick as she was, Kat got a grip and stopped Chambray's pacing with a hand on her shoulder. Moving carefully and slowly, for both their sakes, she turned the irate girl around and gently tilted her head to the light. "Who hit you?" she said softly. "Do I need to take some serious drugs and strap on my six-shooter, or can they wait a coupla days to get skinned alive?"

Chambray just glared at her, her full lips locked together. So it wasn't a client. It was somebody they both knew. Probably Shark, that asshole. Kat sighed. She offered her arm, and Chambray tentatively rested the tips of her fingers in the crook of Kat's elbow. "Come sit on the bed and have a cigar," Kat said, offering the one thing she knew Chambray could not refuse.

Her visitor consented to sit by Jezebel, who was visibly miffed at having competition for her lackey's attention. When Kat presented Chambray with a thin, brown cigar, the cat uttered an obscenity and jumped to the floor. Kat knew the smoke would make her head spin, but she went to sit on the other side of the bed anyway and used a turkey wing to fan it away from her face.

"You ought to smudge this place more often," Chambray said, finally breaking the silence. "Oya would smile on you if you paid her more attention."

"All this African magic is such shit," Kat scoffed. "You're just a nicotine fiend like the rest of us mere mortals, Chambray. And you're goddamned lucky you got a note from your orisha says you can smoke in my house."

Chambray smiled. "Your house is about as chem-free as Spam. The only twelve steps you are ever gonna get will be the tap dance I do on your head. Tobacco is a purifying agent. It is also a powerful poison. And a stimulant. Like most good things it can be addicting. But you got to watch yourself, Kat, my friend, because not letting yourself have the thing you want can be as habit-forming as getting too much."

Kat didn't have anything to say to that. She just kept fanning nice and slow, like the ladies who sat in the front row of the church. In July and August, there was no way Kat could keep awake in church, no matter how often her grandma pinched her, no matter how loud the choir sang. The windows would be wide open and you could hear the bees buzzing in the lilacs outside, and that soft droning just ... made you ... zzzzzzzz.

When she woke up, Chambray had undressed herself, and they were naked in bed together. The smooth feel of female skin against her own automatically stirred Kat to action. She rolled over just enough to get her nose into Chambray's armpit. She smelled like tobacco, Thai spices, and a clean cunt that's starting to get sexy. Kat licked all around that armpit, despite the squirming girl who had come awake around it, and descended to her breasts, snuffling and kissing, using her tongue like a big, wet sponge, while Chambray shrieked and flailed around like a mad parrot hanging upside-down from its perch. Kat kept sliding down, leaving a snail trail across Chambray's flat, brown belly, making tuba-noises by blowing into her muscular abdomen. The tip of her tongue barely grazed Chambray's clit as it divided her sex. But she didn't even slow down. By the time she reached Chambray's feet and put those wriggling toes in her mouth, sharp nails were raking down her ribs and the backs of her legs, wherever Chambray could reach. Kat turned around and sat beside her, reached between her legs.

"Don't do that," Chambray moaned. She turned her face away a little. Kat wondered if she did that to make the black eye less noticeable, and had to fight off a wave of anger and nausea to continue.

"Why not, honey?"

"Damn all, are you as stupid as you are big? You saw who I went home with last night. What do you think we did, bake cookies? Woman has a right arm like a jackhammer."

Kat tut-tutted and slid one finger in. "Tell me if this hurts. Promise I won't move." Chambray did not tell her to stop. So she slid in one more finger. "This isn't much of a stretch for you," she said. "Is it? Is it?"

"Nooo. Oh. No."

"So if I don't move around, if I don't push hard, if I don't fuck you like a jackhammer, you should feel no pain. Isn't that right?"

"Oh. Oh. Oh."

Kat went up on her knees so she had more leverage. "Just want you to know I'm there, that's all. Can you tell I'm there?"

"Yesyes, yesyes."

"Wanna tell me something else? Wanna tell me if this is enough?"

"Don't — don't — don't—"

"Don't what? Don't put this other finger in here, this way? Don't push up a little bit to make sure it fits? Don't wiggle the tips of my—"

"Don't tease me you bitch, you bitch, don't make me scream it in your face, spell it out for you, be my horse, be my horse, I ride you, I ride you — on, oh — on — on — on you!"

Kat fell forward, lying across Chambray's belly, and gritted her teeth as she moved slowly but with lots of pressure, trying to give the girl what she needed without making her sorry later. It was difficult to stay in control with that silky skin rubbing against her feverish, too-sensitive body. Waves of the erotic perfume of a woman in heat kept coming up in her face, inciting her to riot in this flesh. But the tissues under the pads of Kat's fingers were swollen and abraded. No amount of lubrication could make the surface entirely smooth. Chambray threw her hips' harder and harder, cussed at her, and clawed her shoulders. Kat got a bit dizzy. Maybe this wasn't going to work. Maybe she had started something she wasn't going to be able to finish. Dammit, she didn't want to frustrate—

Then Chambray put her hand on Kat's rump and eased two fingers between her labia. "Turn just a little, big girl," she said, and as Kat adjusted her position, she slid in.

The muscles under Kat's fingers smoothed out, the lubrication became thicker, Chambray's movements became more rhythmic and less desperate. So Kat endured the distraction of penetration, allowed it, and was just beginning to enjoy it when the girl underneath her came. So she pulled away, off the invading hand, assuming it was time to cradle the other woman and stroke the sweat from her body.

But Chambray did not assume they were through. She did not want to let go of Kat and tried to come up off the bed after her. Without thinking, Kat pinned her down. Quick as a snake, Chambray turned her head and bit Kat's forearm hard enough to bruise the bone. The big woman hollered and let her go. "What the fuck?" she cried, staring at her injured arm.

"What I give you I give freely, but don't you ever try to ravish me," Chambray hissed. "I am my own woman. Not your slave."

"I could tell you the same thing!"

"Didn't have to tie you down for it, did I?" Chambray snapped, getting out of bed. "What you think your pussy's for, girl, preaching gospel? Got your life savings up your snatch? Is it my fault you're too stupid to hold still and get fucked long enough to make you come?"

"Don't talk to me that way, Chambray."

"Don't talk to you that way? What do you know about being bad-mouthed? Nobody says nothin' to you but what you want to hear. It's all, would you please Kat an' by your leave Kat an' you're so funny, strong, an' sexy, Kat. Makes me want to puke sometimes to watch them fawn over your fat ass while you make a fool of yourself. Seems to me that's about half of your biggest problem, girl, all those drunk bitches you let follow you around with their noses up your crack."

Chambray bolted out of bed, and Kat followed her into the kitchen. She was smarting from Chambray's tart comments, but she was also worried that Chambray was going to do something a lot more serious than running her mean little mouth. The black woman was throwing cupboard doors open and slamming them shut. "Quit makin' all this racket," Kat said. "You're scaring my cat. Ssh, baby, nobody's mad at you, princess. The booze is over there, you rampaging harridan. Pour us both a shot."

They sat and drank together, silently, until Kat finally said, "What are you doing over here anyway? If Shark just turned you inside out you didn't need to scratch my back. Did you guys have a fight?"

Chambray just shook her head and reached for the bottle. Kat took it out of her reach. "No, now. I know that look. Don't bullshit me. Something upset you besides me playing hard to get. We been friends too long to let this go."

Chambray started to cry. It was an ugly sound that put Kat's teeth on edge. For decency, she went over to the sink and turned her back. She ran some water she didn't want into a glass, touched it to her lips, and poured it out without drinking any. By the time she sat down again, Chambray had put herself back together.

"Shark say," Chambray began, getting her voice under control, "the Shark says I should quit letting white girls like you treat me like a piece of meat."

Kat almost hit the table. But for once in her life, she had the sense to keep her temper. This was delicate stuff. The two of them had never talked about color. They pretended that being friends had somehow settled all that. And they didn't talk about sex, either. When one of them got horny, she would drop by the other's place and see what happened. They didn't date. They would never be lovers.

"Shark want to be your one and only?" she said, trying to keep it light. It wasn't. She would miss Chambray badly. But there was a lesbian code that said it was so hard to find a mate that you did not come between a friend and her lover, even if your friend sometimes slept with you. Lovers, even potential lovers, had to come first — even though the friendship would usually outlast the romance. And (at least in the beginning) you don't tell your friend anything bad about her lover, even if you know their story can't have a happy ending.

"Maybe. She wants to tell me what to do. She wants me to want her. She wants to be my only choice. An' if I do all that, who is to say if she will love me or laugh at me? The woman wants to be a hero, an outlaw, some kinda romantic movie-star pimp and pool-hall champion. She is a certified public accountant, Kat. She lives with her mama, who has arthritis so bad she hasn't been able to work for years. If I can get out of her bed as easy as I get in, don't it just remind her she is nobody special, never going to shake things up, never going to be famous for what she does best? It's what they do to us. How we do each other. I hate it, and I hate us."

"Chambray," Kat said, and cleared her throat, "nobody has the right to make you feel bad about what we do together. I don't treat you like a piece of meat. I am very damn fond of you."

"But if I was a white girl, would you make me take my hands off your body?"

Kat did hit the table then. She also shouted. Chambray tried to leave the house, and Kat got between her and the door. "Don't go!" she cried. "Please." She slid down to the floor and put her arms around Chambray's knees. "This is not about color, it's about power. It's about who I let close to me. I haven't let anybody make me come for so long that I just ... forgot about it somehow. I am begging your pardon for pushing you away tonight. Don't go. Or you'll never come back, it will never be the same, and I can't stand it. To have you even wonder — Chambray, it hurts me like a knife in my heart. What can I do, what do you want me to do — crawl into the bedroom?"

"For starters, yes."

Kat froze. She was being called on her grand gesture, and she just didn't have the guts to walk it like she talked it.

"Don't tell me you don't want to," Chambray said vindictively. "I saw the drool runnin' down your face when Reid slapped shit out of Artie and rode her out of the bar. Everybody in Jax could smell what was runnin' down your legs. Why do you think this love stuff is always a one-way street? All the girls you've dragged out of Jax by their nipples know your story, Kat. They know what you really want. Me an' Lady Sage an' everybody else, we laugh at you and take what we want from you because you are too gutless to get down on your knees. But someday somebody is gonna get you good for all of us, Kat. We're all waiting and wondering when it's gonna happen. As far as I'm concerned, it can't be a moment too soon. You can play pony for the whole damn world then and I'll just laugh my sweet ass off."

Kat was pinned to the floor by her fury. She could not speak. She couldn't even raise her fists. Chambray's words would pass right through them. All she could do was wait it out. The last time she'd been in an earthquake was a lot more pleasant.

"Well, I guess I know where I belong now," Chambray said, turning on her heel. "I got somebody who's waiting for me who isn't ashamed to spread her ass or tell me she can't come unless I pull her hair real hard." She paused for one last salvo. "And how dare you think it was the Shark who gave me this black eye, you racist motherfucker? I walked into a door." The slam that accompanied her exit was so loud that Jezebel and her kittens sank to the floor with their ears back as if a gale was passing overhead.

Kat finally let her breath out and took in some oxygen. Now her soul felt as battered as her body. But, strangely enough, she didn't feel feverish anymore. Her head was completely clear. Without letting herself think about it or hesitate, she went over to her bedside table, turned Reid's bloody calling card rightside up, and dialed the number that had been written there in somebody else's pain.

■■

Reid sat in front of the TV with a plate of Chinese takeout and a Coke. She handled the chopsticks carefully. The fingertips on both of her hands were raw from the overly enthusiastic manicure she had given herself for Artie. She had a bad headache from spending the day outside in the sun, drinking Khaliber that she'd lugged to the field herself because concession stands never sold nonalcoholic beer, and watching Artie pitch a no-hitter. She hated fake beer and softball about equally, but knew what you had to do after a scene to keep things friendly with a butch bottom. You had to acknowledge who they were in the real world, and make them feel successful and important, or you might make yourself an enemy who had some dangerous stories to tell about your most intimate habits.

After the game, Artie had been surrounded by her jubilant, dusty teammates, Las Estrellas. Artie asked her if she wanted to go celebrate with a few "brewskies," and Reid shook her head. "I've got three tapes I have to transcribe for a client by Monday," she lied. "Great game, though."

One of the other players butted in, a copper-colored woman with a mop of long, curly hair. "Who's your tiny friend, Artie? Hey, honey, what sport do you play — midget wrestling?" Her Spanish accent made Reid's cunt tingle even as the words made her hackles rise. She liked long-haired butches and (in a slightly different way) boys who wore earrings. But she recognized that tone, and she didn't like girls who assumed they could use it on her without getting slapped.

Nevertheless, this was Artie's turf and Artie's day to be the hero. So Reid tried to keep her sense of humor. "Yeah, you gotta watch out for us little people, we might walk off with your kneecaps."

But the pumped-up jock didn't want to let it go. "I think maybe you're a cheerleader. Where's your pom-poms? Want me to take you back in the locker room and help you look under the benches?"

Reid got a little pale. She was always too full of herself after a scene. It was hard to let go of a vision of yourself as lord of the universe, completely powerful, immediately obeyed, feared utterly. The world was collapsing into a tunnel, and this woman's broad, nasty face was at the other end of it. "Those the same benches the coach gets your ass up on?" she hissed. "Maybe that's where we oughta go looking for pom-poms."

"Uh, Reid—," Artie sputtered. "Barbara — hey, guys—"

"Listen, Artie, I don't know what you see in this pipsqueak, but if she doesn't want to help you celebrate, we can just carry her along for you. Our first-string pitcher oughta have whatever she wants on the day she shuts out the Shamrocks. Bet she'll fit in the trunk of my car." Barbara took one step toward Reid, and Artie grabbed her.

"Quit being an asshole," Artie said. Baseball diamond dust ran in streaks down her chalky face. "C'mon, let's go. Everybody's gonna leave us. Reid, I'll call you, okay?"

Reid sighed, took her hand out of her jacket pocket (leaving the knife behind), and waved goodbye. "Sure you will," she said softly. Goddamn novices, she could never tell them no when they came on so hard and seemed so sure about what they wanted. But they inevitably withdrew after the first scene, getting a little freaked out about the fact that they really could do all those things they'd been jerking off to for so long. Not to mention the shock of encountering somebody who had cooked up a few ideas of her own.

The TV picture went bad for a second. The gay boys upstairs must be running their dishwasher. Reid sighed and rubbed at the bunched-up muscles in her neck and shoulders. This apartment building was okay. It was nice to have faggots for neighbors. They didn't complain about all the thumping and humping that went on in her bedroom. But she missed the house in the suburbs with its carefully kept yard, and she missed Nikki, the woman who owned it. It was easy to forget how much she had hated the long drive to get into the city for leather events and the claustrophobia of living with a trust-fund baby who didn't understand why life couldn't be just one long scene.

Reid sighed again. Annoyed with the old-lady sound of it, she bit her tongue. The room over the garage that was supposed to be her office had never gotten remodeled. Nikki couldn't understand why Reid couldn't write the great American novel on her kitchen table. Her word-processing business fell apart because she kept missing deadlines. When Reid's bike finally quit running because it needed major repairs, her lover refused to spend what had suddenly become "her own money" to fix it. Reid knew what that triumphant smile across the class barrier meant. It meant, "I've got you. I've got control and revenge and I own your ass." It took Reid a week to sell the bike for parts, take the bus into the city and find her own apartment (the deposit came from an advance on her last viable credit card), and call an old friend who had a truck and needed to be strung up and beaten so badly she would just haul Reid's stuff away without gloating about how stupid Reid had been to think true love could ever work out with a chick from the suburbs.

But is all this fucking around any better? Reid asked herself. *Do they respect me the next morning?* Unfortunately, she had no idea what the two triumphant athletes had said to each other on their way to the parking lot. If she could have overheard that conversation, it would have made her feel a lot better than musing over love gone wrong.

First, Artie had put Barbara in a half nelson and faked breaking her neck. "Quit horsing around," she had said grimly, "or I'll have to hurt you."

"You're gonna hurt me? Promises, promises."

"I better, or Reid will, and then you'll be really sorry."

"You have got to be kidding."

"I am not kidding. I finally found out what this S&M shit is all about."

"Stop, you've only been whining about getting into leather for the last six months. And now you're holding out on me. I want to hear all about this. What did she do to you?"

"Not until you learn a little respect, Barbara. That's R-E-S-P-E-C-T. No, dammit, don't start singing the fucking song, I *know* the fucking song. Christ, somebody better teach you some manners before you hurt your silly-ass self."

Artie and Barbara didn't make it to the victory party, but they did drink a champagne toast to Reid sometime in the wee hours of the next morning. It's amazing how much fun you can have with ice cubes, the terrycloth tie off your bathrobe, and a Ping-Pong paddle.

Ignorant of all these ripples, Reid ate the last mouthful of shrimp fried rice, turned off the TV, and went into her bedroom. Unlike most S/M dykes she knew, she kept all her equipment out and instantly available. She couldn't afford a big enough apartment to turn one whole room into a dungeon, but her bedroom was the next best thing. She started to clean up, piling soiled trick towels into the laundry basket, carrying dildos into the bathroom and dropping them into the sink, scrubbing them with hot water and Betadine, going back to the bedroom to toss used condoms and rubber gloves into the garbage, hanging her whips back on the wall. A couple of things (a blade, a cane) needed to be wiped down with alcohol. Her chaps needed to be sponged off and oiled.

The familiar work of putting her tools in order calmed her down, and took the edge off her post-scene depression. Determined to preserve this improved mood, Reid resolutely did not look at the three chain collars that hung together on one hook. Each of them had once been worn by women she'd had contracts with. One of those contracts had been broken by cancer, one by an overdose, and one by dishonorable behavior on the part of Reid's property. She did not use these collars on anyone else. They were in permanent retirement. Reid knew she should probably just pitch them out, but she kept them to force herself to remember, to learn from the things that made her grieve.

For a novice, Artie had not been bad. Actually, for a seasoned player, Artie had not been bad. For the first time since breakfast, Reid smiled. The look on that nosy bartender's face when they rode by playing horsie was just too much. You could live on looks like that. *There* was a woman who never had to ask anybody for anything. Probably just took out a cigarette and didn't even wait for somebody to light it, just knew it would be burning by the time she took a puff. That was a weird little scene she had pulled, getting in their faces about bringing down the tone of Jax. Jax, of all places. Why, that hellhole would make your average longshoreman start cryin' for his mama. After getting all that static, she wasn't sure why she'd left her phone number behind. Hmm. Well, there had been too much blood to let it all go to waste (Artie bled real pretty), and she liked upsetting people. Liked it almost as much as she had liked looking for a hole in Artie's body that her whole hand would not sink into, with enough patience and Probe. Mmm-mmm.

She was sorting all her tit clamps out (pairs on chain hung on the pegboard, little plastic ones in bright primary colors went in the Tinkertoy can, rubber-covered wire ones went in the wooden Dutch Cleanser box, alligator clamps got dropped in the see-through plastic box from Radio Shack with all the handy little compartments) when the phone rang. She answered it without letting the machine pick it up — it was so late, it had to be either a wrong number or somebody she knew. "Sexual Compulsives Anonymous," she chirped.

There was dead air on the other end of the phone. "Put out or fuck off," Reid said politely.

More dead air. Then — "Will you give a person a chance to say hello?" someone said. Someone querulous. Reid knew she ought to recognize that voice. The tone was so familiar. Wait a second — "We don't allow that kinda stuff in here." Bingo.

"That was your chance," Reid said, and went to hang up the phone. A loud squawk erupted from the receiver, and she brought it back to her ear. "Is someone interfering with you, Miss?" she asked solicitously, in her best *Masterpiece Theatre* British accent. "Shall I call in the Yard?"

"Will you shut the fuck up for just a second?" Kat said. "What is wrong with you?"

"You're extremely rude, so I'll try to be brief. Number one, no, and number two, I don't think I want to talk to you long enough to explain that."

Kat did a very quick mental shuffle. She wasn't used to women who played with language this way. If you wanted people to think you were bad, you used short words and pronounced them emphatically. But Reid's whimsy was more intimidating than a truck driver's curse. *I don't think I'm smart enough to keep up with her,* Kat thought. She had to force herself to respond. "That's true. I was rude. Uh. There's no reason why you should explain anything to me. Uh. Uh. Is there any way we could start this whole thing over?"

"It does run counter to policy. Nothing personal, you understand. But I don't give second chances, and right now you're looking at your third."

Kat recognized that ploy. She knew how to be charming when a girl tried to give her a scolding. She ducked her head, even though Reid wasn't there to see how endearing it looked, and whispered, "I'm in big trouble, huh?" She thought she had managed to put just a tiny quiver in her voice.

"Afraid so."

"But I don't even *know* you." That was good, Kat thought, letting her voice crack at the end of the sentence.

"Bullshit," Reid said firmly, and was surprised to discover how much she meant it. "You know everything you need to know about me. The only question is, what are you going to do about it?"

Now Kat was pissed off again. This woman must eat bricks for breakfast and shit out mortar. How could anybody be so impervious to her tact and diplomacy? "Confrontative little fucker, aren't you?" she snapped.

"You're the one who dropped the dime, big girl."

A very satisfactory kind of silence followed that comment. It lay at Reid's feet, glaring and sweating. Reid looked at herself in the mirror above her bureau. She was smiling.

A muffled cry of pain made Reid crinkle her eyebrows. She had no way of knowing that Kat was on the brink of tears. "What is this — phone sex?" she asked, sounding like a schoolteacher accepting a wormy apple.

"I need to see you," Kat choked.

"Ah. Yes. I am sure you do."

"What do I have to do, take a number and wait in line?"

Reid hissed. It was a really nasty noise. Emitting it made her feel like a rabid mongoose.

Kat finally decided to shape up. "No!" she panted. "Don't hang up! I'm sorry!"

"Do we know our *p* word?"

"Please. Please. Please."

"Yes, all right, don't get maudlin. You understand that if I agree to see you, it's only because we have unfinished business. You were a churl, and I don't overlook slights of that magnitude. If you agree to come here, you must understand that I will brook no challenges to my authority. And if you don't show up, I may very well come and fetch you. You owe me, bitch, so don't come over here planning to be coy or jerk me around. Knock the chip off your shoulder and come prepared to pay up like a decent chap. Wear old clothes, and bring a spare set."

"Okay. Just say when."

"The *p* word?"

"Please."

"The *s* word?"

"Sir."

"Shall we go for a complete sentence?"

"Sir, please tell me when I can make myself available, sir."

"I am pleased to note that your descent into loutish incivility is far from complete. Tomorrow. Nine sharp. Memorize this address."

"Thank you, sir," Kat said, writing it in the dust on her bedside table.

Reid did not reply; she just hung up.

■■

Kat put the phone down and looked reproachfully over her shoulder at Jezebel, who stopped bathing one of her babies long enough to give Kat a level emerald stare of disapproval. "Don't be maudlin," she parroted. "You were a churl. I don't overlook slights of that magnitude. I will brook no challenges to my authority. The *p* word. Loutish incivility. Shit. She talks as crazy as a bag lady in a tinfoil bonnet. I'm goin' off to see a nut case." She locked her front door and went back to bed.

The next day, Kat was surprised to find that she seemed to have recovered completely from the flu. *Fighting with Chambray must have burned the virus right out of my system,* she thought as she rang Reid's doorbell. She had only the vaguest memory of what she'd done that day, but she was on time, wearing her oldest, greasiest T-shirt and a ripped-up pair of jeans, and carrying a gym bag with a change of clothes in it, so at least part of her brain must have been functioning.

She was buzzed into the building, climbed two flights of stairs, and rang again at the apartment door, where she was buzzed into a dark hallway. The lights suddenly went on. Reid was at the other end of the hall, wearing a pair of chaps and a plain motorcycle jacket. Under the chaps she wore a leather jock that bulged a little from the cock she was wearing. She was utterly unself-conscious about packing. Kat liked the set of her hips, the way she carried herself, her shoulders, her tool. You could call it having guts, you could call it having gonads, but what it really was, the girl had balls. Taking responsibility for your desire, wearing it where other people could see it, being defiant about your deviance — it was the kind of butch signal, like a shaved head, that Kat recognized and loved, that made her knees get weak. You had to flaunt it. You couldn't change it. You didn't really want to. Because even if you hardly ever get what you want, knowing what it would look like and trying to get it was so much less crazy than believing the lie that you wanted what everybody else wanted, that there was nothing else, no choice. *Fuck that,* Kat thought. *Oh, Reid. You little stud. Fuck me.*

They were the same leathers she had worn to Jax. Kat silently approved of that too. Leathers should be worn frequently, broken in, given a chance to absorb your sex and sweat, get some worn spots, bags and creases. She hated the twits who seemed to have a different outfit every weekend. Their stuff always looked brand-new. She was not into patent leather.

"Kneel," Reid said. She had suddenly gotten very close. The top of her head came up to Kat's breastbone. Then a searing pain hit Kat in the arm, and she went down. That buzzing noise was familiar. Yep, the woman was carrying a dog trainer, a silver, battery-powered wand that was sold in leather shops as a "cattle prod." Kat knew that a real cattle prod would have knocked her through the door. Little masochistic sprouts growing up in the country find these things out. On bad days, Kat used to go to the far side of the pasture, where nobody could see her, and try to climb the electrical fence. The memory made Kat smile, but she didn't think Reid would appreciate that, so she wiped the grin from her face.

"First lesson," Reid said. "Unconditional and prompt obedience. If you stop to think, you're taking too long. If you didn't hear me, it's your fault. So pay attention. You're about to get real busy."

A switchblade clicked open under Kat's left ear. "Chuck the jacket," Reid said. She was putting the dog trainer back on her belt.

She got it into the leather carrying loop without looking. Before Kat's jacket hit the floor, Reid had grabbed the front of Kat's T-shirt and punctured it with the knife. Her booted foot kicked the kneeling woman's denim-clad knees apart. She took her time destroying the T-shirt, making sure Kat got a taste of the blade's fine edge while being careful not to cut her.

"I have a notion," Kat said, screwing her head around to follow the knife, "that we're supposed to be having a conversation right about now. Something about limits and safe words."

"Really. Well, if there's anything you think I should know, by all means tell me now, while you can still talk."

Kat was nonplussed by this flat invitation to spill her guts. She wanted to be prompted, drawn out, fussed over a little. But all she could think to say was, "I need this," and Reid rewarded her honesty by dragging the edge of the knife along her ribs. Kat's air came out all at once, and she thrust her torso into the thin line of pain.

"God, I'm glad I'm not the only one," Reid grinned. Rags that had been a T-shirt were bunched in her fist. Kat was naked to the waist. Reid whistled and used the point of the knife to trace the patterns on Kat's skin above her breasts, stepped close enough to look at her back, and scraped the switchblade over the skin between her shoulder blades. "Scars upon scars upon scars. Fine silver lines and nice fat white ones. You're just a whore for a sharp edge, aren't you, darlin'? Up."

Kat was getting the hang of her style, and was on her way to her feet. Reid's boot toe caught her between the legs anyway, just a little incentive to be quick about straightening her knees. For a moment Kat saw red, and Reid snapped, "Put your hands behind your back." Kat threw her hands back hard and fast so she wouldn't kill the little motherfucker. At the base of her spine, she clenched her fists, reciting silently, *Whodoesshethinksheis, whodoesshethinksheis, whodoesshethinksheis,* while the knife chewed through her jeans. The thick denim came off in chunks. She was so used to Reid cutting nothing but cloth that the sting of a sweeping cut across the front of both legs made her gasp and tip forward. Reid was behind her and quick to take advantage of this minor loss of balance. She kicked one of Kat's heels forward, and kept her moving through the kitchen, into the bedroom.

The room was lit with candles and some track lights with red bulbs turned down low. It was hard to see details, but every wall seemed to be covered with hooks or shelves or pegboards full of equipment. There was only one picture, a life-size photograph of a Japanese woman with a full-body tattoo. She was fighting with sais, short-handled steel tridents. She had been wounded. Blood dripped from one of her arms to the straw mat on the floor. Only the shadow of her opponent's kimono and naginata, the spear-shaft tipped with a crescent blade, fell within the picture's frame.

Kat was so enthralled with this image that she barely noticed when Reid tumbled her to the floor and pulled off her boots and socks. It felt kind of good to be thrown around this way. When you're big, people don't try to propel you in a direction they've selected. Because she liked it, she didn't mind helping. Things sure were happening fast. Then cold metal went around one of her ankles, and Reid was sitting on her stomach, screwing in the key. The bitch didn't bother to take any of her own weight on her own two legs, just sat on Kat like she was a beanbag chair. *Well, okay,* Kat thought, *fuck you, I can take your weight. I could carry two of you around under my arms. It'll take more than this to crush me.* She would have liked to see what the little twerp was doing to her feet, though.

Reid came off her and turned around. Kat had time to see that there were steel circles around both of her ankles. Then Reid sat on her again and grabbed one of her wrists. Kat pulled back. Reid applied enough force to keep her hand in midair. They hung that way in space, eye to eye.

"I'm not a pushover," Kat said finally.

"Really?" Reid said dryly. "You're not a novice, either. So what is your excuse?"

"Fuck you," Kat said, and surrendered her hand.

"That's going to cost you," Reid promised, and put the cuffs on. These were hinged steel bracelets about an inch wide with a hasp that could be locked. She breathed a little easier now that Kat was almost in four-point bondage. Part of the thrill of playing with big girls was the risk that they'd lose their minds and turn on you. Might as well try to calm down a rampaging elephant. Now she felt secure enough to needle Kat a little. "Surprised they fit?" she asked, putting a little sneer into the question.

Kat just glared at her, resenting the way her thoughts had been divined.

"Well, don't be. You aren't the first big girl who found out how far it is to fall to my feet. And you won't be the last one either. Did it ever occur to you that this is probably never gonna happen again? So you'd better show me your best side, badass. I don't particularly care that we don't like each other much, but it seems a damn shame to waste the whole night. I can call you a buncha nasty names, slap you around some, maybe slap you around a lot, fuck you senseless, and then call you a cab. Or I can just call you a cab. You decide. Now."

Kat didn't say anything.

"Silence will not be accepted as evidence of consent. Later, maybe, but not now. You ask me nice or do without. Now!"

"You're a real ball-buster," Kat grimaced.

Reid laughed. "Yeah, I do that, too. Don't try to change the subject."

"You think I would have let you put these on me if I didn't want you to?"

"Okay, that's fair. You in for the duration?"

"Do your worst," Kat said through clenched teeth.

"Oh, darlin', darlin', you do not know what a temptation you are to me," Reid said, and kicked her to her feet, kicked her over to the bed, and shoved her onto her back. The bed had four eight-foot-tall posters and was braced with chains and turnbuckles. There were screw eyes all over the wood frame. A person could get into a lot of trouble here and not be able to do much about it. Kat shivered. If she'd had some rope, she would have been tying herself down.

"See, this isn't about who's tall, is it, darlin'?" Reid said. "It's about who needs it worse. How long you been doing without anyway?" She reached for some chains, started locking them to fetters and manacles.

"Damn you, don't you do me any favors!"

"Oh, I don't feel sorry for you. Not at all." Reid took up some of the slack in one of the chains. Kat felt the pull in her armpit, and realized she was going to be stretched tight as a drum skin across the surface of this bed. "Think I've never been lost in the desert? If we're still speaking to one another in the morning, we can tell each other all those stories. I'm just chewin' on your ass. If I didn't want you, big girl, d'you think I would have interrupted one of the hottest scenes in recent memory to write down my goddamn phone number for y'all?"

"You're lucky I found it."

"I'm lucky I'm alive. You feel lucky yet? No?" Reid chuckled. "Move around for me."

"How?"

Reid pulled both of her nipples straight up and twisted them. Kat found that she could indeed move. Reid took up some more slack in one of the leg-chains. Now there was a steady pull in Kat's groin muscles and down both sides of her chest. The weight came off her lungs, and Reid left her. She actually missed the little creep. Kat thought that was interesting. And she was vaguely worried about what Reid might find to implement her cruelty, out there in this strange room. *I'm alone and helpless with someone I barely know,* Kat thought. Why did she feel so calm and happy?

Reid was suddenly aware of being tired. The hours she'd spent with Artie had taken a toll, and so had all the stage fright she'd felt getting ready for Kat's arrival and wondering if she'd have the guts to keep her appointment. It was important not to get distracted by all the equipment and forget the person it was supposed to be used on. Reid didn't want this to be a perfunctory performance. Kat deserved a more personal effort. So Reid took several deep, slow breaths and hoped the energy she needed would keep on flowing.

"Anybody know you're here tonight?" she asked Kat.

Shit, Kat thought, *you have no right to keep pulling things out of my head.* "Yeah," she said, a little too loudly.

"Paranoid, weren't we?"

"Careful."

"Paranoids always are. Keeps 'em so busy they don't notice when you sneak up behind 'em."

What Reid came back with didn't make Kat feel any less paranoid, that was for sure. It was a black rubber gas mask. It had big bug-eyes of clear plastic, and the curved snout had the look of a pig.

"In for the duration, you said," Reid reminded her. Damning her own weird sense of honor, Kat didn't let herself say a word as Reid tucked her chin into the mask, stretched out the elastic straps at the back, and pulled it over her head. But she couldn't keep herself from breaking out into a cold sweat, and Reid scraped some of it off her flank and rubbed it into her own face.

It smelled awful in there, like rubber and something else, some chemical. The eyepieces weren't very transparent, and they distorted Reid's face. Kat was terrified of getting them fogged up. She tried to draw a breath and realized that the mask fit so tightly, it formed a seal around her face.

Reid said something.

"What?"

"Sorry." The other woman's voice was louder now, the enunciation more precise. "I said, don't gasp. If you draw slow, shallow breaths, you'll get enough air, but if you start to pant or gasp, you'll cut off your own oxygen."

Jesus. That was weird, to smother just because you were trying to breathe. Kat lay there, pretending she was perfectly calm. Maybe it was Sunday morning and she had just barely waked up, wasn't really awake yet—

The chemical smell she had noticed earlier flooded the mask. It was poppers. Goddammit! She did not like that stuff. The way it made her heart pound and the taste it left in her mouth were too much like terror. But Reid was touching her. She had on a pair of black leather gloves, and she was just touching her, gently, all over, it was sort of a massage. Kat didn't want to respond, but she felt her body melting anyway, yielding to those wise hands.

What a treasure, Reid thought, running her hands over the woman chained down to her bed. *So much muscle, and so much heart. Smart, too. Wish she wasn't so goddamn antagonistic. Well, whatever it takes to crank yourself up to go through with it. Bottoming like this would scare the shit out of me.* Reid shook her head, then corrected herself. *Bottoming like this has scared the shit out of me.*

When so many people in the community were obsessed with finding "a real top," it was too easy to forget your own history. Reid spared a few seconds of silent homage for her nervous, awkward, but determined younger self who had been willing to go under for just about anybody. She didn't want to waste any time being angry about the ridicule, abuse, and injuries she had garnered by wearing her keys on the right. It was better to remember the scenes that had been hot, and not add up the price. But she also thanked the Goddess for the naughty girls and obedient boys who had urged her to get on the other end of the riding crop. *I hope,* she thought, *I have treated all of you better than I got treated.*

Reid could tell that the poppers were cresting and the ride was getting smoother because Kat's pelvis was coming up off the bed in little, rhythmic waves of need. She rubbed her sex the way you rub a cat that arches its back at you. Kat rubbed back. She was wet. That was a good sign. Reid realized she wanted to fuck this big, hard body and see how many changes she could put it through. There was something addicting about having someone tough and well built at the end of your arm. It was a test of your own stamina, but it was more than that, more than just a challenge. Reid had always been told that she felt too much, wanted too much, had too much passion and lust and energy. When she was with a woman who was really big and strong, she felt as if she had a place to pour all that intensity without destroying the vessel. Slender, fine-boned women made her afraid that all of her good stuff would overflow and wind up in a puddle, just wasted on the floor.

This wasn't what usually happened. She didn't often want to fuck the people that she topped. Usually it was like being a windup toy. Only she had to wind herself up, and then they got to watch it wear off. All the time you wondered if they would even remember your face if they ran into you at the grocery store tomorrow. Being a top was like being a public utility. But even public utilities have their limits. Reid drew the line at going through the motions of sex unless she felt something for them between her own legs. Or unless they paid.

It was too soon to do that, to turn the scene sexual. But it wasn't too early to inform Kat about her desire. So Reid slid down Kat's body, sat between her legs, and thrust all her fingers between the slick and furry halves of her sex. She pushed slowly, up to the biggest part of her hand, before she felt any significant resistance. Not that there was no response — the poppers were still circulating inside the mask, making Kat's breath come short and sharp. Her nerve endings were raw. The muscles along her torso stood out as she tried to come down on Reid's hand. "This is for me," Reid crooned. "Dessert. For later." She wiped her hand on the bulky thighs. "I'll help you keep it wet," she promised, and slid back up Kat's body to confront her face-to-face.

After tripping alone for so long, it was very odd for Kat to see Reid's determined little face, wearing those stupid glasses, just inches from her own eyeballs. "I know all about you," Reid said, and for the first time, Kat thought maybe that was almost true. "If I do anything you don't like tell me to stop. If you get to me before the beast comes out, I will. But you aren't going to say no to me. You've been looking for me for a long, long time. Let's not waste any time pretending we don't understand one another. You need to be hurt. I need to hurt people. You don't think anybody can hurt you enough, and I'm sure you're wrong. I just want to feed you, darlin'. Till you just aren't hungry anymore. Are we having fun yet? I am. I am. I am."

The first time Reid said, "I am," she covered the snout of the gas mask with her palm. Suddenly, there was no air at all. Kat's whole body thrashed the way a fish out of water flops, and for exactly the same reason. Then Reid gave her life, gave her air. "I am," she said again with devilish glee, and took it all away. Kat's life was literally in the palm of her hand. Then it was back, sweet air, cold air. Kat's face, her whole body was hot under freezing sweat that melted and ran down her sides, pooled beneath her. "I am," Reid repeated with terrible conviction. Kat struggled with the chains, the hooks they were welded to, the wood the hooks were embedded within. But all she could really do was turn her head from side to side, and Reid had no trouble at all keeping the small opening in the mask covered. She kept it up a long time until Kat's field of vision swam with black mist. Then she let her go and leaned in closer still.

"Don't you hope I'm an ethical and compassionate human being? Aren't you glad you're too big to stuff into the trash compactor?"

And she hit the mask again, covered the hole, deprived Kat of the most important thing in the whole world. Oh, it was wicked, wicked, Reid thought, wanting to do this to somebody else. The temptation to take more than Kat would willingly give beat in her cunt like a hard-on that wouldn't go away. Sometimes Reid found that fighting that temptation was more of a challenge than getting the bottom to have a good time. The restraint she had to place on her own sadism had to be stronger than any chain that locked somebody else to her bed.

When Reid let Kat breathe again, it was only to give her more poppers, and when the air left after that, it was even more hellish. Kat's pounding heart demanded more oxygen, she *had* to have it, and it just wasn't there. She was sobbing and pleading, but the medium she needed to form words had been sucked out of the mask. There was only the threat of unconsciousness, Reid's looming face (which didn't look silly at all anymore), and all the things that had been taken away from her that she had thought she could not go on without. Kat felt two small, sharp tears gathering at the inside corners of her eyes. This was not like losing a job or a lover, it was not even like going without a meal or two. It was like dying, it was fucking awful, and Reid was not going to stop, she knew, until—

Reid stopped.

She pushed the mask up off of her face. Kat said, "Thank you, sir" before she could stop herself. She ought to be pissed, she ought to be resentful and wary of this woman, but this was the person who had saved her, who had let her live. The fact that it was also the person who had put her in jeopardy was too confusing to deal with. Frightened people need to feel safe, and they will turn their jailers into saviors if that is all the hope they can devise.

"How you doing?" Reid asked. Kat noticed that there were tiny wrinkles around her eyes. This was not a kid. This woman was her age — maybe older. She was certainly experienced. Had, uh, some exotic tastes. Yes. Because this was her idea of an appetizer. A warm-up. And she, Kat, had invited Reid to do her worst. The extent of her own stupidity appalled Kat so much that her next remark was a little too tart.

"Is that what you call getting lucky?"

The joke took Reid by surprise, and she felt her hackles rise. Was Kat going to be one of those ingrates and hypocrites who pigged out on pain and humiliation, and then just had to find a way to deny their own pleasure and make it look like you, the top, were the pervert, and they had been victimized? Reid broke one of her own cardinal rules and lost her temper. "Look, you don't get to fill out my report card. It's obviously a mistake to lighten up on you for even a few seconds." The defensive sound of this outburst made Reid blush. She had to get off the bed to cool her face off and simmer down.

"No—," Kat moaned.

But Reid was gone. She had left the gas mask on the bed, and by stretching her hand to the limit, Kat could just barely touch it. She had to, there were things she expressed by touching it that she would never be able to say out loud to Reid. Somewhere out there, Reid made the red track lights go off. There was only candlelight now.

Reid came back with a black plastic wand in her hand. It looked a little like a vibrator. She was fitting a glass attachment shaped like a mushroom into one end of it. She bent to plug it in somewhere by the side of the bed, and turned a knob on the bottom. The smell of ozone burned through Kat's dried-out nasal membranes. But she barely noticed it, because purple sparks were shooting out of the mushroom. "This is an ultraviolet wand," Reid said. "Smart girl like you's probably seen a million of them. But I do like to hear myself talk. It generates a field like static electricity. So I can use it anywhere on your body. Except the eyeballs. Oh, well. Here we go." Every time she used an electrical toy, Reid chided herself for being lazy. But her lower back was sore from flogging Artie and sitting in front of the keyboard today. Besides, the three women she'd called to get the dish about Kat had all told her that the bartender was also a mechanic, maybe even an engineer. A technical girl like her ought to appreciate these warped machines. She ached to lay leather across Kat's back, but told herself that would have to be the evening's grand finale.

Reid stroked the hollow globe full of hissing, glittering magic up the inside of one of Kat's thighs. The leg threw itself out and went rigid. Kat said, "Hmm. Goddammit!" The sensation was very odd, almost impossible to describe to herself. There was prickling, and it made a sizzling noise, which probably made the prickling feeling more intense. But it also felt like little needles being driven into her flesh, needles that melted and left tiny seams of molten metal buried in her body.

Reid turned the UV wand up. The purple color got darker, reflected off her glasses. There were more sparks, and they shot further. "Hold still," Reid told her.

Kat could not. Chained in that position, there was nothing she could do to avoid contact with the glass mushroom, but she could not help flinching anyway. The noise of frying was ugly, and the feeling was too peculiar. She could not categorize it with the simple pain she got from a whip, and she could not build sexual tension out of struggling against and then yielding to it. It just made her tense and irritable.

"Hold still," Reid repeated. "Dammit, I mean it, now, pay attention. Do you feel that?" She ran the sparking attachment over Kat's belly, keeping it firmly in contact with her skin.

"No. I, uh, I don't. Not really. Should I?"

"No, idiot. But you feel this, don't you?" And Reid lifted the wand, put it down, lifted it again. Each time the glass surface left Kat's skin, sparks arced from the wand to her body, and there was that buzzing, prickly, piercing feeling.

"The moral to this story," Reid said, "is refer to lesson one. By not doing what I told you, you've inflicted a fair amount of discomfort on yourself. And I'm not sure I should have even told you. It's so much fun to make you jump." She repeated the lesson a few more times. It didn't really help. Kat set her teeth on edge and vowed not to knuckle under to something that wasn't really hurting her. Except that it did hurt. Only she didn't like it. But did she ever?

Luckily, Reid broke in on this introspection. "Well, that's interesting," she mused, "but it's not quite the thing, is it?" Kat turned her head and watched as the glass mushroom was replaced by a little steel pointer.

"This is the same but different," Reid warned. Of course, the first thing she touched was a nipple. Holy smoke! It was, Kat reckoned, about as close as you could come to being struck by lightning if you didn't live on top of a flagpole. The metal point concentrated the purple sparks into a single bolt of pure energy that was excruciating but compelling. The sensation left her speechless. Reid smiled, and began to apply the metal point to other parts of her body. Kat knew she was headed for her clit, and couldn't help but bend her neck and watch. It was a sickening sort of fascination. As the stabbing pain went through her again and again, Kat thought that this was not the kind of thing she was used to at all. You'd think these gadgets would just be distracting. It was like being in a very sick amusement park that was also a sort of prison. *I could get to like this*, Kat thought. Then added, *What the fuck am I saying?*

Then Reid put the metal point at the top of her inner lips, and Kat thought she was going to piss or go blind. That hurt more than anything else she could remember or imagine. She cursed with fervor, but (oddly enough) did not inveigh against Reid.

"Payback time," Reid said. "Remember the incident of the withheld wrist? How many seconds do you imagine you resisted me?"

"Seemed like forever. Five minutes?"

"Well, at least you're honest. If you'd said five seconds, I would have cauterized your clit. But it was probably more like a minute, even less. We'll make it sixty just to be on the safe side. And divide that into threes, that's twenty for each nipple and twenty for down here. In sets of five, I think. You're going to count and ask me for each shock, and then thank me."

It was the kind of thing that would have sounded boring on paper. But counting to sixty can be very dramatic when it is accompanied by intense (if brief) suffering. And the ritual of repeatedly calling Reid "sir," making a polite request to be hurt, and then thanking her for it put Kat back in the submissive mind-set she had acquired when Reid pushed the gas mask off her face. Being rescued was so much more important than asking why she was in trouble in the first place. And if she could not stop what was happening, at least it had some meaning. If Reid said it did.

And what Reid said was astonishing. She got especially eloquent whenever she hurt Kat's sex. "Bet your cunt hurts most of the time anyway" was one of the things she said. "Hurts from not getting touched. Aches to be hurt, huh? Bet you don't like getting fucked unless it hurts. But you like getting fucked a lot. Partly for the pain of it. So how is it to have pain without the fucking? There will be fucking later, but there isn't any now. I bet you could come on this. Shall I make you come on this?" Kat found herself begging Reid not to do that. She didn't want to know if that could be true, she didn't want to be exposed that way.

So of course Reid told her she couldn't help it, she would come the next time she felt the pointer touch her clit, and she did. It wasn't the kind of come that makes you feel finished, done with sex, and ready to go home. Still, it was intense enough to be embarrassing—the kind of thing that makes you feel like somebody else has dirty pictures of what you did in a motel.

Kat looked humiliated. Reid wanted to defuse that. She put her hand on Kat's mound, not to arouse her, just to steady her and draw off the shame. Kat's ability to come from pain filled her with awe and tenderness. Masochists were so amazing. They took her need to hurt and made it beautiful. "Have you played much with electricity?" Reid asked Kat, unplugging the wand and banishing it somewhere off-camera, along with the gas mask.

"Is that what we're doing?" Kat wondered.

Reid laughed. "Oh, yes. That's what we're doing. I have something else here I want to try. This is wonderful. It can hurt so much you'd just cut off your right arm to make it stop. And it can feel so good, like the fastest tongue in the world flickering on the most sensitive spot. Too bad you don't have rings in your cunt. It makes it easier to attach the electrodes. But these will do."

She had a pair of metal clips, trailing electrical wire and plugs, in her hand. "These are alligator clamps, but I've bent the teeth out and sprung them a little. They're just snug, they don't pinch."

"Awww."

"Don't be a smartass, I've got a pair that I left the teeth on. But those are for another time. You're just a baby, I have to be careful

with you." Reid put a dab of ointment inside each of the metal jaws ("conducting jelly," she explained) and then placed a clip on each of Kat's inner lips. As she had promised, their grip was firm, not painful.

But Kat was too busy clenching her fists to pay attention to that. Whenever she started to relax, Reid would say something that got her back up. Kat was damned if she would back down from anything the little redhead could do with the radio-sized black box that she plugged the clips into. It had three silver rheostats and a little red button. After Reid turned it on, she held the red button down. It made a noise like a miniature klaxon. "That tells me how fast the pulse is," Reid said. "You don't feel anything yet, do you?"

Kat just shook her head. She didn't want to talk.

Reid turned dials. "Tell me when."

Kat screamed.

Reid turned dials back a tad. The pain subsided to a dull roar. "You were supposed to tell me when you felt anything at all, not when you were in agony. Of course, if that's what you wanted to get out of this—" She flipped one dial all the way to the end of its rotation. Kat cried for mercy and yanked on her chains until the posters of the bed creaked. She didn't even think about it, she just did it. She had never done that spontaneously before, begged for something to stop. Come to think of it, had she ever stopped a scene? Usually she just toyed with the idea, teasing herself with it, and before she made up her mind, the woman who was working on her had run out of ideas or steam and quit. She wondered if she had even had a real scene before. Reid's formality and formidable arsenal of equipment made Kat's previous experiences look like rough sex with a few fancy touches. It had taken a lot of manipulation and provocation to get most of her other partners to use a belt or tie her hands behind her back.

"Listen to me, now," Reid said, and Kat focused on her face. She looked so serious, like a well-meaning schoolteacher. Kat had a soft spot in her heart for all the sweet, solemn young women who had tried to keep her in school. She had gotten a few of them to take the pins out of their buns before she discovered wilder women whose hair and hearts were free, and had left school for good. But she still remembered how to paste a sober look across her mug and pretend that this time she really meant it; she was going to change her ways and try much harder.

"You've got to get over this macho idea that I can't really hurt you," Reid said. She knew that some of the anger she felt wasn't really Kat's fault. It was old stuff, accumulated whenever somebody tried to help her lift something she could handle on her own, patted her on the head, or tried to pick her up off the ground without her permission. When you're under five-foot-six, other dykes just don't take you seriously. They think you don't know how to change the oil in your own damn car, they assume that any shelf you put up is not going to stay on the wall, and they are always telling you you're "cute" when you're sweating over something difficult and don't appreciate comments from the audience. Anybody who wants to hassle dykes figures you're a safe target. Reid thought that was scary enough without the additional burden of the big girls' ignorance about how quick and mean a little dyke had to be to survive.

Reid dug a fingernail into her palm to bring herself back into the present. "Stop smirking at me," she told Kat sharply. "You look like a juvenile delinquent who's trying to get out of doin' detention. Don't you understand how hard I have to work to make myself behave and keep within some reasonable limits here? If you don't pay attention and help me, I'm going to start playing just to please myself. I know you're big and bad and mean as hell, but I can break you, Kat, in about five seconds, without even breathing hard. So tell me when it is just barely perceptible."

Kat nodded, panting. Reid inched the dial over. "There? Okay. We'll leave the intensity there for a while, and just play with the speed of the pulse and the shape of the wave." She twirled other buttons. "See? Feels different, doesn't it?" Kat was white-lipped, clutching at the sheet. "Oh, you like it slower. Okay. How about this? Yes, I thought so. Now, isn't it like it's just happening inside you, these regular pulses of pain that well up from your cunt, like lubrication? Couldn't you get used to that and start to expect it and even like it? It's a very seductive pain. It's so intimate. And inescapable. Relentless, even. Makes you want to squirm, huh? I bet it does. I can see it does. Oh, darlin', don't blush, I could make a four-star general tell me how to start World War III with this little black box. You're already taking more than most of the little pussycats I lure to my lair. If it makes you purr and grind around, that's a good thing. I told you, I recognize your stuff. You're a masochist. And that's okay, because I'm a sadist, and I like what you've got. I just want to hurt you severely for a long period of time. It'll make me very happy. You too. You too. You too."

She spun the intensity control over each time she said, "You too." It was like the gas mask. Kat couldn't breathe while it was happening. She said something about that, so Reid got the mask and put it back on her. She had been wrong. The two experiences had nothing in common. And together they were devastating. "I wish I knew how to start World War III," she croaked. Reid laughed so hard, Kat thought she would piss. "You're very funny," Reid said. "But you're thinking too much."

She changed something on the box. At first, Kat thought she was just changing the amplitude, but eventually she realized Reid was just turning the intensity up a little at a time. And she was still getting off on it. It was starting to feel like getting fucked, only there was no penetration, just the same kind of throbbing you got after somebody with really big hands stayed in just a little too long and banged around a bit too much.

"You're still hungry, aren't you, darlin'? Yeah. What's going on down here, where this evil little black box is humming away? Ain't run out of batteries yet. Eveready. That's you, huh? Ready now, anyway."

Reid released her ankles so Kat could lift her legs. She had not realized how cramped her calves and thighs were. When Reid saw how Kat's face twisted up as she worked out the kinks, she leaned forward and undid the locks on the wrist cuffs as well. Kat shook herself, putting joints back in place and driving blood into muscle groups that had been operating on less than a full supply. When she had limbered up, Reid handed her the black box, and laughed at the look on her face.

"I think we understand each other a little better now," Reid said. "If I thought you were going to turn it off, I'd never let you have it. I know what you're going to do with it. You don't know yet. But I do." While she was talking, she completed the awkward process of removing her leather jock. It took a lot of digging into her chaps and tugging on straps and snaps. Kat didn't crack any jokes or even smile, and Reid was grateful. Packing made you so damn vulnerable to other women's approval or ridicule.

Reid lifted Kat's legs, put them on her shoulders, and went in, fat and long. Kat forgot for a while what she held in both hands; she was too busy grinding back and grinning.

"Feels good?" Reid asked.

"Yes," she growled.

"Have at it, then," was the invitation, and Kat accepted. Reid had to dig both of her knees into the mattress and clamp her hands around Kat's hips to keep from being bucked off the bed. She could barely reach Kat's nipples, and she knew that messing with them would only increase the buffeting she was taking, but she couldn't resist the temptation to twist those dials. Fortunately, Kat wasn't about to let that spoon slip out of her sugar bowl for a long time. She wrapped her legs around Reid's butt and locked her into place. It took a couple of comes (well, more) to take the edge off the hunger that Reid had created in her. What the hell was Reid saying about a one-woman rodeo?

When Kat became aware of her surroundings again, Reid was softly urging her to check out the buttons on the box. So she started twiddling dials, feeling silly. But what happened to her cunt wasn't silly at all. It was dramatic. Having somebody fuck you while this other thing was going on could be habit-forming. She was terribly curious about how many different ways it could feel. She played with the frequency, she played with the amplitude. And always, always, that dial that governed the intensity of the current seemed to creep up until she had it all the way over to the right and was dammitall shouting at Reid to really fuck her, not bullshit around, put it in, motherfucker, and Reid pulled out her dick and slick-slammed her fist in there, and punched it out and punched it out and made it happen just right, while somebody said, "Come home, come home, come home."

And she did.

When Kat opened her eyes, there was a somewhat greasy and very short person with red hair grinning like a maniac and wiggling her ears. The electrodes dangled from Reid's hand. "Damn, you're good. I'm not bad, either," Reid said. She shoved the electrical box off the bed. "Roll over. I want to beat you."

"What?"

This bleary-eyed question made Reid's heart leap with glee. So it was possible for her to wear this big girl down. "Are you deaf? You didn't think we were done, did you?" Reid was tired of wires and dials. She wanted to move, jump, dance, kick ass, flex her muscles, throw her weight around.

"Well, the thought had crossed my mind, but I can get amnesia at a moment's notice. Hold still. You're makin' me dizzy."

"Uh-uh. Get amnesia now. Do I have to tie you down?"

Kat wondered where her pride had gone. With somebody who was in her own weight class, she could always hide behind the illusion that she was being made to do things she didn't really like. Now she wouldn't even have the excuse of being in bondage. Her resistance dissolved, and she found herself blushing at the thought of how much she craved Reid's severe attentions. She went cold and hot at the thought of giving it up to somebody who didn't look to be her match at all, and she ached to lay her big head on Reid's perfectly shined, little-boy boots. Apparently the old proverb was right. The size of the dog in the fight had nothing to do with it.

"Not if you don't want to," she mumbled with her head down, her mouth against the mattress.

"I'd rather not."

"Okay, but, uh, you can't hit my ass."

"Fine. Nothing on the butt, then." Reid trotted off, no doubt to return loaded down with whips, like a leather Santa Claus. She hadn't asked why Kat's ass was off-limits, and Kat was thankful. Really, now, how many fucking reasons could there be for somebody to hate getting hit on the ass? It wasn't because you loved your dear old dad. She intensely disliked explaining all that old shit to people. "Oh, that's terrible," they would say, and their eyes would get all misty. "I know just how you feel. I'm an addict and an alcoholic and a codependent adult child of alcoholic parents and an incest survivor with terrible food allergies." It made her want to pop them one right in the mouth. Nobody knew how she felt. Not ever. She wouldn't mind telling Reid all about it, sometime, but not right now. They were having too much fun.

Sure enough, the jolly old elf was back, tossing whips onto the bed. One, two, three, many.

"There's only one of me," Kat warned.

"I know. But there's enough of you to make a lot of hamburger. Grab those chains."

At first, Kat kept her head turned so she could see what Reid was using. There was a leather slapper, a riding crop with a very large but rigid flap of leather on its end, and a short whip with many flat strands. Then her neck got a crick in it. She had to straighten out her spine and lie flat. That meant she couldn't see, but Kat decided it didn't matter. It was easier to just close her eyes and let Reid whale on her. She could look later. All she knew was that her back felt as if it was heating up and swelling, rising like bread. She was relaxing and tensing, relaxing and tensing, as if one long muscle controlled her whole body. There were deep, thudding blows and wide blows that landed mostly on the surface. There were sharp, stinging, cutting, burning, and crushing blows — every feeling you could get from a whip. But it wasn't confusing, somehow. Each change soothed the pain from the previous bout and lifted her up another level, into acceptance and excitement. Both of them made occasional silly remarks, kept each other laughing. Kat was purring, rolling from side to side and wanting to be fucked again, but not wanting the whipping to stop.

Reid put one hand on the small of her back, slid it down. Kat's ass came off the bed to soothe itself along that hand. It patted her, and the tips of the fingers barely cupped the crack of her ass. Kat had no fear that Reid would suddenly take a notion to smack her butt or stab a finger into her asshole. This amount of touching was just pleasant — making her aware of her whole body again.

Then Reid shifted position, put both her hands on Kat's shoulders, and swung a leg over her. Her shoulders felt enormous. The slabs of muscle there were swollen and heavy from the whipping. Her skin smarted under Reid's hands, the abraded skin reacting to the salt in her perspiration. The weight on her ass was reassuring, pressed her back into the bed. She was not going to float away. Reid was not done with her.

The switchblade clicked open, the tip of it resting within her ear. It tickled. "Hold still," Reid said, and cut her from shoulder to shoulder. Kat bucked. "Goddammit, don't push up at me!" Reid snapped, alarmed. She slapped the open wound. But Kat couldn't help it. The pleasure and pain were too intense not to roll up and greet them. Steel parting flesh was her favorite sensation.

"Do me again," she hissed, and Reid cut below the first line of blood. At Kat's urgent request, five molten ribbons were laid across her back. The flowing blood seemed to release some big knot that had been buried in Kat's gut, and she began to cry, happy to be freed from its weight. Reid stayed on top of her, hanging on to her shoulders, rubbing her face in Kat's blood and growling softly.

"You smell good," she rumbled, and Kat felt as if she could go to sleep and never wake up again.

Then the air in the room seemed to freeze. Everything was suddenly different. Colors were brighter. The world was back in focus. A sharp, musky odor hit Kat in the face. Was that Reid? "Roll over," Reid said.

Kat hastened to obey. The tone of voice was flat and cold. She looked up. This was not the jolly old elf. No, this was another person entirely, twirling a cane, tipping it end-for-end from finger to finger. She took a closer look. Reid gave her a very unpleasant grin. Why were her canines so big?

"The better to tear your throat out with, darlin'. But not yet. Not yet. What's wrong? Don't you recognize me? You've been calling me out for the longest time."

What had Reid said earlier, something about the beast?

"Oh, yes, it's me. The other face of passion. You're afraid now, aren't you?"

"No," Kat lied.

"Then lock yourself in."

Kat cursed herself for a fool. The headlines would read, "Big Girl Found Murdered in S&M Sex Den." But her hands were already shackling her ankles, using the open padlocks that Reid had left hanging from the links of the chains. Those hands were shaking, but they seemed determined to do their job. She watched what was happening, wondering why she could not stop it. How could she be so frightened? Reid wasn't threatening her. There was no bluster. But there was still something violent in the air, like an apparently peaceful neighborhood that's about to erupt into a riot. Kat locked down her left hand and held up the right for Reid to fasten down.

Their eyes met. Reid licked her lips. Her tongue seemed to loll. The fingers that circled Kat's wrist and put it down onto the chain were very strong. "I need this," Reid said, and Kat heard the echo of her own voice in the hallway, felt again the searing path of Reid's blade across her ribs. Need. A need so bad it could make you take your bike through a red light at eighty miles an hour or get you into a fight you couldn't win, unless you learned how to let it out quietly at home with a razor blade or a lit cigarette or a needle full of smack. Well. This was something she was familiar with, after all. Probably. Maybe. She warily eyed the circling cane.

"Give me this," Reid said, and it was a completely selfish demand. Tops do not usually make such demands. Or if they do, it is only for a mouthful or two of what they really want. Reid was asking to be fed a whole meal. Kat swallowed hard. Her thighs were shaking.

"You can have whatever I've got," she said. "I might need a little help is all."

"Help?" Reid laid the cane across her thighs, sawed it back and forth. "Oh, yes. You mean you don't want to have a choice. But the chains are real, and I'm real, and you really can't just get up and go home. Not until I'm through with you."

She hit her lightly, rapidly, the cane bouncing with dreadful flexibility. There was a rhythm in this that made it a little less frightening. It acquired a predictability. Even if it was getting harder and harder, Kat knew it was going to be just so fast, so many beats per minute. The harder Reid hit her, the slower she went. Just before the blows got difficult to handle, she stopped entirely and told Kat to take a deep breath. Then she brought her arm down. The curve was beautiful, and Kat saw the welt come up before she felt a thing.

That was a good trick. But she was a little too busy to be full of admiration. This was devilish. The sensation started on the surface, went deep, expanded, contracted, and all of it was awful. There was simply no standing still for this. She was really glad Reid had chained her down.

The arm went up again. Kat took a deep breath, released it, and there was the welt oh God where is the pain where is the pain this is going to be bad — there! The pain! *Shit! What was I in such a hurry for?* Kat cursed to herself.

Reid gave her four more strokes, changed sides, and did six from the other side. "I'm a traditionalist," was all she said. Kat had no idea what she was referring to. She had never been caned before. It was not something anybody she knew would do. Maybe if she were British, she would have some memories or some fantasies that would make this easier to take. But she did not. So she fell back on Reid, the look on her face, the perfect concentration, the set of her shoulders, that look of a prowling wolf that was hunting because it had to, because the only way to get what it needed was to go out and find prey and overpower it. She kept making herself say, "Yes, sir, do me again, sir," and that helped some. So did the breathing. Relaxing when she saw that arm go up was an ordeal, but the one time she got hit on top of tensed muscles convinced her it was necessary.

There were deep red and black lines across both of her legs. The marks came in parallel sets. Where the tip of the cane had gone in, it was outlined in red, with a deep blue bruise around it. Some of the cane strokes had bitten deep into the tender inner thigh. One stroke had glanced off her cunt.

"You're so good," Reid murmured, and it was like being blessed. Kat had thought she was doing lousy. So there was hope. This could not last forever. And Reid said she was good. She would be good. All she had to do was stay here, breathe, relax, stay here—

"I beg your pardon," Reid said, "but this is something I really have to do."

The descending arm was too fast to follow. Just as the cane touched Kat's flesh, Reid pulled her arm straight back, so the blow both crushed and cut. Kat screamed so hard she thought her guts would come out of her mouth. But Reid went on until she quit screaming. Then the cane snapped. And Reid instantly stopped, dropped the broken cane, and sat down heavily. Her hands felt like she was wearing concrete mittens, but she managed to fumble the locks open and let Kat go. Then she put her arms around her and collapsed on top of her. "I'm through," she said to the big woman's neck.

"You're not," Kat said. "Let's fuck. Me first. My turn." She rolled on top of Reid, and was surprised to find out how well the small body fit against her torso. She half-expected Reid to bite or slap her and make some pompous statement about never letting herself get flipped. It's true Reid put up a fight, but it was the kind of lazy struggle that a girl makes to turn herself on. It was a covert way of feeling Kat's muscles. Kat knew all about that dance and liked her part in it. At first, she tried to go a little easy on Reid. After all, she was ten inches taller and at least sixty pounds heavier than the other woman.

But Reid didn't want a walk in the park on a sunny day, she wanted a steeplechase. Reid got fucked the same way she topped, with her teeth bared. "Talk to me!" she insisted, digging her strong thumbs into Kat's biceps. "Tell me what this is, tell me what we're doing. *Talk to me.*"

Kat snarled, "Now you know how big I really am, because I really am on top of you, I really do have your hands pinned down, and you really can't get away until I'm done with you." At that, Reid grabbed Kat's ears, wrapped her thighs around Kat's forearm, and came, damn near pulling off all three appendages.

"Your turn to catch," Reid said when she got her breath back. "Gimme the Probe."

"I think the bottle's empty," Kat said apologetically.

"It better not be, or I'll shove it up your ass." Kat growled, and Reid laughed. "With your kind cooperation, of course," she drawled.

"That'll be the day, even for you, Miss Wonder Dwarf. Wouldn't it be easier to just let me get in my bag and give you my extra bottle?" Kat scooted off the bed and went to find her duffel.

When she got back, Reid accepted the new lube with a little bow. "Nice to know how you expected the evening to end," she said.

"Fuck you, Reid."

"No, I'm afraid it's your turn now."

■■

Later, while they ate some Top Ramen (Reid had scrambled an egg into it, saying, "I need some protein," and Kat thought it looked disgusting, but she ate it anyway, trying to be polite) and drank nonalcoholic Coors Cutters (which really made Kat gag), Reid told her the story about Artie's obnoxious teammate. Kat grimaced. "Where can I get my season tickets for midget wrestling?" she asked.

Much later, after they had shuffled around the topic of sleeping arrangements and decided Kat would stay over and sleep in Reid's bed, the big girl said, "How can I thank you?"

Reid said, "You can take me to dinner tomorrow night. I'll wear my strapless black velvet sheath."

"Oh, fuck all," Kat said. "There is no Goddess. There can't be, because I'm in more trouble than even She could think up."

"But not more than you deserve," Reid said.

"Close."

"Not even close."

Daddy

■■

I'm getting dressed for my daddy. She is waiting for me in the living room, sitting on the couch, drinking shots of Jack Daniel's and chasing them with beer. She just got here a few hours ago. Because we live so far apart, we only see each other two or three times a year. Of course, if we quit spending so much money on long-distance telephone calls, we could probably pay for a few more plane tickets. All that aside, now that she is here, this apartment has become our world. We probably won't go outside until I drive her to the airport. For the next few days, we will talk, have sex, and eat. We will do all three of these things as if we were starving. I already feel a little crazy: confined, determined to get under her skin even though the end result is that I will lose her, and angry because I know this is as good as it will ever be for us. Our story will not have a happy ending.

What a big suitcase that word "daddy" is. It's jammed so full of stuff that I never seem to get it closed. There's no time to unpack the whole bag now, but the most important things, the ones I use the most often, are close to the top. A few of them have toppled onto the floor, and they demand to be recognized. I have to name them before I can put them away and play. (Play? I don't think I do anything more important than this, or more serious.)

At the age of twelve, I stopped calling my male parent "daddy" and referred to him only as "father" and "sir." It was my first attempt to get revenge by following the rules just a little too closely. Since he overtly demanded nothing but respect and subordination from me, I gave him that, and worked hard to withhold the trust and affection that he also wanted, but could not ask for. That was difficult. My father is a very charming man. He is funny, flirtatious, expansive, and generous; tells great stories; makes perfect strangers fall in love with him. It was hard to be at war with him. As an adolescent, I didn't understand why I couldn't keep sitting on his lap and giving him mashed-potato-and-gravy kisses. I wanted to ask his advice, tell him my secrets.

But my father has no control over his temper. When he is angry, he throws whatever he has in his hand, slaps the closest person (sometimes more than once), and says something caustic and crushing. If he knows anything about you that will wither your ego or deflate your self-esteem, it comes out then. His rage is terrifying. It comes without warning, for no good reason. My father selected me for a target because I fought back, I fought well, and because I deliberately put myself in his path to keep him away from my mother and my younger brothers and sisters. I was not very old when I realized that I wanted to kill him. I had help figuring this out. Because after we fought, we would make up by going downstairs to the family room and cleaning his rifles and pistols together. He always made sure I knew which bullets fit which guns.

I knew my father would kill me, if he could make a suitable accident happen, because I would not submit to him or get out of his way when he needed to terrorize somebody. On some level, he probably realized that having a hard-on for me meant that he was turned on to something queer, strange, and masculine. I never went deer-hunting with my father. I never went driving with him alone. I never turned my back on him.

I wanted to be grown-up so I could take my mother away from him. He thought this meant I did not love him. And it's true, my love for him was very hard to see. But if I pretended to be more her child than his, it was only camouflage. I hated my mother's religion, her prudery, her shyness and rigidity. Of the two of them, she was less crazy, but only marginally so. He punished me for no good reason, but she wanted to squeeze all the joy out of my life to prevent God from punishing me later, forever.

I knew this whole situation was really her fault because she married him and she stayed with him, and I had utter contempt for those choices. When she was angry with him, she would try to seduce me into thinking I was her best friend, her only friend, her boyfriend. When she decided to forgive him, I was supposed to shed this adult, male identity and become a subservient, compliant, ignorant girl-child. These flip-flops were every bit as dangerous as his rage. My mother taught me how to figure out what women really want, and she showed me how vicious people can be when you tell them their own truth. I also learned that I have no control over my desire to protect others. Even if they are stronger than me, even if there is no way I can win, even if they don't deserve my help, I have to try to put my body between someone who is hurt or frightened and the thing that threatens them.

I did not want to take my mother away from my father for her own sake. I wanted to possess her because I understood that would make me like him, his equal, another man. And then, I thought, we would be able to touch each other again and our house would not be full of anger and sexual tension. I blamed my tits and pubic hair and pimples for giving me a sex and driving my father away from me.

My mother was not the one I wanted to come to my room at night and teach me what to do with the desire that shook my adolescent flesh. She was not the one I wanted to show me how someone else's hands could make me feel. He was my hero, the strong one, the one who risked his life every day by going to work so far underground, setting off dynamite and digging tunnels in the treacherous earth. I learned how to touch other people by giving my father backrubs when he came home from work, slipping my hands under the light, one-piece garment that all adult Mormons wear to remind them of their temple vows. I ignored the way my mother rattled pans and slammed the oven door in the kitchen while I loved his muscles and inhaled his Old Spice cologne.

Now I am older, and so is he. Just four years after I left home, my mother finally found her backbone because of my father's unrelenting cruelty toward her youngest son, my baby brother, the sissy. She told him he could get a divorce if he wanted one because he was not living in her house anymore. So he married a tart-tongued, busty woman my age who is half-Mexican and half-Basque. When she's angry with him, she makes Mexican food that's too hot for him to eat. She never goes to church. She matches him drink for drink and won't give up her job. They read each other *Penthouse Forum* in bed. There are no more children in his house. He's happy with her, I think. She doesn't add to the load of guilt he began to accumulate when his own father abandoned him, his mother, and his sister in the middle of winter, and he was not old enough to work the farm by himself and keep them all fed.

I do not see him very often. But he is with me every day. Sometimes I think all of us are incest survivors, because we take both of our parents with us every time we go to bed. I don't believe my father ever came to my room at night. But I sometimes wonder if it would not have been easier if he had put an end to my fear and simply done what we both knew he wanted to do. Every time I flirt with a waitress or buy a woman a drink, I am doing what my father taught me. Does that make me a rebel or a collaborator?

After the beatings I took from him for being queer, no gay basher can make me turn aside from another woman's hips. And I do not intend to let the desire I felt for him go unnamed or wasted. I deserve a daddy who needs and wants and admires me. I deserve a daddy who will touch me until I come. As one of my friends who is a convert to Christianity told me, "I need to have at least one loving male figure in my life."

So here I am, getting dressed for someone who is not afraid of me or my desire, someone I can trust with my life and my back and my sex.

I wad up the white knee socks, cram my feet inside, and unroll them over my calves. I hate them. I want to wear nylons, but Daddy won't let me. Daddy says I'm trying to grow up too fast. So I have to wear these stupid, thick socks and oxfords instead of high heels. He says, "The nuns wouldn't let you wear high heels to school anyway." But I'm not going to school right now, and I think excessive consistency is bad for sexual fantasies. Hot with resentment (and nothing else, do you hear me?), I pull up white cotton briefs, eager to cover my shaved pubic mound and outer lips. The thin fabric rasps delicately across my clitoris, which is exposed, unprotected, always getting bumped and rubbed.

Daddy says I'm not old enough to wear a bra, so I tug on an undershirt. My breasts make it bulge, so I hurry to button up my shirt. It is plain cotton, white, with one breast pocket. In the pocket I put a folded hanky. The pleated wool skirt that I drop over my head is a cream, green, and brown plaid. I used to wear a cream-colored cardigan with it, but Daddy found a green wool jacket for me in a thrift store. On the left breast pocket it says, "Holy Name Academy." The motto is embroidered below: *Serve and Obey.*

There are cigarettes inside the jacket. I don't smoke, but Daddy put the cigarettes there along with a handful of rubbers, so there they stay, next to the catechism booklet. I have not memorized today's lesson. But it's too late for that. I fasten a gold chain around my neck. It has a little gold cross dangling from it, another gift from my daddy. Because I am angry about the lesson, I march into the bathroom and slather some lipstick onto my mouth. Daddy won't like that at all.

When I present myself in the living room, Daddy ignores me. This makes me bite my nails and study her; try to figure out how much slack I will have tonight. If Daddy's other girls, the grown-up ones, the hookers, have been making their quotas, I can expect to be humored a bit, allowed a few mistakes. But something is usually going wrong in Daddy's life. The fences take too big a cut, the cops are greedy, the goddamn car needs repairs — and I am the safety valve. Which is why I don't feel safe at all. Steam is about to whistle through me, and I am going to get scalded. I am not tough enough to take this. That's why I got the job.

My daddy has short black hair and is wearing slacks, a man's shirt, and a tie. A black leather trenchcoat, suitable for concealing a sawed-off shotgun or a boosted carton of cigarettes, has been thrown across an armchair. I want to sit down and wrap myself up in that long coat, but I'm not allowed to use the furniture unless I'm told to sit down.

On the coffee table is a shot glass and a bottle of Jack Daniel's. On the floor is a dog dish. Daddy pours and drinks a shot of whisky. The dish on the floor is empty.

"My little girl," Daddy says, and I am very frightened. This is not an endearment. "Get over here."

I do not come quickly enough. Daddy grabs my arm and pulls me, hard, so I fall. There will be a thumb-shaped bruise above my elbow tomorrow. I stop myself with my hands, but the floor is still hard against my knees. I spend a lot of time on the floor when my daddy is around. I remind myself that getting there is the hard part, that once I get used to it, I am going to want to stay on the floor, and it is going to take another sharp yank to get me up on my feet again. Still, there is a part of me that dreads the whole evening. If I can get through this scene, I promise myself, I will never do this again.

"Wipe that shit off your mouth," Daddy says and slaps me in the face with his cock. While I was giving myself that pep talk about overcoming my resistance to kneeling, I noticed his fly coming down, the hand (that hand that can be folded in half lengthwise and go impossibly deep into me) fishing within Daddy's trousers. It was what made the pep talk work, probably.

So there it is: the reason why I am here. Not my daddy's dick (which is, after all, dispensable), but my need for it. The need that makes me open my mouth, tongue the rubber head, and try to get as much of it down my throat as I can before it is taken away. Sucking a dildo is so perverse, evoking a series of emotions and images that ought to be confusing, but that make perfect sense at the time. I am sorry the instrument that moves in my mouth is not flesh, because then I would be able to give my daddy pleasure beyond the visuals, the way it makes him feel to see me choke, cry, and struggle to expand my physical capacities to accept him. I am also (more selfishly) sorry because a real cock would come long before my daddy will get tired of this game and withdraw. Then I would be off the hook.

On the other hand, I am glad this is a dildo and not a cock, because I don't have to worry about STDs and because its presence means I am with a woman, which is consistent with my sexual identity, allowing me to sample the pleasure of oral violation without violating my sense of myself. And I strive to make this act as physically pleasurable as possible. I know the base of the dildo is riding against my daddy's cunt, and the hand that I have wrapped around the shaft of his cock is there to manipulate that point of contact as well as to keep me from being smothered by my own enthusiasm and Daddy's hands on the back of my neck. Then there is the point in time where I lose awareness of my daddy's gender, or even my own. It is an infantile state. I am sucking, and this is what I must do to live. It is all that life is.

"You're such an incorrigible slut," Daddy says. "Advertising that pretty little mouth. Trying to get yourself thrown out of school? Who's that lipstick for, huh? The boys? You got a crush on some pimple-faced high-school dropout who's going to take my baby to the drive-in movies and pop her cherry on the backseat of his car? No way, honey. Your daddy takes better care of you than that. Doesn't he? Don't I?"

The shaft in my throat is gone, and I miss it. I try to find it again (my eyes blinded by tears), but I am getting slapped, and this ruins my sense of direction. Snot, spit, and tears fly off my face beneath the glancing blows from my daddy's hand.

"Answer me!" Daddy says.

"What's the question?" I squeal, shamed by my weakness (I hate pain), my undignified, wobbly voice, my inability to remember the simplest thing.

"Doesn't your daddy take better care of you than any of the local punks?"

"Yes, Daddy, you love me best of all."

"Do you have a boyfriend?"

"No, Daddy, I'm your little girl."

Daddy reaches under my skirt. My belly arches, and I make it easier for him to hook his fingers under the crotch of my panties and feel me. I want to be touched. It means no more hitting. (Although I wouldn't enjoy this respite if I thought that meant no more hitting, ever again.)

The shaved flesh is smooth; the cleft and its protruding inhabitants are wet. "That's why I keep you shaved," Daddy says, "to remind you that until you're all grown-up, you belong to me, and you have to do what I say. You have to take good care of your daddy." Then she slaps me again, a really hard blow that makes my head snap. "So I don't want to see any more slutty red paint on your face. If you're going to act like a whore, I'll have to treat you like one. You may think you're ready for that, you might think you'd like it, but I know better."

The tone changes from nasty to wheedling. "Come and sit here by your old man."

Daddy slides over a little, and I sit as far away from him as I can get. For that, I get slapped again and dragged over to the other end of the couch. "You're not going to make this difficult, are you?" Daddy says. "Don't tell me you've forgotten everything I've taught you. Do I need to teach you a lesson?"

Daddy unbuttons my jacket, "finds" my cigarettes and condoms, and shakes his head. "Lipstick. Smoking. Rubbers, even. Ready for anything, aren't you? You're hanging out with the wrong crowd. I haven't been strict enough with you. From now on, you have to come straight home from school. Here. Where I can keep an eye on you. You're grounded for a month, young lady."

This tirade sounds pretty middle-class, coming from my non-nuclear-family dad, and for some reason the lack of obscenity in it makes me really mad. I know that isn't the end of my punishment, but there's nothing I can do to hurry this up or delay it. Daddy is the only one who knows the script for the evening. I have to just sit here and play my part.

My green wool uniform jacket has been removed. Daddy pours and drinks another shot. Now he is unbuttoning my blouse. His cock is still exposed. I want to touch it. I do not dare. My daddy wants to touch me now, and I have to let him.

"I'm so good to you," Daddy says, feeling me. "Showing you what to expect when you grow up. Showing you how to make me happy. Taking care of you." Those long fingers have found my nipples and are making them a curse. How can something that goes on so far away from my cunt make it awash in sensation? "Don't pretend you don't like this," Daddy says, close to my face. I smell whisky and hair oil. I wish Daddy smoked. I like the way cigarettes smell.

"I do like it," I whimper. It is the line I have been taught to say, and I learned it quickly because it was true. Is true. No one will save me from this. The only person I can tell the truth to will use it against me.

"You're getting so grown-up. Pretty soon all the boys will be chasing you. Touch me," Daddy whispers.

He exposes my breasts and begins to suck on their tips, pushing them together so the nipples nearly meet. My breasts are so big that he has to push hard to squash them together this way. They ache inside from being shoved together. I want to cry, so I do, a little, and pick up my daddy's cock. I stroke it. "Do you remember when we used to play this game, when you were little?" Daddy says.

"Yes, Daddy," I gasp. I want to spread my legs. I want the thing I am handling to be shoved inside of me. But I can't stop handling it, not yet. And I have to keep my knees primly together.

"But we play other games now, don't we?"

"Yes, Daddy."

I am pushed off the couch and land on my rump, skirt awry, blouse tugged out of my waistband, undershirt wadded up in my armpits. A rude word almost issues from my lips, but I bite it back.

"Get on your hands and knees," Daddy says. I comply. "Pull down your panties." I comply. "Spread your legs." A moment before, I longed to do just that. Now I hesitate. I hear Daddy's belt leaving its loops. I don't know whether to obey now or not, since spreading my legs will make it easier for him to hit my poor shaved pussy. Of course, after I have been hit (only six times, that is all I can stand, I really have no willpower at all), I spread my legs and get hit there anyway, which makes me really cry.

"I hate you," I say, knowing it is not wise.

"I know," Daddy says. "Hand me the doggie dish, since you're going to be such a bitch."

"Fuck you," I say, getting dumber by the minute.

Daddy takes the dish. "You know I don't like it when you use bad language. Turn around and keep your head down."

I know Daddy has dropped her pants and is pissing in the dish.

"If you'd been a good girl, this would be Jack Daniel's instead of nasty hot piss," Daddy says smugly. That will be the day. I know little girls don't get to drink hard liquor, unless you count what comes out with the piss.

The bowl waits for me. I imagine there is a little steam rising from its rocking surface. Maybe I could drink her piss with my mouth up against her cunt. It would be an extension of cunnilingus. But I can't do this. Can't and won't.

"Aren't you thirsty?" Daddy asks, sounding concerned, and straps my ass before I can answer. Oddly enough, the beating does make my throat dry, perhaps because I am howling like a monkey. It takes a while before being belted seems worse than drinking piss out of a dog bowl on the floor. As I lower my head and stick my tongue out, I hear the click and hiss of the Polaroid. Another picture for our family album. The liquid surrounding my tongue is salty and bitter, but luckily still a little warm. Could anything be more revolting than cold piss? Then Daddy's boot comes between me and the bowl, and it slides away.

"The fact that you're willing is enough," she tells me. She is speaking out of role, in a kind voice that recognizes who we are when we are not steeped in these alternate personas. She has a knack for this, knowing when to back off and go easy on me. She is not this nice to the full-time bottoms (most of them butches or female-to-male transsexuals) who are always tugging on her jacket.

Sometimes I wish I were a masochist. Other people might think they're sick, but nobody snickers at their scars. Submissives embarrass even other S/M people. It's ironic that the kind of scene we're doing now — butch top, femme bottom — which is probably the most common kind of play is also the one that leather dykes talk the least about. Very few of us admit that we want a daddy, and an even smaller number of us can say out loud that we want to be Daddy's little girl. Even perverts think if you put on a skirt, you must be a candy-ass.

I'm lucky to have a daddy who isn't put off by my closet full of evening gowns and my drawer full of bustiers and black stockings. The gleam in his eye has mended my broken heart. My mother was wrong; the queer-haters who call me an ugly dyke are wrong. I'm capable of being a pretty girl, and I don't have to give up my feistiness to do it. I know that most people can't see any power in putting on a dress or makeup. Most people would laugh at me right now, or go off and be sick. But the only thing that really matters is how this makes me feel, and how it looks to my daddy. I have to concentrate on that.

"No, it's not," I say, full of a quiet fury about all of this. "Just being willing is never enough." I stalk across the floor (if someone can be said to stalk while she is on all fours) and chug the contents of the bowl the way my daddy throws back his shots. A masochist's pride is based on their ability to turn any extreme physical sensation into pleasure. A submissive's pride is based on their ability to obey any difficult order without hesitation. "You have to live out the things in your heart, or you don't deserve them," I tell the floor, speaking a little too loudly for somebody in my position.

"Then come over here and show me what you've got," Daddy says. Her tone of voice is lazy, but I can tell I made my point. I turn around and scoot across the floor to where he is reclining on the floor with his head on a pillow. Once he is sure that I am looking at his dick, he rolls a condom over it and lubes it up. I wish that dick were just a half-inch shorter. When we do it this way, it goes in just a little too far.

We've only played this game a few times, but I know what parts of it excite my daddy too much to be left out. I know I will be made to fuck myself. Daddy likes making me work for what I want. Sometimes I have to sit on my daddy's lap, facing him, so he can hurt my nipples while I rise and fall upon his dick. But tonight I have to kneel on the floor, and my tits bounce against my thighs as I rock on the shaft that I have coveted all night. Now I ride it with a fury to be rid of it. My daddy likes fucking me when I am angry. He likes knowing I can't do anything about it except come.

But before I am allowed to come, I am penetrated again. Daddy sinks two, then three greasy fingers into my ass. Now I will say whatever it takes to get this woman to keep on being my daddy, to keep my daddy fucking me until I come. I believe I would do anything to make this continue. I do not care what it looks like. I do not care what somebody else in the room might think. And this freedom from my ambivalence, my self-consciousness, is as precious as the physical pleasure of being perfectly fucked and mind-fucked, the treasured object of my daddy's amusement and contempt and cruelty, only a toy, but an irreplaceable, priceless toy.

Daddy says, "You dirty girl, you're dirty here. And you don't care, do you? I think you like it this way. With your ass full of shit." Then I am coming the only way I know how to come and be finished, done, spent, satisfied.

Of course this is not enough for Daddy. Daddy has other plans. The night is young. There is still the matter of the cigarettes, the catechism lesson that I have not memorized, and the lipstick. Daddy grabs me by the elbow, twists my arm painfully behind my back, and marches me into the bedroom. I am told to take off everything. On the bed is some black underwear. On the floor, high-heeled shoes.

"Since you want to be a whore, I'm going to train you to be one," Daddy tells me. "But I still love you too much to put you out on the street. You'll have to be my whore, my own sweet, private fantasy."

Daddy dresses me. First he puts me into a black bra. I am speechless with admiration. She has so much patience, this woman I love, to painstakingly dress me in these fragile and intricate garments, just so she can have the pleasure of removing them later. It is a reassuring ritual, proof that she likes to see me this way as much as I like being seen. It is also a way to preen and get petted without Daddy having to be sucky and sentimental.

The bra has an underwire that holds my breasts up. It fastens in front, to make it easy to take off. There are black panties. They fit funny, and I tug at them, trying to adjust them, until I realize they feel different because they are crotchless. I imagine her buying these things for me to wear, and I blush. It took guts as well as good taste. I know how tacky the clerks in lingerie departments can be to butch dykes. There is a garter belt, stockings with seams. Daddy brushes my hair out, then holds my face with one hand and paints it with the other. I sit on the bed with my legs akimbo, feeling relaxed, luxurious, and doomed.

"Whore," Daddy says. "That's what you'd like, isn't it? You'd like to be out there letting everybody stick it to you. But I know what would happen to my baby out there. It's better for you to get it from me. I can show you things nobody else can. I only want to do what's best for you. Besides, this is my pussy. I made it. So it's mine. I can do anything I want to it. Including fuck it. Or hurt it."

"No, Daddy!" I cry when I see the clothespins. I clap my knees together.

"Don't tell me no," Daddy says and forces my legs apart. In between the shaved lips, my clitoris is prominent, easily pinched up between his fingers and placed between the jaws of the clamp. There are three of them. My sex is painfully compressed. The clothespins protrude through the crotchless lace panties. I cannot bear to put my legs together now, nor can I bear to be used.

Daddy takes me to the bathroom. I have to crawl. Crawling hurts my cunt. It hurts my pride, too. I have an unreasonable amount of pride. It keeps coming up, like the national debt, distracting me when I want to do other things. In the bathroom, there is an enema bag. A series of nozzles have been laid out on a towel. The smaller ones are there to make the last one look even bigger. It is black, and has a rosebud tip on it. Daddy puts it in my mouth.

"Get it wet," he says. "Daddy doesn't want this to hurt when it goes in. Do you remember? This is how Daddy taught you to suck on things, to let me put things in your mouth, so you could get them wet before Daddy put them in you. When you were little, you were naughty a lot and wouldn't go every day. I had to put you on a schedule. I had to train you. It's important not to forget your training. I don't want to spoil you."

Daddy withdraws the fat nozzle from my mouth and jams it into the hose on the bulging red enema bag. The clamp on the hose responds to his thumb, much like my clitoris. He inserts the nozzle into my mouth again and lets a little warm water squirt against my tongue. His voice is persuasive. "Suck it. Drink it. Taste it. You'd like to suck my cock, wouldn't you? You'll get it later, little-girl whore. Suck this for now. You'll do whatever I tell you to do with that pretty mouth. Do you like your lipstick now? Do you? Then tell Daddy thank you. Thank Daddy for making you be his pretty slut."

I repeat the ritual. It's much better than reciting my catechism, although there are some odd similarities. But no amount of verbal acquiescence can prepare my bottom for the cold KY, the invasion of an enema nozzle that is very nearly the size of a penis. I imagine water flowing into me before any is released, and yelp. "Crybaby," Daddy reproves, and lets it gush.

Once again, my resistance is shattered. No matter how I plead, the entire bag is emptied into my bowels. As soon as I can, I must rush to perch on the bowl. There isn't even time to get myself into trouble by asking Daddy to leave the room. I can't help myself, I have to empty my cramping belly. Daddy hugs me because my stomach hurts and rubs my shoulders while I whimper. Then he flushes for me, removing some of the smell from the room, and lets me wipe myself. Somebody who would stay with me through all this, see me this way, must love me.

I feel giddy, but Daddy has refilled the bag. It's time for another trip to the floor. This time the nozzle goes in more smoothly, and the water disappears quickly. My ass is plugged, and Daddy crops me. I scream, but only because it hurts. I am not really fighting now. I know if I scream really well, Daddy will only hit me a dozen or so times. And I like the way it feels a few minutes after each blow. My ass feels hot, big and hot, and I want to rub it up against something, anything. Every now and then my thighs bump the clothespins between my legs, and I mew. But I can barely feel them unless they are touched directly.

Daddy fixes that. He has me position myself with my thighs apart and uses the clothespins to jerk me off. I am instructed to come on the pain. When I do, I am surprised and pleased. Then I have to extrude the butt plug and drop my water. Daddy lets me do this in private. After I wipe with paper, Daddy gives me a wet towel. I stand up and clean myself carefully.

Now I am positioned on the bed, on all fours again. My hands are cuffed together. Daddy works his cock into my ass. The head sliding past the sphincter seems to make a popping noise, but it is probably only in my mind. Being considerate, Daddy holds still once he is in, to let me get used to this awful urgency. I am the first one to move. Of course. I have no self-control. That is why my daddy is always restricting and punishing me. I can't seem to learn my lesson. I just can't seem to behave myself.

"Can I come, Daddy?" I beg. "Let me come, please."

"Take off one of the clothespins."

"No!" I shriek. Daddy has been handling my welts. Now his hands dig into them. I do not heed the warning. Several hard slaps on my butt make the crop marks burn. I take off one clothespin, yell, and cry. Daddy fucks me harder. I want to come, I think I might come even without permission. But Daddy knows this and stops moving. "I'm not going to start moving again until you take off another clothespin," he says. I know he means it. Still, it is several seconds before I can nerve myself to revive the sensitive flesh of my sex by taking all the pressure off it. It is so terrible I think I will die, but then I do not, so of course I forget about dying and try to come again. "You can come as you remove the last clothespin," Daddy says, and I say bad words, but do as I am told.

Good girls do what they are told, but good girls are never told to do the things my daddy tells me to do. I don't care, I would rather be a very bad girl, being fucked this way, even after I've come, my clitoris feeling as if it's been cauterized, lucky girl, dirty girl, I love my daddy, I do, I do.

It is the kind of sex that makes you feel as if you will never need to have sex again. I imagine that all I want to do is curl up with my head on her shoulder and go to sleep. I shed what remains of my finery and creep in between the covers. Then she stands up and undresses and takes off the dildo and the leather harness, and I discover that I may need to have sex again sooner than I thought. Much sooner. She slips into bed beside me and shoves my head down, toward the foot of the bed.

I know her clit will be so hard it will seem ready to burst, her vagina so wet I will hardly need to add lubricant to my fingers. And this is what makes me love her as well as want her. When she brings her cunt to me and puts it in my face, I know that this scene, the fantasy characters we've lost ourselves in, are as hot for her as they are for me. She demands that I make her come. She does not let me lie around in my sweat and get lazy or paranoid. She puts me to work, fucking and sucking her, and lets me earn my keep.

Do we sleep? Do we eat? If we do, I don't remember, because it doesn't matter. I feel myself changing inside, energy shifting, my fantasy selves shuffling themselves like a pack of wild cards and jokers, trumps and Greater Arcana. I am becoming someone else. It's time to change reels, but it won't be the same movie.

■ ■

My boy has gotten dressed for me. Maybe it's the following night. Maybe it's just later in the same day. But I have issued instructions, left the room, and transformed myself. Now I am back to see how well my orders were followed.

These are the clothes I always ask for: a white T-shirt, faded 501s, black cowboy boots. No belt. Those pants aren't going to stay on long enough for him to need anything to hold them up. Under the jeans, there will be no underwear. I know this because my boy takes these details seriously. There is something touching about this. He has good reason to distrust all putative masters. Still, he has certain ideas, certain standards — a code. And in his heart, he has kept faith with it, despite many disappointments. I am also moved by this complete shift of role and attitude. Nobody can make my boy ashamed of what he wants, and he would never resort to the cheap tricks of bottoms who try to provoke a top by being lazy or rude. His position is, *If I am going to do this thing, I will do it right, to the letter, perfectly.*

Tonight I am a sadistic daddy. I've been many different kinds of dads for boys of all ages. Sometimes I take little boys to ballgames, barbecue hamburgers for them, and put Band-aids on their hurt knees. Sometimes I take older boys to that house on the edge of town where young men lose their innocence, introduce them to the madam, and remind them to use some protection when they get the girl they've chosen up the stairs. Sometimes I beat the snot out of young bucks who've gotten too big for their britches. All these daddies have one thing in common — an unmanly willingness to give unqualified approval and affection. I can't be somebody's daddy if I don't love them.

I have other ways of being a top, but they are more clinical and much less sexual. When I'm Daddy, I want to get my dick into something hot and tight. I want to show that boy what his cock and his butt are for and fuck the come out of him. If a boy needs to be thrashed before he knows I love him, I'll wallop his ass until he cries. But then I want to take him in my strong arms and ride him till I'm coming dry. So many dykes grew up longing for rites of passage, ways to test their courage, systematic training in how to be strong and capable, scrappy adults. When I am Daddy, I take care of that need. Unlike most real daddies, I never make a boy feel ashamed of being afraid or queer. Good daddies turn out boys who can be brave and strong as well as excellent cocksuckers.

But this particular boy doesn't want a daddy. (At least, not yet.) While he was away from me, he gave a lot of women pleasure, but he didn't get much back. It's hard to define the quality in a bottom that makes a top reluctant to undress or get off. It's probably not a rational decision. I'm sure I've turned down bushels of orgasms, just because a whisper of a chance existed that I might hear about it later in a less-than-kind tone of voice. God knows even a charity fuck might be less demeaning than some of the hot sex I've had — we've both had — with the psychos and losers that our cunts decided they had to back into. When I refuse to let a bottom get in my pants, I'm not sure if I'm protecting myself from sexual shame or perpetuating some of its foundations. All I know is, we won't put out if somebody doesn't scare us and yet somehow convey the message that it is safe to let down our guards.

The part of this boy that is willing to say it needs anything is buried deep. Deprivation has turned into denial. If I tried to comfort him now, he would mistake it for pity, and bolt from the room. My job is to break him down. Get him to confess to being human. But before this boy will accept any warmth from me, I have to be a mean son of a bitch. Masochists are often like that. Most people need to be tenderized with arousal and sensual teasing before they can accept any pain. Masochists don't really like being caressed or entered until they have been hurt in the particular way they prefer, for as long as it takes to convince them you mean business and will not abandon them or judge them. I will not be able to get or give much tenderness to this boy until I remind him that I can make him suffer for every sin he even imagined committing. I wonder if I can make this work. Having someone else's body and soul under your hands is terrifying. It's so easy to make mistakes. Do I still have what it takes?

He is waiting for me in the middle of the floor — the exact middle of the floor. This is a task I give every new boy, to go and place himself in an appropriate position in the exact center of the floor. Very few of them figure it out. This one looked up before I had even left the room, saw the light fixture, and knelt smoothly below it. I like that kind of intelligence. Most of the people I play with are just smart enough to get themselves into trouble. This one is smart enough to get me into trouble.

So I tell the daddy part of my persona to be patient for a while and pour my distilled need and attention into the sadist. Colors get brighter. My hearing seems sharper. I swear I can taste new smells on the air. My body feels quicker, more precise, more obedient to my will. I pause for a moment after entering the room and examine the raw materials I have to work with — the strong ropes that hang at each corner of the bed; the whips, restraints, clips, knives, dildos, and a dozen other kinds of toys; the boy. Under those jeans is a pair of long, slender legs. I've never seen those legs in black seamed stockings (and I probably never will), but I know they'd look perfect.

Those fashion-model legs give her a height that I find very attractive. They also give her a mean and accurate kick. Always I see her with this strange double vision, the elegant and severe woman who exists at a tangent to the young male rebel.

We don't deal with her female persona very often. The lady inside her is street-weary and knows only one thing to do with sex — trade it for money. I've seen a picture of her, and she's very beautiful, but her eyes are mad and vacant. She doesn't occupy her body unless it's been flooded with enough junk to make it seem safe to be there. The only reason she's alive is because she never trusted anybody. As far as she's concerned, people who make promises are pimps, dealers, users, and con artists. It's hard to argue with that experience. But sometimes, if the sex is really good, I can say a few words to her, in between strokes, just enough to feed her and keep her alive. I want to let her know I'm out here waiting if she ever feels like coming out and letting me touch her. She has closed a lot of doors between us, but there must be peepholes in every one, because I feel her watching me, trying to figure me out, hating me and wanting me at the same time. But I know this is not her night. This is just one more round in a long fight to prove myself worthy of an audience with that chilly, regal, lonely bitch.

Anyway, I don't believe in the phony equality that says, *If I wear a dress, you have to wear a dress.* We do what's hot for each of us. Our needs are not identical. There's no way I could cope with the terrible things I'm about to do to this woman I love. So she doesn't inflict them upon me.

Then I stop thinking and start kicking and slapping. My boy has been waiting for me for a long time. Being down on his knees is not intrinsically exciting for him. Being shoved around and forcibly put someplace is. I hate to think what would happen to my nose if we ever got into a real fight. But we're doing this together. So he avoids me, twisting to make sure my kicks land on muscle instead of on joints, and he puts his hands up so I have to knock them aside to strike his face. He only tries to get up once, but I am quick enough to snag him by the hair and slam him back down to the floor. Now we are both breathing hard. A little sweat is starting to sprout on our upper lips, under our arms. This is a good place, loose and almost out of control.

I kick him in the crotch, letting the top of my foot catch the fleshy part of his cunt. It makes a nice, solid noise and sends a shock up through his torso that rattles his teeth. "What's the matter, boy?" I say. My voice is distorted because I'm out of breath and low because I'm so horny I hurt. I swear that each kick brings the smell of her cunt up into my face, even through the thick denim of the jeans. "You wouldn't be trying to get away from your old man, would you, now? You know that's not a good idea. You know that's not allowed."

My fingers are folded over the handle of my knife. I don't remember taking it out of the sheath, but I transfer it to my left hand so I can slap him again, harder, daring him to hit me back. It's so difficult to sit still and let somebody hit you in the face. It's the kind of thing that makes you want to spit and lunge at your tormenter. I couldn't get away with it if he didn't know that much, much worse things could — and will — happen. "Be grateful it's just a slap," I say, and we both know what I am talking about. "Take off your boots, you dumb shit. You know you aren't allowed to wear any boots in here." In fact, this is a new rule I just made up, but his lack of protest is evidence of how quickly and surely the scene has gotten off the ground. He reaches behind himself, with those long, pale arms that are almost double-jointed, and slides the cowboy boots off, kicks them into the corner.

I drag him up on his knees with one hand twisted in the front of the white T-shirt. It's so old and thin that it tears, making an injured sound. I put the knife away and shred the shirt with both of my bare hands. It's a ridiculous, Hulk Hogan kind of gesture, but he knows that T-shirt is a substitute for flesh, and it makes his eyes go wild.

The half-naked body in front of me is too thin. All those years of junk, methadone, lithium, Elavil, and whatever medication she's on now keep her looking starved. I don't usually like angular women. But it looks right on her. The bone so close to the surface reminds me of the connections between death and pleasure — how the imminence of death drives us to pursue oblivion, bliss; how our pleasures kill us. The clear outlines of her skull remind me that we don't do recreational drugs; we don't have casual sex.

"You been working out," I say, touching the exposed chest. The skin is vampire white. "That's good. I like thinking about you throwing those weights around." There is absolutely no subcutaneous fat. The chest muscles are so hard, they seem to be made out of plastic or stone, not living tissue. I move away for a minute so I can take my jacket off and arrange it on the bed. When I come back, I test his upper arms, grasping them hard enough to bruise, and hoist the boy onto his feet. I turn him around, get his pants unbuttoned, and somehow manage to simultaneously strip them off his butt and legs and throw him backwards onto the bed.

There are cuffs waiting to be molded around wrists and locked in place, then locked to chain. I will start out tonight with my meat on its stomach. His torso rests on the cool, slick surface of the armor that I wear every day to warn people to keep away from me unless they really want my attention. He puts his face into my jacket and refuses to watch me imprison his limbs.

Sometimes I omit the ankle cuffs because it's fun to watch them kick, but tonight I want to see him stretched out on this bed tight as a deerhide being scraped clean for tanning. So I buckle on the padded ankle cuffs, and I drag him down and chain him up so snugly it makes him gasp. That's perfect. It makes me giggle when people assume that bondage is somehow lighter than other kinds of S/M, or isn't about pain. Good bondage is stressful, and the bottom has to struggle with their own discomfort to endure it.

I am wearing my boots, my chaps, and a black T-shirt. Underneath the chaps, I have on my dick and my jockstrap. Some of my friends wear fake mustaches and strap their tits down with Ace bandages or plastic wrap and tape to do this kind of scene. I'm impressed and turned on when somebody's makeup and drag is good enough to get them into a gay bathhouse or allow them to use the men's room. But I don't like being restricted that way. I associate compression of my torso and an inflexible waist with wearing a corset, not having cut pecs and a hairy chest. Any illusion of manhood I create is based on my stance and voice. Being read visually as a man in public is less important to me than administering the proper combination of blows and threats in my own bedroom.

A few of my friends are taking male hormones and using male names full-time. Sometimes it's tempting to follow them. I love their big muscles, deep voices, and furry faces. Sometimes it seems to me that being a man would make my life a hundred times easier. I know that some of the people I sleep with don't like my ambiguous gender and wish I would choose one side or the other. But I'm not a man or a woman. Sex reassignment would be as crazy for me as aversion therapy for homosexuality. The things I hate about being female come from outside of me, not from within. I don't want to be a little dude with a big ass and a dick that doesn't work right. The thought of giving up my tits makes me nauseous. I cling to my female body, even in the middle of this genderfuck fantasy.

My trussed-up victim looks so good, I just *have* to reach under the tight-stretched banana-shaped curve of my jock and squeeze the hard shaft inside it. He is watching me, head turned to the side, eyes in slits, fists clenched. "Don't start thinking about dessert before you've had your main course," I caution. Then I throw a leg up onto the bed and lower my body onto his. My cock presses into the back of his thigh. I have my teeth hooked in the rim of his ear. Black hair, full of pomade, curls in a perfect juvenile-delinquent DA under my hands. This is a smell I will remember later, when I'm jacking off, after she is gone.

"Do you know who you are?" I whisper.

I get a vigorous shake of the head.

"You're the punk that gets beaten and fucked on my jacket. That means you belong to me, asshole. And if you're worried about fucking this up, don't bother. Because I am not going to allow you to be anything less than perfect. Tonight I get what I want. And what I want is to see you in pain. In pain and then stuffed full of cock. So get your shit together." I have my fist in his hair, and I gently raise his head and mock-slam it into the mattress. "Better grab that jacket. Hang on tight. Bite it if you have to. Because right now that jacket is the only friend you've got."

I move away, stand up, and go to the wall to select my first whip. I have three flat, unbraided cats I like to use to start a scene. One is very short and lightweight, another is short but weighs a little more, and the third is long and heavy.

I pick the easiest instrument and start lightly circling it above his back. His hair is so full of greasy kid's stuff that it doesn't even move in the breeze I'm making. It's hard to tell exactly when the whip makes contact. I want this to be slow and careful. All I want is to remove a few dead skin cells, get the blood circulating, wake up the body and its appetite for struggle.

"It's been a long time," I say, and he groans and pushes his hips into the bed. "If you've forgotten who you are, maybe you don't remember me either. Do you know who I am?"

He turns his head and shows me his teeth. He is impatient for the whip. All these questions make him nervous. He doesn't want to talk, he wants to get beaten. But I shake my head. I will not let the whip land until we finish this conversation. The last time we were together, I visited the city where she lives. And I noticed a few things there that I want to use now.

"No," he drawls, to see if insolence will hurry me along. "Who do you think you are?"

"I'm the person who's going to make you scream and try to get away." He grunts cynically. "Oh, believe it. I will. But I'm more than that. I'm not just your jailer. I'm not just your master." I lean down to whisper in his ear. "I'm your daddy."

This evokes a wordless wail of protest. The bed creaks as he thrashes around. I am relieved to see that all the screw eyes remain sunk deep in the wooden frame of my bed. The chains hold. He gives me an indignant look that says silently, *You betrayed me.*

"Don't try to bullshit me," I say contemptuously. "It's not hard to figure out what you really want. Did you think you could just keep it to yourself, that I'd never notice or try to make you say it out loud? I met your friend Jackson, remember? You took me to his shop. But I think you wanted to look at more than a new motorcycle jacket. What is he, fifty? I saw you take off your keys and shove them in your pocket. I saw you scrambling to find something — anything — that you could do for him, whether it was get him a fresh cup of coffee or sweep up the scraps on the floor. I saw him looking at your butt, wondering why his dick was hard. He really cares about you, even if the only thing he dares do about it is squeeze your arm or make you hang around and try on vests and harnesses and talk about bikes. Jackson is never going to beat your ass. Wouldn't you rather have a real daddy, somebody who would let you suck his dick?"

He does not answer. I hit him a few times with the whip. It's not very long or heavy, but I make the blows count. "Answer me," I insist.

I get my response, but she will not look at me. "All I want is for you to beat me as hard as you can for as long as you can. If you want to make up stories about what you think it means, I can't stop you. But I will never ever call you ... that. You can't make me."

Because she will not look me in the eye or even say the offensive word, I know I am on the right track. "We'll see," I say.

I've been gently whisking the surface of his back, butt, and thighs. Now I let a few strokes land harder. I get an affirmative grunt. So I stop the circling motion and strike overhand and down instead, a simple thudding chop that makes a fair amount of noise and hardly stings at all. I pause to run my hands over the skin. I already want to fuck him, shove my cock between the ass cheeks that are flexing in doubt. *Is this what I really want?* I hear him thinking. His body hasn't had enough time to get its endorphins circulating. I sympathize. Neither one of us is very good at taking pain without chemical assistance.

I don't want to leave him alone with this anxiety or let him get impatient. He's had too many aborted scenes with tops who chickened out at the crucial moment, threw down the whip, and pleaded to be held. That's such a rotten thing to do to a masochist. Being a whip tease is every bit as bad as the other kind. I hope there's a special hell for people who make carnal promises that they can't keep. I am old-fashioned about keeping my word. You could call it a fetish. And I have promised this boy quite a drubbing.

So I take the whip in a circle around my head and bring it down hard, flicking my wrist so it sends a wave down the blades that peaks on the right side of his ass. I keep on doing this, taking a breath between each stroke, until the ass and shoulders are uniform sheets of red. A white belt of untouched skin rings his kidneys and lower back. I haven't missed once. Good for me.

"You're beginning well," I say. I separate the cheeks and spit, let my finger follow the white bubbles down the crack. I spit again and apply the blob of water and slime to the sphincter. His hips are absolutely motionless. This lack of response makes me feel bitchy. I shove three fingers up his cunt and gently frig his clit. This gets a rise out of him. He slams the bed with his fists, and his upper body curls up in protest. He really wants to be fucked, but I haven't hurt him nearly enough. What a dilemma.

"Let's get serious now," I say. I skip the other warm-up cats and select a whip with a long, braided stock that splits into two tails. It's a combination quirt and blacksnake. It's noisy, and I can pick precise spots to hit with it. I love the way using it makes my body feel. The stroke starts in the soles of my feet and rises up my body like a wave of sexual tension. When it lands and snaps, I feel as if I'm going to come in my pants. I use this beauty on his shoulders, butt, and thighs until my arm starts to ache.

Now his breathing is harsh and ragged, and there are a few red stripes, but no broken skin. I use the long, unbraided flogger to bring more blood into the tissue and start breaking it down. When somebody is this muscular, it takes a lot of effort to mark them. Mostly this part will just feel good to him. It's like getting a massage. By the time I'm done, I'm panting, and his toes are curled. Both fists are wrapped around the chains, and I'm impressed. I didn't think I'd left enough slack for him to be able to do that. I love girls who can stretch chain.

"Are you trying to get away?" I ask softly. I prefer not to raise my voice in a scene. It forces the bottom to keep paying attention to me. I don't like it when they space out and start imagining they're all alone in a world of disembodied sensation.

"No!" she spits.

"Liar. I saw you try to get away. What else was it I said I would do?" Her balkiness makes me angry, so now I shout. "Answer me!"

"You said—" (rattle, rattle) "—you would make me scream."

"I told you I would make you do something else too."

"No!"

Making him think about it is, for now, every bit as effective as getting the forbidden words to come out of his mouth. I look to my weapons. The braided cat is next. I have several of these, too, in different widths. The thinner the braid, the faster they move, and the more they cut and burn. The authority is in the knots. They are like tiny fists. I try to remember all the rules about pacing and buildup, but I'm getting so excited that I want to take that motherfucking whip in both hands and go up on my toes and just bring it down as hard as I can until the walls are spattered with blood.

"This is how we get high together," I say. "You're getting me very stoned. Do you know how much I like to hurt you? When I hurt you I feel like I'm getting fucked. All I want to do is hurt you until my head explodes."

"Do that," she snarls, clawing at my jacket. "Do it harder. Do it some more. I thought you were going to make me scream."

"Sounds almost as if you want to scream," I reply. She laughs and shakes her head, tries to muffle it in my jacket. Striped and bruised, shaken and battered, she laughs at me. This is a good moment. We are in this together. It makes me laugh too.

I use my belt, another quirt, an assortment of implements. But I'm delaying the grand finale, and we both know that. I finally draw a cane out of the stand.

Women who can take the cane are an elite group. If somebody has a genuine enthusiasm for the cane, she will not have much trouble persuading me to pick one up. I don't care what she looks like, who she is, or why she wants it, as long as she can hold her butt up and wait for my stroke. The first time I was handed one of these supple, wicked scepters, it immediately became an extension of my arm and my libido. I've never had a bad time caning somebody, and, no matter what emotional price I've had to pay for it later, I've never been sorry.

But to do this with somebody I love — well, that's a very different thing. Normally I run off my own narcissistic energy within a scene. Voyeurizing, watching myself is the hottest part for me. But this is someone who has me by the short hairs. I want her to like this. I want him to tell me he needs it.

"Tell me you want to be beaten," I say. "Boy," I add.

There's no hesitation. His head comes up, the lips move. "Please — I want to be beaten." The voice is definite and clear, even though the eyes are glazed. It's impressive.

"Tell me who I am."

"You are my master. I belong to you. Please hurt me."

It's not exactly what I want to hear. But it's close enough. So I do what she tells me.

The cane eventually breaks the skin. I know I am going too fast, but I don't care. I can't stop. I know my lips are drawn back in a snarl, and my arm is a blur of motion. If anybody tried to stop me now, I would rip their throat out. I have to have this. Somewhere in the middle of this, I have taken off my boots and chaps so I can move more freely. This is what makes masochists dangerous. They get to see this part of me. They know how much I need to raven, rend, and ravage them. It gives them quite a hook to twist.

But this woman will not punish me for being a sadist. She never will. We may come to hate everything else about each other, but I really believe we will always honor this exchange, and be proud of ourselves for going this far with each other.

My boy is twisted on his side. His face is full of tears, his mouth stretched open in an O of disbelief. I go to my dresser, take a bandana out of the top drawer, tie a knot in it, then dunk the knot in the glass of water I keep by the bed. I shove the wet bundle into his mouth and tie the bandana behind his head. He shakes his head no, no, but right now it is my job to say yes, yes. "I thought you didn't want to scream," I snicker. "I'm just helping you to keep quiet. I don't want you to embarrass yourself. Besides, if you scream now, I'll have to stop, and you'll be so disappointed."

This is why he keeps coming back to me, because I know better than to quit when he thinks he's had enough. If I unchained his feet, knelt between his legs, and rode his ass right now, he'd come within minutes, but he'd be disappointed. This isn't about good sex. I'm not sure how to describe the place that lies beyond that. You have to use the body to get there, but it's a state that seems extraphysical.

I pick up the short quirt and move closer, wrap my arm around his hips so I put him back on his stomach, and hold him in place. Then I strap his butt without mercy, lacing into flesh that has already been cut by the cane. I do not spare the thighs. Only the back I ignore, because it doesn't have enough padding to withstand this assault. Besides, it doesn't have the same psychological impact, hitting somebody on their shoulders. They are used to carrying the burdens and tensions of their life there. It feels good to get some of that weight beaten off your back. But being struck across the buttocks makes someone feel younger and more frightened. It is more sexual. It is a breaking point.

It's hard to scream with a mouth full of wet cloth. I spare a look over my shoulder so I can relish the outraged expression that's common to all gagged faces. The cheeks are strained, the eyes are wide, the throat is tight. But I do not stop until my arm has gone dead and numb, and several strangled screams have died against the gag. They don't count.

So I take off the gag. My next-door neighbor is a pervert, and the apartment downstairs is vacant. I reach for the cane again. When he sees it, his body slumps. He knows I am going to win, but it has not yet occurred to him that this means he wins too. "Try not to cry out before the last stroke," I tell him. "Because there will be six of them, no matter how much noise you make." Despite my big talk, a tiny part of me is afraid he may be able to tough it out and keep still. So I aim for the sorest part of his butt, and I pile all six strokes on top of the same quarter-inch-wide ribbon of scored flesh. It bleeds as freely as he screams, for mercy and for joy.

I unchain his hands and feet and get myself a drink of water and a hit of my asthma inhaler. The straps of my harness are cutting into my ass. My pubic mound is sore from having the rubber base of the dildo pressed against it, and underneath my cock I am wet to my thighs. I offer him water, and he has a little, but doesn't really want to be bothered with it. His ass keeps coming off the bed. Some of this is a shock reaction to all the pain, but most of it is heat.

I understand that. We've waited long enough. "Jack off for your dad," I say, unchaining his hands. Both paws immediately slide under his belly and get busy. He doesn't even think about the tacit agreement he's just made. He has been hurt enough, and now he is hurting to come. Standing close to the bed, I slap his swollen and bloody ass. "You're gonna let me in here," I snarl. "Isn't that right? You're going to let your daddy fuck you."

He is licking my jacket, biting the collar. That alone is almost as good as sex. "Uh-huh," he says. "Uh-huh." He reaches for me, frees my cock from the elastic pouch of the jockstrap, wraps his fist around it, and swallows it whole. Nobody else has ever gotten my entire cock in their throat this fast. I swear I can see the shape of my shaft below his jawline, a swollen line along his trachea, the head of it wedged far past his soft palate. I can't help it, my hips jerk, and he has to cough up a little of my cock so he can breathe.

"I'm going to fuck your face," I say, and he grabs my butt and hangs on to it as hard as I hang on to the back of his head. I repeatedly tell him he is sucking his daddy's dick, and right now he can't argue with me. We move like the pieces of an engine, and I know it is not physically possible, but I come that way, come so hard I think I might tip over. Only his hands, clamped around my thighs, keep me on my feet. My cock comes out of his face, looking slippery and a little mauled.

"Did you get hurt enough?" I ask, climbing onto the bed.

"I don't know, I don't know anything anymore, just put it in, please sir, put it in."

I lube up my cock, rolling my fist up the crack of his ass. I love the dark fur that grows thick all over these long legs, the thighs, and lines the cleft I am about to pummel. With two fingers I press down on the head, angling it toward the sphincter's lower lip. There is a brief catch. I can't tell which one of us moans, as if in protest. Then— "Daddy, please!" he sobs, and all resistance dissolves. There's a smooth descent, and the heat from that opened asshole warms my belly, too. I am where I want to be, physically, emotionally, psychologically. This is home.

I have a looped choke chain in my left hand. It's got lube all over it now, but I don't think I'll stop and wipe it off. I throw the loop over his head. The long end is in my fist, and I yank. Instantly his entire rectum contracts, compressing me, just like I'm compressing his throat. I laugh, delighted to have this much control over something so important. Can I be trusted? Maybe. Probably. Maybe not.

My sadism has been fed, so now I feed his ass. I pack that butt, moving slow, lost in the ozone until some curses remind me that there's a person connected to that asshole. "Can I come now?" he screams, meaning, "Fuck me harder, you dipshit!"

"Tell me what I want to hear," I insist, panting so hard I am not sure he will be able to understand what I am saying.

"Let me come, please, Daddy!"

I change gears abruptly from a waltz to a slam-dance. The hand that isn't keeping the choke chain taut is clamped over his hipbone, and I'm using it to keep him from sliding off my cock in his frenzy to be penetrated. I feel myself coming seconds before I hear the harsh noises that mean my boy is losing it, and somehow make myself keep moving even though my thighs have turned to rubber. For a split second, I feel sorry for him. It's so hard to come when you can't really catch your breath. It makes the orgasm last longer, but in some ways you feel like you didn't really get to come.

Now the choke chain comes off her neck. I grease it up. I roll my boy onto his back. There's more. There has to be more. One fuck can't possibly use up all the energy we've generated. One link at a time, I push the chain up his ass, leaving the two large rings at either end of it dangling outside the sphincter. The chain is very smooth, but each link pinches a bit as it goes in. I remove my harness. My boy doesn't like being dick-fucked in the cunt. The leather straps are slimy and there's shit on the condom, but I don't want to bother with cleaning it up now. It goes somewhere, off the edge of the bed into never-never land with all the other discarded toys.

Finally, I touch her cunt. "I love to fuck the come out of you," I smile. "I love it when you can't help it, when you have to come." I separate the inner lips. There's so much juice, they are plastered together. Even the hair on her cunt is wringing wet, and has broken up into little curls. Her clit, always large, is rigid and outrageously big. The shaft and hood are two inches long, the glans the size of my little fingertip. "Can you take Daddy's fist? I have to be inside you now. I have to own you. Take you and use you. Fuck every single one of your holes." This is classic dirty talk. I don't think I ever fuck without saying this. But lust transforms cliches into poetry.

My hand slides in with very little trouble. I stroke the wall between cunt and asshole. Links of chain move behind the thin membrane. Every time I put my hand deeper into her or draw it out, I put pressure on the heavy, metal mass in my boy's ass. I love fucking someone on their back because I can see their face and watch their nipples get hard. But he can't come this way, so eventually I have him roll over, back on all fours.

"Fuck you from behind like a bitch in heat," I say. It's an old, reliable line, but it always works, like calling somebody a cocksucker. I reach forward and pull on his nipples. "You get hard when I handle your tits. You like being played with like a girl. Getting fucked like a girl. Make your asshole my pussy, boy. Use every hole you've got. Take your breath away and maybe I'll never give it back. Give it up, now. Give me what I want or I swear I'll punch a hole in you."

Those long, slender hands are a blur over her clit. I feel contractions starting to flutter. It's time to draw out the chain. Link by link it slides, each link making the asshole open and close and open and close, and each link is another small orgasm, each small orgasm becoming a slightly bigger orgasm, until somebody is shouting my name, telling me I am a bastard, he loves me, he is my boy, his cunt belongs to Daddy, and I know I'm going to have a bruised wrist in the morning.

Except that it's morning already. One more day out of the precious few we have is gone. I can't help but ask myself if I've done enough, if I've used each hour as completely as possible. I don't know when I'll get to do this again.

I stagger into the bathroom and wash my hands, find the bottle of rubbing alcohol and a handful of cotton balls. I go back into the bedroom. She's curled up on one side, breathing lightly. Her face looks peaceful. She stirs a little when I clean off her right shoulder. The rubbing alcohol is cold, and its strong smell makes me feel a little sick to my stomach.

There's a number-fifteen scalpel by the bed. I peel it out of its sterile wrapper and snap the plastic backing off the blade. Slowly, carefully, biting my lip, I cut the runes into her shoulder that say, *We are of one blood, you and I, outlaws together, one folk with the same dream.*

Then I lick the blood from her shoulder, rub it on my face, smear it into my hair. It's not safe sex, but nobody lives forever, and I can't stand to deprive myself of this iron taste, her heart's fuel.

Like the stone butches who used to scare me so much when I was seventeen, I don't want to be touched right now. I came while I was making her come, and all I want is to be a peaceful witness to her satisfaction, a guardian of her slumbering body. We sleep tangled up, disowned children, and we do not dream our parents' dreams.

*fi*X Me u*p*

■■

Lena plastered her body, thin as a zither and as tightly strung, full-length against the big window. It gave her a silly little rush to know that nothing but a thick pane of glass held her up, fifty stories off the ground. It was late Sixday afternoon. Rain had been pissing down all the dismal day. The moment the sun fell, a wind would come up, a mean wind that would pour itself through the canyons between the ziggurats and gleefully slice through the poor, wet drones and plugs trying to slog their way home. She was up too high to see the bright colors of the advertholos, chasing pedestrians, or hear the illegal ads blaring bad music and squawking about their wares. The neon and pastel shades of the commercials and the shop windows would be reflected back by the puddles on the street, making rainbows like so much spilled snake oil. Lena never went down to the street if she could help it.

The rain thickened, darkened, blew in diagonal lines like a shower of poisoned abo spears. Lena smiled, and felt her teeth click against the glass. No matter how devil-may-care David's streetboy act was, he would get his cute little ass inside before that wind bit him on the butt.

She had spent the last hour just tidying up. Nothing major like floors or laundry. She had meant to go down to the twenty-fifth floor breezeway and get a few groceries and some tequila. But it had been a busy week, so she called down and had everything delivered. The delivery charge was almost as much as the bill for her food and liquor, but she could afford it.

She wasn't waiting for David. He wasn't that important. She was just wandering through her apartment, sucking on a lemon and a shot glass, touching this and that, arranging things, making sure she knew where everything was. During the week it was so easy for the smaller props — the vibrators and dildos, wigs, her stethoscope, the rubber hood, the pacifier, the nurse's cowl, the bug-gloves and bug-face, the military cap, the riding crop, the poppers — to get misplaced.

She had covered the computer terminal and unplugged the video camera, the earphones, and the sensenet. Today had been surprisingly busy for a weekend. She did most of her business between official working hours, when office plugs could make surreptitious use of company lines or stop in a private booth during lunchtime. There was another flurry of biz for an hour before and after corporate rollcalls, when sweats could use the databooths on the way to and from home for a quick fantasy fix. Today, she had done two baby calls, a cross-dresser, one pioneer-and-aborigines scenario, a full set of military calisthenics, a castration, a bug collector, and six straight fucks in various imaginary positions and costumes — seven men, five women, and a herm. The Virgin alone knew how many of them were transies.

She was pretty quick at the keyboard, but she still needed to do some costume changes to augment the visuals, or customers complained. One of them had called from home with deluxe, full sensory plug-in, which meant she had to create three hundred and sixty degrees of erotic experience incorporating all five senses. She hadn't had much practice with the software for taste sensations or smell. Lucky for her, this client hadn't ever stuck his nose, much less his tongue, in somebody else's crotch, and he was happy with a sweet-but-sour flavor Lena lifted from her favorite no-calorie dessert and a whiff of musky perfume.

Lena felt like a worn-out drive that had been erased, reformatted, and written on so often that its ability to retain data was deteriorating. So she did not want to look at the terminal tonight — or tomorrow, if she could help it. She moved involuntarily toward the keyboard to check her credit balance, but restrained herself from lifting the dustcover. She made herself just sit in the comfortable work chair that gave perfect back support no matter which way she tilted. Without really processing what she saw, she stared into the mirror behind the computer. Tonight's events had nothing to do with sex, but everything to do with desire. After so many hours of catering to other people's rituals, her own (no matter how arbitrary, no matter how destructive) seemed very precious.

No, she was not waiting for David. That was the difference between them. He was the one who waited on his missionary, who waited until it was late enough in the day that he could drop by her place pretending he was on his way to someplace else — a show, a party, a jump-off. And she knew just what he would say when he came in the door. Every time he saw her, he said it sooner and sooner, with less and less preliminary conversation.

He would say, "Fix me up, Lena."

And she would. After he paid the price. That was one factor that carried over from her job — the expectation that everyone who wanted her had to give something up in return, at a rate she calculated and demanded, without negotiation.

She ran a finger over her eyebrows, and made sure the peak was still there, that crooked place in the curve that made her look so dark and disapproving when she raised one brow. Even when she smiled, her face had a sharp, satirical look.

She got up and stretched for the mirror, bent over, and looked at her own ass. She was wearing her favorite pair of shimmerlegs. The inside seams, the ones along the upper thigh that always wore out first, had been mended with wide leather patches, a dull black that absorbed the colored lights that twinkled in the fabric. Mirror studs ran down the outer seams, emphasizing the length of her legs. Tonight she wore a mirror for a belt buckle, too. Her knee-high boots were silver, and the spike heels were studded with rhinestones. She was wearing a very old, neon pink T that had been worn down to the thickness of a sheet of paper. In the right light (or if it was wet), you could see her tattoos through it, the black spiderwebs that spanned her shoulder blades and breasts and collarbones, and the red jumping spiders that waited there for a thrumming touch on the web to bring them to life.

These were primitive engravings, made by actually implanting pigment beneath her skin with an electric needle. The process was illegal, but you could always find some ex-con, derelict, or artist with a passion for quick cash and live canvas. She had no patience for the ornamental holos that other people wore because you could take them off, like a bracelet or a mask. Her tattoos were not jewelry. They were an alteration of the map of her body. They were her way of saying: *Be careful. This comes with the territory.*

David had never commented on the way she looked. Still, why would a top-bunk boy approach you in a bar full of his peers when you looked like an old witch, especially when you wore your pistol in a very visible shoulder holster and a large buck-knife in one of your boots, if he did not find you attractive? He had brought her a drink back from the bar on a fucking tray. Hadn't spilled it, either. When she did not take the drink, he had disappeared into the crowd and returned with something a lot more interesting. He had had the good sense to precede her out of the bar — not get behind her and make her nervous about her back. And he had touched her only once, on the back of the hand, an instinctively submissive gesture that had charmed and irritated her.

She had not been back to the kite bar since. And it had been much longer than she liked to think since she had actually strapped herself to the crosspieces of one of those dangerous, fragile contraptions and accepted an aerial duel. These days, it took a serious stretch of sobriety or celibacy to make the walls of her home seem more dangerous than the outside world. She had to be forced onto the street by furniture that resented taking her weight, mirrors that were adding years to her face, kitchen drawers and bathroom cabinets full of ways to take her own life.

She had picked the Third Spur because she knew there would not be any other women there. There weren't any covens anymore; a room full of women would have made too tempting a target for a rape gang or bridal slavers. Still, dykes managed to claim corners of other people's clubs. But she would rather be among resentful male strangers than run the risk of taking a woman home. Lena had another bad habit she preferred to romance. She knew she could not give it up for the sake of love. And when you combined lust with religion — well, it was just too dangerous. She had been just a kid when she learned that, dumb enough to believe somebody was going to save her.

It was tricky, finding a good old pioneer place that didn't want you but wouldn't throw you out. Women were rare but not unheard of in the kite scene; Lena was careful to be neither obnoxious nor servile. Her presence titillated some of the men, and made most of them skeptical. It seemed to her that the hetmen who got hostile with her were painfully attracted to machas, but assumed they were not available. No wonder they were nervous. Since the plague had killed half of the planet's women of childbearing age, most females had been locked up by their families or husbands. If you saw a woman on the street, she probably carried a sidearm. Rumors that woman-lovers were somehow, perhaps by magical means, invulnerable to the disease had made any woman who was perceived as a witch the target of gang rape. This was still a frontier planet. The law responded by authorizing members of protected classes to carry firearms at all times. It was cheaper than paying the cops or the courts or a commission to take care of the problem, and satisfied the vague requirement that members of the Planetary Trade Co-operative "recognize human rights issues."

The whole society was just inches away from martial law anyway since the bugs had come out of nowhere, disabled a freighter, and removed its crew. Rumor had it that the bugs were responsible for the plague. It was germ warfare from outer space. Another rumor attributed it to the government. Something it had cooked up to kill the aliens had gotten loose by mistake. Lena found trips to the firing range and a heavy investment in rubber goods more productive than such speculation. It seemed only fair for the bugs to kill her species when the human settlers had been the death of every abo on this planet. What did it matter where the plague came from? The fact was that getting stuck with somebody else's dick or spike could give you a slow and ugly death. Just believing that, the simple truth, was more than most people could manage.

Lena had always been the kind of woman who went places men would rather keep for themselves. She felt immune to their threats — the verbal ones, anyway — because she didn't consider herself so much unavailable as undesirable. She hadn't found that many women who were interested in what she had to offer, either. So she was amused by the occasional startled look on the face of a breeder boy who had just felt a pang of desire that would make his buddies guffaw. Let him feel freakish and undesirable, too. Do him good, it would.

But then again, Lena thought, *I am not just a dyke, and David is not just a cunt-lover.* She unrolled her bed-of-nails, a leather hide liberally studded with metal prongs, across her tatami. She touched a silver point to reassure herself of its sharpness. *David and I have something in common that brings us together. It's rather touching, in a way, his fear of needles and my fascination with puncturing the skin.*

Maybe Joey the Bag is right, she mused, *and David is just a repressed little manjacker who needs a daddy with a big dick to put him on the proper path to submissive, cock-sucking clamhood. But somehow I doubt it's that simple. Might work if he could find a daddy who came Angel Piss. The Bag is just jealous 'cause I got me a better-looking boy than he does presently. Not that I want to be anybody's daddy, you understand. And where is the kid?* she asked herself. *My mind is wandering. Time for more tequila. It helps me focus. Where's the damn bottle?*

■■

The doorbell rang, and Lena jumped. She hated the sound of bells. Telephones, doorbells, sirens, curfew, ambulances, fire alarms, anything like that made her grit her teeth, hold her ears, and will it to stop. She was standing by the speaker plate at her front door. It would have taken only a few seconds to press the buzzer and let him in. Lena placed her finger on the button, but didn't push it down. Let the little fuckhole sweat it. The pisser. How much longer, she wondered, was he going to be able to keep these visits down to a weekly thing? She had told him in the beginning that she would only see him once every ten days, and if she ever caught him letting anybody else stick a plunger-and-point into his arm she would blot him out of her retina file.

The doorbell went off again, and this time she didn't wince. She counted to ten, fifteen, under her breath, and then hit the buzzer. The door in the lobby crashed shut. The stairs rattled as he came up. When she had met David, he was wearing lace-up shoes, cheap sidewalk shock absorbers. But the first time he came back to her apartment, he was wearing steel-toed boots. She wondered if he had done that on purpose. But people like David tended not to make conscious choices about how they appeared to others. They just let things happen.

Which is how she got away with little mind-fucks like making him wait again at the front door of the apartment, making him wonder if maybe he'd hit the wrong button by mistake and got buzzed in by somebody else. *What if the bitch has gone out?* she imagined him fretting, and when she popped open the peephole, there did seem to be a little extra shine around his hairline. Sweat, maybe? Sweat was almost as good as blood, just more difficult to obtain in quantity.

The peephole signaled recognition of the pattern behind his eyeball. She smiled sweetly and threw the door open. "Get your sorry ass in here," she snarled, and kicked it shut. "You smell like a wet dog."

"Aw, Lena, didja have a bad day?" He was already pleading with her. His blond hair needed cutting. His hands were filthy. And had he lost some weight?

"You look like shit," she said, ignoring his question. "When did you eat last?"

"I hadda samwich," he mumbled. One of his worst nights with her had started when she caught him eating some cold leftover soup out of the refrigerator, without her permission, with his fingers, yet. "I'm not going to feed you," she had shouted. "You damn well better eat before you get over here, pinhead, pincushion! This is not a date, boy. I'm not running a baby wagon here!"

"You hadda samwich," she mocked him. "When? Twoday?"

"Aw, Lena, don't be mean."

"Aw, David, don't be stupid. If I wasn't mean you wouldn't be here."

"I brought—" His hands were shaking when he pulled the zipperbag full of glassine envelopes from the front of his red leather jacket. Was it new? She liked the way it looked on him — its color, the quilted shoulders, the fur collar and the tight, corseted waist. Under the jacket he wore his usual gold-and-black leopard-spot T and tiger-striped tights.

Her eyes narrowed. There were many more glassine envelopes in the bag than usual. How had he gotten this much religion? Probably sold some major piece of his comfort — a cycle, a music console, one of those appurtenances that seem so expendable when you are turning yourself into a convert, a true believer, a steady user. It always seems to you that you are on the brink of getting something so much better and bigger, but you never do, you just learn to live on less and less. And more and more.

She took it away from him. *Really, there has to be something wrong with me,* she thought, *that I get such a rush in my crotch over these little struggles. He does not want to let go of his dope, but he has to, if it's going to do him any good.*

"Party favors, sport? Offerings to the three-faced Goddess?"

"No, no. Um, they were going to be a present."

She did not understand. "What?"

"If you want it."

No matter how well you think you know your chattel, he can still surprise you. Lena looked hard at him, not exactly pleased.

David sighed, hunched his shoulders, and pleaded with her again. "You always say I have to bring enough for both of us, so, well, I thought maybe if I brought extra, um, well, that you would, well, like it. You could get high without me underfoot, if you wanted to. After I go home. Maybe. Lena?"

She slapped him. He started to cry. It was one of the most touching things about him, the fact that he actually shed tears in her presence. They just jumped out of his eyes while he looked surprised and humiliated, and wiped at his cheeks.

"Haven't you got it figured out by now, asshole, that the best way to get yourself in big trouble is to think for yourself? You little freak. Just because I keep you company with your lousy habit, don't you try to make a believer out of me. Did you figure you could get some more control over me this way, by giving me more religion than I can handle? What other favors did you think I might start to do for you to keep you preaching? Got visions of yourself as some big-time switchboard cowboy with a stable of operators? Shit! Think again. You are talking nothing but shit. Bug shit."

She slapped him again, and he staggered a little. Her arms were hard and long. His own body was more muscle than fat, but she had never seen him raise his hands above his waist while she was hitting him. He didn't even make a fist. He just hugged the outside of his own thighs and kept on crying.

It was enough to make you want to come.

"Go clean up," she said roughly. "There's some potato salad and cold cuts in the fridge. Eat some if you can quit bawling long enough. Boil some water while you're at it. Then get your butt in here and let's get this over with. I got things I have to do."

■■

In the shower, David soaped his body for the second time that evening. He would never dream of showing up on her doorstep dirty. She had some kind of thing about hygiene. The whole apartment looked like she cleaned it with a toothbrush. But then, if you hardly ever go outside, he guessed you had a lot of time to keep everything spotless. Sighing, he picked up the fingernail brush and scrubbed his hands again. Cabinet-making left a perpetual black stain on his fingertips, cuticles, and knuckles. Sometimes he had burns or patches of epoxy stuck to his skin. He didn't blame her for shying away if he made the mistake of trying to touch her. His hands looked awful. He scrubbed them until they were bleeding a little, then rinsed them under scalding water. Come to think of it, she probably didn't even know what he did for a living. She never asked him any questions. He must have walnut-stained three hundred keyboard benches this week. It was a bug-headed fad, people wanting good, clean, durable plastic to look like something that gave you splinters and rotted away. But overtime pay was double-time-and-a-half, and all that had gone into the zipperbag that had just gotten his face slapped.

So why am I happy? he asked himself, stepping out of the tub and toweling off. His cock stood out in a shallow curve, no more than the beginning of a proper erection, but when he thought about her hand connecting hotly with his cheek, it jerked upright so fast it took his breath away. But he didn't touch it. *If I was going to do something that simple,* he thought, laughing quietly at himself, *I could have stayed home.*

He put his stripes and spots back on, slid his feet into his boots, padded into the kitchen, and filled a glass with water. While it cooked in the hotbox, he stuck his head into the refrigerator. There, as promised, was a tub of potato salad and a plate of cold cuts. He ate some of each, although he wasn't hungry. He wished Lena would let him take her out to dinner sometime. But she always did this weird thing of pretending she had someplace else to go and was gonna kick him out as soon as they got the angels to come down. Every Sixday night for the last three months, the same damn routine.

She had lost weight, he thought, rolling up a piece of ham and sliding it into his mouth. The circles under her eyes kept getting larger. Animal protein, for War Mother's sake, and being able to afford it was no excuse. Didn't she know what it did to your heart? There wasn't a slab of soy or a sheet of seaweed in the house. She didn't get enough sun or exercise. He checked the vegetable bin. It was full of single servings of carob and cola pudding. She didn't have any vitamins, either. He had checked every shelf in the kitchen. But try and tell her she ought to take better care of herself, just try. Worth your life. Damn woman would rip your arm off and beat you over the head with it just to prove she was in better shape than the Big Bug Queen.

"Hey, you looking for an escape hatch in there?" she jeered from the living room. He put the lid back on the potato salad and licked his fingers. His stomach tightened. She was in fine form tonight. Maybe the dope would slow her down. About as much chance of that as getting off on derms. Which are legal, yes, all you have to do to get them is sign up at your local health center and get three extra digits punched into your ID. Being on the government's narco list makes you exempt from the draft so you don't have nightmares about being trapped in a ship with a hull about as thick as a balloon while aliens uglier than centipedes take careful aim, disable your vessel, come inside, and take you all away. Carefully. Tenderly. Alive. While they taste you with their mouth-parts, full of pulpy pieces that look like rotten fruit, and tickle you with their antennae and stick their jointed, chitinous limbs that are covered with fine hairs down your throat and up your—

Those three extra ID numbers entitled you to pick up so many derms a day at the pharmacy of your choice. If you wanted more, you had to go back to the health center and sit around most of the day until you saw a doctor who would tell you to consider cleaning up before he doubled your 'script. But you had the time to sit around once you got registered, because there were so many jobs they wouldn't let you do if you were on the list. Like the job he had now, for instance. Let an addict handle power tools? Joke.

The skin patches were always reliable because they were made under carefully controlled laboratory conditions. Nothing like the unpredictable, kick-ass stuff that loco alchemists cooked up from flowerbeds of illegally cultivated seraphim that could give you a heart attack or bring on the rapture. Bless the double-sexed aborigines for showing us that trick before they all died of the common cold and venereal warts. By comparison, the synthetic heroin-fourteen in derms is about as much fun as an artificial vagina. Even one that can talk dirty to you. Give me Lena any day.

Whatever you want, he said silently to himself. *Whatever you want. Just so I can look at you and be here for a little while, I don't care. Do whatever you want.*

"Coming, Lena," he said patiently, and walked into the living room, carrying the glass of boiled water.

■ ■

Lena had her T off, and was wearing a leather vest that was open in front. It made his perineum ache when she did something like that, take her shirt off like a man and just walk around completely unconscious of her tits and what they did to him. He liked the whole shape of her, lean and somehow coiled up, springy, inside her tight, glittering clothes. And he could see the spiders. The first time he had ever crashed at the foot of her futon, sleeping on a pile of cold, greasy chains, he had dreamed of being held captive by big and extremely intelligent spiders who intended to sting him repeatedly and then eat him a little bit at a time. It had been unpleasant but fascinating, the kind of thing that made you shiver half the day and wonder how shit like that got into your brain.

The witches seemed to like bugs. They all wore jewelry and laserpix with crawly things on 'em. Well, why not? The deep-space bugs never took women. Just crawled right over 'em to drag out the dudes. He'd heard a rumor that Major Aerospace Corp. was going to start hiring women only on their security teams. The union would have fits over that. Any day now the army would probably start drafting women. Wouldn't that shake things up, now? Oooooh-eee.

Lena had looked a little like a soldier, the first time he saw her, or a b-vid space pirate. He had actually gone up to her at the bar instead of just looking because some prick-pisser had made a very bad-taste crack about a bunk wearing a chain-mail vest and dueling spurs. Though he must have been just a novice kiteboy himself, because he still had all his fingers and none of the nasty facial scars you got from glass-impregnated string sawing across your face. Not to mention the damage the spurs could do, although those scars tended to be invisible in most social situations and created odd rumors about the sexual kinks duelers had to develop to compensate for the loss of vital parts.

Instead of uniting them in joint distaste, the insult had suddenly made David's own tastes very clear. *That*, something inside him had said, *is one fine woman. Put on your welfare office manners, junior, and go find out what this is gonna cost you.*

"Shall I light the candles?" he asked.

"Yes."

He liked asking her what to do and waiting for her response. When she said yes, it was as if he had anticipated a need and provided for it without challenging her supremacy, and that made him feel a little proud. It was a good trick. When she said no, it was as if something had reached out and held him in check, and it was annoying, but also reassuring. It told him she paid attention to what he said, evaluated it. It gave him a place in her regard.

So he lit candles, trying to move quietly and not bump into anything. He knew better than to light the lamp on the table where her paraphernalia was laid out neatly as a surgeon's tray. She always lit that herself, striking the match with one hand while she held the spoon full of water and powder in the other — a piece of arrogance that had pissed him off in the beginning, her taking a chance of wasting that much of his salvation. But she had never spilled any yet, and by now he didn't care. It was her ritual, and it meant so much to her that it made the whole thing mean something to him, too. That sense of doing something important, following a plan, got him off as much (well, almost as much) as the needle.

He noticed the spiked hide on the tatami and got a lump in his throat. He had not seen that before. New games kept things interesting, but you never knew how you were going to perform. The probability of fucking up increased. And fucking up increased the probability of more new games. Sometimes David thought Lena didn't like him very much. But to be honest, most of the time he didn't care. Did he?

The anxiety became a little much. "I don't want to hold you up," he lied, placing the spent matches in her single ashtray. "Lemme have my shot now?"

"Follow the form," she reminded him irritably.

"Lena," he breathed, "please, would you fix me up?" It was so embarrassing.

"No. Not yet. Tell me how bad you want it."

Now he discovered that the cold fire of a spike sliding into his arm, and the subsequent diffusion of warmth up to his heart, his head, down to his loins and his toes, was something he wanted more than he could stand. "Please," he whispered. Then he whined. "Lena, I really need to get out of my head. I've been working so hard this week. And you know I can't do it for myself. I always mess it up, please."

"Not yet. There are a few things I want you to do for me first."

This was the form. He was on familiar ground, but he was miserable. "Do I have to?" he cried.

"No. You can leave."

"I can't."

"Then get down on your knees."

Nations have surrendered with less grief.

She had told him to get down on his knees. He fell like a bird shot in midflight. Now she told him to strip, something that was hard to do in that position. But he contrived to make it look pretty. Enticing. He took his boots off first, giving up the whole idea of protection along with their steel toes. His fingers lingered over the riptabs at the shoulders of his leopard-spotted T, and it fell seductively, revealing his well-defined, smooth-shaven chest and the small, inverted nipples. Without being told, he rolled the T up and tucked it neatly into one boot. He had never needed to be told to fold his things and stow them out of her way, take up as little room as possible. Sometimes it seemed to her he even breathed considerately in her presence, careful not to use up too much of the good air. She thought about his deftness, the strength of those hands, and her knees went a little weak. It made her want to slap his face bloody. When he pushed down the tiger-striped expandex tights, he had to straighten his thighs, then lift each leg and peel the stretchy, clinging material off his calf, and maneuver it over the awkward angle of his ankle and foot. Then the tights were folded once, rolled, and stuffed into his other boot.

His liberated dick was a fat sausage. It could hardly swing from side to side, it was so heavy and swollen. But he was careful to keep his hands away from his genitals — another habit (along with keeping himself shaved) that she had taken pains to reinforce. He came here to have her do things to his body that he could not do for himself. Very well, then, let him relinquish all attempts to give himself pleasure. It was just part of the price. And she loved to see him in need.

Looking at him felt like getting rich. No vid could ever approach the glory of doing it in person, or making somebody else do it. It was such a pleasure to look her fill instead of dressing, posing, acting, editing an image to be seen. Everybody knew you couldn't catch the plague by just being in the same room with somebody else, but that "knowledge" didn't quiet the visceral fear that the virus would crawl into your bloodstream via the mere presence of lust. One of her clients had even demanded that she put on rubber gloves before she touched the keyboard to upload his fantasy.

Was David crazy? Because he didn't seem to care, he was shameless. Even now, he was crawling toward her with his tongue out, as if there was nothing to be afraid of. She let him lick the leather patches on the insides of her thighs. In a minute or two, he would try to wheedle her out of her 'legs, start talking about how much he loved to eat oysters. Why did hetboys always think that was what machas were looking for?

I am shameless, too, but I'm not careless, Lena told herself. *I want to live forever. Sure, he says he doesn't do this with anybody but me, but people lie to get sex. They lie to get anything that makes them feel good. So he can do what I say and we'll both stay healthy, or he can go to the local*

piece-a parlor and fuck in a body bag, or he can ask death to go dancing.
Even through the shimmerlegs, she could feel the heat and wetness inside his mouth. It must hurt to lick the fabric — the metallic threads were sharp. But he lapped at her repeatedly, until the pressure became uncomfortable and she slapped him away. Tears ran down his cheeks. "I could make you feel real good," he said, and the next slap bloodied his mouth and tossed him onto his side. She kicked him then, and took her time about it, walking around him to pick her spot, sure he would not try to get away. He didn't even curl himself into a decent ball or cover his head, just kept his hands on his thighs and bit his lip and moaned. Mostly she used the side of her boot, or the sole. But a couple of times she planted the pointed toe deep into the muscle of his naked buttocks, then she kicked him over so he lay on his belly, and literally walked all over him. He bore her weight patiently, even though the spike heels were making bloody holes in his back. He did not scream until she stepped off — onto his upturned palms.

From there, she went to her favorite chair, and sat, legs crossed so she could squeeze her thighs together at the sight of him crawling, dragging himself forward with his injured hands, to cradle and kiss the boots that had hurt him. He could take the entire heel into his mouth. She liked this spurious fellatio, his Eve's apple bobbing as he struggled to cope with the intrusive object in his throat. Maybe it would help him develop self-control. The Virgin knew he needed some.

When she took her boot away from him, he rolled over onto his back, and she rose to her feet, balanced on one foot, and placed the other foot on his face. She did not have to put much weight on it to make him hyperventilate and squirm. The toe was pressing on his mouth and chin, and the sharp heel rested in the hollow of his throat. "Do you want it?" she teased him, and he could not say yes or no. "Would it get you off, or is it just too big, David?" She saw from the look in his eyes that he understood the reference perfectly. When she lifted her foot and walked away, his sigh of relief was loud.

You won't be glad for long, sucker, she vowed to herself. *It's going to take you a long time to get off the hook tonight.*

It was his job to crawl after her. Tonight this was coming easily. That was a relief. Sometimes he froze. Hands and knees refused to carry him, and she had to drive him forward with pain or threats. That was baffling as well as mortifying. David suspected it was the little, nagging discomforts — the pain in his ankles, the irritation of the carpet against his palms, the soreness in his lower back — as much as the humiliation that sometimes stuck in his craw. Why did Lena have to make him crawl? He would have been glad to run to the bathroom, if the mood was on her to make him suffer there. He would even have sprinted to the leather bed of nails on her tatami, which was where she led him now.

He chuckled at himself, silently, deep in his throat, afraid she would see it on his face or hear it and think he was deriding her. *If I wanted to crawl, she would make me run,* he told himself. *All we both want right now is to pump as much religion, chapter and verse, as we can before we get too fucked up to find a vein. And it's dangerous. It's a desire that cannot be consummated. If you try, you engender nothing but more desire. So Lena won't let me do anything just the way I want, for a long time. To prove we have enough control to finally do it, do the thing we want, and handle it, stay in control. She is taking care of me, a perverse nurturance, training me in denial to prepare me for indulgence.*

The calves of her long legs, swaying ahead of him, were plump in the tall silver boots. He wanted to sink his teeth into them, taste the flesh encased in the metal. The rhinestone heels that had worn his tongue to shreds winked sardonically at him. Would Lena taste of flesh, or of mylar and zircons? His mouth was dry, making it hard to swallow the little bits of dirt left there by her soles. *Does she notice me?* he wondered. *Does she care that I am crawling well tonight, that I do not hesitate or stumble? Or does she only notice me when I fail?*

■ ■

Behind her, Lena heard the slight, rhythmic scraping of his palms and shins on the rug. She made him stop at the low table by her tatami and hand her the bowl full of rubbing alcohol and used needles she had placed there earlier. She had been saving the points she used on him ever since he had started seeing her. But the way she would use them now was something new. She wondered how he would respond. "Keep your hands down, David. Don't move."

She pinched up some flesh at the side of his upper arm, pulled it away from the bone, and ran a needle through his skin. He winced, but did not cry out. She repeated this on the other side. He looked at her mutely, begging, like a dog who has done something wrong. She smiled and put a third needle in below the first one, then inserted a fourth one in the loose skin of his other arm. When she had six of them in each arm, she put eight of them in the front of each thigh. The skin was not so loose there. The skewered flesh bled. He was shaking and making noises that were not quite words. When she started to rub and pinch his nipples, his bloated cock swung up like a tusker's trunk, and he blubbered for mercy.

"Later for you. This is for me." She could smell the blood. It made her mouth water, and she clamped her lips together. Too bad she was old enough to have developed a taste for it, before the plague. *Look all you want, touch, smell, but don't swallow,* she told herself. *You can always make him bleed a little more to make up for it.*

She thought it was best to restrain herself to a pair of needles per nipple. She ran them parallel to each other, at the top and bottom of the brown nubs. Here, too, there was bleeding as soon as she put the points in. Now, wasn't it a good thing she made him shave? Hair would distort the thin red paths, soak them up, make them less vivid. "You're making such a mess," she said. "Straighten your back." It would make the blood flow in straighter lines.

He was coming along nicely so far, but she didn't want to lose him. So she turned around and made him bend over and unzip her boots with his teeth. Then she stepped out of them, took her belt off, threw it on the tatami, and rolled her 'legs down over her hips. Unlike David, she didn't fold them up neatly and stow them away discreetly. She wadded them up in her hand and tossed them into the corner. He spread his thighs in anticipation, and she stepped between them, pressing his nose into the latex bikini she wore under her clothes.

"I'm tired of hearing you brag about how many oysters you've swallowed," she said. "So put up or shut up. Now."

She was wet enough to feel his tongue gliding over her, despite the thin sheet of rubber between them. When he sucked at her clit, it was wonderful. But there was no reason to spoil him. She turned around again, and bent over.

"Spread my cheeks," she said, then thought, *Have you gone crazy? Letting him paw you with his sweaty little mitts?* But his hands on either side of her furrow were surprisingly gentle and dry. He opened her only enough to allow his tongue complete access, and he didn't try to cheat and get a taste under the strap. Getting rimmed this way was much better than having him go after her clit. She let him do it until she was dizzy from hanging upside down. By the time she turned around, the blood was dry on his chest and thighs.

But his cock was still up, and she crouched between his legs to grasp it. Her erect nipples grazed his cheek, and he pulled his face away from her vest, afraid of seeming forward. But his mouth was still open, and a thin string of saliva fell from his lower lip. "What a good hungry dog," she said. "What a good boy. Oh, David, do you really want to be a good, good boy?"

He nodded, and she ran the first needle through the underside of his dick. He jerked, and she laughed, low and sexy, and said again, "What a good hungry dog." Then she pierced the loose skin of his shaft again. She put one in every inch, and his erection just got firmer, his balls tighter. With praise and with pain, she kept him pumped up until he would have let her put a needle through his tongue if she had promised to kiss him first.

Then she produced a ball of black-and-silver twine. First she wound it in figure eights around each set of upper-arm piercings. Then she cinched each nipple to its mate. The long threads that were left over from binding his tits were woven back into the piercings on his arms. She drew the twine so tight that his shoulders were cupped forward. The holes in his arms began to bleed, and his wounded nipples opened and released more thin threads of scarlet.

She laced up each of his thighs. He guessed what would come next, and shuddered, but could not form a coherent protest. It was awful and wonderful at the same time. Thigh was bound to thigh. Then his cock was bound — twine going completely around it, up and down — and his nipples utilized once more as anchors, to keep his pisser pointing toward the ceiling.

Lena stepped back and regarded her handiwork. He was holding absolutely still. To move at all would cause him excruciating pain. The idea of having his skin penetrated and violated so often had put him in a near-catatonic state. The piercings themselves were not that painful, but the stress the twine put on them jacked the pain up to a level that she found erotic to witness. *I actually want to play with myself,* she thought, *I want to make myself come just watching him kneeling there, trying to save himself some hurt by not breathing deeply. And resisting is absolutely out of the question. That would just pull everything out, split the skin in a dozen places.*

She put her fingers under the latex strap of the bikini and manipulated her own thick sexual lubrication, the thin and rubbery lips, the spongy mouth of her opening. She let him watch her. Let him know, let him know, let him know — what this did to her. It was a reward. It was a threat.

David shook, and willed himself not to shake. Every needle blazed. Every needle froze. The skin around the piercings heated and swelled. The rest of his skin was clammy and cold. And she was perfect, in front of him, her face a bestial mask of sadistic lust. Lena was masturbating at the spectacle of his willing vulnerability, the suffering he offered up to her, the bleeding wounds he had held still for her to make, and allowed her to bind. He wanted ... everything. Consumption. To be used, to be used up completely. To be absorbed into her eyes, her mouth, her sex, to become part of her substance.

When he tried to tell her this, stumbling over the inadequate words he could barely string together, she pushed him over onto his back, onto the bed of nails. He choked and cried her name. She laughed again, and picked up her crop. She struck him on the piercings. She was careful, aiming the crop in such a way that the needles would not be caught and ripped out, but she hurt him a lot. She even found his nipples, within the hollows of his shoulders, and beat them. She made him lick his own blood off the crop. And she used the large flap of leather at the tip of it to flog his cock and balls. The stock was used to beat him across the thighs. He saw white light every time she hit him. The force of the blows sent him back into the sharp points embedded in the leather. Slivers of pain went deep into his back and buns and upper thighs. He had never done anything so difficult.

Then Lena said, "Roll over, David."

Oh, the bitch, the bitch, the unfeeling loveless heartless dried-up cunt of a bitch. She wasn't even going to help him by kicking him over. He was going to have to do this all by himself. He did not deserve this, he did not know how he was going to obey, it was hard, too hard.

He must have spoken at least part of this aloud, because she was reaching inside the black latex bikini and smearing something on his face. "Oh, far from dried-up, David dear," she said. "Of course it's hard. But it gets you off, too. I know you. So do it, David, do it now. Do it because I want to watch you. I promise I'll make it worth your while, David. Lay on your pain, boy."

With a groan, he went over, and screamed. There was no way to help himself land. He simply fell on the piercings, and there was nothing but more needles to fall upon. He was held up in the air on spear-points. Broken. A victim.

Then she beat him. Hymen! As he howled, he thought, *When she cropped me before, she was toying with me. Trying to scare me. Now she's just trying to cut me in half. I hate this, I hate her, and there's nothing I can do, because I want what comes later, I want — I want — I want this, even this. Even this. Because she cannot cut me in half, she cannot diminish me, even this I can survive, thrive on, so go ahead, you bitch, I can take it, and more than that, I can love it — almost come from it — but I can't stop screaming. And I can't scream any louder. When will it end?*

He could not get up by himself. He could only roll from side to side. And that meant rolling on the needles, rolling on the spikes in the leather. He hated that riding crop. Hated its thin, leather-covered, flexible stock. Hated the noisy, floppy piece of leather on the end of it. Resolved to buy her something thicker and less stingy, a razor strop, maybe. Then she threw down the crop and started to use her belt, and he changed his mind. Let's not buy Lena anything. Let's not give Lena any ideas. Let's just hope we live through this.

When she was done, she rolled him over with one hand on his shoulder, and the other in his hair. She showed him his own face in her belt buckle. He was a mess — tears and snot, hair every which way. But his eyes looked serene; his face was relaxed somehow. *Virgin, Birth Mother, and War Mother damn it, she always does it, she makes me feel ... safe. If she's crazy, we're a pair.*

Lena let him rest while she untied the twine. She removed the needles carefully, spraying alcohol on each point before pulling it out so the stinging antiseptic would be drawn through the wound. Then she put on rubber gloves and dabbed antibiotic salve on the punctures. Had she really let him put his mouth on her panties earlier? Or had he dreamed that?

She was bending over him with another needle in her hand, a different kind, just a slender, hollow tube of chrome with no plastic end to connect it to a syringe. And a gold ring. "I want you to wear this, David," she said. "Just for tonight."

On his finger? What? "Okay," he mumbled.

She grabbed his right nipple, shoved the needle through it, fit the end of the ring into the hollow butt of the needle, and pushed it through. A tit ring? Indignation almost made him bolt off the mat. "Just for me, David, just for tonight," she reminded him. "Nobody else needs to see. Nobody else needs to know."

A ring, going through an actual hole in his body. Might as well say in public, *I'm a hype*. Nobody else wore them. They were too fucking primitive, permanent. An advertisement that you liked to put needles in your body. Unsanitary. Spreads disease. Spreads the plague. Unnecessary. Illegal. Sick.

She was bending over him, closing the ring. Her vest fell open enough for him to see that her nipples were still hard. And why not? He was still hard too, and she was squeezing him, making him gasp as the astringent powder on her glove made contact with the fresh needle-marks.

Then she left him, and he was so lonely he cried out for her. "Lena!"

"Don't worry, I'll be right there. Time you met the heavenly host, boy. Lay still."

She returned carrying the alcohol lamp, the water, and her wooden box. This was another break with tradition. Before, she had always fixed him at the table. If they got really inspired, they would slide to the floor, but they started out facing each other, sitting primly on chairs. David was confused. He decided the best policy was to be absolutely passive. As usual. Lena knew what she was doing. He didn't know. So he should just hold his tongue and watch.

She handed him a foil packet. "Put this on."

It was a condom. She had made him wear one before. She liked to make him jerk off in them, then save the contents to punish him with later. Come tasted terrible when it was cold. He rolled it on.

■■

Lena sat down at the little bedside table. She took a mirror from the wooden box, tipped half of the contents of one of the glassine envelopes onto its silver face, and began chopping the yellow flakes into powder with a single-edged razor blade. When it was fine enough to suit her, she slid the razor blade beneath the tiny heap of gold dust, and dumped a portion of it into the ornate silver spoon. The bottom of its bowl was permanently blackened, and the handle had been bent to make sure the precious liquid in it stayed level when she put the spoon down on the table. She lit the alcohol lamp, drew some of the clean water into one of the syringes, rinsed the blade off into the spoon with careful, tiny squirts, ejected the rest of the water into the glass, and held the spoon over the flame.

"Keep it up," she warned him. The air over the spoon sizzled. She put it down and pinched a bit of cotton off one of the large white balls of fluff, rolled it tight, then dropped it into the spoon. David handled himself, watching her chase the cotton and finally pin it down with the needle, and draw the plunger on the syringe back, filling the glass barrel with piss-colored fluid. The slow masturbation wasn't necessary. He wouldn't lose his erection or shoot until—

Lena was shimmying out of the black latex bikini. He gaped at her shaved sex. She put one foot on each side of him, and spread herself with her free hand. It looked like a woman wearing a hooded cape ... or a woman with wings.

"Hold it up for me," she said, and sank onto him. There was no time to be grateful or surprised, and barely enough time to be helpful. David tried to position his cock so it would go into her smoothly, at the proper angle. "Help me," she said, waving the rubber tourniquet at him. He put out his arm, and she somehow managed to pull it tight and tuck one loose end under, so it would put just a little pressure on his bicep. She shook the syringe, flicking it with her forefinger to get rid of the air bubbles. Between two fingers, she felt for his vein, held it still, and rested the point of the needle where it should go.

But she did not put it in. Instead, she moved on him. He stopped caring about the spiked hide under his back if that was the price he had to pay for being ridden this way. Lena had put down the needle and had both hands on his shoulders. Her eyes were closed. He lifted his hands, knowing this was an unpardonable crime, and slid them beneath her vest. Her breasts were small and firm, and he touched them as lightly as he could, hoping she would ignore the touch or maybe not even feel it.

But Lena did feel it. Her eyes popped open, and she showed him her teeth. "Better get a decent feel while you can," she hissed. "Grab them, stupid, pinch them, hang onto them, you might never get another chance." Yeah, so a real mistress always insists that her submissives treat her with absolute respect and gentle tenderness. Shit on that. She hated being touched that way, the way you pick up something disgusting — tentatively, afraid to make contact. He was almost mauling her, but it felt good, good, and that was what he was there for, to make her feel good.

She was fiercely happy to have David inside her. Show him what that big thing was good for. Something besides getting it slapped around, punctured, and jacked off. She was breaking too many of her own rules, but she did not care, not yet. She could worry about it later. She never had to see him again. After tonight, she could send him away. If she hadn't finally scared him off for good. She rested one hand on his pectoral, heard him groan, and looked down to see the ring. She would make him give that back first, of course. It was 24-karat gold, and he'd never dare keep it in long enough for the piercing to heal. She tugged on it anyway, just to remind him that he was a marked man, then leaned on his other pec, the intact one.

He wouldn't be able to resist coming for much longer, and neither would she. The only difference was, if she came now, the party could still go on. If he came, the party was over. Might as well perform the rest of the experiment. She picked up the hypodermic and got his arm in the right position again. This time, there was no tease. She slapped at his vein, and it bulged the way his cock did when she hit it. All she had to do was lean on the needle a little, and it broke the skin. She had barely retracted the plunger when a miniature geyser of blood appeared. He was so easy to do. She gave him nearly three-quarters of a cc, more than his usual dose. He wouldn't be able to come now until his drugs wore off a little. He could lie there and get a head start on salvation while she sat on top of him and cooked up a fix for herself. It would be awkward, but interesting.

Then she began to hear music — or almost hear music. Or was it her own voice, singing? Somewhere something sounded delicious, heavenly, and there was a golden light around everything. David looked as if he were miles below her, as if he had fallen from a great height and landed on his back, his wings spread out behind him. Maybe they weren't wings, exactly, but a nimbus, a radiant cloud of ... benevolence and goodness and warmth, a blessing, a ... melting. As if everything bad or painful or confusing was dissolving, running out of her, out of the whole world, disappearing, evaporating, and what was left behind was so simple, so good, it was no wonder she could hear everything singing, glorious music everywhere.

The power of so much beauty made her want to cry. When she touched David's hair, light came off it in rainbow glints. It hurt her eyes. And when she closed them, the visuals turned instantly into a rush of heat in her gut, between her legs, and she used him hard, again and again, knowing he could not prevent her, did not want to, would have given his life to see this look on her face, her helplessness, pleasure, his tormentor losing control while she still controlled him absolutely. When she finally tired and slowed down, he put his hands under her hips and helped her keep moving, and the drug had filled her with so much sweetness that she did not mind. She knew that even now, David would not come until she allowed it, released him from her service. And so she pounded it out of him, demanded it, and he obeyed this order like all the others, not knowing why both of them were flying together, seeing, being angels together.

It wasn't until the music faded out of earshot that she got mad. For her to catch his rush, there had to be skin-to-skin contact between them. The drug could pass through one mucous membrane into another, especially if there was enough friction to wear away the outer layers of protective cells. She wasn't sorry, and that was what made her so angry — that she had needed him, needed him to pleasure her, but also needed him to go on and reach his own climax. How could this have happened? He was a toy, he was recreation, he was like your favorite vid program or a hobby. This was not a relationship. She did not have relationships. Especially not with boys half her age who were stupid enough to be hypes and bent enough to love getting spanked.

This could not be her fault. Somebody would have to pay.

David was out of breath, panting, watching her through half-closed eyes as she came up and off him with a wad of rubber in her hand. "Broken! Shithead! Can't you even put on a scumbag right? What is wrong with you?" She threw it at him, and David winced as it hit his chest and smeared slime across his nipple.

His chest contracted. He felt as if he had just murdered someone. "Lena! No! I was careful."

"Are you arguing with me?"

"Yes!"

It was the first time he had ever crossed her. They stared at each other, furious. He started talking again, fast, afraid she would find a way to shut him up. This was too important. "Lena, I am sorry. But I have been using those things since I was eight, and I've never had one break yet. Maybe it was old. Maybe we just got carried away. But it shouldn't matter. I had a blood test just a month ago. I am clean. And I have not been fucking or shooting up with anybody but you. I swear."

He remembered the bad teeth and bald head of the bartender at the Third Spur, whispering in his ear when he came up to get Lena's drink, "Better take her something a little more potent unless you want just a handshake. Talk to Shaky over there, that drowned rat character with the shoulder pads. He knows what her usual is. Hope you know what you're doing, son. She's a fickle wind." It seemed like such a long time ago. Giving Lena her drink, trying to look like he really did know what he was doing, figuring if you want to be cool you talk as little as possible, so all he said was, "If you really want a party I'll go talk to Shaky." She had just glanced up at him and barely nodded. And him afraid to ask the missionary what was in the envelope that had cost too much money, afraid to ask Lena, too, just letting her take the lead. Until now.

"You swear?" she shouted. "You swear? You pisshole. If I hadn't had the brains to shove some foam up there before you got here, you would be dead, sucker. I would call the cops and report you."

"Report me? That's hysterical. Have you lost your fuckin' mind? You better grab the rest of this religion and flush it down somebody else's toilet before the sheriff kicks down your door. You better wipe your hard-drive and cook an extra set of books to hand the tax-man, unless you're the first sex-jockey since the first moron microchip got stuck on a board to give Caesar his due. You better pray real hard that nobody in this building hates you enough to claim that you been seeing johns on premises. The very nicest thing they'll do is revoke your license, Lena, and you can work off your fine down at the corner of Fifth and Grand, and hope Joey the Bag will buy you a drink once in a while so you can get off your achin' feet. You'll have to leave your nice, clean nest, Lena. You'll have to touch people you don't even know!"

David realized he had gotten closer and closer to her, until he was yelling at her just inches from her face. He grabbed her hands, backed up a step, and lowered the volume. "Don't make a bug raid out of a bat bite. This is going to be okay. You want me to get tested again? I will. Come with me. I'll sign for you to get the results, and you can tell me if I'm clean or not. Lena, please, it was so fine, don't make it ugly, it was an accident. I would never do anything to hurt you. Please."

She twisted out of his grip. "Oh, yes, you'll get tested," she hissed. "Tomorrow. And a month after that. So will I. And you will stay here with me until you do. So I know where you go and what you do. And if I get sick—"

"If you get sick, you can shoot me up with a needle full of your own blood. You can do it now. I'm that sure I'm clean. Are you? Are you that sure?"

She didn't answer him, just grabbed her knees, put her head down, and rocked. He left her alone, went into the kitchen, and found half a bottle of tequila sitting by a sticky shot glass. He rinsed the glass, looked in the refrigerator for a lemon, couldn't find anything but cans of lemon-flavored iced tea, and settled for taking the tequila and a clean glass out to the tatami. He poured her a shot, made her drink it, and persuaded her to give him one of her feet to massage. Finally she started to cry. He wondered if that would make it better or worse. Would it ease her terror, or would it make her ashamed?

Lena was panicking. He was being too good. But he had done something awful. Hadn't he? Had she? He was picking her up, moving her off the tatami, putting her down, and unrolling the futon. Her bed. She never let him up on her bed. And there was something extremely scary about how easy it had been for him to lift her off the floor and put her someplace else. She didn't like being reminded that he was that strong, that he really had a choice about obeying her. Then he picked her up again, put her on the bed, and stretched out beside her. His naked hip was warm. She wanted to stroke it, she wanted to touch his cock. She made a fist instead and tried to get up, off the futon.

David touched her shoulder, gave her a tissue and some more tequila. He was kissing her, making her lie down while he cooked up some more religion. "Secondhand can't be as good as the real thing," he said, reaching for her arm. He looped her belt around it, cinched it tight, gave her the end to hold. Lena was too heavy with grief to stop him. She realized then that she had never actually seen him fuck up his own hit. He didn't seem to be having any trouble doing it for her.

His hand was in her. After everything that had happened, the idiot had put on a rubber glove. And he was touching all those places that a cock never reaches. All those places inside her that only women had touched. That was why women were dangerous. They could make you do anything, say anything, buy them anything, follow them anywhere for their attention, their smiles, the sex, this sex—

Just one woman, really, Lena thought, *because all the women who came after her were just reflections and imitations of that original obsession. She looked so elegant when she came up to me at the transit station, with her face painted like a poet's and her hair put up with a dozen silver throwing spikes. She wore a dress made out of hundreds of little, multi-colored silk scarves. I hid my hands behind my back because I didn't want her to see the dirt. That dress made her look like a flower or a bonfire, something that was wild or dangerous but still beautiful. She had the courtesy to pretend that she had not noticed me grubbing in the garbage can. "Where is the nearest Vend-A-Meal?" she asked, and pretended not to understand my directions. "A penny if you'll guide me," she said, then frowned. "Isn't that the going rate for guide services?" After that, we were together for ... a year? Six months? Six weeks? So much was happening, who could keep track of the calendar?*

She was an adult, the first free person I had ever met. She knew how to make me happy even if I wanted to die, knew where to get it, the doses, showed me how, laughed at me for being such a goon the first time I got religion and I knew this was something that could take over the rest of my life. She claimed she never would have sent me to heaven if she'd known how young I was. But then she said it was better if I did it with her, at home, so she could take care of me. And what did I know? I was a kid. I was running away from a place that was not home, had never been home. I guess there were worse places I could have wound up. Worse people who could have taken me in.

David, cooking up and administering his second dose, barely noticed that Lena's gaze was fixed on an empty corner of the room. Her lips were moving, but she didn't make any noise, so he didn't try to follow her monologue. Her facial expression was shifting from grief to joy to anger, but that was normal when you were this fucked up. So he left Lena alone in the grip of memory.

And all she could remember was that woman. The one who carried a gun before it was legal and swore she would shoot the man who made little Lena leave home if she ever ran across him on the streets. He wasn't Lena's daddy, but he made her call him that all the time, even when her mouth was full of — no, that was too much to remember. That was going too far back. That was a memory with poisonous spines. It was easier to think about the woman who had a beat to walk every night, in shoes that should have been worn only in bed. While Lena waited all night at a dirty table, feeling squeezed by the vending machines that lined the walls and the fluorescent light that beat down from the ceiling so hard there were no shadows, not even under her chair. Waiting for her keeper to come back and give her some more cash and take a few more rubbers. The woman would tell Lena to wash her face and ask her what she was reading, then promise to take her back to the library tomorrow. Lena didn't really mind having the same conversation three or four times a night. It was kind of like looking at your watch. It told you the time was passing smoothly and predictably, the same way it had the night before.

There were times when the night did not go smoothly, when they had to go find another hotel room without going back to get their stuff at their old place. Or a friend would drop by the diner to tell Lena they had to go to the hospital. Or somebody would tell Lena to give them bail money, and she would have to decide if it was a legitimate request or a hustle. It was dangerous work. The woman dealt with it by telling stories. There was a story about vice cops who tried to shake her down. She convinced them she didn't have any money, talked them into accepting sex instead, then serviced them in the dark. She didn't tell them she was bleeding. Lena had heard the moral to that story ("If I'm going to die, some of them are coming with me") dozens of times, and always nodded and smiled. She knew that the story might not be true. The spirit behind it — the defiance and trickery — was the truth it conveyed.

Then there was the night when the woman decided not to turn anybody with the numbers three and seven in their license plate because she could swear the bastard who'd tried to choke her yesterday had a license plate with those numbers. Or was it eight and nine? They went hungry that night, and for several nights after that. She had broken some of the bones in her right hand beating that guy up. He had tried to take his money back. That was when Lena learned how to do her own preaching, because her girlfriend's hand was out of commission, and it hurt so bad, Lena had to do what she could to make it better.

But there came a night when Lena, young as she was, realized that the woman and her sore feet, the woman and her kabuki makeup and clown wig and chipped purple nails, the woman with a dagger tattooed between her breasts, the woman who laughed at her own horrible stories, the woman and her habit could shatter your whole life, if you ever got a chance to have a life apart from her, apart from the messed-up adults who could not help themselves, could not help but be predatory, unpredictable, draining.

Lena was afraid of the religion that was supposed to be the answer to all of their problems, but at the same time ate up every bit of spare cash and complicated all of their interactions with the other people on the street. Any of their possessions, their friends, or their promises to each other could vanish in a minute if they could be traded for more drugs. Feeling that good couldn't be good for you. *Oh no, oh no, not me, not me,* Lena told herself. *I am an atheist, I am an agnostic, I can take this or leave it. So I left her.* By then, Lena knew other ways to get a bed for the night. You could join a gang of kids that boosted stuff from the market. Find a rent-a-daddy and hold his cache. Get some fake ID, chase some other rooster out of a bar, and keep the patrons supplied with anything it was illegal for the bartender to sell. Break into cars, co-ops, street vendors' booths. Sell expired film, bootleg vids full of static, and broken designer body holos to tourists.

But Lena vowed she would never walk into the headlights and stop her own drivers or keep her own paranoid list of license plate numbers. Never pour her whole life into the spoon and the needle. And never be able to do without it, either. Because the pain of living does not go away. You need to treat that pain. Or you need to die. Lena did not want to die.

The spate of memories made Lena's breath catch in her chest. They hurt her. Perhaps she had gotten it wrong after all. *Was it really her who left me? Forgot to come back for me? Until I got sick of chugging vending machine coffee and couldn't face the place in daylight, and went off on my own? Did she find somebody older and smarter who could take care of her, or was it somebody as young and scared as I was when she first met me? How could she abandon me? We had absolutely nothing, but it was still more than anybody ever wanted us to have.*

Every other woman in Lena's life had her own story, but it was the same story. She is jealous because religion means more to you than she does. Or you get jealous because of the things she does to get to heaven. You have been trying to clean up only she asks you to hit her because she has the shakes, and then she tells you how good you are to her and she has extra, let's get off together, let's party. Please. She is scared, and you are so strong. Strong enough to do without it. Then you do, you fix, and she says now she knows you will never leave her. Only later she leaves you to clean up. Or she leaves you for somebody who can get her high three times a day. And the only reason you are surprised, the only reason it matters, the only reason you stick around for the end of the story is because you care. Loving her makes you stupid. So when she hurts you, you have no one but yourself to blame; you should have known it was coming, you shouldn't even feel sorry for yourself. You're sick and you need medicine, even if taking the medication is your sickness, and it all makes about as much sense as falling in love because you don't want to be lonely.

And now all the places where women used to strut and tussle, flirt and fight, were gone. Just when Lena could have gotten in without a fake ID, they disappeared. Nobody had to bust them. They closed because the women were gone. Lena tried not to think about those places. She had visited them only a few times anyway, hiding behind the woman, who occasionally sought out a little cash or a missionary there. Lena had a dozen confused, fragmented sensory impressions of big dance floors full of colored lights, sur-rounded by booths you could rent if the music made you too passionate to wait until you got home; crowds of women in their finery, always talking, always touching each other; their insanity, their feuds, their ridiculous acts of kindness to total strangers who could not be trusted; the lengths they went to dress lust up in pretty clothes and call it by more trivial names.

Now if Lena saw another woman on the street, she was probably wrapped from head to toe in viricidal gauze and protected by a bodyguard of her husband's younger brothers, toting automatic weapons. Lena had even seen women in chains on the street. They were actually chained to their male protectors, so nobody could spirit them away and sell them to a family that was desperate to marry off its heir. If you saw another woman who was an outlaw, who was still free, she didn't want to talk to you. She would keep one hand on her gun and the other on her wallet. When young girls ran away today, where did they go? Who took them in? *Not me*, Lena thought. And finally she knew what people meant when they talked about sin and guilt and repentance, because the knowledge of her own cowardice suddenly made her ashamed.

David's hand fell on her nipple, and it was full of strength and love. The touch was angelic, too sensitive, too completely plea-surable to be human. "Hush, Lena," he said. His honeyed voice was resonant; set off vibrations that hummed in her belly, tickled her throat, and made her thighs roll apart. Her body was hollow, it was tuned to his voice, he was like a clapper in a bell. "Listen. Hear the music? Good, I'm glad. I'm so glad. Fly with me, Lena. The War Mother herself never flew this high."

Lena realized that the spaces in between the words were even more delicious than the sounds that David was making. She wished he would just shut up and let the sweet silence hum around her. But he kept on talking. "You're so beautiful when you smile like that. All I ever wanted to do is make you happy. Would it be so terrible, having me around? The shop owes me two months of vacation. I wouldn't get in your way. I know you have to work. But I could feed you, Lena. I could cook you really wonderful things to eat. At night, you could sit down and relax and have a hot, nutritious meal for a change instead of all that takeout crap. And I'll clean up after myself. I could keep the whole house together. You'd save so much money. And we could fly together like this every single night."

Lena put her hands up to cover her ears, but David intercepted one of them and carried it to his breast. "I'm not going to take it out, Lena, I'm going to leave it in. The ring. Feel it? I'll leave it in. And I'll take care of you. It'll be okay, sweetheart. I'm a big, strong boy, and there's nothing that I can't fix for you, if you'll just let me."

She opened her eyes, and everything in her apartment was a weapon.

UNSAFE SEX

■■

Malcolm loves me for myself. If I put on fifteen pounds, he worries — not because it's unattractive, but because it's not good for my health. I'm sure Malcolm doesn't jack off in a frenzy, yanking on his tits while he visualizes isolated parts of my body — my dick, quivering to hold itself up, my asshole spread wide with both my palms flat against my cheeks, the little smear of hair that decorates my booth-tanned crack.

In fact, I'm not sure he jacks off at all. But wouldn't it be peculiar if he didn't? Malcolm probably masturbates just often enough to be well adjusted. Then I bet he gets up and changes the sheets.

No, what we have is a mature, adult, gay relationship. As k.d. lang says, "Sex is an important thing, but it is not the thing." It is my whole self that engages Malcolm. He is patient and considerate, thoughtful and kind. He never forgets anniversaries, birthdays, or holidays. He even sends out cards to my parents for Mother's Day and Father's Day.

I am the perfect other half of this perfect relationship. Malcolm and I live in a midtown Manhattan co-op. Every square foot of it cost a few thousand dollars, and we deserve it. We've decided it's okay to take good care of ourselves. We need our home to be a haven, a retreat from the dog-eat-dog, mercenary atmosphere of the business world. We can afford security. That's because we work hard at our respective professions. Malcolm is an attorney; I own a travel agency. We have health insurance, medical powers of attorney, and wills that we update every two years. We are each other's beneficiaries on our life insurance policies. Our prosperity counselor has helped us to create a safety net for our old age.

Malcolm and I do not use words like "fabulous." We do not own pets. There is nothing more ludicrous than grown men slobbering over small, fluffy dogs. We do not go disco dancing (although we did when we were dating). Only ten percent of our video library is porn. We keep the KY and the condoms in the bathroom. Sexual paraphernalia on display in the bedroom is just a little gauche, don't you think? We had our six weeks of mating frenzy, but we're safely past the honeymoon phase now, thank God. Our relationship is held together by much more than just fucking.

We walk with Dignity in the annual Christopher Street march, but we would never be caught dead at one of those poorly planned, inflammatory temper tantrums that the little boys with the nose rings and the Doc Martens are so fond of staging. Do they really care about anything besides getting on the evening news? I don't think gaining personal notoriety is necessary to promote social change. Malcolm's family in Connecticut would slit their wrists if we got ourselves on the front page of the *Daily News*.

We make an annual donation to the Gay Men's Health Crisis because we have to take care of our own. Malcolm and I would really love to find some time for volunteer work. But if we had time to volunteer, we wouldn't be able to afford that sizable contribution, would we? Oh, and we don't give handouts to panhandlers. The taxes we pay to provide welfare are quite enough, thank you. I'll grant you, the homeless are a terrible problem. They make it so hard to get into the subway stations. So I give my spare change to cabdrivers instead. At least they're working. Although you'd think if they planned to stay in this country, they'd have the courtesy to learn to speak English.

Like so many other hardworking men who just happen to be homosexual, all Malcolm and I want is our little piece of the American dream. We have to take responsibility for proving that the stereotype of the promiscuous, narcissistic clone is false. We are men first, gays second, but we don't want to make a fetish out of our masculinity, either (although Malcolm needs to add a few more squats to his routine to build up those flabby calves). Oh, and you should have seen the look on his face when I told him I wanted a diamond ear stud for our last anniversary! I must say, I was more than happy to take this Rolex instead. We don't want to be bitchy, but we deplore those members of our community who continue to live out mainstream America's flamboyant and perverse images of the gay lifestyle — the Queer Nation kids in their kilts and pierced eyebrows, the tattooed leatherboys, the diesel dykes on bikes. I will admit it makes us a wee bit resentful that their freedom to slander the rest of us was won at our expense, through the efforts of decent, ordinary men like ourselves.

But you shouldn't think we're dull. We try to keep the playful and spontaneous spirit of our limerence phase alive. We don't want to lose touch with the child within. We have our wild and crazy side. We're even thinking of buying a Miata.

Malcolm is working late again. I wonder when that new assistant of his is going to get the hang of the firm's filing system. It's too bad Malcolm's not trying to teach him his numbers instead of his letters. They could use Malcolm's dick for a yardstick, then they'd only have to go up to six.

When Malcolm phoned with this news, I told him I might not be in when he gets home. I have to take care of a sick friend. And it's the truth. How could I ever lie to sweet, decent, open, trusting Malcolm? Let's be real. My dick is the sickest friend I've got. If I asked him, I'm sure Malcolm wouldn't dream of trying to isolate me within our relationship. Outside interests enhance a couple's intimacy.

Tonight, I want somebody who does not love me for myself. I want somebody who does not love me at all. And I want someone I can adore blindly. Someone to worship. It has to be just the right person. Not everybody can be an icon, even for the ten minutes it usually takes for me to suck them off. No, it has to be a big man with a hint of brutality, more than a hint of the animal, the bestial. Somebody strong and domineering who will be deaf to my comfort or my history, somebody who doesn't care about my taste in restaurants or the location of my seat at the opera. But he can't be too smart. I don't want to talk to him, for Chrissake. And no kissy fags who will ask me for my phone number. I don't want to found a cult, y'know, I just want to throw myself down, grovel, get used, and get up and go home.

I take a cab to the meat-packing district and walk around. They closed the Mineshaft a long time ago. I have no idea what took them so long. But honestly, what do they think went on there that doesn't go on now in the alleys and cul-de-sacs that surround that foul pesthole, that shit-encrusted and semen-drenched toilet, that fire-trap that was probably saved from going up in flames only by the hundreds of quarts of piss that were sprayed upon it every night?

Most of the streetlights are busted. The streets are paved with brick and cobblestone and garbage. Mud and less palatable things clog the storm drains and gutters. It isn't dark yet (I'm not that much of a fool), but the hookers are already starting to stake their turf.

I can't help but stare at one whose starved-looking midriff is a moon crater between her metallic silver halter top and a cracked, black vinyl skirt. I can tell she's a girl because she doesn't have any cleavage, just an exposed collarbone and knobby shoulders. The only ones who still have tits are the queens on hormones. Boys or girls, their stockingless feet are crammed into thrift-store high heels. All of them wear a score of rubber bracelets and probably have a tattoo. Some of them come out in tattered lingerie. It makes you wonder what on earth they change into to go to bed — if they ever sleep in a bed.

Why do whores put all of their makeup on their eyelids or their lips, and nowhere else? It makes the ornamented part of the face jump out at you. The effect is rather frightening and carnivorous. How can anybody let that into a car with them? I can only believe that the act of paying is much more important to their johns than the indifferent blowjobs they will get from these strung-out crash cases.

I give up trying to figure out which ones are really girls and which ones are boys. They might as well all be fish to me. When I see them, I don't feel that pull in my gut as if somebody were trying to make violin strings out of my intestines. I don't feel my teeth set on edge and grow points. I don't feel my knees tremble and my throat get thick with the phlegm I'm about to be forced to cough up.

Still, the hookers glare at me. They fold their arms, plant their feet, and give me looks as sharp as the razors in their ratty wigs. Tricking for free offends their morality. Little do they know what I am willing to pay for this evening's adventure.

Then I see him. It never fails. I have sometimes wondered why the fates always send us out together, me and the object of my desire, and how they manage to guide us so that our paths will cross. He is a big, black man wearing boots and leather pants, a police shirt and a Sam Browne belt. No badge. That's good. Phony police badges are such a turn-off. His leather cap is pushed so far back on his head, he must be a little drunk. His face does not move to acknowledge my presence. But he hesitates a split second before stepping off the street into an alley, and, once around the corner, he makes enough noise to let me know he has stepped behind the first dumpster.

I come upon him pissing up the wall. The yellow jet is so fierce, I imagine he will hit the fire escape. It is quite honestly one of the biggest dicks I have ever seen. He smiles at me, obviously expecting me to be impressed. I have a master's degree in sociology from Columbia University. What kind of brainless twinkie does he think I am, to be swept off my feet by that old chestnut, that tired staple of stale pornography, the muscular, mean, black hunk with a monster piece of sex-meat?

One of my knees lands on something mushy and wet. There is a piece of gravel under the other. I shift to avoid both of these unpleasant trifles, and shuffle (crawl, really) onto blessed dry, dirty brick.

"Why, lookee what we got here. We got us a cute little cocksucker, just look at the doggie hang his tongue out and beg. Wanna chase this bone, white boy? Wanna get force-fed some real man-stuff? This is gonna make you pant for sure. Open wide and show me you want it, white boy. Beg for me."

While he is saying all this, I am making the appropriate whining noises. I've never done this before, but I discover that I know how. It's a latent ability, sort of like my talent for collecting on delinquent accounts. He reaches into his jacket pocket. The only way out of this narrow back street is the way we came in. I wonder nervously what the hell he has in there. A knife? Tear gas? A stun gun?

Something much, much worse. A condom! I can't believe it. I actually back away half a shuffle.

"What the hell do you think you're doing?" I say. Actually, I'm afraid I snarl. It's not the best way to encourage a topman, but my libidinous dreams are going up in latex-scented smoke.

"Wrappin' my joint," he says matter-of-factly, as if this was a natural part of what we are about to do with one another.

"That's really not necessary," I say.

"Who asked you? You think I want your white-bread fag disease?"

This blatantly homophobic remark from a leather freak who is so obviously queer in his butch drag compared to me in my casual J. Crew clothes makes me choke. I like being called a cocksucker and a fag as well as any other man fortunate enough to be born with a throat like an Accu-Jac, but this is too much. I wonder what he'd do if I called him the *n* word?

He continues to put on the rubber. "Oh, come on, it won't even go all the way up!" I protest. "Look, it only covers a third of your dick."

"Tell you what, if you can get anything besides the head of this big banana in your mouth, I'll peel it for you, baby. Now get over here and do your job."

Before I can tell him this is not safe, sane, and consensual, he is fucking my face. I squirm and twist, but he has me by the hair. All this resistance means that his erection isn't getting enough traction. "Stop that," he says sharply, cuffing me, then grabs me again. "I'm gonna kick your nuts up around your ears if you don't cut that shit out and suck my dick, you pussy-face fag. You know you want it, and I'm gonna make sure you get what you want and a little bit more."

He is wearing heavy boots. Their steel toes can probably do all the damage that he promises. When rape is inevitable, you might as well relax and enjoy it. I try, I really do.

"Don't like the way that tastes, do you, punk? Tell me what you like, you scum-sucking cunt. Do you like uncut dick that's gotten really raunchy, grown itself a real crop of cheese? Or would you rather drink rank bitter piss out of truck drivers' hoses? Or is your thing just plain old spunk, huh, white boy? Seems to me a gourmet like yourself ought to be relieved to have nothing on his breath after he gives a blowjob but a clean old condom."

I'm trying to prove that he was wrong about how much of his dick I could get down, but it's hard to point out my success when he's so busy enjoying it. I'm losing my tonsils to the Roto-Rooter man. But nobody wants a piece of rough trade who's using protection!

"I wanna fuck you, baby. You got a cute ass for a white boy. That's a nice little bubble-butt that's restin' on your heels. Bet it's even tighter than your throat, ain't it, cocksucker? Drop your pants, bend over, lemme see that tiny pink hole."

I'm only too happy to oblige. But I make sure I position myself facing the main street, so he is not between me and an exit. Surely now, I think, now he will want to plunge all the way into my aching furrow, and he will have to dispense with that ridiculous barrier. But when I hint at this, he says, "I'm getting real tired of your bullshit, princess. Whatchoo want me to do, tear you a new asshole? Let's just go for a ride and you quit your bitchin'."

I make one more attempt to get what I really want, and he slaps my butt. Hard. So hard it takes my breath away. I hate that. Of course, it also makes my asshole open up like an umbrella. He's a marvelous fuck. It takes a lot of skill to drive something that big.

Too many well-hung men think all they have to do is the old in-out. But this man is teasing me, stroking all points of the compass, doing everything inside me except turn cartwheels. I wish it were enough, I really do. But I know he isn't going to lose his stinking, filthy load in me, really use me, soil and despoil me. And without the fillip of that violation and defilement, I can't let go.

"You like come so much, I wanna see yours," he pants. "Get it out and jack it off, boy. Show your master how much you love taking his hard dick."

The stupid thing is hard, of course. It apparently doesn't realize we aren't having a good time. I told you it was my sickest friend. So I dutifully beat my meat, agreeing with everything he says, echoing the names he calls me, swiveling my butt as if I were Catherine the Great and this were the last member of my guard who could still get it up. He is Sir, he is Daddy, he is my Master, and he owns my ass. I am a dirty bitch, a high-pocket slut for hard cock.

"Don't you dare come without permission," he hisses, but it's too late. I flood my palm and the ground below us. He shoves even further into me, which gets him close enough to grab my wrist. He forces my hand up to my face and smears my sticky fingers across my nose and mustache. "You like jizz so much, lick that off your lips," he sneers. Then he yanks on my hips, bucks three times, and comes.

There isn't even time to say, "I hate you." I see them coming long before he does — a small gang of undernourished urban youths carrying baseball bats, car antennas, and what looks like a brick tied in a pillowcase. I have to get away! I push him and all the disappointment he represents away from me and hear him fetch up against the dumpster as I bolt out of the alley. I sprint to the corner, whistling and yanking on my trousers. A cab miraculously pulls over. There is no time to look back, only time to throw open its door and escape.

During the ride home, I brood about how safe I will feel once I am back in my own space with its Persian rugs, Shaker furniture, and David Hockney prints. I mustn't forget to take my Elavil tonight. I will brew a pot of chamomile tea and listen to Debussy. Do you think it's really possible that Malcolm loves me for myself?

†HE bOuNtУ hUnTEr

■■

The bouncer was at the foot of the stairs and Bel stood on the landing at the top of them, but her broad and sensitive nostrils had already picked up the smell of fight that came off him. Her coal black, almond-shaped eyes dilated with joy at the prospect of combat. He came up the stairs like a cannonball — surprisingly quick, for a Vesh-ya. Bel barely had time to put her ears back before she had to duck under his fist. He was so short that this was a difficult feat. She came up into his stomach and used her shoulder to heave him over the bannister. He landed heavily on his back, sprawled on the floor of the entryway, the wind knocked out of him. Bel descended at a leisurely pace to see if he needed another drubbing.

From the top of the stairs, the yellow-haired Vesh-ya whore who had started all this trouble clutched a dingy pink robe about her thin shoulders and deliciously oversized breasts and continued to berate her departing customer. "Vesh witch! Pervert! What does it take to make you understand that enough is enough? I'm not made out of steel, you know. I'm flesh and blood, and I've got to rest sometime. What am I supposed to do, let you fuck me to death? You don't want a girl, you want a fucking machine! I have plenty of other customers, you know. *Grateful* customers! *Satisfied* customers! Customers who give me *a lot of money!* You're no gentleman, my lord!"

Despite the whore's curses and signs that the bouncer was recovering (he was up on all fours now and shaking his head — he was tough, for a pinky), Bel took the stairs at her usual deliberate clip. She'd taken the time to pull on her leather breeches and green shirt before allowing the poxy bitch to eject her. Her tall, intricately tooled brown boots made a rude comment about this place, the Belled Cat, and the town it was in, River's Mouth, every time their heels hit wood. Only two things betrayed her nervousness: a back-and-forth flick of her pointed ears and the fact that her knife was all but out of its scabbard. Once drawn, it would have to drink blood, and that always made trouble in towns.

The cult of the sword and all the other old ways were dying, but Bel remembered. She had not always been a mere scavenger, a bounty hunter who even took money from Vesh-ya to settle their feuds. Since a neighboring lord's treason had prevented her mother's estate from coming into her hands, the only heritage Bel had left was an old-fashioned sense of honor and the memorized steps of a dozen formal dances. Bel held her face very still, remembering the drill master who had pounded the codes of combat into her hard, disrespectful, young head. Bel missed her teacher's scarred face, and remembered her crippled hands with more tenderness than she had felt for her own mother. *Ah, well, a good mother can't be trusted,* or so the aunties always said. And also: *A good mother is as kind as the greenwood.*

The madam, bouncer, and customers of the tavern had all come out of the taproom to see what was the matter on the stairs. They were all Vesh-ya (which means, "not human," "small," "obscene," or "silly"). The lot of them were pale as puddings and had hair the color of a potter's poorman clay. Some of them clutched mugs, pieces of bread, or greasy joints in their soft paws. How they could hang onto anything with their short, brittle nails was more than Bel could guess. She despised their round ears, which might as well be deaf, and their even teeth. You had only to open a Vesh-ya's mouth to know they had more in common with grain-chewing herd beasts than they did with an honest predator, who needed prominent canines.

They were not at all pleased to see a six-foot-plus, olive-skinned, dark-haired, yellow-clawed, pissed-off Vesh (which means simply, "us") descending into their midst. "For love of the Lady, she's a big 'un!" somebody said. The crowd withdrew a few paces, but Bel did not like the fearful, angry smell of them. She grimly drew her blade and loosened another which was seated in her left boot. All of Bel's knives (one at her belt, two in her boots, a couple more in secret places) had bone handles — spares in case she broke a limb or a finger. And around her neck she wore two strands of teeth, braided into silver chains — more spare parts.

"She has murderer's eyes!" one of the herd bleated, and all of the rest of them moaned. "Don't look at them! They'll turn you to stone."

The superstition made Bel raise her upper lip in a contemptuous snarl. On each temple, she wore a blue eye which had integrated itself with her optical nerve. The extra eyes gave her almost 360 degrees of vision. *Give the people what they want,* Bel thought, and turned her head to one side and then the other, making each "murderer's eye" wink gravely at the Belled Cat's clientele. Sadly, they remained flesh and blood.

The blue eyes were all that was left of her brother, who had been cast out at puberty (as all Vesh males should be) and left to survive as best he could until his sister hunted him down and proved her right to rule her dead mother's land and people.

At least, that's the way it always happened in legends. But Bel's brother had been sheltered by their mother's deceitful lover, an acquisitive neighbor who falsely claimed he had sired her heir. Bel had pursued him anyway, and forfeited her inheritance. Before she took his life, she took such parts of him as might prove useful later when she must live as he had, an outlaw at the mercy of the wild green.

But it had been far too long since these Vesh-ya had known the exacting discipline of life on a Vesh estate. Town Vesh-ya had taken to calling themselves "settlers" lately, even though they had fallen uninvited out of the sky to this planet's surface, and had lived and died at the whim of Bel's people for five generations. When they had first arrived, armed with superior technology and a lust for precious minerals and metals, they knew that another intelligent species already occupied these forests, but they did not care. It seemed only natural to them that a meeting between planet-bound aborigines and interstellar travelers would mean extinction for the natives. But there had been no genocide of these aborigines.

It was only within the last half-century that Vesh had allowed Vesh-ya to live off the great estates and congregate within their own villages. But Vesh-ya bred prolifically, and what had been a few sanctuaries for escaped or unwanted slaves had exploded into a large network of towns. The idea of Vesh-ya independence and the trade they set up as effortlessly as Vesh took on new body parts were still controversial, and younger, land-hungry daughters sometimes organized raids on the smaller townships, putting their inhabitants to the sword or leading them off in coffles to clear the ground for a new estate. The towns were magnets for rogue Vesh males, who found it easier to survive if they could pick up some of their scraps. The lords didn't like that much, either.

The Vesh-ya had a fatalistic attitude toward these raids, although some hotheads talked (not within Vesh hearing) about the day when they would stand up to the sinister people of the forest and win. Most free Vesh-ya were wiser and more conservative. They concentrated on making themselves useful to Vesh. Bel foresaw a day when this parasitic way of living, commerce, would bring down the grand, self-sufficient plantations. She hoped to be dead by then.

Within River's Mouth, there was a strong feeling that everyone should stick to their own kind, except for the meetings demanded by commerce, religion, or lust. Bel's occupation involved all three. Until this particular trip to this town, when she discovered her favorite brothel had changed hands, she had been welcome here. She spoke a language that every Vesh-ya understood — the language of the unclipped coin. No one whose wits were handy willingly antagonized one of the Fair Folk, especially one who hunted heads for her daily bread and entertainment.

Bel did not hunt for sex when she was after some unlucky culprit's head, any more than she gave heed to what she ate or drank, or where she slept. But when her quest was complete, the bloody proof of her success delivered, and the bounty money fell into her hands, she felt an imperious rush of need in her crotch, and left her patron immediately to begin a marathon celebration which lasted until her money ran out or a particularly tasty commission dropped into her lap.

Once outside the tavern, Bel relaxed a little. No one was going to follow her and pick a fight for the sake of a whore's exhaustion. The liquor at the Belled Cat was not that good. To satisfy the honor of her blade, she pricked a few drops of blood from her arm. Then she used its point to scratch a certain symbol above the lintel of the door. Let its patrons' privy parts sleep as deeply as the Vesh-ya blonde who had ejected Bel after only one day and one night of gaming in the sheets.

Imagine a daughter of Tamara not being trained to keep pace with a Vesh in real need! Her mother's concubines had all been able to stay awake and ravishing for three days at a stretch. Bel yawned, her people's equivalent of laughter, and licked her canines. Motivation was the problem. The Vesh whore had lacked proper motivation.

She shook her head in disgust, and then set off down the dark, quiet side street. When Lira was the madam, she had handpicked a girl for Bel, usually an intelligent and saucy wench whose curiosity was piqued by the prospect of playing slave to a Vesh noblewoman, albeit one who had fallen on hard times. Knowing the preferences of her best customer, Lira had always tried to find her a plump, well-endowed blonde. Bel was allowed to keep the girl upstairs for as long as she liked. There was no sordid conversation about the individual price for each act of passion. When Bel was finished, she sent the slut downstairs with her price in her bodice, a smile on her face, and enough scratches on her back and thighs to inspire pity and awe in the other girls. Bel would turn over in the stained bed and enjoy the closest thing to sleep her people had — a brief postorgasmic trance that sometimes included disturbing hints of the future or other living beings' thoughts.

Who was that foul-smelling, raddled harridan who had usurped Lira's place? The place had reeked of narcotic weed and gum, the bedding was not clean, and the whores were consumptive. The puny Vesh-ya still had not developed immunities to some of the planet's most common ailments. The town needed culling worse than an unlicensed slaver's caravans. Lira's place had been full of rosy-cheeked, well-fed country girls who seemed eager to be tumbled any place more comfortable than a hayrick or a freshly plowed field.

Damn my pride, Bel told herself, and kicked a slow-moving rodent out of her way. *I just couldn't leave until I had what my money entitled me to. And damn my weakness for big-breasted blondes. I probably got the stupidest, meanest one of the lot. She had no capacity for surrender and no ability to charm pleasure out of my toes. I knew the minute she flipped up her skirt and fell onto the bed like a pole-axed milker that she was nothing but an in-out girl. Thank the Lady I did not mold my brother's most precious gift to my pubes and cut myself to bring his parts to life. What would she have called me then?*

The part of her that was determined to die of old age chose this moment to give the rest of her a little lecture: *Bel, Bel,* said the auntie's quavery old voice, *you are far from home, creeping down dark back streets, and these so-called settlers have never felt the whip across their faces. They do not know their place under this moon. Be calm, be patient. Go onto one of the main streets and find another house with a merry madam. Ask where Lira has gone. You still need to come. Until you're satisfied, your pants won't fit quite right, and you won't be able to walk a straight line. Turn left here and walk toward the lights. The night is a festival that will last until dawn.*

Bel knew she should listen to this counsel, but she hesitated, dawdling to enjoy the crisp autumn breeze. She realized with a little panic just how dependent she had become on Lira and her establishment. There were dozens of brothels here, but she no longer dared enter one and risk another disappointment or an ugly confrontation. It was too late and she was too tired to teach another madam how to pander to her tastes. She was too far from the forest and its friendly voices. She felt ... lonely.

Bel's skin prickled. She broke into a cold sweat. Was she getting ill? Waves of heat seemed to roll outward from her lower belly, making her skin feel rashy and irritable, then cold under a thick layer of sweat. Could it be? How old was she? Bel counted on her fingers. Forty-five. Young, but coming upon adulthood, and greatly overdue for pairing. No wonder she was having all these poignant memories. This was what traveling did to you. You lost touch with the rhythms of life, the grand calendar of the seasons.

This would not have happened to her if she was not so far from her natal estate. Where were her sisters, her sweet aunts, her demanding and distant mother? There was no one here to comfort her, read her, and sift through all the nubile Vesh-ya on the estate until one was found who could be bound to her. Bel's mother had been especially fond of the pleasures of the pillow and the claw, so her estate had housed more than the usual number of concubines, bred to retain the unique beauty of their species, and trained to provide safe companionship and pleasure which the Vesh, with their constant internecine feuding and brother/sister dueling, could not give each other.

Bel forced herself to remember the follies of her aunts as well as their faces. None of those inbred and hidebound warriors, farmers, and artisans would have known how to quiet the burning in Bel's heart and loins. One by one, she recalled the male and female Vesh-ya in her mother's kennels. None of them had suited her then, and none would now. She did not want a country brat, trained from infancy to think its highest fate was to be collared and kept at the heel of one Vesh lord. An ignorant child who knew nothing of the forest, who had been only two places in her life, the kennel or the mating room, would never be able to keep up with a bounty hunter.

And it was a little brother's tale, the idea that a Vesh female at the peak of her need and maturity would bond forever with the first being who touched her. If that was so, the busty blonde at the Belled Cat was about to find herself a belled and captive pet. The prospect made Bel retch.

The Vesh bounty hunter found herself on the broad and busy main street. Her feet must have been moving while her mind was spinning. She bought a skewer of grilled meat and vegetables from a dark-skinned vendor with very muscular legs and arms. Bel admired him. He noticed, grinned broadly, and made a quick "come closer" gesture that troubled her more than a little street flirtation should. Bel backed away, barely keeping her lips down over her teeth.

She looked around thoughtfully while she ate and walked, wondering what kind of face she might want to see every day for the rest of her life, what kind of body, what kind of walk and laugh and sex. Mostly men were on the street, but a few women capable of taking care of themselves were also strolling in the throng of mercenaries, vendors, whores, street cleaners, drivers, and thieves. The air was full of the smell of frying food and smoke from the torches that children carried, for a few coins, before Vesh-ya bravos who wanted to see where they were stepping. The moon was almost too big for Bel's comfort. It lit up every nook and cranny of the gutter, the alleys, and the doorways that lined the street. Once in a while, a surge of wind from the sea would clear away the thick stew of town air, providing a few minutes of relief from the stench of too many Vesh-ya left to their own filthy devices for far too long.

A crier in red-and-gold livery went by, beating a drum tucked under his arm. He was announcing an auction at the House of Fatman Fler. The merchandise was Vesh-ya. One had only to follow him and be brought into paradise, where the most young, beautiful, and ingenious performers would demonstrate their erotic artistry and plead to be taken home by a virile new master. Bel wondered why this news did not incite the crowd to fury. Did they buy and sell their own kind as readily as Vesh penned them? She noticed a few other Vesh in the trickle of folk who followed the barker. But most were Vesh-ya men, and none of them would meet her cool black stare.

She grabbed steamed buns from another vendor, beer from his neighbor, and let herself be carried along like a fingerling in a brook. Waves of heat and freezing cold kept rolling over her body. She wanted to hide herself in the crowd. Elbow to elbow, the citizens kept one hand on their purses and another hand on their weapons, and had little energy left over to notice her weakness. Her knees and elbows ached. The little pains became big ones, and then twinges attacked her wrists and ankles. Soon her entire spine was outlined in fire, and Bel had to bite her own tongue to make herself keep walking. Inside, there would be a place to sit down, at least. If she could simply rest for a moment, she could compose herself and summon the energy to leave the town or find an inn for the night.

But the House of Fatman Fler was hardly a restful experience. The slaver had commandeered a warehouse down by the docks. Cranes, piles of hauling rope, spools of chain, hooks, big wooden cargo cribs, and other equipment needed to load and unload a ship had been shoved against the walls. Fler had not wanted to waste a lot of time or money on atmosphere. Worn carpets which had once been expensive works of art had been thrown down helter-skelter on the stone floor. Cushions were few and far between. Bel didn't much like the look of that. If she had to fight or flee, she didn't want to start from a supine position. She strolled along the left-hand wall, looking for a crate small enough to sit on. By the time she found one, she was close to the front of the room, where a rough stage had been erected. She took one of the cushions out of a pile being hoarded by a Vesh-ya family, and made a hand-gesture that said "thank you" when the mother turned to glare at her.

Bel plumped up the cushion on top of her box and perched there, feet balanced nicely on the floor, ready to bounce into an aggressive stance. Now she was almost comfortable. The aches and pains, fever and chills that had been plaguing her withdrew. She knew they would be back again, so she planned to enjoy this reprieve. She was suddenly very hungry. The greasy rolls and sour beer were long gone. A naked girl draped in purely ornamental chains was circulating through the crowd, and Bel whistled her over. She was serving tiny cups of tea and offering bite-size sweetmeats from a tray. Bel gave her a coin and said, "I'll take that tray. Leave the pot and a cup."

The broody-hen sitting next to Bel turned around and made an aggravated noise. Apparently she coveted some of those wares for herself. Bel yawned. She lifted one of the dainty snacks. "Your man does not feed you, perhaps?" she purred. "Let me feed you, then. Go to your knees like a properly hot little Vesh-ya bitch."

The vendor blushed red from head to toe, and fled. The Vesh-ya mother nudged her husband in the ribs. He took one look at Bel's glowing eyes and weaponry, gathered up the children, and moved to a safer part of the room, leaving his mate to scamper after him.

Word about the generous and hungry Vesh warrior spread among the vendors, and Bel was quickly surrounded by a flock of beauties bearing ewers or trays. She soon had her fill of chilled wine, fish marinated in hot spices, and cut fruit rolled in colored sugar. Bel richly enjoyed the attention, but when one of the girls became too flirtatious, she warned her away. "Do not touch me," she said, and her voice was so surly that they all abandoned her.

Then the auctioneer was climbing onto the stage, and Bel's attention focused on him. He was a big man, almost as tall as she was, and she wondered if this could be the Fatman himself. Probably not — he would be at that table to one side of the stage, where successful bidders piled up their coin and took away their new toys. Unlike Fler, the man onstage was handsome, with a thick coat of body fur and big shoulders that promised an ability to bear a lot of weight. He had even allowed the hair on his face to grow, something that Bel found repulsive but fascinating. He wore almost nothing but a wide belt, which held a whip and a leather pouch for his sex. He cracked the whip, which made Bel shudder with rage — a beautiful, sexual weapon like that in the hands of a Vesh-ya — and the first girl almost tumbled onto the stage. Her long, blonde hair was gathered to the top of her head and caught up in a silver scarf. Bel raised an eyebrow. That could easily be a fake length of hair which would come off in the new owner's hand.

The auctioneer moved quickly to clamp his hand around the dizzy girl's upper arm. *Too much wine or snort in that one,* Bel thought disgustedly. Who could tell what a slave was really like if she was dosed? But the crowd around her did not seem to mind. The auctioneer lifted, turned, and posed the girl, keeping up a hearty, bawdy patter all the while, implying that the audience would be poor sports indeed if they did not enjoy this fine party and spend their money freely. The first wench was quickly disposed of. At a crack of the auctioneer's whip, she went to a bowlegged man in sailor's whites who seemed every bit as deep in his cups as his new chattel.

Now, here was a sultry bitch — a long-legged redhead who had been allowed to keep a length of black silk around her hips. She stalked around the block, daring anybody to pull her off the stage and have her right there, legs kicking, jaws snapping. The wench would probably put your eyes out if you let her. Bel laughed. The woman was obviously kennel get, probably trained with goads to attack anyone who attempted to have her. All her resistance would melt away as soon as you gave the signal, which the House of Fler supplied when you purchased her. Of course, there were some owners who foolishly thought they would not need a hand signal to tame a female slave, so they forgot it. Tragic stories were always circulating about careless (or masochistic) owners who let their beautiful spitfires rip them to pieces.

Bel enjoyed a good struggle in bed, enjoyed it tremendously, but there was something artificial about buying a slave who had been trained to fight before you gave her a good reason. She didn't like the idea of being able to compel obedience by using some signal that had been planted deep in the slave's reflexes by painful training. Bel preferred to make a slave behave because she was afraid, or because she longed to please her lord. Still, it was an effort to take her eyes off those pouting, peach-colored lips.

Here was another one, a cuddly little cub with sweet brown eyes and light brown hair. She never even rose to her knees, putting on a show on the floor of the stage that made even the auctioneer randy. Butter wouldn't melt in this one's mouth, but your sex probably would, and she would be so pleased you'd made her a present of it. Bel shook her head. This girl was not as stupid (or as submissive) as she seemed. Goddess help you if baby didn't get as much candy as she wanted. Who could live with tears and sulks for days on end or, worse, little puddles of piss by your bed? Trying to punish a girl like that would be like spanking a baby. She would be helpless to stop herself, too silly to understand you, too self-willed to quit persecuting you until she got her own way ... or had to be sold. No, that cinnamon-syrup bun was not for Bel.

Twin sisters a trifle past their prime were brought out, and they fought energetically for a piece of taffy the auctioneer tossed between them. But when he ordered them to kiss and make up, their passion lacked conviction. Even a warning touch with his whip failed to stir genuine ardor, and the big man was forced to let them go for one coin less than the amount at which he'd tried to start the bidding. A boy took the stage, his training obvious from the fact that he was sold here with women. But this was not the right crowd for him, and he went for a mere whisper of gold more than the minimum bid. Then two big men with two equally hefty women were offered as litter-bearers. They looked healthy and willing enough to Bel, but this crowd wanted more glitter thrown in its eyes. No ripe vegetables flew at the stage, but a few people booed. Some folks near Bel got up, shook out their robes, and left.

Bel wondered if the House of Fler was already down to its less desirable merchandise. Her wrists tingled, and she was afraid that real pain was about to follow. Her stomach felt odd. Had she eaten too much? Then why was she still so hungry? Those damned vendors, where were they when she needed them? Perhaps it was time to go.

"And now," said the auctioneer, making his voice boom to the back of the warehouse, "something very special. Not to everyone's taste, oh no. Just for those who have the sophistication to really appreciate a truly unique offering." The crowd fell still, and Bel abandoned her search for vendors to look at what had quenched their chatter. A woman was brought out with her hands fettered. She was short even for a Vesh-ya, no more than four-foot-ten. Bel frowned. Those were the heavy, iron cuffs used to restrain big bulls — miners or galley slaves. They looked far too bulky for the narrow wrists they contained. Her shoulders were bowed from the effort it took to carry them. Where did they think this sprig of a girl was going to go?

She refocused her eyes and took a closer look. The woman for sale moved like a sack of flour, barely keeping upright. If the first slave to be sold here had gotten one dose of happiness, this one had been given a half-dozen. Bel thought she could discern the outline of a black eye under thick makeup. When the auctioneer turned the girl, Bel snarled. Her very long hair (so pale it looked blue in this light) parted to show a host of livid weals on top of old bruises across her buttocks. This was not discipline, it was brutality. As the auctioneer moved her about, one of her feet came off the stage, and Bel dug the claws of one hand into the palm of the other. No wonder she was having trouble standing up. Her feet were swollen and had turned dark blue from being beaten.

The auctioneer was struggling to open the captive's mouth. "For those of you who have the courage to sample the forbidden—"

"No!" the manacled girl shrieked.

Bel was surprised that she could speak, much less struggle with a man who was easily three times her weight. But then she realized that this was not the standard offer to show prospective buyers the health of a slave girl's teeth. Bel was willing to bet that if she strolled onstage, the girl would open her mouth like a well-trained mount being offered the bit. And her tongue would be pierced, ready to hold a jeweled stud that would enhance her Vesh lord's pleasure. This was no Vesh-ya village doxy. This was someone's high-caste concubine, somehow kidnapped and brought to this dingy, flea-ridden, mildewed, backwater market.

The drugged girl had actually bitten the auctioneer. He let go of her, more from surprise than from the incidental pain. "My mouth is not for the likes of you," she hissed at him. Her voice was musical, even if the words were slurred by pain and chemicals. The short speech was too much for her. She collapsed, unable to stay on her feet. Still, she struggled away from the auctioneer, crawling toward the edge of the stage, using her hands and arms to drag the rest of her body along.

The crowd was not pleased. Cries of "Vesh lover! Animal fucker! Pervert! Filth! Succuba!" rang through the warehouse. Bel cleared her throat. Was she to be turned out of doors again in one night? The odds were considerably worse here than they had been in the Belled Cat, but this circus of hooting inferiors was too much for her pride. She pulled her little knives from here and there and began to juggle them. Some of the rowdies realized that a tall native woman stood within easy throw of their throats, grinning at them through flashing steel, and they swallowed their tongues. Bel followed the silence as if it were a path through the crowd, and it took her neatly to the foot of the stage.

But one Vesh bounty hunter could not silence all the heads of this beast. "Fraud!" was the cry that came now, albeit from the back of the warehouse. "I wouldn't touch that with my boot!" one Vesh-ya male, less drunk or less intelligent than his peers, shouted.

"Friends!" cried the auctioneer. "The House of Fler defrauds no one. This little flower would be the prize blossom in any good-man's pleasure garden. Her tongue will heal in time. If the strange places where it has been displease you that much, cut it out. Are you saying you do not have a strong enough arm to teach her to respect you as well as any—" Here he faltered, because Bel gave him a little warning growl, and he looked down to see her knives whirling beneath his feet. "—her previous owners," he finished weakly. "This is a superior female, tempting, useful, delectable, compliant!"

The "tempting" and "compliant" female had almost reached the stairs by now, and the auctioneer was forced to cut his speech short to retrieve her. When he hauled her to her knees by her hair, she spat at him, and the crowd laughed.

"Where did she come from?" Bel asked. Her voice carried easily to the block, and to the ears of every customer around it.

"The House of Fler obtains all of its merchandise in full compliance with the laws of this great city," he blustered.

"Laws," drawled Bel, and everyone there heard her say the word she really meant. "Laws flow from Vesh-ya towns like pus from a boil. I care not one piss for the stinking breath that issues from River's Mouth," Bel told them all. Then she addressed herself specifically to the auctioneer. "Arrogant and foolish man, you stand upon this ground and sully the forest's clean air by the good graces of me and my sisters and my aunts and our mothers and grandmothers. That is all the law that Vesh-ya need to know."

"I do not care to bandy words with you about the lease to the lands of the, um, the esteemed and famous township of River's Mouth. I am here as a duly licensed auctioneer, and I am conducting a legal and proper sale for a reputable house."

"Then answer me. Where does she come from?"

The auctioneer looked for help to Fatman Fler, who was hastily counting coins at his table, shoving them into sturdy canvas pouches, and urging subordinates to take them away. The auctioneer got no answer but a hand-gesture of denial, a "don't bother me now" sort of signal. His face flushed with rage, the big man onstage coiled his whip and stowed it at his hip. "I know not," he said finally. Bel thought she could almost like him for that. He was not a liar or a coward, even if he was in the employ of one.

She smacked her lips, a Vesh expression of satisfaction with the food one has caught and is about to devour. "But I know where my money came from," Bel told the entire warehouse. "I was well paid just this morning for cutting the head off a big buck like you, who had soiled a virgin without her parents' permission. And I will give you a fair price for your mysterious merchandise — the exact value I place upon your life if you tell me no." Bel stowed her tiny knives and fished two green coins from her pouch. It was the sum you needed to buy a brief stop in a public pissoir. She threw it at the auctioneer, and he caught it without thinking. The crowd laughed again. Then Bel was onstage, scooping up the pale-haired, much-marked girl.

When the bounty hunter's bare hands made contact with the wench's back, something like fire or strong drink flickered through her veins. "What is your name, lass?" Bel asked, keeping her voice soft and gentle.

"Sylvana Tamarasdotter," she said, then her eyes rolled up. She had fainted.

Bel desperately wanted to wipe her property's face clean, comb her hair, and tend her injuries. Dirty Vesh-ya had such an unpleasant smell. But the crowd had an ugly feel to it, and was gradually moving closer and closer to the stage. The assembled Vesh-ya might not want this girl performing upon their sleeping mats, but they did not like the idea of a Vesh lord taking her away from them.

Bel jumped onto Fatman Fler's table. It took her weight and the weight of her captive without complaint. The slaver was not that complaisant. His jowls trembled, and he shook as if he had swamp fever. His robe was stained with food and drink. Bel wrinkled her nose at him and his leftovers. One more jump put her on the floor, nose to nose with him. "My papers, churl," she hissed. He signed the deed of sale with a hand that longed to throttle her. "The key," she prompted, tucking the folded sheet into her pouch. The merchant's hands went below the table.

A Vesh male materialized at Fler's elbow, pointing a tiny dart at his neck. Bel recognized it at once — an arrow small enough to fit into a blowgun and find its target, riding on the archer's breath.

"One scratch, and you'll be as dead as you are ugly," he whispered. "Give my elder sister her due, or my brothers and I will return you and your band of vermin to the cleansing bosom of the sea." He and his fellows wore shirts of hunter's green, not the bright colors favored by males who had a home. Still, Bel was glad to see them.

The weapon that Fler hoped to draw clattered to the floor. He knew all about blowguns and their miniscule, but deadly, missiles. During one of his meetings with Vesh hirelings, he had unfortunately accepted an invitation to witness an archery contest. The loser was tied to the target post so the winner could test a new poison upon him. Given the Vesh ability to regenerate after almost any injury, the experience had not been fatal, but Fler had seen many ways to die that were a great deal more pleasant.

"Take her," he said thickly. "May she trouble your house as much as she has troubled mine." He slid a long, dark key across the table.

With the Vesh male and his friends keeping watch, Bel felt easier about taking her time to fit key to lock and free the girl from her heavy chains. The irons had worn deep sores into her ankles and scraped her wrists raw. Bel half expected her to faint again, but after she picked up the manacles and dumped them on the slaver's table, cold green eyes met her stare. Bel realized with a start that the little chit was appraising her. The temerity!

"Please accept our company to the door, elder sister," the Vesh male murmured, and Bel graciously inclined her head. Like a procession of princes they made for the exit, just four Vesh shielding one Vesh-ya girl, but a crowd fifty times their size did not dare lay a finger upon them.

Fatman Fler knew better than to let the show end upon this sour note. The pretty girls in pretend chains were soon circulating through the crowd with free glasses of twice-distilled spirits, and three dancers took the stage. Even the auctioneer recovered enough to start making jokes about shaking his tambourine.

Only one bully boy did not choose to let the merriment override his patriotism. He moved to block their way. "This is our side of the river," he told the bounty hunter, hooking his thumbs in his belt. "Don't let us see you here again."

Bel stopped to hear him out, and her escort danced on the tips of their toes, impatient to be gone. She ignored them. Males who survived the quest were, of course, very fretful and anxious creatures. "Have a care I don't order the river out of its banks to wash this midden clean," she told the pompous little rooster, who probably thought his friends were clustered at his back instead of giving him their backs. She dropped her voice to a confidential level. "Because if I do, you will have to run into the forest to escape the flood, and I will be waiting for you there. After I've cut you open and strung my harp with your overfed, overweening guts, maybe I'll let you run away again, as soon as you can grow back what you've lost."

The fool fell back as if his belly was already slit from side to side, and Bel's companions urged her toward the big double doors, propped open in case some stray customer wandered in. "I could offer you passage to the trees," the Vesh male said, his lips an inch from Bel's left ear. The warm wind created by his lips tickled, and sent erotic shudders down her shoulders. She shook her head, reluctant to feel so drawn to him. He noted her reaction and withdrew an inch or two. "I am only thy little brother, and my ship is not worthy of you," he added, careful to keep irony from his voice.

So Bel followed the archers toward the docks. Their little ship (which looked more like a raft to her) was berthed nearby. That was a bit of luck, because in between the bewitching odors that came off the Vesh male's body and the jolts of pure pleasure that every contact with the slave's skin sent through her, Bel was having a difficult time keeping her head clear and her feet moving. Sylvana was a restless bundle. "Put me down," she told Bel. "You are tired. I delay you."

"Be still," Bel said, giving her a little shake. "I am in no danger. You weigh less than a hunting bird's feather. And I will not have you sullied by any further contact with this place."

Getting Sylvana on board was difficult. Bel refused to hand her to the anxious boys who stood at the top of the ladder. Their leader finally solved the problem by positioning Sylvana upon Bel's back and tying the two of them together, so Bel carried her up the ladder like a baby. This contact was even more disturbing than bearing Sylvana in her arms. The girl's legs were wrapped around Bel's hips, and the pressure of her little sex against the small of her back made Bel want to come or bite something soft until it bled.

It took all of her self-control to hoist the two of them up onto the deck. She did not protest when the men carefully arranged them side by side under a canopy that had been rigged to provide a little shelter from the wind. "The forest comes down to the river between this noisome place and the ocean," the Vesh male told Bel. "If we do not take you there, we will have to pole the boat upriver, and that would take far too long for you, I'm thinking."

"Yes," Bel said. "Once I'm in the trees, no one can touch me."

He smiled at that, and left the two women alone. Bel must have slept, Sylvana's pale head pillowed on her arm, because her "little brother" had to actually touch her arm to let her know it was time to disembark. "As the trees grow thicker and the land rises, there are many caves in the hill," he said. "We've left our blankets, water, and some firewood in one of them. You will know the way — we've been there often, and left our scent."

"Who are you?" Bel thought finally to ask. "Why have you been helping me?"

He knelt in the damp sand at the river's edge. "My name is Frick," he said. "And I knew the moment I saw you that a life spilled between your hands would be sweet indeed. Not all of us have forgotten the old law, elder sister."

"My dueling days are done," she said bitterly. "My brother did not escape my blessing, but it did me little good." She gave Frick her hand to press between his own. His blue eyes seemed clear of any deceit or malice, but who really knew what a man was thinking? With a start, Bel realized that if her change continued, within a few days, she would indeed know exactly what Frick — and everybody else — was thinking. She almost missed his response.

"Then think of me when you need heirs of your own," he said, bowing his head over her hands. "I am not so besotted by your beauty that I would dare tell you what house reared me, but my lines would not displease you, lord. We will meet again, I think."

His courteous caution almost made Bel yawn. "Have you need of this?" she asked, indicating her money belt. Frick and his crew seemed well fed, but their clothing was a little shabby. She did not want to offend him, but he had already threatened his own survival by adhering to natural law. Bel would reward him if she could.

He pretended to be insulted. "If I were in need, elder sister, I would be ashamed to come before you, since it would mean I must come without a gift for you."

"Then let your underlings take this," Bel said, and tossed the largest coins she could find to his men.

Frick pretended he did not see them catching her money. It was neatly done, he thought. She had added to the coffers of his group without forcing him to admit that he was in need. No honorable captain of a band would deny his subordinates a reward. He had to admit that Bel was much smarter than his own vicious but unimaginative sibling. He was annoyed with himself for the way his heart skipped a beat when Bel got closer than a foot or two to him. What did he care if the fine hairs in Bel's ears were a lovely shade of russet, or if her dark eyes held flecks of gold? After so many years of running from his sister assassin, surely he was disillusioned enough to abandon all that romantic nonsense about succumbing to a strong, cunning female hunter.

Frick returned to his crew, yawning at his own folly. He told them, "Shove off, boys, let's pole this barge upriver and see if we can't sell it back to the same dumb pinky who let us steal it. And thank your lucky stars, my darlings, because we have just ferried a lord on the brink of her transformation into the forest with a new and untried companion. And yet we are unscathed."

His fellows' jaws dropped at that. "I thought she seemed ... most attractive," little Magee ventured, afraid to give offense. He had been forced to leave his home when his mother died without a daughter, and willed all to one of her sisters rather than see a male run her estate. The sister was an aristocrat of the old school, and she would not tolerate males who were not her direct descendants on her grounds. Some of the younger houses had passed into the hands of sons, but the notion of running an estate would have made Magee panic. He had been happy with his hounds and concubines, his music and his garden. All he wanted was to know his place, have his basic needs provided for, and trust that yesterday was the only pattern for tomorrow.

"It is not right to leave the lord alone," Cam, Magee's younger and more impetuous brother, dared aver. If he had been allowed to stay on under his aunt's reign, Frick thought Cam would surely have gotten himself killed in a race or a gambling dispute. He did not have the sense the Lady gave a flitter, and could see no difference between dying because someone slapped his face or being cornered by a hundred grim pinkies with rusty pikes and shovels. "Her companion will be too occupied to forage for the lord or stand guard when the change begins."

Frick rolled his eyes, although part of him envied the brothers' unthinking admiration of Bel. They had never heard the hunter's horn pealing to set the pack upon their heels. They really thought that nothing but courtliness motivated him to act as Bel's champion. He grinned like one of his predatory ancestors who had roved the plains on four feet instead of two. "I think we will dig up the gold we've cached upriver and double back to see if we can make ourselves useful."

Only one of his subordinates complained. None of them knew why dour Tupper, who was built like an old tree and could lift one man in each of his mighty arms, had joined their band. Frick suspected he was a throwback, a man who could not content himself with other men or Vesh-ya concubines of either sex. If the old stories were true, the lords had once given a little of their love to their menfolk. Nowadays, a sworn companionship between a Vesh man and woman was rare enough to be an aberration. He doubted anyone at home had even noticed Tupper's departure. *If I had the coin,* Frick thought, *I would gladly buy Tupper a place in some childless lord's affections. If I ever get to stop sweeping out my own tracks, of course.*

Tupper spoke slowly, as if each word pained him. "Once I left my mother's gates, I never thought I'd turn again to lick a female's boots."

It was time to give his followers a little taste of the back of his hand. "I do not plan to live the rest of my days in terror of my elder sister's blade," Frick snapped. "Until she has my head, she will not be able to call any bed she sleeps in her own. So she will not rest until she has me by the throat. And other tender parts of me, which perhaps I am overfond of!" he cried, grabbing his crotch. That made everyone but Tupper laugh nervously. Then Frick spoke more seriously. "She has come at me three times, and each time, I escaped by the lashes of my eyes. If I am bound by blood to another house, she must leave me be. I cannot be both her brother and the father of another lord's child."

"This landless lord will never give us sanctuary," Tupper protested. Cam and Magee were pressed against one another like whelps seeking comfort, fearful that it was true.

"There is land under our feet everywhere we go," Frick replied. "Why shouldn't some of it go to the House of Bel? Do you not fancy the sight of some of those plump burghers working off their excess bulk with pick and shovel and hoe? I know I do. Break out some wine. Poling will be weary work. And we must hurry. I will not have one of my own hunted by the exceptionally silly Vesh-ya of this town."

They were good lads, more afraid of losing his leadership than anything else. Soon he had them singing and poling their hearts out. With any luck, Bel and Sylvana would go to ground where he had sent them, and he would be back before anything could threaten the lord and her companion.

Once she heard the raft leave the river's edge, Bel sank to her knees and nearly fell on top of Sylvana. Who would dream, to look at this tiny creature, that her frame would be solid enough to take Bel's weight? She smelled like a feast after a rainy day of hunting, a clean bed full of potpourri, restful yet agitating. Bel murmured, "Sylvana," and nipped her neck, licked down to the full breasts and the nipples that were as big as her own nose. She put her claws in between the girl's ribs and dug in just hard enough to make her wince and throw her arms around Bel's neck.

Sylvana wished she had not spread her legs. Now she had no leverage to shift Bel's weight. A raspy tongue was honing her nipples into fine, hard points, and she knew she would yield to this strong and magnificent lord who had come out of the crowd like every lost hope to save her from a slavery that had no meaning, no love, and no honor.

She desperately wanted some time alone to weep for the love she had lost, but this was not the time. If she allowed herself to remember, she would see the broken fragments of the ritual cup, only just filled with the potion that opened the very different minds of companions to the Vesh lords who sought to bond with them. The shards of glass lay on the ground in a circle like the petals of a strange flower. As she screamed, they filled up with a new and darker liquid, the magenta blood of her slain lord. Oh — she would surely go mad!

Sylvana had no idea how many days she had spent, drugged and beaten, dragged along by the renegade Vesh-ya who had sold her to one of Fler's outriders. But she would not weep in front of them. She would not even tell them her name. Her captors had sensed the need that had built to a peak during the interrupted ritual, but she had refused to let their clumsy attempts at violation ease her suffering.

Now relief was being offered to her, and she did not think she could refuse. "Give me your lips," Bel said, and Sylvana dug her small, white hands into Bel's black mane and let her drink. If Bel's high cheekbones brushed the bruises around her eye, Sylvana did not care. It was no shame to feel pain at the touch of one's lord.

It was a deep kiss that displaced many breaths. Soon they were both drunker than a winebibber staring at the bottom of his biggest cup. Bel's tongue was large and rough, her teeth sharp, and Sylvana could well imagine what damage the hunter's mouth could do. But Bel wished her no harm, unless being pleasured this much was also a kind of damage.

Bel's claws raked her carefully, lightly, from her shoulders to her ankles, and Sylvana turned from side to side to offer new skin to her lord. It was exquisite, just on the edge of pain, like being tickled and cut simultaneously. And Bel continued to feast upon her nipples, which made Sylvana's furrow beg for harvesting. Bel touched, squeezed, licked, bit, and scratched every part of her except the part that needed the most attention. Sylvana literally wept for mercy, but

Bel was adamant. Let the Vesh-ya learn to wait for satisfaction.

Vesh took several hours of stimulation to reach their first climax. Bel knew that Vesh-ya could be quickly appeased, but she preferred to torment them. It made them angry at first, but later they were grateful, as full of love as a ripe berry was full of juice. Sylvana was using all of her muscles, trying to entice Bel into giving her relief, but she was so small that it was easy for Bel to keep her pinned, not quite exploding. Bel liked the smell of furious, wet Vesh-ya bitches. It was better than fresh blood or her own piss descending upon an enemy's boundary marker.

Sylvana had been schooled from childhood to yield readily and sweetly to the Vesh who desired her. Now she felt an odd separation between her training and her wisdom. Her breasts and hips responded helplessly to Bel's increasingly rough caresses. But Sylvana had been told again and again that she was responsible for watching her lord's back, even in the most heated embrace. She knew this place was dangerous. She could never survive the shame of losing two lords in one lifetime. And so she tried to talk sense into Bel, to push her away. "We must go away from the water," Sylvana whispered. "We need more trees around us. There is no safety here, no time for me to pleasure you."

"But there is time enough for me to make you call my name in prayer," Bel said, and sank her face between Sylvana's thighs. Sylvana devised enough prayers to start a million new religions, but Bel could not hear them. She was drowning and deaf, locked between two thighs that were much stronger than she had guessed. Bel did not trust herself to penetrate her prize. She did not think she could control her claws. But Sylvana did not seem to think anything was lacking. With tongue and perhaps a bit more tooth than was wise, Bel put Sylvana in her debt again and again, until the smell of fresh-turned earth told her that the girl had clawed up the turf.

Bel's own parts were moist, the horns rigid, but she did not want to begin something here unless it could be finished properly. She lifted her head and listened hard, snuffing the air, tuning out Sylvana's shallow panting and damp skin. She heard only the music of flowing water and dancing leaves. But Sylvana was right; it would never do to remain here.

The bounty hunter hoisted both of them to their feet and sought out higher ground. Once the scent of the river faded, she picked up hints of Frick and his men, and followed them as doggedly as an undertaker trails a rich widow. As the way got more difficult, Sylvana staggered, and Bel picked her up again. "No!" Sylvana said. "We have to be hidden away before dawn."

"The rat-folk of River's Mouth would never dare track us into the forest," Bel said, wondering if she was right. "I can go faster with you in my arms than I can if I must wait for you to crawl along. Do not make me waste my breath on one more argument."

Frick and his three followers had indeed marked the way. In the second hour of hiking, their scent became much richer. They were all healthy, young males, and Bel kept wanting to stop and lose herself in a dream, inhaling their strength, their hunger, and their innocence. But Sylvana kept plucking at her sleeve, keeping them both moving forward.

Soon Bel thought she could discern hints of the goods that had been left in the outcasts' cave. But perhaps that was wishful thinking. She put Sylvana down and said, "See if you can walk a little way." When Sylvana put her arm around Bel's waist, the bounty hunter did not shoo her away. Leaning on each other, they struggled up the face of the hill. The ground was littered with stones, and Bel was afraid Sylvana would turn her ankle, but it was as if the girl could see through Bel's night-wise eyes, and placed her poor battered feet accordingly.

"Is there a change in the darkness?" Sylvana asked, and Bel squinted up, between the big, red trunks of two giant conifers. Yes, there was a patch of smoother black. Bel took two more steps, and a slight breeze from under the earth kissed her face and made her sneeze. Sylvana was tugging her toward the cave, and they went in on hands and knees. Fifteen feet from the hillside, the cave bent to the right. They found Frick's stores and a rough hearth just past this bend.

A sudden wave of nausea made Bel double over and clutch her stomach. Sylvana was busy with some bundles at the cave wall, striking flints together. Soon there was a little fire. The wench shook out a blanket and wrapped Bel in it. "There's water," she said hesitantly. "No," Bel croaked, reaching out with one arm. "You. Hold me." A red mist swam before her eyes, and Bel wanted to seize the girl and force her mouth to service her aching horns, but she lacked the strength to move.

"Let me make the fire safe." Sylvana put a block of slow-burning fuel over the kindling, hoping it would not smoke too much. She had already filched a stick of jerky from the cache of food. She worked a bit of it loose with her sore teeth and settled down alongside Bel, wrapping another blanket around the two of them. "Are you sick?" she asked, hoping the Vesh would not take offense and do something violent to prove she was fit.

"No. Not sick." Bel's teeth were chattering so hard, Sylvana could hardly understand her. "I think I am changing."

"Oh! Lady defend me," Sylvana blurted, then hissed at her own stupidity. She was safer with a Vesh lord, even one in the throes of transition, than she was back in River's Mouth at the House of Fler.

"I ... will ... not ... hurt ... you," Bel said, painfully articulating each word. "Yet," she added, with a cruel smile.

"We have to keep you warm," Sylvana said, trying to remember everything she knew about the change. She was supposed to be a pleasure slave, not a healer, but it took many hands, working from one sunrise to another, to keep an estate running. She would rather make herself useful and learn something from other servitors than sit playing with her cosmetics or admiring her own costumes. "And you're going to be hungry, from time to time. Ravenous. I think we have enough food to get through the night. Tomorrow, when it's daylight, I'll see if they've left any snares or darts behind. Or I can go back to the river. I'm not much of a hunter, but I do know how to fish. You'll get feverish, but you must try to keep well covered. But you're supposed to have medicine for the pain and there's supposed to be a ceremony—"

"Be not so busy," Bel said, slipping into a dialect that lords used to address their intimates and children. "Join your flesh to mine. That is all the potion I need for what ails me." Sylvana sank down beside her, and Bel brushed the pale hair back from her face. "Never did any lord have a concubine fairer than thee," Bel said. There were beads of sweat on her upper lip. The courtly use of that honorific made tears appear in the corners of Sylvana's eyes. "An' we live," Bel said, "I will buy thee a brush and matching combs to set in thy hair. D'ye ken how to braid it, lass, into a golden crown? It is an old-fashioned fancy of mine, I do confess it. Long hair is no pleasure if you do not put it up so I may take it down again. Oh, the color is fantastic. It is like a veil of moonlight. I wonder if you should ever wear aught but your hair."

Then waves of heat chased away the nausea, and Sylvana had to wrap her arms about Bel's body to keep her covered. The Vesh's hands prowled her body, alerting every nerve that trouble was on the way. Bel turned on her side and wrapped one hand around the back of Sylvana's neck, immobilizing her. The other hand went between the girl's legs, and this time Bel did not think about her claws. Being fucked this way was always dangerous, but Sylvana had never been truly afraid of a Vesh before. She took their cruelty for granted because she had only seen it lay other slaves to waste — slaves who surely deserved it.

Now it was her tender parts that were skewered by strong fingers, tipped with nails that could slit the bark from a tree. Sylvana squirmed, afraid to move and afraid not to move. Then the things that Bel did inside her made it impossible to choose. She moved, and made Bel the guardian of her life. It was like coming at the point of a knife, or being tossed on the horns of a rutting stag. The curving passage of the cave shielded the sight of their fire from passersby, but Sylvana's cries would have betrayed them to any tracker.

Lucky for her, a hard chill gripped Bel, and she withdrew her hand to hug her own body. "It is like insects, stinging my flesh!" she cried. Once more, Sylvana had to wrestle with her to keep the protective cocoon intact. When the fit passed, she persuaded Bel to take a little water. The Vesh seemed to doze after swallowing the liquid, so Sylvana conducted a hasty search through their meager supplies and found a little pipe, caked with black gum. She woke Bel up and put the pipe between her lips, then lit it with a straw from the fire. "This will give you a little peace," Sylvana promised, and hoped she did not lie. While Bel smoked the soporific, Sylvana splashed some water into the smallest cook pot and crumbled a piece of jerky into it. The broth would be salty, but she did not dare give Bel solid food. The Vesh would surely choke on it.

Now Bel was sitting up, wearing her blankets like a shawl. Sylvana touched her boots, but Bel gave her a little kick. "Leave them on. They keep my feet warm. Besides, we may have to quit this place in a hurry."

Sylvana did not think much of their chances if they had to run, but she silenced that thought.

"Talk to me," Bel said. "Where do you come from? What tragedy brought you to the groves where I hunt?"

"I belong to Harrier House," Sylvana said. The sudden look of fury in Bel's eyes made her cower. "Forgive my stupid tongue. I am only a slave. It was where my life began, where I thought I would end my days. And I was pledged to the heir's youngest sister, who was the master of the forge. I knew my place and loved it."

"Approach me," Bel said. Sylvana trembled, but she obeyed. The bounty hunter took her by the upper arms and shook her viciously. "My name is Bel," the Vesh lord said, her canines gleaming in the firelight. "My sisters no longer remember my name. I slew my brother out of season, and lost my mother's land to the lying bitch who claimed him as her stud. You are my house. It is by my side that you will end your days. Never forget." She tossed Sylvana away. "Now tell me the rest," she said curtly.

"I — the ceremony was nearly complete," Sylvana said, finding it progressively more difficult to hold back her tears. "The cup had been poured. It wanted only a little of my blood and the blood of my lord before we would drink it down and become one forever. But the rebels came — they cut her throat with the ritual blade and took me away — I fought, I screamed, but it did no good, everywhere there was burning and murder, rape and riot and confusion—"

Bel gathered Sylvana in and made another cave with her own body, a dark place where it was safe for a heartbroken Vesh-ya to sob and curse fate. Vesh did not weep. They used the same word for sorrow and vengeance. If they could not take action against someone who had hurt them, they sometimes stopped eating and died of grief and shame. So Bel found this display a little alarming, but charming, and certainly educational. How could anyone survive such strong emotions without taking action? No wonder Vesh-ya were so easily conquered.

"And was your lord handsome?" she asked, when the tears had turned into sniffles.

Sylvana considered this question carefully. Vesh could always tell when you were lying. Their keen senses detected the subtle physiological changes that accompanied prevarication. And Vesh valued loyalty. Sylvana did not want to make herself appear faithless just to flatter Bel's vanity. On the other hand, the Vesh were also famous for self-love. "I thought so at the time," she said slowly. "And I would not think much of myself if I ever forget her face. But valor is the mother of beauty. I do not think she would have plucked me from that dreadful place, my lord." Then she knelt in the dirt and made a formal obeisance, a move taken from the bonding ceremony. It pained her sore ankles and wrists, but it was better to open old wounds than acquire new ones.

Bel seemed placated. She grunted, and did not ask another difficult question. Sylvana succeeded in making her drink a cup full of hot water flavored with jerky. The nourishment seemed to make the gum work more strongly. Bel lay down, and only minor tremors shook her body for the next hour of the night. Sylvana even caught a little sleep herself, in between wrestling the blankets back into place.

She awoke during the eeriest portion of the night, when the soul is trapped between midnight and dawn. The Vesh-ya with a gift for doctoring called it the graveyard shift. It was when the hurt or sick left their suffering bodies behind, and new Vesh mothers gave birth to children who would not live. It seemed as if light would never come over the hills, and Sylvana was chilled to the bone. Even Bel's fevered body could not warm her. She sat up, put another block of peat on the fire, and had another strip of the tough dried meat.

Then the voice of a little, lost child came out of the dark. "Tell me a story," it said.

Sylvana jumped and dropped her jerky. She cursed, picked it up, and brushed off most of the ashes. It was only Bel, who sounded as if she were in a trance, speaking out of the visions that harried Vesh "sleep." Sylvana thought it must be awful to never be able to cut your ties to the real world completely, to sleep deeply and escape into pleasant dreams of adventure and freedom.

"A story?" she asked, trying to get some clue about where Bel thought she was or what she wanted.

"Tell me the tale of Tamara," Bel insisted.

All Vesh-ya knew the legend of their foremother by heart. If it were not for Tamara's intervention, the Vesh would have slain every interloping human without even asking why. Before meeting Bel, the slave girl's full name was "Harrier's Sylvana, Tamarasdotter." Now she supposed it was "Bel's Sylvana," but she remained Tamara's child no matter which Vesh she served. The legend (well — the part that Vesh-ya recited for Vesh ears, at any rate) was supposed to be accompanied by drums, flutes, and rattles. Professional chanters were sometimes hired to recite it when wealthy Vesh took a companion.

"Never mind that folderol," Bel said impatiently. Sylvana tensed. The change must be heightening the bounty hunter's ability to filch a thought from another's mind. "Tell it plainly, without the flag-waving and twittering, the way Tamara must have told her own sisters and daughters. And sit by me. I want your hand here while you speak."

Sylvana hesitated only long enough to make sure the fire would not go out, then she repositioned herself at Bel's side. The Vesh threw off her blanket and put Sylvana's hand upon her laces. "Reveal me," she ordered, and Sylvana undid the soft, suede pants and eased them back from Bel's hips. "Slip your hand in — yes! So!" Bel cried.

A thick pelt, glossy as the hair on Bel's head, guarded her sex. Sylvana had to comb through the wet fur with careful fingers before she found the instrument she would play to accompany her story. A Vesh female's pleasure organ was larger than Sylvana's tiny bud, and differently shaped. It protruded just enough for Sylvana to grasp it with her thumb and forefinger, and instead of a plain, rounded head, it had two little horns. She began to perform the caress known as "teaching the young dragon to blow fire."

Despite the fact that her teeth had been loosened and her lips bruised by the slavers' fists, Sylvana felt her mouth fill with water at the thought of feeling Bel's dragon swim across her tongue. But it would never do to begin with her mouth. Her lips and tongue would give out long before their job was done. A wise concubine started pleasuring her lord with one hand, then with two, and saved her kisses for the grand finale.

Bel was bewitched by the girl's soft touch. It was as if her parts had decided to move of their own volition. She felt a surge of gratitude for all the lords who had schooled this Vesh-ya's hand. This was not the sort of pleasure one could buy. Sylvana's touch made the itching, nausea, fever, and teeth-clenching cold withdraw. "Tell the story," Bel said, growling from the good feeling of being stroked and stoked. "Or I will find another use for your pretty mouth, and we will both be sorry."

■ ■

"In the beginning," Sylvana said, "there was fire. Vesh were given fire by the Lady who made the water, earth, and sky, made the first trees touch the clouds, and sent animals to live in them. The Lady gave Vesh fire because She knew they would rule it wisely. Without fire, life would be possible, but it would not be comfortable. But if fire is not contained, everything in its path will perish. From tending the fire, Vesh learned respect. Fire created duty and honor. And from fire, the Vesh learned that every change has its price, that the power to create is wedded with the power to destroy. So is death buried in our living flesh, closer than any lover. And Vesh think it is an honor to have death so close at hand, reminding them to live completely.

"But one night, fire came out of the sky, and this fire was not the gift of the Lady. This fire did not go out like lightning, but continued to burn, like an enormous torch. And it pushed a little world ahead of it, a world full of beings that the Lady never made. You would think that anyone who lived in the midst of such magnificent flames would be wise and fearless in battle. But these travelers were not wise. They were not fearless in battle. They were the slaves, not the guardians, of the fire that drove them, and when they touched the Lady's fair earth, they did not have the sense to put it out."

A flint in Sylvana's slow-moving hand would never strike a spark, but her languid fingers made Bel's horns burst into flame. The Vesh rocked like a child being sung to sleep, always craving more, always receiving it. Sylvana's touch was sure, steady, and relentless. Bel longed for just a little more pressure, just a brief bit of contact with the tips of her nails, and Sylvana obliged. Each time she let her hand slip down to gather more moisture to ease its work, Bel growled at her, but did not attack.

Sylvana spoke in a soft, even voice, giving Bel the substance of the legend without any melody or poetry. "A Vesh lord's quest had taken her far from her mother's lands, but she was forced to stop and order her retainers to extinguish the fires that the strangers had allowed to escape. Luckily, there were not many of these little fires, and they had not joined together. The Vesh lord marked well where these fools had made camp, and she vowed to return and extinguish them as well, when her quest was completed."

Her forearm was complaining. Sylvana shifted position a little and told the tired muscles that their task had just begun. "The lord's name was Dylan. Dylan was a great hunter, and she easily took her brother's head and left his companions with wounds that would hold their interest for several days. But her triumph was marred by the thought of the forest that had been laid to waste. And so she rode back to see if the Lady had taken these intruders' lives.

"Alas, they had established the beginning of a small estate. In those days, lords traded their younger sons for the handsomest offspring of another estate so that they could have companions.

Dylan's favorite concubine was such a man, and she opened him to take the omens. The Lady told her that the strangers were a gift, so Dylan resolved to take them prisoner."

Sylvana brushed hair out of her eyes. Bel's eyes were closed, her olive face flushed with sexual heat. Still the patient, minute movements must continue. "Dylan deployed her retainers just before dawn. The strangers had erected a fence, which seemed like an easy thing to scale because it was low and made of wire. But the fence was full of poison, and one of Dylan's cousins actually died when she touched it. So Dylan sent her women into the trees, and they dropped from the branches inside the fence. The sentries felt nothing but a wind at their backs, and saw nothing but the trees before they fell. Dylan's company was angry about the death of her cousin and threw one of the guards into the wire fence, where he died, and then one of his fellows made it clear that he knew how to make the poison stop flowing through the wires."

Bel wondered if this was poison spreading through her veins. She longed to take Sylvana by the scruff of her neck and shake her like a coney. One hand was not enough. And surely her horns would burst if this feather-light fondling did not end. Sylvana smiled, a Vesh-ya expression that Bel usually thought looked sly. But the triumph, the control implied in that smile, made Bel want Sylvana even more. Now Sylvana raised her other hand, the one that was not buried in Bel's suede trousers, and wiggled its fingers, loosening it up. But she did not slide it into Bel's pants to join its mate. She let it go walking up Bel's chest, inside the dark green shirt, heading for the right-handed row of flat, dark nipples. The bounty hunter wailed, full of despair and good fortune.

Sylvana had to think a moment to remember where she was in the story. Oh, yes, Dylan (like most Vesh most of the time) was offended. "Dylan was disgusted by this male's cowardice. She thought he would make poor sport indeed upon a quest. And she thought even less of their lords for trusting their lives to the care of fools and traitors. So Dylan had everyone in the camp rounded up, and when dawn came, she gave them a demonstration of the kind of treatment that toughens the Vesh male. She picked six of the tallest, heaviest males, and tied them firmly to the trees so they should not escape their training.

"But none of them lived. Then Dylan understood that these were not real people. The Lady rejected them. She would not sustain or heal them. So the lord told her servitors to end their weak and miserable Vesh-ya lives.

"But there was one woman among the strangers who was wiser than all the rest, and no wonder. Her name was Tamara. She was named for a tree that grew on the world where she was born, a tree that could bear fruit even in the desert." *Ah, Tamara,* Sylvana thought, *perhaps we, your children in exile, would have been better off if you had not been so tough-minded.* The Vesh thought their concubines prayed to Tamara as an avatar of the Lady, but usually when Vesh-ya said, "It is as Tamara wills it," they were not being thankful.

"Now, the Vesh-ya had planned to look for jewels and ore, and if they found any, they intended to rip great holes in the earth and take away her treasure. The people who planned this foul mission knew that even Vesh-ya could not perform such ugly work without being rewarded. Tamara and her male and female companions were the prospectors' reward for being vandals and thieves.

"Tamara was the only one in the crew who loved the forest. She had slipped outside the fence to walk among the trees, and she had gathered any plants that she found beautiful or aromatic. She was tired of the ship's food, so she experimented with some of these plants, drying them and using them as spices or tea. She had discovered that one of the plants she had gathered heightened her empathy, and almost made it possible for her to read her crew members' minds. Using this herb made it much easier for her to satisfy her visitors so she could have more time alone.

"Tamara had always had the ability to subtly plant a notion in someone else's head. But the Vesh herb had increased this ability as well. This talent allowed her to elude her guards. But Tamara did not try to escape. She returned to her quarters and made all of the herb that she had left into tea."

It felt as if Sylvana was pouring hot water down Bel's chest. The Vesh-ya was playing the bounty hunter's nipples like the holes of a flute, and being rewarded with just as many notes. Vesh always claimed their nipples were not sensitive, and ridiculed Vesh-ya for succumbing to stimulation of their teats. But none of the Vesh that Bel had bedded seemed averse to having their tits stroked and licked, so surely it must be all right to allow Sylvana this liberty.

"Just as Dylan's soldiers were unsheathing their swords and selecting their first victims, Tamara came among them, walking slowly, carrying a white cup upon an ebony tray. She was also wearing black and white, a simple gown that did not close in the front. It had long, square sleeves and a red lining. She had taken down her hair. Tamara's hair was a marvel. It was black as pitch and came down to her ankles. No Vesh had ever seen hair that long."

And so, Sylvana thought, *we are obliged to wear it long to this very day.* She had a rueful memory of her mother scrubbing some abrasive mixture into her scalp which was supposed to make her hair longer and thicker. Some of her Vesh lovers had paid so much attention to her hair — washing it, brushing it, braiding it, kissing it, wrapping themselves in it — that Sylvana wasn't sure they would remember her face. The slavers were the first Vesh-ya she had ever seen who dared cut their hair. *If they had offered to free me from this weight,* she thought ruefully, *I might have been a more profitable piece of merchandise.* She tossed the pale mass over her shoulders and kept massaging Bel's horns, but her touch became progressively firmer.

"Tamara knelt at Dylan's feet and offered her the cup. 'My lord,' she said, 'will you not drink with me before you slay your servant?'" How seductive Tamara's voice must have been, how dark and liquid her eyes must have seemed, to make that fierce barbarian look at her with curiosity instead of loathing. No wonder actresses as well as courtesans, Vesh and Vesh-ya alike, prayed to Tamara for a little of her skill.

And now one of Sylvana's hands prepared to drink from Bel's cup. The Vesh knew she was passing through each phase of excitement much more rapidly than normal. Her aborted visit to the Belled Cat and the change made her body quick and pliant. One of Sylvana's hands remained at Bel's helm, keeping the nose of the ship turned into the wind, and the other hand went deep into the sea. Vesh were made inside as they were outside. The pocket ended in two horns, each of them big enough to shelter one of Sylvana's little paws. But Sylvana made Bel anticipate that pleasure. Her strong, slender hand prepared the gate, again and again, until Bel thought it must be yawning as wide as the mouth of the cave that sheltered them.

"Dylan's attendants thought the cup was poisoned, but when the lord lifted it to her lips, she could only smell the wholesome herb. Once the cup was lifted, it would be rude indeed to let it fall untasted. So Dylan drank, and as she drank, Tamara opened her mind, and Dylan found herself lost in wonder at its strangeness. Male and female Vesh knew each other only too well. But Dylan found no hatred in Tamara, and very little fear. Tamara cared naught for her fellows. Indeed, she despised them. But Dylan interested her greatly."

The reasons Tamara and her colleagues despised the "visitors" they serviced on board the mining ship were legends that Vesh-ya mothers passed on to their daughters, and these stories remained a source of bitterness between Vesh-ya males and females. The idea of sporting with a male of her own species did not appeal to Sylvana. Why do something so intimate with someone so unattractive, unless you expected to get something besides pleasure out of it, like a child?

"So Dylan took Tamara into her tent and told her servitors to guard their captives well. Vesh and Vesh-ya waited uneasily while Tamara's cries of pleasure divided the air. For one day and a night, and yet another day, Dylan made Tamara sing, and then that bird lost its music. For the first three watches of the night, no sound at all came from the lord's tent. Dylan's sisters were about to rush it, because they feared the wily Vesh-ya had assassinated their lord.

"But when they gathered at the tent flap, Dylan ordered them to stand back and tend to the captives. Two more watches passed. Just as the sun came up to warm the tips of the trees, Vesh and Vesh-ya alike heard Dylan shout for joy, as if she had seen the Lady. Until that day, no Vesh had known anything other than silent pleasure. You do not cry out when you are stalking your enemy."

Bel did not care if she was in the presence of friend or foe. She hissed and yowled at Sylvana, noisier than a kit toying with the first food she has caught all by herself. Sylvana had sunk one hand within her, and was opening and closing it. Instead of squeezing Bel's horns in her fist, she was drumming lightly on them. The rhythm was maddening and delicious.

"But that was not the end of it. Dylan called her chief lieutenants to the tent, all four of them, and ordered Tamara to cast her spell upon them. The lord wanted to make sure that the unique pleasure she had just taken was not due to some weakness or flaw in her own character. By this time, the troops had grown restless, so Dylan left her chief officers to their pleasures and ordered some of her other servants to harvest as much herb as they could carry.

"When they returned, every Vesh-ya in the camp was made to drink a double dose of it. And Dylan sorted through their minds. Some she almost rejected because they were not drawn to her. But when she led her eldest son past them, their hearts melted. And so she spared them for the sake of her son, because she loved him and wanted his short life to be wild and carefree. Most of the Vesh-ya had twisted, hateful souls, and these poor misfits were beheaded.

"By the time the Vesh-ya had been dealt with, Dylan's lieutenants were besotted with Tamara, unable to walk, unable to defend themselves against her unflagging attentions. But Dylan took her away from them and showed her what had been done. Tamara wept, but the lord did not know the meaning of her tears. Before he was executed, one of the Vesh-ya males had shouted, 'You won't get away with this! Others will come after us.' Dylan wanted to know what he meant. Tamara tried to close her mind, but Dylan had more of the drug made and poured down her throat, and plucked the truth from her thoughts."

Sylvana thought it was time to put both of her hands in. Her weary fingers abandoned Bel's horns and plucked at the engorged sexual flesh that surrounded her other hand. Bel quickly put her own hand where Sylvana's had vanished. Now fingers were sliding in beside the already-planted fist. Bel tried to draw the second hand in, but this made her pelvic muscles tighten. Sylvana was not discouraged. She pushed back, and the opening gave way.

Sylvana's mouth was dry, but there was no stopping now. She wondered what she would do if Bel did not climax soon. Perhaps she had misjudged her work. But Bel's response steadily increased, so Sylvana kept on pumping and talking.

"Dylan took Tamara to the ship that had carried them here with its lawless fire, and the lord made Tamara give the ship a tale to bear, that nothing of value had been found here, and all the crew was dying from a strange disease their doctors could not cure. Then one of the new concubines, a male who could hardly perform his task because he wanted to be used again by his Vesh master, told the ship to rise up into the sky and circle the Lady's world forever."

The fact that a ship existed which could take them home, if only they could reach it, had caused many a Vesh-ya to fall off the narrow catwalk of servitude. Underground slave cults worshiped that ship and taught that when the people had purified themselves, it would return and take them home. Sylvana had no patience for such dangerous nonsense. Slaves who sneaked away to secret meetings in the forest were only asking for trouble. If she wanted to have an orgy, she could do that in complete safety, with her lord's permission, as long as the Vesh got to watch. Why give some old woman whatever coins you'd managed to filch from the masters in return for being told you were still full of sin and undeserving of rescue?

"Dylan allowed her people a few more days of sport with their new concubines. Unfortunately, many of them died because Vesh did not understand the Vesh-ya's preference for carrion or their need for sleep. Nor had it occurred to Vesh that any of them would willingly take their own lives. So Tamara begged Dylan to begin the long trek home. By then, she had learned to speak a little of the Vesh language. So the lord let her walk among her fellows to teach them the art of love and inform their masters when they were in dire straits.

"And so it was that Vesh-ya came to sit by the fires of the Vesh, and will never be allowed to leave."

Then the second hand was in, entering its place like a mount returning to its stable. As Bel cried, "Sylvana!" a beam of sunshine crept across the dirt floor of the cave and touched the hearth. Bel thought the sun was coming up within her belly. Her triumphant shouts rang down the cavern walls and, seconds later, made stalactites vibrate in faraway chambers no Vesh had ever entered.

"You are the girl for me," Bel said, and slipped into a trance which told her where some frisky little beasts had hidden their winter store of nuts, and that Frick and his comrades were only a few miles away.

Sylvana slept far more deeply, relieved that her already-abused mouth had not been required. She would not be so lucky on the morrow. Fortunately, she healed quickly. And she had learned during this adventure to steal sleep wherever she could, no matter how brief and uncomfortable it might be.

■ ■

Bel did not regain normal consciousness until the sun was at its highest point. It was getting hard to tell the difference between trance and waking. The power that had slumbered within her for half a century was coming into its own. But it fluctuated painfully. She would be fully cognizant of the doings of all living things within a mile of the cave, and then the field would shrink and she would feel nothing that was not a stone's throw away. Her perceptions went through other bizarre changes. First flying things would overwhelm her with vertigo; then she would feel as if all the birds had died, and the busy creatures who lived in the bark and fruit of the trees would harangue her. Then they would be silenced, and swimming things would shed their scales across her mind, burrowing creatures would throw dirt past her shoulders, or grazing animals would grind up food in her mouth.

She knew that this cacophony would continue until her talents stabilized. When she knew their limits, she could set about teaching herself to screen out unwanted information and focus her mind. A few unlucky Vesh never completed the change, and either lived in the maelstrom or gave their lives up to a friend's loving kindness. And a very small minority found themselves burdened with other abilities — the power to move objects without touching them, fire starting, rainmaking, appearing simultaneously in two locations. Vesh males and at least half of Vesh females never experienced the change, and Bel almost wished she did not have a long line of gifted ancestors.

Sylvana was also waking up. She kissed the base of Bel's throat, whispered, "By your leave," and went outside to relieve herself. Bel staggered after her, hoping no visions of fisher-birds diving after their silvery prey or insect-catchers cutting upside-down figure eights to snap up their lunch would interfere with her balance. A three-legged pot full of cooked grain, a loaf of bread, and some cheese and fruit had been left within a few paces of the cave's mouth. There was also a bucket of water, which Sylvana was dipping into to clean herself.

Bel staggered into the brush and found a sapling she could lean against while she voided. Her waste smelled of sickness and fear. When she came out of the scrub trees, Sylvana had built a little fire and was waiting for her with a hot, wet towel. Bel allowed the girl to undress and bathe her. "There's a new shirt and breeches here," Sylvana said uncertainly. "Do you think they will fit?"

Frick and the boys had obviously come calling. Bel caught a shadow of their floating minds. They had pitched their hammocks a decent distance away, among trees big enough to support them. Tethered mounts grazed peacefully within sight of their exhausted riders. Well, that explained how all this food came to be here. She felt better with clean clothing, and even better when Sylvana gave her a warm bowl of porridge and a bit of bread to scoop it up with. "Feed yourself," she told the wench. Sylvana gave her a little bow and took some fruit and cheese.

"They left a tent for us, my lord," Sylvana said with a full mouth. Bel hoped she didn't choke. Bless the child's hearty appetite. Love was hard work for a Vesh-ya. "It would probably be a lot more comfortable than the cave. And there's a bed cover for the floor. If you can help me get our shelter up, I can cut some branches or gather some of that long grass we walked through. It should make an easy laydown when it's stuffed."

Bel could never remember enjoying a breakfast more. Could it be that the change was through with her? She briefly considered taking one of the men's mounts and quitting this place.

"You aren't thinking of leaving, are you, my lord?" Sylvana said, a trifle too sharply. "There's no way of knowing how ill you might feel in just a few hours. Unless you sense treachery in your adopted brothers, I think it wise to remain here until you are more sure of yourself."

Bel was offended. Sylvana's tone of voice reminded her of the bossy, self-important way her mother's Vesh-ya majordomo had spoken to her about stores that had gotten low or beasts that needed branding. "You are right," she told Sylvana, "but be not quite so familiar with me."

Sylvana flushed. She had deserved that rebuke. "I beg your pardon," she said. But Bel intercepted her before she could sink to the ground.

"Perhaps I have been solitary for too long," Bel said. "I am in need of your faithful care." It was the closest thing to an apology Sylvana had ever gotten from a lord. "Now, let's see if we can get that tent up," Bel said briskly, "before the Lady's thumbprint squashes flat my tiny mind."

The shelter was too complicated for Bel's taste, but Sylvana seemed to have no trouble sorting out its parts and putting them together. They erected it in plenty of time for Sylvana to gather bedding. A warning wave of nausea took Bel by surprise, and the concubine fetched the blankets from the cave and made her lie down upon them. "I will stay within call," Sylvana said before leaving.

Bel could hear Frick and his men rousing. One by one, they swung from their hammocks and performed their morning rituals of elimination and cleansing. They must have taken time to sport with one another before lying down, because all of them had a sort of orange glow about them, a faint, warm light of satiety. Only Tupper had seemed uneasy in his swinging bed.

Tupper's mind was ... unusual. Old-fashioned. It was like a block of well-seasoned wood. The grain of it was puzzling and pleasing to the eye, and it felt smooth and strong beneath her examination. It was raw material waiting to have something beautiful made out of it. She left off inspecting him because she felt his consciousness turn toward her with a feeling of welcome that made her cringe. Cam and Magee were much simpler, like little flames, leaping from place to place, gleeful, always on the brink of doing damage. But Frick — Frick was a deep one. His mind was like a cold lake, purple with its own depth, full of wily fish that fed near the bottom, too ancient to be fooled by a hook-and-lure at the surface.

"Eat up," Frick told them. "We're on holiday, my darlings. We've nothing to do except a little hunting while we keep watch on the lord and her chosen one. It's a fine day to be alive, is it not?"

Magee yawned, rubbed his nose, and responded, "A fine day to die, indeed. Frick, when you sit at the lord's left hand, will we still be dear to you?"

"As dear as you are today," Frick promised.

Only Bel saw / felt Tupper scowl at that cheery statement.

"Then may I have a red coat again, and a big pack of white hounds, and as much land for my flowers as I can walk around in a day?"

Cam cuffed his brother. "What foolish toys you pant for. Frick, I want a big salon with a gaming wheel. And cards, and dice, and lots of lovely girls carrying pipes full of the darkest gum to refresh the players. And I want a shooting range. An indoor one, so no one gets rained on. And lots of dances. Dances with fabulous music, so the young lords for miles around will quit their mothers' skirts and come to step a measure with us."

"And what about you, Tupper?" Magee cried. "What would it take to lift that sour look from your big mug?"

Tupper was restacking the woodpile, somehow making it neat and square. "Let Frick give me what he will out of his largesse," Tupper said, speaking so slowly it made Bel grit her teeth. "I expect our captain will have many a surprise for us when he comes into his own."

Now it was Frick's turn to be dismayed. But it lasted only a moment. "Eat, eat!" he insisted, rubbing his hands together. "Tupper, when we have broken our fast, you will take Magee down to the stream and string our net. Remember, we're fishing for six. Cam and I will scout out a location for the sauna. The lord will want a good sweat when this beastly change releases her."

Cam and Magee were nudging each other off a large, flat rock that each of them wanted to use for a chair. Cam stopped pushing for a moment to ask a question, and lost his seat.

"Do you think the lord will be fearful after she changes?" he asked, and made a sign to avert evil.

"What? You mean one of those hags who summons tempests and lights the neighbor's hayrick on fire?" Frick had already fed himself and was bending over the fire to get a light. Bel liked the stimulating smell of his cigar. He straightened with a burning twig in his hand and turned his back on the company to ignite his smoke. Bel saw a glowing shape twist in his mind, and the fire leaped from the twig to paper before the two touched. "Did the mean old aunties make you wet your bed with gruesome tales about monsters under the floorboards? That's just a myth, my pretty lad. No such shadows of the Lady walk among us."

Bel's consciousness was abruptly dragged back into her body. She hugged her belly as cramping and nausea returned. Now she was grateful for Sylvana's fussing. She was cold, cold enough to make her body tremble, and she jammed a fold of the blanket between her teeth to keep from gashing her own mouth. Sylvana was near enough to call, if only she could make a sound. But her throat was full of ice and sand.

There was more light, then less, as the tent flap parted and dropped. "Bel!" Sylvana cried. She dragged the makeshift mattress into the tent, helped Bel onto it, and rolled them both up in blankets. "Don't worry, I'm here," she said. "I'm here."

By the time Bel's chills faded, it was dusk. Sylvana had made her drink something bitter that eased the pain in her joints. It also seemed to hold her maddening new sensitivity at bay. Bel's temperature was mounting by slow degrees, but she sat up and ate some of the steamed fish and vegetables that Frick's boys had left for them.

"Bring me my purse," she told Sylvana after she had swallowed several dry and tasteless bites. The Vesh-ya fetched the leather pouch that usually hung from Bel's waist. Inside it was a smaller bag, which up till now Bel had never opened in front of another living being. In fact, she seldom thought of its contents at all, unless she was full of drink and self-pity. She took Sylvana's hand in her own and tipped its contents onto the narrow little palm.

First Bel picked up a coiled strip of fine leather which had been taken from a large reptile prized for its blue-and-silver skin. "Since I cannot stand for this ritual, you must at least put your head lower than mine," she told Sylvana. The Vesh-ya girl flattened herself before Bel's crossed legs. "I have taken thee to rule and to cherish," Bel said. "As long as you love me, you shall never lack for anything. I will keep you close as death by my side. This collar is my token. Once closed around your neck, I am bound to slay any fool who trespasses upon you. So now decide. Will you wear my token, or will you not?"

"I will wear your token," Sylvana whispered. "I will be your shield. My hands are yours to command. And I will ever strive to make myself useful and a joy to you, and never betray this sacred trust."

The metallic blue band looked good upon Sylvana's slender throat. It made her pale hair seem even more ghostly. Bel was pleased. Now Sylvana handed her the second thing that the little suede bag had held. This was a single large, blue stone, set atop a flat spiral of gold. The stone was cut in a traditional, complex pattern called "the eye of love." It picked up the light from their lantern and reflected brilliant squares of sapphire color onto the dark walls of the tent. Sylvana could not resist reaching for it.

"Soon enough," Bel said. "You will wear it for a long time, precious thing. First let us drink from a single cup."

Sylvana had to duck outside the tent and brew the tea. She was surprised to find that the fire was perfectly healthy. She did not remember putting that many sticks into the hearth. She put a deep-sided pot full of water above the flames, and as soon as she released the handle, it moved an inch or two closer to the hottest part of the grill. "Oh!" she gasped, then slapped her own face for being a silly girl, and measured out the dried leaves that Frick had left among their supplies. The water heated far more quickly than she expected, so it seemed only a moment had passed before she was kneeling again in front of Bel, offering the cup of companionship.

Sylvana didn't quite see the little knife come out, but Bel had already pricked her own thumb. It was thought to be a lucky omen if both drops of blood entered the tea at the same moment, so Sylvana thrust her hand at Bel, praying it was not shaking too badly.

She didn't even feel the knife, just saw two ruby drops fall and mingle in the golden tea. Bel held Sylvana's chin and poured the Vesh-ya's half down her throat. A good thing, too, because it was so bitter it made Sylvana's stomach lurch. Bel finished the cup without flinching.

"Now," she said, and Sylvana bent toward her and opened her mouth. Without pinching her tongue, Bel deftly inserted the jewel. It was a finely made piece. The back part rested easily on the floor of Sylvana's mouth, causing her no discomfort, and the blue stone did not bother her any more than her own teeth.

Bel and Sylvana sat cross-legged, facing one another, looking into each other's eyes. The potion was already changing both of them.

Sylvana had disturbing flashes of the way the world seemed to Vesh senses — keener vision, but with muted colors that Sylvana's brain kept trying to correct; a confusing wealth of sounds that she could not sort out; more odors than it seemed possible for a little tent to contain. Then she began receiving more than sensory data. Bel's anger, fear, and pain came through in hot flashes of red and yellow. Sylvana kept her breathing slow and deep. Her job was to function as a channel, to draw off the overwhelming aspects of the change and allow them to pass through her.

It was hard to let it all go. Her Vesh-ya curiosity kept prompting her to investigate, retain, and question. Her ego was also a problem. It kept bobbing up, trying to claim the flow of agony and creation as its own property. Sylvana felt as if she were trying to stay seated on an inflated ball, floating in a river swollen by spring runoff. Moment by moment, she barely kept her equilibrium.

Bel experienced a growing sense of relief. Instead of relentless physical pain from the too-swift changes in her psyche, she got occasional moments of respite. At first, being linked to Sylvana was like having a little soundproof room she could step into. Then, as the link between them strengthened, it felt like having a large, empty room where she could store whatever she could not absorb. As the herb took full effect, it created other metaphors for what was happening, and Bel could feel Sylvana's cool touch here and there in the streams of lava that seared her aching head.

Sylvana felt Bel's hands on her shoulders. The two of them sank side by side into the fragrant bed. The sweet smell of new grass and freshly cut branches was comforting, cleansing. "Your bondage to me will not be an easy one," Bel whispered in Sylvana's ear. "Do you think you can serve me perfectly, without protest, without resentment or even a rebellious thought? Because your mind is an open meadow that I can walk through at my leisure, and I will know every blade of grass therein."

Sylvana did not think it wise to point out that the doors to Bel's mind were also thrown wide open, and her thoughts would probably always remain accessible to her concubine. Instead, she laughed. "Is that what you want? A companion who never protests, never pouts, never says you nay or argues? I think such 'perfection' would very quickly drive you from my side."

"Saucy wench," Bel murmured, putting her teeth delicately into Sylvana's shoulder. "You have a lot to learn, I think."

"And is it not my lord's pleasure to instruct me?" the Vesh-ya said lazily, putting her hands under Bel's shirt.

They undressed each other. Bel's long, olive-skinned, furry arms and legs twined around Sylvana's smaller, white, hairless body. The potion and the change enhanced the pleasure of skin-to-skin touching. Each of them inspected and approved the difference that they saw in the other. Sylvana arched her back as Bel's thigh came to rest between her legs. She rubbed the wet pillow of her mound against the Vesh's coarse skin and hard muscle. "Give me your lips," she told the Vesh, and they kissed each other hard enough to draw a little blood. It had taken Vesh-ya a long time to teach the predatory Vesh how to kiss. And Vesh swore they were still teaching Vesh-ya how to properly use their puny claws.

Outside, the wind came up, bringing a patter of rain. At first the drops were few and fine, like a very thick, wet mist. But soon they began to come down in earnest. Bel and Sylvana, lost in the change that now had both of them in its talons, barely noticed. But a few hundred yards away, a tiny band of Vesh males cursed and struggled to erect a little shelter. Luckily, the rain was warm — an oddity that only Frick noted.

Under the lean-to, Cam and Magee shed their soaking clothes and then stripped Tupper and Frick. "You can't get any wetter," Cam said reasonably. "Besides, my thing is feeling frisky." He put his hand around Tupper's forked tool and made the older man groan as he squeezed the two sensitive tips together. "Lay with me," Cam insisted. He knelt and lapped at the bobbing wand until

Tupper gently tipped him onto his back and knelt between his thighs.

Magee stretched out beside his brother. "Ride me," he said to Frick. "Make it hurt this time."

Frick's jaws gaped with Vesh laughter. "Is this the same lad who walked bowlegged and complained he could not sit down for three days the last time he had me?"

"I only pretended, to make you feel like a big, strong brute. Are you angry?"

"No," Frick said, putting his weight on top of Magee, who pouted. "Yes, then, I am furious," the captain said, putting on a grim face. "Prepare for your punishment, you lying slut."

Magee sighed with contentment, and wrapped his arms around Frick's broad shoulders.

The rain came down harder, hotter, bruising the leaves on the trees and flattening the grass, drowning out the sounds of hard-used flesh. In Bel's tent, Sylvana writhed upon her back, brought to yet another peak of pleasure by the Vesh's big hand, nearly buried inside her. There was no more pain inside Bel's head, no more terror locked in her chest. The change ran now on tides of lust, but if anything, it ran faster and stronger now, awakening every mind, however small, for miles around, and swamping them all with desire.

Bel licked the sweat from Sylvana's flank, bit her nipples, slapped her thighs. The pale skin was marked now with light red scratches and patches of pale blue. "Love is hard work for a Vesh-ya," Bel said, yawning briefly at the trite sound of the old proverb.

"This isn't *work*," Sylvana taunted. She pummeled Bel with her little fists and showed her short, blunt teeth. "You're too easy. Too kind. Push me. Push me!"

Bel slapped her face, turned her over, reddened her ass with an angry hand, then placed the tip of one clawed finger against Sylvana's anus. The puckered skin recognized the threat and fluttered, trying to escape. The bolt of fear made Sylvana's pelvic muscles loosen, and Bel's enormous fist finally found a home within her. Sylvana came up on all fours to receive her.

Bel left off terrorizing Sylvana's asshole and groped through her clothing for one of the little knives. Its hilt came to her fingers like a tame bird trained to take seeds in its beak. "Hold still," she warned Sylvana, and ran the sharp edge up and down her spine. A fine spray of shaved blonde hairs coated the edge of the blade. Bel fucked her for a few minutes, making her really feel the weight of her hand, and stopped when she could tell that Sylvana was about to come again. "Turn over," Bel said. "I want you to see my face."

Sylvana tumbled in slow motion. As she landed on her side, she lifted her ankle neatly so Bel did not have to remove her hand. Bel had to admit there were some advantages to getting an estate-trained bed girl. Sylvana's eyes were fixed upon her, and Bel's addled time-sense made a necklace of this moment and all the similar moments in their future when Sylvana would wait to see what her owner would do to her flesh and mind.

"Be very still," Bel said. Then she cut her initial into the Vesh-ya's inner thigh, bent, and licked the scarlet design. The blood coagulated within seconds. Vesh saliva would turn the scar blue. But Sylvana was in no mood to think about aesthetics. Vow or no vow, a collar could be taken off, and a jewel could be removed from your tongue. But this mark was permanent. She cursed Bel as Tamara once cursed Dylan and won the lord's heart with her surrender and her fury.

As Sylvana came, the muscles inside her body shoved Bel's fist out, and an enormous crack of thunder divided the sky. The lightning that followed was so bright, it lit up the interior of their tent.

The change was circling Bel now, like a bird, high in the sky, descending in slow circles. She stretched out on the mattress to receive it. Sylvana crawled over to her, using Bel's legs for hand-holds to drag herself along. She ached all over. The very pores of her body felt exhausted. But she had just one more thing to do. Just one more thing, one more, just one. Bel's hands on each side of her head welcomed her in, showed her the destination. Sylvana put her lips around Bel's horns and allowed the jewel to press into the sensitive spot between them. The contact seemed to send a current of energy through her body. There was another crack of thunder, and lightning danced around the tent.

"Begin," Bel said, "with the movement of the predator circling the herd."

Sylvana obeyed. She followed with the movement of catching snowflakes on one's tongue. Then there was the movement of removing a nut from its shell, the waterfall, contemplation of a new dish, stirring honey into tea, the feeding bird, icing the cake, the spear, the potter's wheel, making what is rough smooth, making what is smooth rough, catching the grasshopper, stoking the fire, and a dozen more refinements of the mouth-dancer's art.

Bel opened herself to everything. The storm within was one with the storm without. Thunder seemed to issue from her mouth, lightning from her outstretched fingers, and still the bird circled, descending, its plumage like the colors that stream through a prism. She could see its fierce black eyes and the wicked curve of its sharp black beak. Sylvana's tongue and its ornament moved in time with the bird's broad wings. Bel floated, full of pleasure and knowledge, aware but not afraid.

Several trees away, Frick had collapsed on top of his fellows. They labored, without much conviction, to roll him off. He found it difficult to believe they had not toppled the lean-to with their erotic acrobatics. The desire to continue, to keep fucking, to somehow wring more pleasure from his body, was still keen, but his flesh would not respond. "Release us!" he shouted at the storm. "Lady damn you, Bel. Let us go!"

Sylvana's face was smeared with Bel's ardor. She could not catch her breath. Her neck and shoulders felt as if she had been pulling a plow. Bel had nearly come a hundred times. Sylvana thought she could not continue for one more second. Then Bel's hands came down upon her shoulders, kneading them gently. "Wonderful dancer," Bel said. She sounded drunk. "Your tongue could persuade the very stars to fall in homage at your feet." Her powerful, clawed hands adjusted Sylvana's face, moving her tongue up just a fraction of an inch. "Now put your jewel there, my darling, my dancer, and I will be your falling star."

Bel closed her eyes. Sylvana simply pressed her tongue against the spot she had been shown — pressed hard. The bird folded its wings, put its feet together, and descended like a stone. It fell into Bel's heart, shredding her chest, then the warring pieces of her psyche came together, joined, and healed. She came like a conquering army, and the rain stopped more quickly than a barkeep closes his keg to a customer who's spent his last bit of brass.

"I should go and have a smoke with our brother Frick," Bel said thoughtfully. "There are plans to be made. The lords and little brothers of the forest cannot allow pinky slavers to murder our sisters and steal their bond-maids. You shall have vengeance for your loss, Bel's Sylvana Tamarasdotter." The bounty hunter turned over and fell deep into a trance. Sylvana covered them, molded her body to Bel's side, and slept safe in the shadow of her love.

*w*HA*t* G*i*RL*s* a*R̃*e mA*d*E O*f*

■■

Bo (née Barbara, known as the Yeti in high school because of her fondness for snow) had just shuttled her last set of papers from one office to another. Not a moment too soon. Downtown traffic was about to change from hellish to terminal. Instead of putting thousands of people who hated their jobs and hated each other in cages and letting them race each other home, Bo thought they should just give them loaded guns and let them duel it out at twenty paces. It sure would thin out the freeway. It had been a very busy day, even for a Friday. Every piece of paper she had delivered was an emergency, although how anything that wasn't bleeding could constitute a crisis was beyond her. The clerks and receptionists she'd dealt with today weren't getting enough fiber in their diets. Cops were giving away parking tickets like they got to put the fines in their own pockets. And every taxi in the financial district seemed determined to eat a motorcycle for lunch.

Before she went home to her microwave and a freezer full of Stouffer's frozen entrées, Bo decided to detour through the Tenderloin and visit one of the porn shops. She had a hot date this weekend. Maybe she would buy a dick. The thought of putting it to somebody else made her feel a little taller, a little meaner. Yeah. That was a really good idea. Just walk into the porno shop and buy a dick, like it was something she did every day. They were just lying there behind glass, in a counter next to the cashier. A dozen of 'em, like big, pink, deformed rubber hot dogs. The clerk didn't give a shit. Who cared what he thought, anyway? Who cared what some jerk thought who worked in a dirty bookstore? It would be easy, Bo told herself, and backed her bike into the curb, between two cars that were far enough apart to leave room for her soft-tail.

"What are you looking at?" she snarled at a lanky old wino who had accidentally pointed his face in her direction. He blinked at her but couldn't quite get her in focus. He mumbled, "Spare change?" because that was about all he said to people anymore, other than, "Gimme a pint of Thunderbird."

"I haven't got any," Bo said. "How about a cigarette?"

"Sure," he said, putting out a hand that shook so bad, Bo didn't see how he ferried liquor from a brown-bagged bottle to his lips. She took two cigarettes out of her pack, put one in his stiff shirt pocket, lit the other one, and waited while he found it.

Now he could see her just fine. She was five-foot-six and well fed. Her light brown hair was cut like a Marine's. But Uncle Sam would never have put up with that ring in her nose. "Did that hurt?" he asked.

"No pain, no gain," Bo said, and backed away from the conversation and his bouquet.

"Be good," he admonished her, and let the building prop him up again. The wall was freshly painted, which in this neighborhood meant only one thing: it housed an adult bookstore. Bo glanced up at the sign. The letters hanging on the marquee's wires spelled out XXX SUGAR AND SPICE XXX. She pushed the heavy glass door and went in, already wincing at the thought of her boots sticking to the floor.

The shop was in the front. You had to walk past racks of hard-core magazines in shrink-wrap covers and cases full of Hong Kong's finest marital aids to get into the rest of the place, which featured REAL! LIVE! SEX! ACT! GIRLS! A big guy who looked like he might have been a biker before he lost one hand was there selling tokens, one for a dollar. Sometimes groups of women came through on "feminist tours of the red-light district." He always told them, "Ya can't go back there without an escort." Sometimes one of the customers would offer (with a leer) to provide that service. Bo wondered if he would tell her that. She imagined herself saying, "This is my escort," and whipping out a switchblade. That would make them all step back. She stuck one hand in her jacket pocket to make sure her Swiss Army knife was still there.

She loitered by the glass case full of dildos. It reminded her of a cage at the zoo. "See the wild, endangered, artificial phalli," the sign by the exhibit might read. They looked like dismembered organs in the fluorescent light. The bored clerk flicked a glance at her, said, "Back again?" in a bored tone of voice, and went back to his racing form. Bo blushed as red as the hanky in her back pocket. *Oh my God, he recognized me!* How could she possibly figure out what she wanted with this homophobic jerk cruising her? Well, he wasn't getting any money out of her today.

She turned away and walked toward the magazines. She touched some of the covers with the tips of her fingers, but what was the point in picking any of them up? You couldn't turn the pages and see what was in them. A small group of guys, including one man in a wheelchair and two men who were at least as old as her grandpa, were studying the racks anyway. One of them looked up, saw her, and edged away. *All I get from these straight assholes is constant harassment*, Bo thought bitterly, and headed for the bouncer guarding the turnstile. Just let him try to keep her out of the back. He'd find out pretty soon that he'd picked on the wrong kind of woman.

"Getcha tokens here," he said. "Hey, guy, how you doin'? Wanna spend some money on the foxy ladies? We got a red-hot trio today. One blonde, one brunette, and a real exotic little Asian fox. You friends with summa the dancers?"

Bo had counted on being stopped. This geek obviously thought she was a man. She didn't know what to do. If she corrected him, he might throw her out, and that would be humiliating. She glared at him, daring him to hassle her.

"Getcha tokens here," he said, talking over her shoulder, addressing the entire room. "If you wanna see the show or watch a movie, you gotta getcha tokens here," he told her confidentially.

Bo felt as if everyone in the bookstore was waiting to see what she would do. She decided to just act casual, like this was something she did every day. She gave him a twenty. He wasn't impressed. "Getcha money's worth," he said, sliding four stacks of five tokens toward her, and motioned her through the turnstile. Looking at her back, he thought ruefully, *Why do all the cute ones have to be dykes?*

This part of the store was much darker. Bo was afraid to stop moving for fear she wouldn't be able to get herself going again. Why weren't her eyes getting used to the dark? She was going to bump into some guy, maybe some jerk who already had his dick out. Then she remembered she had her Ray Bans on and slipped them into the pocket of her overlay. The light was still dim, but she could see well enough now to know that she was in a maze of little booths with plywood walls. Most of the doors stood open. There were pictures on each door that looked like the photos on video boxes.

The temptation to cop a few minutes of privacy was too much. She went into one of the cubicles and shut the door. There was a machine on one wall of the booth. She stuck a token in it just to see what would happen. It made a sound like a coffee grinder, and then a square of color appeared on the opposite wall. A surprisingly attractive young woman was down on her knees, licking a surprisingly homely man's cock. The picture quality wasn't very good, but Bo could see enough to tell that he wasn't getting it up. Nevertheless, the sight of real people having actual sex right there in front of her was oddly arousing.

Then she noticed something moving around at the bottom of the screen that didn't seem to belong in the movie. Was that a couple of fingers, poking through a hole in the flimsy wall? "Hey, dude, put it through! Best suck job in town!" somebody whispered.

The guy on the screen was hard now, and the woman who was blowing him had wrapped her hand around the base of his dick to keep it from going all the way into her face. Bo wanted to kill him, but she also wanted to wrap her hands around that bitch's neck and shove her head — where? Meanwhile, there were those beckoning fingers, the brave and weird offer to give a stranger pleasure. She should probably break his fucking hand, but it wasn't like he knew who was in here.

"Uh — I'm resting," she said, pitching her voice as deep as possible.

"Maybe later," the voice said. The fingers slid out of sight faster than a vanilla dyke who had just found poopoo in her girlfriend's anxious rosebud.

Bo thought she'd better get out of there before he saw her. As she rattled the door, she became very aware of her cunt. It was pressing into the seam of her jeans like a cat that leans on your leg to let you know it's breakfast time. *Why,* she wondered, *is there no word in English to describe this? I can't exactly say I've got a hard-on, but I bet this is sort of like what it feels like to have your dick get hard. I don't know if I want somebody to suck on my clit or fuck me, but I sure don't feel passive or receptive. It's an aggressive kind of feeling, demanding, and it's not all in my head either. It's very physical.*

This was turning into quite a trip. Maybe she should have gone to the feminist vibrator shop and purchased a leaping purple silicone dolphin. Or a pink ear of vibrating corn. Or told her trick she'd have to bring her own damn treats! Bo staggered out of the peep show section and headed for the next attraction — a round, slightly elevated, glass-enclosed stage that was surrounded by more little booths, like one of those lazy-susan Plexiglas spice racks that yuppies bought at Macy's Cellar.

The public-address system burped (a sound that momentarily returned Bo to high school), and an unctuous female voice said, "Gentlemen, fill your pockets full of *tokens*. The performance starts in *five minutes*. Three of the hottest, *wettest*, sexiest girls on *earth* are about to *shake it* just for you. These ladies are uninhibited, they're *bad*, they're ready to cut *loose*. They also take *requests*. So *buy* those tokens *now!*"

Men started coming out of the peep shows and clustering around the bouncer. He made change really fast for a one-handed guy. Somebody tried to sneak under his arm and pilfer a token. The bouncer lifted him with one arm and shook him until his teeth rattled. "Don't do that. It upsets me," the big man said mildly, and handed over tokens for the five-dollar bill he was offered in lieu of an apology.

The P.A. system crackled again, and the female voice repeated exactly the same announcement, putting identical emphasis on the words "tokens," "five minutes," "wettest," "earth," "shake it," "bad," "loose," "requests," "buy," and "now." Bo shook her head. "Sucker born every minute," she said ruefully and headed for the nearest booth.

■■

Backstage was a mess. Three dancers were supposed to get ready in a space that was only slightly bigger than a walk-in closet. There was only one chair and a small mirror that was losing its silver backing. The floor was cluttered with gym bags, carryalls, and discarded street clothes.

"My mascara came open in my lingerie!" Crash (née Lisa) wailed. Her blonde hair was only half teased-out, so she looked like a "before" ad for a PMS remedy. "Where's my hair spray?" She dug through her dancer's bag, throwing shoes, press-on nails, lace gloves, and anything else she needed over her shoulder.

"So wear black, Crash. Nobody will notice," Killer (née Brenda) said, rubbing lip gloss into her cheeks. She was already wearing a leather miniskirt and studded leather bra, but she hadn't finished zipping up her thigh-high boots. An asymmetrical, purple-streaked, black ponytail sprouted from one side of her mostly shaved head. "I have to make a lot of money today. The fucking manager's been harassing me about my eyebrow again. I think I'll get the other one pierced tomorrow. *And* my nipples. *And* my cheeks. *And* the spaces in between my fingers and toes!" She kicked the can of hair spray over to Crash.

"Toilet's stuffed up again," Poison (née Candy) announced, squeezing into the room. She wore only a gold G-string. The metallic fabric nearly blended into her old-ivory skin. She was shorter than the other dancers, but her body was solid from hours of dancing lessons and soccer. Her long, black hair had one eccentric platinum-blonde stripe. "Where is that boy, anyway? She's supposed to take care of this shit for us."

"Literally," Killer snickered, painting big Egyptian eyes around her own. She snapped on her favorite wristbands. Their large pyramid studs matched the ones on her bra. Then she reached for the high pit-bull collar that completed her outfit. "Come on, Poison, get dressed. We go on in five minutes."

"I'm really sick of Bad Dog's lame excuses," Crash said, shimmying into a cherry red merry widow without bothering to unhook the back. She'd left the stockings attached to the garters and crammed her feet into them like they were an old pair of jeans. Miraculously, they did not run. Poison lined up her scarlet patent pumps so Crash could step into them. "Are you trying to tell us you feel like being the victim today?" She grabbed a comb, elbowed Killer out of the way, and started flipping her hair back into a lacquered bouffant.

"Sure, I'll do it. Just don't get too rough. I wish they'd at least put a piece of carpet down on that stage. It's a hard place to fall."

Killer stood and zipped up her boots. "There are no easy places to fall," she said. "Where the fuck is your costume? I am not going to get docked again just because you like to wander around forever in your underwear."

"I don't have to dress up. I'm a China doll, a submissive geisha, every sailor's fantasy. It drives the white boys crazy." Poison sang, "Such a gentle way about you, Singapore girl." Killer shot her a nasty look. "I'm just going to wear my kimono," Poison said hastily, taking it off a hanger that dangled from a nail in the cracked, industrial green plaster wall. Hints of gold embroidery still glittered against the old, white silk. "Don't worry, Killer, I have a lot of toys in my pockets to keep the customers satisfied." She untangled her obi, printed with a green chrysanthemum pattern, from the mess on the floor, wrapped it around her waist, and then fished out her gold stiletto heels.

A knock on the dressing-room door shook the cubicle. "Ladies," the manager said, and came in before anybody gave her permission. Her name was Carole, but everybody just called her "the manager." She was a former dancer who always noticed when they were late and often failed to notify them that their time onstage was up. She was always pressuring them to do without a lunch break or work overtime on lame shifts. The dancers hated her even though she didn't demand sexual services like the men they'd worked for. "Where's your charming assistant?" she asked snidely.

"Flaked," Killer said briefly.

"Tell me about it later. You're on."

She closed the door, and Crash sent her a gesture that has been getting people killed in Sicily for hundreds of years. The three dancers filed into the hallway and opened the stage door. "We need some music!" Killer shouted, and their tape came on. Crash had made it. She called it "my tribute to popular culture's fascination with vicious bitches." The first song was the Waitresses, singing, "I know what boys like." The manager hated it.

They distributed themselves around the perimeter of the stage, dividing up the customers. If somebody started tipping, all of them clustered there, unless the customer indicated a preference for just one of them. The stage was about three feet higher than the floor, which put the customers' faces at a level with the dancers' knees. Sliding windows went up and down between the booth and the stage, and the men had to keep feeding tokens into a machine to keep the window up. There was also a little hole in the Plexiglas, to make it possible for folding money to get shoved through. Dancers got paid minimum wage because tipping was allowed. They put on two twenty-minute shows every hour, for eight hours, and on a really good night, they might each make $500. Usually, they made just enough money to make dancing seem a lot more attractive than being a secretary. They were supposed to receive a percentage of the token sales, but they all knew the manager shorted them.

The three of them had been working here for three months, three days a week. Nobody danced full-time. Theater owners were not about to dip into their profit margin for health insurance or other benefits. They had finally managed to get "promoted" to a weekend evening shift, when you made decent money, so they were probably about to get fired. Managers did that routinely to make room for new bodies and faces onstage. But they always found nasty, personal excuses — "You're late, you're on drugs, you can't dance, the customers don't like you, your tits sag, you're too fat." Smart dancers moved on to another theater before that happened, but nobody looked forward to working up another act or performing with strangers. Some of the straight dancers were uptight about dykes, and transsexuals were so competitive. It was unusual for three friends to get work together. The specter of dancers cooperating with or protecting one another made managers nervous.

You could make more money as a street hooker, but that was a lot more dangerous. There was no customer contact here. A girl on one of the other shifts had been followed to her car after work and raped, but that could happen to anybody. One of the adult theaters a few blocks away featured lap dancing, and the money was supposed to be fabulous, but it sounded like a very difficult job. How many different ways could you say, "Give me some more money or I'll go away" and make it sound flirtatious?

Killer had tried working as a dominatrix, but it was boring. "All I did was sit on my ass all day and wait for the phone to ring," she complained. "The other mistresses thought I was really strange, and most of the clients hated punks. It's so bogus. All the domination ads say, 'No sex,' right? But they all gave handjobs. I made the mistake of talking about it, and after that, the tacky comments about whores just kept coming. One day I had a slave down on the floor jacking off, and he came all over my shoe. I snapped. I took off my other shoe and went after him. I got him good a couple of times, too, before the woman who owned the place threw me out."

Today all the booths were busy. It was a Friday afternoon, and the working man was ready for some fun. Each of the girls danced, trading places onstage, for one more song. Poison had shed her kimono already, after taking some tit clamps and a small, battery-operated vibrator out of its pocket. Crash took some money from a guy who wanted to see her ass, turned around, took down her panties, and waved it in his face. He showed her a $50 bill and said, "Give me those hot little panties, honey." So she inched them down, bent over to take the $50 in her teeth, and pushed the scrap of red satin through the hole. *Baby gets new shoes tonight,* she thought.

Poison somehow managed to keep gyrating on her high heels while she worked the vibrator in and out of her pussy. Her other hand was busy yanking on the tit clamps. She didn't have a free hand to take tips. Crash danced over to her, started playing with her nipples, and used her free hand to collect the cash. "Honey, don't do that," one of the men said. "Don't hurt yourself like that."

"Fuck you," Poison said, sticking her tongue out at him. "This is the only part of this show that I like, asshole." He let his window come down and stay down.

"You just broke that piggy bank," Crash said, yanking on Poison's chain. "At this rate, you're never going to finish law school."

"Hey!" Killer said, tossing her head so her black-and-purple ponytail whipped through the air, "you're supposed to be *my* girlfriend!"

Poison snickered. You had to hand it to Killer, she always came up with an excuse for a little girl-wrestling onstage, and the boys loved it. "So what?" she yelled. "I want her to fuck me, and you can't stop us!" She did a little end-zone, in-your-face dance while Crash took over manipulation of the vibrator. Then she grabbed Crash and tried to smooch her.

"Get your hands out of my beehive," Crash said irritably, smooching her back. "It'll look like shit if it comes down over my face."

Killer stormed over to them, looking genuinely pissed off. The bright lights above the booth made it a hot box to work in. Crash and Poison could see the perspiration on her shoulders and breasts, above the leather bra. She pretended to slap Poison, who did a neat stage-dive onto the floor. While the customers shoved tokens into the machines like they were cops eating donuts, the blonde in her red corset and the brunette in her leather skirt struggled onstage, with Killer finally gaining the upper hand and administering a not-so-fake spanking.

"I'm sorry, I'm sorry!" Crash wailed, trying to protect her beehive. Poison floor-danced around the perimeter, running her obi back and forth between her legs and pretending to whip herself with it, picking up money, making sexy ooh-baby faces at the customers and feigning masturbation for the ones who gave her something bigger than a single. "Don't be so mad at me, lover girl," Crash said to Killer when she got tired of having her hair pulled. "We can both have her!"

Poison couldn't stop giggling as her two friends picked her up and tossed her back and forth between them. Even with an audience, it was a good time. "You don't scare me," she told Killer. Then it was Crash's turn to collect tolls as Killer "forced" Poison to her knees, slowly removed her studded leather bra and skirt, and "made" Poison go down on her.

Normally Crash didn't check out the booths too much. All she saw were hands and green paper. But one member of the audience had pissed her off. The window on his booth had been open since they came onstage, and he hadn't tipped once. So she stomped over to that cubicle and glared at its occupant. "What do you think this is, Catholic Charities?" she snapped. Then she saw the tits. "Hey, there's a girl over here!" she yelled. The click of spike heels told her that Killer and Poison were on their way.

■ ■

There was just enough room in the booth to stand up and whack off. Bo wondered why there was a machine on one wall. Who wanted to watch movies if there was a live show? Then the three space tramps came onstage, and she thought she would die. They looked like the beautiful, come-fuck-me straight girls that she didn't dare talk to in the clubs. Because the stage was higher than the floor, she could look right up their dresses. But their shoes were even more intriguing than their pussies. Bo loved high-heeled shoes. The tall, thin spikes looked like they should punch holes in the floor. How could anybody do all those turns and kicks in them? Her heart was in her mouth, for fear one of the dancers would slip or fall. But they kept their balance. It was magic.

The first time her window came down, it scared her so bad she almost peed. What was she supposed to do, leave the booth and let somebody else have it? She opened the door a crack, but nobody else was exiting. "Are you going?" asked a hopeful onlooker who'd been too slow to get a booth.

"Well, I don't want to, but I can't see anything."

He gave her a strange look. Bo braced herself for a homophobic comment. But all he said was, "You gotta put a token in to make the window come up."

Feeling like a complete idiot, Bo muttered, "Oh. Thanks," and closed the door. It was warped, so she yanked it into place. With the window down, it was really dark in there. She had to feel for the token slot. When the window came up, it revealed something even more wonderful than solitary dancers. They were tussling with each other! She got out another token and held it over the slot, ready to drop it in the minute her view was threatened. The leather girl with the black ponytail sure had a hard hand. But her friend in the red corset seemed to like it. A lot of girls had hinted around about kinky stuff like that with Bo — like the one who was coming over on Saturday night. It made Bo happy to know she was projecting the right kind of tough image. But when it came down to actually tying somebody up or getting rough with them, somehow the timing was never quite right. Either they wanted it too much, or she wasn't sure they really wanted it after all. Too much pressure or something. Besides, she didn't *really* want to hurt anybody. Did she?

Meanwhile, all the hair-pulling and slapping onstage was making Bo's stomach feel funny. It was awfully hot in there. She reached for her right pocket to get her bandana, realized she was keeping it in the other pocket this week, fished it out, and wiped her face. She shouldn't let herself get conned like this. It was just an act, breeder chicks faking lesbian sex, but she pulled her T-shirt up anyway and pinched her own tits. Hard.

The window began to descend, and she dropped a token. As it came up, Bo's zipper went down. She had to work her jeans down over her hips to get her fingers in between her lips. She had a moment of panic, imagining cops barging in, but even the threat of being caught here with her pants down around her ankles made her cunt wetter and plumper. If she put one finger on her clit, it would take a little longer to come, but that would leave one hand free to work her tits. If only she knew why they'd put a glory hole in the Plexiglas. What was it for, kissing the dancers? Gross!

She was so close to coming. Of course, that little Asian girl wasn't really eating out the cat lady, but Bo knew what it would feel like. She knew what it would taste like. To be that helpless — to have all these people watching—

Her vision was blocked again, but not by the window. An angry blonde in red lingerie was plastered against the Plexiglas, looking like she might use her long red nails to claw right through it. "There's a girl in here!" she cried. Bo's arousal was swept away by a flood of shame and fear.

"Hey, what about us?" one of the guys yelled as the other dancers converged on Bo's window. *I have to get out of here,* she thought, dragging at her clothes. She pushed on the door, but it was stuck.

"Leaving so soon?" the brunette crooned. She had taken off everything except her boots, wristbands, and collar. "We were going to put on a special performance just for you. We don't see other dykes in here very often."

"Don't bother, I was just leaving!" Bo panted, wrestling with the door.

"Chicken," said the Asian girl, who was wearing only her gold spike heels.

"Enjoying the show?" the blonde jeered, rotating her hips. She had taken her breasts out of the cups of her merry widow. Bo couldn't stop staring at her bush. All this blatant female nudity and aggressive attitude were making her sweat.

"No," Bo lied, trying to sound defiant. "I'm not enjoying the show."

That offended all of them. "But we're working so hard," the blonde pouted. "Is there something special you'd like to see? Want me to stick that vibrator through the hole so you can lick it?"

"This is sick," Bo blustered. "How can you stand to do this? It's degrading, letting a bunch of men jack off while you squirm and wiggle around."

"Ooh, Crash, degrade me some more!" the Asian girl crooned. They started French-kissing, hands between each other's legs. The sight completely exasperated Bo.

"Cut it out! That's disgusting. You can't fool me. You're just a bunch of mercenary straight bitches. You don't know anything about making love to a woman."

The door shrieked as Killer forced it open. "Is that so?" she hissed, dragging Bo out by her belt. One minute, Bo was staring at the pissed-off vixen's pierced eyebrow, and the next minute she was on the floor, staring at her boot heels. Then her hands were being cuffed behind her back, and she was up on her feet again. The rapid changes in altitude made Bo dizzy. This girl ate her spinach.

The bouncer left his post by the turnstile. "Have we got a problem here, Killer?" he asked, eyeing Bo.

"Not anymore," Killer told him. "We just got a new whipping boy. Maybe this one will be a good dog instead of a bad dog. Are you a good dog, honey?" She punched Bo's upper arm. "Huh? Answer me!"

"Well, you'd better get her in back before the manager sees her," he said. "She just went out to get a prescription filled, and she'll be back any minute."

A buzzer sounded, signifying the end of the act. Bo thought about putting up a fight. But where was she going to go in these damned handcuffs? Killer shoved, and Bo went. Men were coming out of the stage booths, and most of them had hurt feelings. A few of them looked like they might complain, but Killer said clearly, "The first one of you bozos to whine at me is eighty-sixed. The show's over."

"You could do that to me," one of them said wistfully, ogling Bo's handcuffs.

"You'd like it too much," Killer said scornfully. Bo couldn't believe her ears. This girl was *naked*. How could she talk to a room full of men like that when they could see everything she had? Wasn't she afraid of anything?

Killer hustled Bo into the dressing room and tumbled her onto the floor. Bo's face was buried in a pile of nylon, spandex, lace, PVC, satin, and suede unmentionables. Something — probably a pair of high heels someone had left on the floor — dug into her stomach. The tiny room smelled like perfume, makeup, hair spray, girl sweat, and pussy. Bo thought she might suffocate. She much preferred the smell of motor oil and bourbon. All these filmy, stretchy, whispery, see-through, tight, gauzy, wispy, shiny, femmy things undid her. Clothing should be durable, comfortable, sturdy, and protect you from the elements. How did they get in and out of these rags? Where did they find the moxie to walk around half-naked? How could they trust garments that were held together with itsy-bitsy hooks and eyes or skinny pieces of elastic?

Then Killer kicked her lightly in the ribs. "Look at me, home boy."

"I am not your fucking home boy," Bo said hotly. But she refused to roll over.

"You're right," somebody else said, "but it's not very smart to argue with Killer. Hey, get off my torts textbook! Do you know how much that damn book cost me?"

The next kick was not so gentle. Bo gave up and rolled onto her side, just far enough to see all of them. God, they gave off a ferocious aura, like the three witches in *Macbeth*. "Take off these cuffs," she said, without much hope that they would.

Everybody laughed. Bo did not enjoy being their punch line. "You know my name," Killer said. "This is Poison, and the B-52 girl is Crash."

Bo refused to play along. She wasn't telling them anything.

"I guess we'll just have to call you shit head," Poison said.

"Or pig boy," Crash added.

"Or dead meat," Killer concluded.

Such lovely options. "Bo," the butch on the floor muttered. "My name is Bo."

"That must be Bo as in 'Boy, am I stupid,'" Crash said thoughtfully. "Don't you think it's rude to call a girl a tramp when she's only trying to show you a good time, baby boy?"

Killer snorted. "Baby boy is right. What are you, lover, all of seventeen?"

"I'm twenty-two," Bo snarled. "And you look old enough to be my mother."

"That's one," Killer said softly. "We'll just run a tab for you, shall we? Poison, what's she got on her?"

Poison knelt and rummaged through Bo's pockets. The Swiss Army knife drew gales of hilarity. "I'll take custody of this," Poison said, shaking it under Bo's nose. "This little toad-sticker won't protect you from us, sugar."

"Give me back my knife!" Bo shouted.

"Shut the fuck up!" Crash snarled, looking nervously over her shoulder. "The walls have ears."

Killer leaned down and spoke to Bo. Her lips were an inch from Bo's nose. "Don't be dumb, my little lamb. None of us happens to like your little toy, so when we're done with you, if you're a good boy, you'll get it all back. *Capeche?*"

"Look, this is getting completely out of hand," Bo said. "If you let me go *right now*, I won't call the cops. Okay?"

"Woojums," Crash said tenderly. "If you do absolutely every little thing we say, *we* won't call the cops and report you for breaking and entering. Okay?"

Bo muttered something under her breath.

"Was that an epithet?" Poison asked, her eyes wide. "I believe it was a sexist epithet, Killer." She took one step closer to Bo and slapped her across the face. The stinging blow brought tears to Bo's eyes. "This is a very small place. We simply don't have room for inflammatory hate rhetoric in here."

"I don't know about you girls, but dancing always makes me horny," Killer said, giving Bo a very unmotherly smile.

"Oh, yes, I feel almost compelled to have an orgasm," Crash affirmed. Poison didn't say anything, so Crash nudged her.

"Ouch! Definitely."

"So let's just fix our little boy toy up here so she has some back support," Killer said, and backed Bo into the corner. "No escape attempts," she warned her, and showed her the handcuff key. "Crash has got a gun in her purse. Don't you, dear?"

Crash obediently stuck her hand in her purse and pointed it at Bo. "Yeah. Don't move, sucker."

"Oh, bullshit, she does not have a—" Suddenly Bo was looking down the muzzle of a Beretta.

"It's licensed, too," Crash explained. "I used to be a security guard. If I ever get off the waiting list, I'm going to be one of the city's finest. Think I'll look good in blue?"

Killer took advantage of Bo's surprise to remove one of the cuffs and lock it around a water pipe. "Don't do any Samson imitations," she warned Bo. "It's a hot-water pipe. All you'll do is scald yourself. Now suck me off. And make it snappy. I have to be back onstage in five minutes."

They stared at each other for several long seconds — the triumphant bitch goddesses and their flustered, hijacked tourist. "Maybe she doesn't know how to eat cunt," Poison said helpfully. "Maybe she's one of those awful straight girls who gets a short haircut and hangs out in lesbian bars pretending she belongs there."

"Well?" Killer said impatiently. "What about it? Do you know what to do with a piece of cherry pie, stud, or is your tongue just for making rude comments to your betters?"

They were not going to let her go. It was no use fighting them. Whoever would have thought that girls in lipstick and pushup bras could be so mean? "No," Bo said finally, looking at the floor. "I'll do it."

It was hard to get her tongue all the way into Killer's silky inner lips. Handcuffed to the water pipe, she couldn't get her neck to bend at the right angle. But she did her best, and Killer's flexible dancer's hips and slender legs made it easier. Out of the corner of her eye, she noticed the other women changing clothes and refreshing their makeup. Geez, if Bo was going to humiliate herself this way, the least they could do was watch.

"You're good," Killer said, tugging one of her ears. "Do it faster. Not harder, idiot — just faster!"

Killer's inner lips were thin and long, like the two halves of a razorback clam. Her teardrop-shaped clit was very small, like a seed pearl. She seemed to like having Bo's tongue go around it without actually touching it. The thought of biting her was very tempting, but then she'd probably stay handcuffed to this pipe until she starved to death.

"Oh, yes, that's it. Do that!" Killer said, squeezing Bo's head. There was a knock on the dressing room door. One of the other girls told somebody they'd be right out. Killer came silently, biting her own hand. Bo was shaken by the sexual electricity that passed through her own body when Killer peaked. She barely noticed the dancers filing out and shutting the door behind them. They had left one of her hands free. It was the wrong hand, but nothing else was in sight. Wait — there was Poison's vibrator. She'd left it on the floor. Bo had to strain to reach it with her boot toes, but she managed to nudge it within reach.

There was no way she could come sitting down with her pants on. Bo somehow managed to pry her boots off, undo the jeans with one hand, and wiggle out of them. Lucky she didn't believe in underwear. She closed her eyes and tried to remember the exact shape of Killer's clit, the way her palms fit over Bo's ears, the other girls breathing faster as Killer got more excited, how she couldn't escape, couldn't get away, and had no idea what would happen next.

The awkward fingers of her left hand kept rebelling and cramping up. Frustrated, Bo switched the vibrator on and held it against her outer lips. She was embarrassed to even touch the thing. She had seen them in porn shops often enough, in boxes that always had these dopey pictures of women running them over their faces. It felt good, but it kept getting caught in her pubic hair. She tried to point it at her clit, but she was so wet that the head of it somehow slipped down and went into her. It seemed content to stay there, purring away, while Bo stroked her clit.

It just wasn't enough. She needed more, something, anything, to push herself over the edge! She stared around the room, wild-eyed. Right by her left thigh was another love offering from Poison, the discarded pair of tit clamps. Bo could sometimes make herself come just by twisting her own nipples. It was hard to get them on one-handed. Her nipples kept wanting to slip out of the clips. But finally she got both sides to catch.

Oh, God, she was going to come. It was inevitable. Even if the building blew up or her hands fell off, so much pressure had accumulated, Bo knew she would explode. She didn't have Killer's self-control. She heard herself whining, panting, and then saying, "Please, please."

The door opened and Killer walked in. "Yes, you may," Killer said, and jammed her high-heeled shoe between Bo's legs, pinning her hand and the vibrator in place. Bo came with the sharp heel of the dancer's shoe against her perineum. "Come again," Killer said, and jerked on the chain that connected the clamps. She also rocked her heel into Bo's tender flesh. And Bo came again, in terror and shock. "Still want to call the cops?" Killer asked. "No, I didn't think so. Stick around. Pets always get smarter when you play with them."

"Good boy," Crash said, replacing Killer in front of Bo. "Now it's my turn to ride the pony."

Bo guessed it was kind of stupid, but she'd never really noticed before that women liked to come in so many different ways. Crash had coarse pubic hair that made her face burn. Instead of Killer's elegant Art Deco genital geometry, her cunt was built like a '50s diner. It was robust, with shorter, thicker inner lips. The head of her clit was perfectly round and the size of a pencil eraser. She didn't get wet as quickly as Killer. She wanted a lot of long, slow, light strokes with a teasing little flutter at the end. Nobody told Bo that she couldn't, so she kept masturbating while she tried to get Crash to come. For some reason, she kept thinking about the short porn clip she'd seen in the video booth. Was this exactly like that woman sucking cock, or was it completely different? Probably both, Bo decided, though she couldn't have explained why. She was too busy jamming her face into Crash's thighs, sucking her clit like it was a straw buried in a milkshake. The dancer had finally gotten really juicy, and Bo was afraid she'd have to go back onstage before she got off. Finally Crash started pulling her hair — quite a trick, since Bo's flattop was less than an inch long — and tilted her pelvis so Bo's tongue was moving in and out of her cunt. "Yesyesyes," she sang. "Good dog, good dog, good dog," and finally, "Sweet Jesus, yes, good boy!"

Bo felt quite pleased with herself. She leaned against the wall panting. But Crash was looking at her through narrow eyelids. Had she done something wrong? "I always have to tinkle after I come," Crash said delicately, and placed two fingers of her right hand on either side of her clit. The V-shaped fingers lifted her lips a little, and a golden arc of piss sprang through the air.

"Hey, don't pee on my clothes!" Poison snapped.

"Don't worry, I never miss," Crash said sweetly as the last few drops soaked into Bo's T-shirt. "Don't forget us while we're far from home," she smirked, and the dancers left to put on one more show.

"Here," Poison said before she walked out, and dropped a long, thick dildo in Bo's lap. "That teeny thing is only good for fooling around in front of the customers. A big, strong girl like you needs a substantial tool to fuck herself with. There's some lube in my dance bag — the pink one — if you need it."

Bo covered her face with her one free hand. How had she gotten into so much trouble? And why was she having so much fun? Poison was right, she probably didn't need any lube to get that truncheon in her cunt, but it was too embarrassing to go without it. So she wrapped her toes around the straps of Poison's hot pink carryall and dragged it over.

"Who says size doesn't matter?" Bo growled, and worked the head of the dildo in. It was wide enough to make her gasp. The wet T-shirt was going to give her a chill if she didn't keep moving. It sure was funny how things didn't feel the way they looked. Getting slapped looked like the worst thing in the world, but it was actually pretty exciting. It stung a lot, but it made her heart beat faster and her PC muscle jump. The thought of getting pissed on would have made her gag this morning, but now all she could smell was Crash's cunt and her own sex. The wet shirt was like a badge or a medal. She had something that belonged to Crash now. The dancer had given Bo a part of her. You couldn't just abandon somebody you'd pissed on, could you?

She jabbed the dildo in, remembering how it felt to have Killer kick her between the legs. The spike heel was like the point of a knife. It was cruel and relentless, like ... like a woman, Bo realized. Cruelty was a feminine quality. The dancers' willful ways suddenly made sense. Of course they were bossy and nasty and liked to hurt people. Femmes always wanted to be in control. But you weren't supposed to notice it. No, that was one way to get yourself into shit up to your nose hairs. You were supposed to do everything they wanted, before they asked you, and make them think it was all your own idea. Nothing was ever their fault, it was always *your* fault because you were the butch and it was your job to make sure everything went smoothly.

Bo thought she preferred this up-front sexual assault to that silly game. The dildo hurt a little. The hurt made her want to come. But maybe she shouldn't come. Killer seemed to take it for granted that she would wait until she had permission. Maybe she was supposed to wait. Maybe if she waited, it would make Killer happy.

As soon as Bo thought about resisting orgasm, it became much more likely. Of course, she could just quit touching herself, but it was so boring being stuck here with nothing but a broken chair and a cracked mirror for company. She strained her ears, trying to see if the last song in the dancer's set was playing yet.

It was hard to wait. Hard to wait. Hard. Hard. So hard. So big. So—

"You *are* a pig," Killer said, amused. "Look at you, jacking off all covered with piss, just waiting for somebody to come and use you or hurt you or tell you what to do. Aren't you lucky that we bother to take an interest in you?" She stalked over to Bo and removed the tit clamps with one smooth jerk. Bo had forgotten they were there. Her nipples had gone numb while she was eating out Crash. She wanted to shriek, but Killer was waiting to slap her if she did. So she just whimpered a little.

"Well?" Killer said. "Answer me!"

"Well — what?" Bo stammered.

"Aren't you lucky that we're training you?"

Is that what's happening? Bo wondered. "Yes, I'm lucky, ma'am."

Killer looked even more amused. "Now I'm a ma'am. I suppose it's a step up from being your mama. Just call me mistress. I think Poison wants to check you out."

Poison was chewing a large wad of gum. She nonchalantly blew a bubble that was bigger than Bo's face, popped it, and sucked it back into her peony red mouth. "You betcha," she said, sticking the gum to one corner of the mirror. Crash peeled it off with the tips of her fingers and dropped it in the trash.

"Put some lube on your hand," Poison told her. Bo managed, awkwardly. "Now put your fingers up my ass," the dancer ordered, and positioned Bo's head so her tongue was poised in just the right spot. She wanted a hard, flicking motion just above her clit, which was slightly pointed, and a lot of in-and-out work between the cheeks of her muscular behind. Bo's arm rapidly got tired, but Poison was not about to let her rest. "Come on, you can do anything for twenty minutes," she snapped at Bo. "Fuck me like you mean it, put your shoulder into it, and keep that tongue busy too. I want to come all over your face, I want to suck your arm into my ass, I want to eat you alive in little bloody chunks, slave boy, boy toy, bet you never really fucked a girl in your life. You're probably used to taking it up the ass, not dishing it out. Lowlife trash, you come sneaking in here thinking you can get your rocks off and then sneak out again, serves you right getting caught. Fuck me! Fuck me! More! More! More!"

She came briefly, but very hard. Bo's shoulder hit the wall. "Okay, stop it, I'm done now," Poison said, and walked off to change her G-string.

And that was how it went for the rest of the night. Killer eventually took the dildo away from Bo, saying, "We don't want our puppy to get spoiled." Bo gathered from the high energy the dancers brought into the dressing room that they were doing very well out there. She was startled when Killer took the handcuffs off, made her strip, and said, "Go in the bathroom and clean yourself up. Then come back here and we'll dress you up. Make it snappy. Poison already called the limousine."

"My bike—," Bo said weakly.

"I already had somebody take it home for you," Killer said.

Bo gave her a horrified look.

"Well, your keys were right in your jacket pocket," Killer said impatiently. "And you do live at the same address that's on your checks, right? So what's the problem? Eddy's wife knows from Harleys. She's been taking him to runs for years. She isn't going to fuck your bike up. Look, if you don't want to go out with us, you can always walk home. Naked."

Once again, doing as she was told seemed like much the best option. Bo tiptoed into the corridor, and hoped the only door she could see led to a bathroom. The toilet seemed to have indigestion, but a few minutes' work with the plunger fixed that. The sink wasn't very clean, and only the cold-water tap worked, but Bo doused some paper towels and sponged herself off. Shivering, she crept back into the room, and was astonished to see that all the mess that had covered the floor ankle-deep had vanished into three little bags.

Killer, Crash, and Poison looked ready to hit the streets of a sex zone on some perverted, faraway Amazon planet. Killer was wearing a strapless black leather dress with a studded bodice. The purple tips of her ponytail swept her white shoulders and back. Bo wanted to bite her, to leave a round red mark on that fair and very fragile-looking skin. The skirt was slit so high in the back, you could almost see Killer's buns. Her black stockings were decorated with a cobra on each ankle. The snakes had rhinestone eyes. And the heels of her pumps were even taller than the boots she'd worn onstage. Poison was wearing a body-harness made out of leather straps and fine silver chains. The carefully draped chains hid her nipples, and a tiny leather strap just barely concealed her sex. Her shoulders were covered with spiked leather pads, and she wore matching spiked gauntlets on each arm. She had traded in her gold pumps for a pair of knee-high engineer boots with steel toes. Bo wondered where the dancer got such butch footwear in tiny sizes. She had to wear three pairs of socks with *her* engineer boots. Crash was in a high-necked, long-sleeved PVC catsuit that had zippers in its crotch and over the nipples. She had combed out her beehive and had pulled her long, blonde hair through a hole in the back of a patent-leather helmet. Bo couldn't tell where the suit ended and Crash's boots began. Her outfit was a seamless piece of glossy midnight, except for the zippers that protected and flaunted her erogenous zones.

"You didn't have any underwear," Killer said, "so you'll have to wear these."

"These" were a pair of lilac tap pants with black lace around the waist and legs. Bo's whole body went rigid. "I will not!" she said.

Crash sighed and put her in a half nelson. Poison picked up Bo's feet, one at a time, and Killer smoothed the lingerie into place. "We can't have you running around with a bare butt," Killer soothed. "You'll catch your death of cold. Nobody will know what you have on under your jeans. Now get into your Levi's and your boots."

"You can wear my tank top," Poison said, tossing Bo six square inches of black spandex.

"I don't think that's big enough for me," Bo said weakly, tucking the cuffs of her jeans into her boots.

"Let's dress the baby," Killer said. "Put ooh widdle awms up, diddums. There we go."

Bo was afraid to look at herself in the mirror. But Crash turned her bodily to face it. "Nice delts and lats," she said approvingly. "How come butches have all the cleavage, Bo?"

"I hate you all," Bo said unhappily.

"Aren't we the lucky ones?" Killer said coldly. "Just for that, you can wear some lipstick on your way out. So everybody knows who you're with."

Bo tried to struggle, but Poison and Crash held her in place. How could they get so many muscles just dancing? With a firm and practiced hand, Killer made a bright red Cupid's-bow mouth on Bo's trembling lips. "They ought to be that red anyway, considering how much pussy you've chowed down today," Crash snickered.

The dancers hustled Bo to the front of the store. Bo noticed that Crash and Killer were taller than she was. Must be the shoes. A black stretch limousine was parked in the bus zone in front of the store. "Easy come, easy go," a middle-aged woman told them bitterly, staring at the luxurious car.

"Oh, you're welcome, we loved making all that money for you," Crash said, blowing her a kiss.

"She knows a hell of a lot more about going than she does about coming," Poison muttered. The chauffeur was opening their door. "Next time that'll be your job," she said, jabbing Bo in the ribs. *Next time?*

■ ■

The seats in the back of the limo were so wide that the three dancers sat side by side. "Put her on the floor," they had told the chauffeur, and he did as they asked as if there was nothing unusual about their request. So Bo was lying on the carpeted floor, listening to the engine, watching Crash put a tape in the stereo while Poison uncorked a big, green bottle and Killer took three shrimp cocktails out of the little refrigerator.

"Where to first, ladies?" asked the chauffeur. He must be using an intercom. There was a pane of soundproof glass between him and the passenger compartment.

"Over the bridge and back again," Killer said. "We need to unwind. Then we'll visit the club."

"Very good, madam," he said, and did not speak again.

"Impressed?" Killer asked, nudging Bo with her toe.

"Yeah, I guess I am," Bo had to admit.

"Sex workers make a lot of money," Poison bragged. "Especially if they have somebody like Killer to invest it. You should see our coop. It's a nice place, but it's too big for us to keep up with. Too bad you aren't looking for a job. We need a new houseboy. Somebody who won't put my lingerie in the washing machine because they're too lazy to get out the Woolite."

"Somebody who can cook something besides pork chops and baked potatoes," Crash sighed, digging into her shrimp cocktail. "Somebody who dusts."

"Shut up," Killer said sharply. "This little asshole has to make it through the night without disgracing us first."

Bo couldn't see any higher than the ankles of the women who were taking her for this wild ride. Her eyes went back and forth between the poisonous snakes that sprang from Killer's six-inch heels; Poison's carefully polished engineer boots; and Crash's spike-heeled boots. She was mesmerized by the rhinestone eyes of the snakes, their enraged, inflated hoods; the hint of a reflection of her own face in Poison's steel toes; the spurs that Crash cheerfully dug into the carpeted floor of the limo. Inside her 501s, the lilac-colored tap pants bunched up and slid around. The lace scratched. What would her friends think if they could see her now?

"Hey, good dog," Killer said caustically, "want a shrimp?" She held out a piece of seafood, dripping red sauce. Bo opened her mouth and took it carefully from her fingers. "Don't muss your lipstick," Killer added. "What would your buddies think if they could see you now, Bo?"

Poison and Crash laughed. Bo startled like an animal that's been hit with a BB gun. "I think they'd laugh at me," Bo said slowly, "just like y'all do."

That shut them up. "Yeah, they probably would," Killer said judiciously. "But they'd be jealous too, honey, and don't you ever forget it. More shrimp?"

Bo let the dancers feed her crackers smeared with brie, pinches of caviar. Poison tilted some liquid from her glass into Bo's mouth, and she swallowed before realizing it was champagne. "Hey, I can't drink that," she protested.

"What are you, allergic to sulfites?" Crash asked. "You gonna keel over dead if we let you eat at the salad bar? No trips to the Sizzler for you, sissy boy."

"No, I—"

"She doesn't drink, asshole," Killer snapped. "Here, Bo, this is Calistoga. Wash your mouth out."

It seemed only appropriate to kiss Killer's shoe to thank her. Bo didn't think she could feel it through the finely crafted leather. But Killer rolled her foot to the side and pressed the toe into Bo's throat. "You have good instincts, baby," she said. "But you're supposed to ask permission."

Bo hesitated. "It's a great way to get the lipstick off your mouth," Poison pointed out. That kind of spoiled it.

"I wasn't thinking about that," Bo said. "I'm just not used to asking for things."

"Oh?" Crash said bitterly. "You think butch girls like you ought to just grab whatever they want, without asking?"

"No," Bo sighed. "Usually I don't grab anything, I just wait and hope whatever I want will come to me. If you don't want anything, you can't get hurt when you don't get it. It's dangerous to ask for things, Crash."

"That's Mistress Crash to you," the blonde said loftily, and rested her boot heels on Bo's legs.

"Aren't you the deep one," Poison said, cuddling the hard shells of her boot toes into Bo's stomach.

"Quit thinking so much," Killer advised, and stroked Bo's cheek with her soles.

"Can I kiss them?" Bo whispered.

"Honey, it's what you were born to do," Killer replied. "Just don't slobber on me. I hate it when my shoes get wet."

Once more, Bo lost track of time. She was busy creating new yoga positions to gain access to the footwear of all three women. She had never imagined doing anything like this. She had watched a leather boy set up a boot-shining stand at a benefit once, and wondered why the crowd of men who surrounded him seemed so intense, like a pack of coon hounds. The boy's daddy had made Bo get in front of the men who were waiting and ordered the kid, who was kneeling, wearing nothing but a jockstrap, his hands and face streaked with black polish, to make her cowboy boots shine. The boot boy had stoically done his job, but Bo didn't find it very exciting. She knew Daddy Rick from meetings, and he always greeted her with a smile, but they weren't exactly friends. She couldn't tell if he was doing this to let everybody know he thought she belonged in this bar, or to subtly punish his "son."

This act of worship was very different. It was like taking somebody's panties off with your teeth. You had to be delicate. Not biting — not tearing anything — was what made it erotic. If you were really lucky, the girl you were with got so excited that she forgot to take her underwear home with her. Bo blushed when she thought about the secret collection she kept tucked between her mattress and the box spring. She didn't think anybody would forget their shoes that easily. And who would have guessed that the smell of perfume and leather, mingled with a little sweat, could be such an aphrodisiac? It shouldn't be as exciting as smelling somebody's wet cunt and knowing you made it juicy. But above the foot (which might kick you away), there was the ankle, and above the ankle the muscular calf (which would feel so nice draped over your shoulder), then the knees, which might part, then the thighs, round and soft with promise, and after that—

Maybe after that came even more work, more personal service, for a good dog who had a careful, soft, and respectful mouth. Bo hoped so.

"Enough," Killer said firmly. "Stop it, Bo. We're here. We're getting out now. Oh, don't look so upset. We're taking you with us. Poison, would you do something with our guest?"

Bo had to force herself to stop staring at the two spots of color that decorated Killer's cheekbones and look at the other dancer. The two leather bands around Poison's upper arms came off, snapped together, and went around Bo's neck. "It'll have to do until we get our real collar back from the bad dog," Crash said, attaching a leash and extracting Bo from the limo.

Get what back from who? Bo wondered.

"We'll page you," Killer told the driver. "Why don't you go get dinner?"

"Certainly, madam," he replied, and the car floated away.

"Charley would kill to be in your place," Poison snickered, tapping Bo between the shoulder blades.

"Charley can go fuck himself," Killer said. "The last thing I want after I get off work is one more prick hanging around looking for a freebie."

This looked like an industrial zone. The streets were empty. But the block around the bar was crowded with motorcycles, parked so close they almost touched. The three dancers strolled into the club, which Bo recognized as one of those places that was always getting shut down by the city for violating the fire code or selling liquor to minors. What was it called, Jack's? Something like that. No, Jax! That was it. Bo's date for Saturday night had talked about coming down here for a drink, like it was some kind of big deal to walk into this joint.

The bouncer waved them through without asking for ID or a cover charge. The bartender — one of the biggest women Bo had ever seen — shouted, "God help us all, it's the Furies incarnate."

Bo's captors waved back, looking smug. "We're regulars here," Poison explained, adjusting her chain harness so her nipples showed. "Kat likes us because we're troublemakers."

"There's a table," Crash said, pointing somewhere into the crowd. Somebody snatched at one of the zippers on her catsuit, and she elbowed them in the face. "You're a bigger asshole than your asshole," she told the unlucky and unsuccessful woman who had dared touch her without permission. That poor soul was clutching her nose. "I'd put some ice on that if I were you," Crash sneered.

"Go save that table for us," Killer ordered, slapping her gloves against her palm. Crash put the end of the leash in Bo's mouth, and she went without thinking. A couple of the patrons barked at her, but she kept on going until she saw the vacant table. She stood behind one chair and put her hands on the backs of the other two.

"Perfect," Poison said, positioning her hard little rump on the seat. Her legs were too short for her feet to touch the floor, so she propped her engineer boots up on the legs of the table. Bo thought that was pretty cute. "I want more champagne."

"I am not holding your head while you puke all night," Killer said severely. She had seated herself like a grand duchess, and Bo was trying to figure out how she managed to sit down in that tight skirt without splitting it up the back.

"If you make me switch to something else, I'll get sick for sure," Poison replied. "Dom Perignon for me, Bo. Want to help me out, Crash?"

"Whatever," Crash said. She had not taken a seat. She remained standing, drumming her red claws on the back of a chair and scanning the crowd. Apparently she did not find the party she was looking for, because she suddenly blew air out of her nose, picked up the chair, turned it around, and sat on it backwards. "Champagne is as close as I'm going to get to Paris tonight, girlfriends."

"I'm sure Bo could take a few lessons in French," Killer said coldly. "A Virgin Mary, with extra Tabasco," she told Bo. "Go on! Don't *worry* about the *money*, Bo, we run a tab here."

Crash intercepted her before she left the table and unsnapped the leash. "Be prompt, or this goes back on," she warned.

More barking followed Bo to the bar. She wondered what that was all about. It didn't sound unfriendly. It was more like a cheer. The next time somebody howled at her, she howled back. This caused a moment or two of relative silence. She was still close enough to the table to hear the three dancers chortle. "Still think she's going to embarrass us, Killer?" Poison demanded.

Bo fought her way to the bar, where a short, redheaded dyke in a leather vest and jeans was arguing with the mountainous, blonde bartender. "You have to quit covering up for Lolly," the redhead said. "Look at this mess. How are you supposed to tend bar all by yourself on a Friday night?"

"Aw, Reid, ease up, I'm doing okay. You're just mad 'cause I can't take a break and sneak out to the patio and give you a blowjob. We weren't supposed to see each other tonight anyway. Why don't you go home and take a nap? I'll come over after I get off work."

"Fuck that," Reid said. "This is not the way friends treat one another, Kat."

"What do you want me to do, get her fired? In case you haven't heard, there's a recession out there. I am not going to be responsible for somebody getting laid off when there's no place else for them to go. Lolly's in love, and when she's in love, she's just not herself. She'll be back again as soon as the bitch dumps her or they run out of poppers."

"Codependents are a pain in the ass, aren't they?" Bo said sympathetically to the redhead. Reid turned around quick, like somebody had bitten her in the ass, and snapped, "Who asked you?" The keys on the left side of her belt jingled.

"Nobody had to," Bo replied. "It's a free country."

Reid snorted. She turned her back on Kat and her talkative customer and leaned against the bar, scanning the crowd like American radar looking for Russian jets. Kat shrugged, almost stuck her tongue out at the back of Reid's head, then thought better of it.

"You need a tray, right?" Kat asked. "Tell me what your keepers are drinking. No, I'll tell you. One bottle of champagne, two glasses, and a Virgin Mary, right?"

"Extra Tabasco," Bo added, trying to process the idea of these two women being in a relationship and the bartender being a bottom.

"You look like a Southern Comfort girl yourself," Kat suggested.

"Calistoga," Bo said, smiling.

"We don't have any more that's cold," Kat said, sounding harassed. She arranged other beverages on a tray. "We need some ice, but it doesn't look like anybody's going out for any."

"All right!" Reid shouted. "I will get on my friggin' bike and somehow find a place in this godforsaken neighborhood that has ice, and try to convince myself I don't look like a complete and total dweeb running errands for you because your coworker had to pick this week of all weeks to go out on a toot!"

"Don't do me any fucking favors!" Kat snarled. But Reid kept shoving through the crowd. "Don't let those hellcats get too riled up, now," the bartender told Bo, pushing the tray toward her. "I got enough on my hands tonight without them swingin' on the chandeliers and slashing people's tires."

Bo put the tray up high on one hand, the way real waiters did it, and bayed at the women in front of her. It didn't exactly sound like a wolf pack baying at a National Geographic film crew, but Bo figured she could refine her sound effects as time went on. The patrons of Jax let her cut through like the pointer on an Etch-A-Sketch.

"What took you so long?" Poison complained. "Don't let that cork fly — oh, you know how. Never mind."

Bo unwrapped the little, white towel from the neck of the green bottle, put the cork on the table, and poured two flutes of champagne without releasing all of the bubbles.

"Kat and Reid are having a fight, huh?" Crash said. "I knew it could never last. Butch-on-butch is such a joke."

"Shut up," Killer said. "What about your little fling with Belinda, huh? Surely you remember her — the girl who did the snake act at the Manslaughter Brothers' Cow Palace." She took a sip of her Virgin Mary. "Hot!" she sputtered. "Good," she added, biting on the celery stick. It snapped like a little bone.

"That was hardly butch-on-butch," Crash said, holding out her glass for some more champagne. Bo poured carefully. There was no chair for her, so she guessed she was supposed to just stand up and wait on everybody. She filched a bowl of peanuts from the closest table and offered them to Killer, who took a few but did not put them in her mouth because she was too busy hassling Crash.

"Yeah, well, how would you have responded to the suggestion that you get a crewcut if you were going to strap it on with her, huh?" she asked. "I mean, that *is* why you broke up, isn't it? Because one of you wasn't butch enough?"

"No," Crash snapped, putting her glass down almost hard enough to snap the stem. "We broke up because she gave me crabs, if you must know. Did I forget to mention the torrid night we spent in your bed, darling?"

"You're awful," Killer said, smiling happily.

"I think we're all pretty awful," Poison said contentedly. "Isn't it wonderful? Bo, do you smoke cigarettes?"

"No."

"No what?"

"No, uh, mistress. I don't smoke cigarettes. I do carry a few around with me, though, for the street people. So they'll leave my bike alone."

Poison gave Killer a significant glance.

"Stop that," Killer said irritably. "I know it would be nice to have a boy who doesn't smoke. I'm as sick of Donna's dirty ashtrays as you are. But for godsake, Poison, she can't even say the word 'mistress' without stammering. She doesn't know a single thing about the scene. Do you really want to clutter up our lives with a novice who will probably cut and run the first time somebody teases her about giving it up for a bunch of girls?"

Crash, still smarting from Killer's sarcastic remarks about her affair with another dancer, saw her chance to get even. "Well, I'm so glad you were born with a bullwhip in your hand," she said lightly. "I think Poison's right. If we ever see Bad Dog again, we ought to sic Bo on her. Winter's coming. It's time for indoor sports. And I can think of a lot worse ways to spend evenings in front of the fireplace than some training sessions with this little hunk. She knows enough to wear her red hanky on the left. That's all the etiquette I want out of my houseboy."

Bo looked from one woman to the other as they took turns talking. Nobody looked at her. That seemed a little weird. Shouldn't somebody ask her what she thought about all of this? Or explain it? "Hey," she finally interjected.

The silence was frosty. "Yes?" Killer finally said.

"Don't you think it would be a nice idea to ask me what I want before you all go dividing me up like a pizza?"

The three dancers exchanged amused and outraged glances. "No," Killer said firmly. "That would not be a nice idea. Shut up, Bo. We'll let you talk later."

Bo shrugged and let her mind wander while the bickering resumed.

"See that stool over there?" Crash asked her, reeling Bo in by her collar. She ran her fingernails down the skin between Bo's breasts. Even through the spandex, Bo's nipples became visibly more firm.

"I want you to grab that empty bar stool and drag it over by this table. Do you understand me, butchy boy?"

Bo nodded. Her only fear was that Crash would keep hanging on to her collar so long that somebody would sit down on the bar stool. But Crash gave her a little shove, and she got to the only empty seat in the house just a split second before somebody's fanny descended upon it. The crowd hooted at her as she wrestled the awkward piece of furniture back to the table. *Why does everybody in this place seem to know somethin' I don't know?* Bo wondered. *Maybe 'cause they do. Shit.*

"Bend over it," Crash instructed Bo, speaking over her shoulder.

"I — I — what?" Bo sputtered.

"Bend over," Poison piped up. She pushed her chair back and walked over to Bo, who was trying to follow directions and feeling like a horse's neck. Poison stood by Bo's head and leaned forward, pinning her shoulders down. "Remember me?" she said. Her soft belly was plastered against the top of Bo's head, and the smell of her juicy, bossy little cunt made Bo's nose itch with lust.

"Just what do you think you're doing?" Killer said flatly, trying to make Crash back down.

"Come on, dearie, she already has one demerit. You said so yourself in the dressing room. So let me give her a spanking. That should make it pretty clear whether she's got the right qualifications for the job."

Bo could barely hear this conversation. Poison's thighs were partially blocking her ears. But she heard Killer and Crash's high heels clicking as the two friends came to stand beside her. Bo thought it was Killer who touched her on the small of her back, sliding her hand under Bo's spandex shirt and grazing the skin with her long fingernails. Then Poison moved away from her, and Bo could tell it was definitely Killer who was talking.

"You've had a very busy day," Killer said. "I'm sure when you walked into Sugar and Spice, you never expected to find yourself in this position."

"Butcha are, Blanche, ya are!" Poison crowed.

"Be quiet, please," Killer said severely. "Bo has some very serious thinking to do. When I gave you a demerit in the dressing room, I really had no right to do that. You have no agreement with us that gives us the right to discipline you or order you around. So now you have to choose. If you want to stay with us for the rest of the night, you have to let Crash spank you. Right here in the bar. If you'd like to go home, I'll give you some cab fare. No hard feelings, but if we run into you again, we probably won't remember who you are. There are so many butch bottoms who would give their eyeteeth to be where you are right now that I'm sure we won't have any trouble replacing the bad dog who currently calls itself our house-boy. If you can take the spanking without trying to get up off the bar stool, we can talk about a more permanent arrangement. If you find that you can't tolerate being paddled, I'm afraid we'll have to put an ad up on the bulletin board here and start interviewing applicants. Crash and Poison mostly care about your strong right arm, darlin', but I want to make sure your hide is tough enough to deal with my strong right arm."

Now Bo knew what that phrase "got your tit caught in a wringer" meant. What the hell was a butch bottom? She was so wet that she wasn't sure she could stand up and walk away from the bar stool. She would probably slip across the floor like somebody who just stepped on a bar of soap. She looked at Poison. The dancer gave her a wicked smile. No wonder she had a white stripe, that little skunk. She obviously didn't care if Bo succeeded or failed. Either outcome would entertain her. Bo sighed and glanced at Crash. The blonde's attention was focused on Killer. So Bo looked that way too. Both of Killer's eyebrows were raised. "Well?" she demanded. "All you have to do is choose."

"Then I choose to ask for a spanking," Bo said defiantly. "Please, ma'am. Uh, ladies."

Poison applauded and scampered over to the bar stool, where she once again pinned Bo's shoulders to the padded seat. Crash threw one arm across the small of Bo's back. She let her other hand rest on Bo's denim-clad butt.

"No," Killer said meanly, deliberately pitching her voice so that Bo and probably everybody else in the bar could hear her. "No pants."

Bo froze. That meant everybody would see the lingerie the dancers had forced her to wear. She was mortified. But her clammy fingers were already unbuttoning her jeans and pushing them down. "Fine," she said, and left it at that. If she made a longer speech, her voice would shake.

Crash ran her palm over the slippery, pastel purple cloth. God, she had big hands for a girl. "We'll do one soft, four medium, and one hard," she decided. "On each side, of course."

Bo kept her teeth together, anticipating the use of great force. She was surprised by the mildness of the blows. Was Crash going easy on her, or did she simply not hit people as hard as Killer had hit her? Could it be that she was actually disappointed that it didn't hurt more? Wasn't that a puzzle! It didn't occur to her that Crash was playing a little mistress game with Killer, making sure that the new boy didn't flunk out of class.

Bo's face was bright pink when she straightened up, but she figured that was only natural. She'd been hanging practically upside down. The three dancers were back at their table, sipping their drinks. Crash looked like a kitty with canary feathers up its nose, and Killer was obviously fuming. Bo tried not to look beyond that little table. But as she raised her britches, Bo came face-to-face with the big bartender. Kat's knowing eyes made Bo blush tomato red. To hell with those mean, if entertaining, bitches. Kat had seen the shameful undergarments. Another butch — a senior dyke — knew what she had let these femmes do to her. Bo wanted to run and hide.

"Hey, there, little dog," Kat said softly. "You're a good boy. Did you know that? Well, you are. You're being very good."

Bo squared her shoulders, took a deep breath, and whispered, "Thanks." But Kat was already at the other end of the bar, waiting on customers, and probably never even heard her. Bo took another deep breath and then dared to look around at the other dykes in the bar. Nobody seemed to be pointing or staring at her. Was that scorn she saw in the few faces that turned toward her — or was it envy?

"Did I pass your little test?" Bo demanded.

Killer looked ready to jump on her for that. But somebody rammed her from behind, and the table slid forward. Drinks slopped out of their glasses. "You!" Killer said angrily.

"Donna!" Kat called out warningly. "Don't go stirring shit in my bar!"

"What do they expect, dressed up like that?" Donna jeered. "They're a walking advertisement for sexual harassment! They just get so excited, I can't help myself. I have to let them know how they really make me feel." And she grabbed her crotch.

Bo thought this must be the bad dog that the dancers had been complaining about ever since she met them. Donna was as tall as Killer and outweighed her by at least forty pounds. She had short hair that curled like black sheep's wool and liquid, dark brown collie eyes. Bo had last seen that look in the eyes of a dog that belonged to an uncle of hers. Whenever it came around to lick your hand and fawn on you, you could bet that it had killed another chicken. Bo wrinkled her nose at the smell of marijuana and gin. What an uncouth combination.

"Why all the long faces? It's not like I *raped* anybody," Donna jeered. "I'm just sayin' hello." She leaned into Killer's face. "Hello!" she shouted. "Where have you been? You're all *late*. I thought I'd have to take a doorknob home if I wanted to get laid tonight." She took the cigarette from behind her ear and held it under Poison's nose. "Gimme a light," she whined. "Who do I have to fuck to get a match around here?"

"You're fired," Killer said firmly, pushing her away "So give us back our collar, Bad Dog, and get out."

"Fired? You can't fire me! I'll sue. Besides, who's going to pay my tab?" Donna blustered.

"From now on, you'll have to pay your own fucking way," Poison told her.

Donna took a simple leather dog collar out of her back pocket and threw it at Killer, who caught it in one hand. Then she pursed her lips and spit at her.

Kat was hustling down the bar with a sap in her hand. But Bo was faster. She reached out, grabbed the interloper by her earlobe, and twisted. Donna shrieked and fell to her knees.

"You're pulling out my earrings!" she yelled.

"I certainly hope so," Bo replied, and dug her fingernails in a little deeper. She took off toward the front door of the bar, and Donna followed her, duck-walking on her knees.

"You bastard," Donna swore. "I hate you. What did they do, promise to let you kiss their asses? Well, they're nothing but a bunch of dirty little whores, and you know what that makes you. Let me go! Stop it, stop it!"

Apparently Donna was well-known at Jax, because there was scattered applause as the patrons became aware of what Bo was doing. The clapping grew to standing-ovation proportions as Bo reached the door, hauled Donna to her feet, and sent her outside with a boot to her backside.

But the wretched Bad Dog wouldn't go quietly. "I bet you lick their assholes!" she shrieked, just outside the bar. "I hope they shit in your mouth! Whores! You run around with—"

Bo heard a roaring noise behind her head, and white light flashed at the edges of her vision. She took two steps forward, grabbed Donna by the front of her shirt, and punched her in the mouth. "Where I come from, we don't talk that way to ladies who are paying for our drinks," she said, letting her opponent crumple to the pavement. "You've lost. Go home."

Reid pulled up to the curb, three bags of ice held across the back of her seat with bungee cords. She undid the cords and threw a bag of ice at Bo. "Help me get these inside," she told her, stomping into the bar. She gave Donna one unpitying glance. "Have a little trouble, did we?"

"No trouble," said Bo. The ice felt good against the split knuckles of her right hand. She let Reid walk ahead of her, afraid Donna would rush both of them. But when the disgraced dog got up, she kept herself pointed in the opposite direction, as if Bo were a bad smell she was determined to ignore. She took some change out of her pocket and headed for a pay phone across the street.

Inside, Killer, Crash, and Poison took the bag of ice away from Bo and practically heaved it across the bar at Kat. "You're hurt!" Crash said, cradling Bo's battered fist.

"We could have taken care of that rowdy little jerk ourselves," Poison muttered.

"Yeah, but why should we have to?" Killer smiled. "We have a much bigger and better dog taking care of us now. A pit bull, I think. Do you feel like a pit bull, Bo?"

From behind the bar, Kat gave Bo a thumbs-up. "What the hell is going on here?" Reid grouched. "I leave you alone for twenty minutes and World War III breaks out. One of these days somebody in this lunatic asylum is going to hurt you, Kat, and I'm going to have to—"

"Page Charley," Killer told Poison. "Let's take our baby home."

"We'll find out how you like your red hanky when it's on the other side," Crash promised, pressing into Bo's side. Her perfume made Bo dizzy. She wished to hell she knew what that red hanky meant, but after finally getting this lucky, she wasn't about to ask.

Sᴸɪᴘᴘɪɴɢ

■ ■

A gay man tells me that he thinks lesbians have AIDS envy. It makes him impatient when women talk about safer sex because it isn't really a problem for us. We are, he thinks, just trying to jump on the bandwagon.

■ ■

I am in Cynthia's kitchen. I have to swallow some aspirin. I take a glass full of water off the table. "That's mine," she says, warning me. "I just drank out of it."

"I know. I don't care."

This is our ritual. When we eat sushi, I dip my tekka maki in her sauce. I steal slices of ginger off her plate. "Don't worry," I tell her, "I don't have a cold. You won't catch anything."

She is my friend. Once she was my lover. She has AIDS. I will not let her drift beyond the world of human touch.

■ ■

I am holding a dental dam over my cunt. It is too wide and not long enough. The rubber sticks to my pubic hair, and when I move the dam around, trying to stretch it tight over my clit, it pulls out a few of my hairs. The woman who is going down on me through the dam is my lover, but we're not getting along. I will have to move out soon. She won't get a job, and I'm tired of paying the rent. This is not sex; it is an experiment. She sucks on my clit, which I hate, but it's the only kind of stroke I can feel through the dam. It reminds me of every bad fuck I've ever put up with in my life, the times I've lain there high and dry in the dark with somebody's mouth working on me, hating her for doing it, hating myself for not responding. When oral sex does work, it's sheer bliss, but I am never going to do this again.

I host sex parties for leatherwomen. Only safe sex is allowed. To make this easier, I put out gloves and dental dams and condoms. Before every party, I have to buy more condoms and gloves. But a year later, the original box of dental dams is still full. At least I'm not the only one.

■ ■

It's Monday. I'm having an argument with Michael, one of the gay men I work with. He's pissed because of an answer I gave somebody in my advice column. I told a reader that giving somebody a blowjob without a rubber was not safe. Michael had a date this weekend with his only steady trick, a man with a really big dick who loves getting sucked. Normally Michael is moody and touchy. Today he's happy, buoyant. He's been smiling all day — until he read my column, that is.

The argument makes me defensive. "I can't tell him to do something that will make him get sick," I protest.

"But a lot of cocksuckers aren't getting sick," Michael says stubbornly.

I start to say something about the long incubation period of AIDS, then I bite my tongue and leave the room. Michael doesn't go to the baths anymore. They've all been closed. He doesn't cruise the parks. He doesn't get fucked anymore. This is what he has left. It makes him happy. And the truth is that if he has a choice between sucking a bare cock and not having any sex at all, I'd rather he got down on his knees and swallowed come. And I hope for his sake that his trick has at least ten inches and comes in pints.

■ ■

When I first started reading pornography, I was afraid to go into adult bookstores. I bought the paperbacks that you find in regular bookstores under "A" for "Anonymous." Grove Press had reprinted *The Pearl*, a risqué Victorian magazine. At the time, I was in a monogamous relationship with somebody who did not want to have sex with me. *The Pearl* and my newly purchased vibrator were keeping me sane.

I loved all the descriptions of randy uncles plugging their nephews, decadent rakes seducing virgins in private dining rooms, and nuns copulating madly with each other and their father confessors. But there was so much misinformation about venereal disease and pregnancy! People were always employing odd methods of birth control — like douching right after sex — or telling each other they'd been sick last week but were just fine now. There were strange breaks in the narrative. All the female characters would leave England and go to Paris, have their babies, then come home and go straight to the next orgy.

It took me months to figure out why these passages were included. They were the authors' sometimes clumsy way of helping the reader to suspend disbelief, creating an atmosphere in which it was possible to believe that men and women actually felt free to have these ribald adventures. To me, they were anachronisms, but to the intended audience, they were a necessary antidote to perilous times.

Sex has always been a life-threatening experience. Sex has always been a high-risk activity. Because of the pill and penicillin, we forgot that for a little while. But for most of human history, people have had to close their eyes and hope they're lucky before they put it in or let somebody else stick it in.

The Victorian solution to this was to preach a single standard of chastity for men and women. But I have always been on the side of the whores and the rakes. The people who smoked opium, collected pornography, and had illegal abortions. The hustlers and the unfaithful wives. The sailors and their ladies. Colette's waltzing lesbians and passing women, and the street queens who always know everybody's dirty secrets.

■■

I read about the first lesbian case of AIDS in December of 1986. The letter in the *Journal of the American Medical Association* was curt and all the more frightening because it contained so little information. The *Village Voice* ran an article that included a few more personal details. One of the women was dead already. She'd been an intravenous-drug user, had sex with men. The implication was that she was a junkie and a whore. Her lover had ARC. She had not used drugs. She had sex (with condoms) with one bisexual man after getting involved with her female lover. So nobody called her an innocent victim. The two women, the *Village Voice* said coyly, had had "traumatic sex" that caused bleeding.

I wondered who those women were. How did they meet? Were they black, Latino, white, Asian, Native American? How long had they loved each other? Did they love each other? Who was taking care of the survivor? Did her family know? What the hell was "traumatic sex," anyway? It sounded suspiciously like something a doctor would say about my sex life. Did either of them own a leather jacket?

■ ■

On bad days, I don't think safe-sex education is working. I think a few gay men are using condoms, but most of them have just quit fucking. It's probably harder to get AIDS from sucking cock, but by now we've had so much bad news that I can't convince myself that it's safe.

Lesbians still don't believe that AIDS has anything to do with them. The best-educated dykes will grudgingly concede that the disease might be able to pass from one *woman* to another, but not from one *real lesbian* to another. We already knew that real lesbians don't have sex with men, for fun or for money. But because of AIDS, the pool of women-loving women, pussy-eating, cunt-fucking women who also qualify as "real lesbians" has grown even smaller. Real lesbians don't shoot drugs, share needles, or play sex games that expose them to somebody else's blood. We're all in twelve-step programs, but none of us are junkies. Real lesbians don't sleep with straight women or bisexual women. Real lesbians don't have heterosexual histories.

If a woman has AIDS, she must not be a real lesbian. She's not our problem. We can keep ourselves safe if we don't touch her.

It reminds me of the way good girls never talked to the girls who were easy in high school. As if it were a contagious condition. Girls who got pregnant just dropped out, even if they got married. As if they carried some deadly disease.

I remember the conversations I had with my gay male friends early on, when this disease was still being called "gay pneumonia." All of them wanted very much to believe that only the fist-fuckers were going to get sick.

■ ■

In the April 23, 1992, issue of the *Bay Area Reporter*, Bo Huston interviewed Sarah Schulman. She's had a lot to say about AIDS since the epidemic began. Some of the dykes I know call her "ACT-UP's Poster Girl." Huston asked her, "OK. This lesbian safe sex business. What is your position and why are people mad at you?"

She replied, "Well, it's complicated. Somebody in the lesbian community introduced this idea of dental dams, without any substantial discussion — scientific or social — about whether or not they were necessary. And because the community has historically behaved in a very faddish manner, people just went for it. And also because it really fit into a lot of people's shame about their sexuality.

"But the fact is, there isn't any evidence that HIV is transmitted through oral sex between women. And when you look at the four or five cases of women who claim that that was their mode of transmission, the stories don't work. There's always needles or men lurking in the background.

"But, secondly, even if you did have proof that HIV was transmitted through oral sex with women, dental dams have never been tested for efficacy. So we don't even really know if dental dams would inhibit the transmission. Yet people just went on the bandwagon with this thing, and created a climate in which to criticize it meant you were, quote, jeopardizing women's lives, unquote. ... If HIV could be spread by oral sex with women, straight men would be getting it, and they're not."

■■

Gay Men's Health Crisis doesn't like dental dams much either. I called their hotline several years ago, when I first heard dams could be used to make rimming or cunnilingus safe. The man who answered the phone said, "Oh, we don't recommend that people use them." When I asked him why not, he told me that one little square of latex wasn't going to prevent anybody from getting contaminated vaginal liquids in his (!) mouth because when women got excited, they began to secrete large quantities of fluid that just went *everywhere*.

Gay Men's Health Crisis has a brochure called "Women Loving Women." It advises us to "use latex gloves when masturbating" and tells us not to use "Plastics such as those used for ... household wraps" during oral sex because "Many of these materials also contain toxic chemicals." More toxic than HIV? They've produced one safe-sex audiovisual aid for lesbians, and I can imagine what Jean Carlomusto had to go through to persuade them to produce it. *Current Flow* is a great video that stars Annie Sprinkle and a very hot black dyke named Shara. It's also only five minutes long. A lot of dykes won't watch this movie because Annie Sprinkle is a porn star, and they don't think she has anything valid to say about their intimate relationships.

A San Francisco company that distributes sex-education films, Multi-Focus, has a 22-minute tape called *Latex and Lace* that's described in their catalog as a lesbian safer-sex movie. It features brief interviews with women who talk about AIDS and then shows some of them having a safer-sex orgy. None of them identify as lesbians. Lesbian safer-sex is never defined. Any educator who tried to use this film for a lesbian audience would first have to deal with the negative reactions to straight and bisexual women "pretending" to be lesbians for a sex movie, then cope with the audience's hostile response to the idea that lesbians could have public, anonymous sex with multiple partners.

The San Francisco AIDS Foundation has no movies about lesbians and safer sex. They do have a pamphlet, "AIDS ... and Lesbians," which has good information about cleaning needles, plastic wrap, and S/M. But I can't help thinking how many woman-hours have been donated to this organization and others like it. Seems to me we should get something in return besides five minutes of videotape and two pamphlets.

■■

In 1987, Dr. Margaret Fischl at the University of Miami reported that 119 women with AIDS survived for an average of 6.6 months after diagnosis, compared with an average of 12 to 14 months for men with AIDS. She said, "AIDS in women may be a different disease." In 1992, the Centers for Disease Control still refuse to make official a new definition of AIDS that would include the pelvic and vaginal infections that are unique to HIV-infected women as criteria for an AIDS diagnosis.

■■

Lesbians know why gay men get AIDS. It's a natural consequence of male selfishness and dirtiness and violence. A hard cock has no conscience. Men just want to be able to stick their hard dicks any place they feel like it. They have no sense of responsibility toward their partners — or themselves. They can't think past an orgasm to its consequences.

Every dyke knows that semen is dirty and vaginas are clean. Menstrual blood can't be equated with the blood in a dirty syringe or scum in a queer boy's butt. If we are at risk — if this clean community of young, attractive, feminist women has been contaminated by a foul male disease — it's because I and women like me have encouraged other dykes to imitate men. We've encouraged promiscuity, S/M, bisexuality, drug use, working in the sex industry.

Of course, all this stuff was happening before, but those goddamned leather dykes have insisted on talking about it, and once you label something, you have to admit it's going on. You have to admit that lesbians are not exempt from giving each other chlamydia, herpes, trichomoniasis, hepatitis, even AIDS. You have to talk about the sweaty, messy stuff that lesbian solidarity is based upon — the sound of bellies slapping together in the dark, the taste another woman leaves under your tongue, scrubbing shit out from under your fingernails, the mean way women sometimes have of saying no just because you really do want them, taking her tampon out with your teeth, wondering if buying a sex toy will save your marriage or make her finally leave you, thinking about somebody else while she makes you come, wondering how much longer it's going to take to make her come, getting wet just because she looked at you.

The essential ingredients of lust are awkward and embarrassing, and they remain the same whether you are into leather, vanilla, cherry, chocolate, or some other flavor of lesbian sex. There is no such thing as a sexual encounter in which you don't have to deal with power as well as germs. It's interesting that the girls who are into exchanging power are the ones who are the least likely to be exchanging viruses. If she has handcuffs on her belt, chances are she has some gloves in her pocket. Prophylactic paraphernalia has become a new signifier for S/M. In the larger lesbian community, if you ask somebody how she feels about safer sex, chances are good she also expects you to ask if you can tie her up. Women who refuse to talk to S/M dykes don't seem to want to talk to each other about AIDS. They would rather pretend it is somebody else's problem. No wonder they don't want leather dykes at the Michigan Womyn's Music Festival. But, like New York City, vanilla dykes are quickly running out of places to put the trash.

■■

Cynthia is in the hospital. I know she is never going to leave. This is the second time she has had pneumonia. She has tubes in her arm. She has tubes in her nose, and I don't want to think about where they go after that. I have talked to the people who hold her medical power of attorney. I have insisted that they stop giving her nutrition and antibiotics. I have insisted that they increase her pain medication. Her boyfriend has accused me of "starving her to death." I keep reminding everyone that it's AIDS that is killing her.

The nurse comes in to brush her teeth. She puts mouthwash on a little pink sponge that's stuck on a stick. Then she runs the sponge between Cynthia's gum and her lip. Cynthia doesn't like it. It hurts her. She tries to turn her head, but she is too doped up to be able to prevent it. Then a technician comes in to take her blood. They want to monitor the levels of the drugs in her bloodstream. She isn't even conscious, but she tries to pull her hand away. I will always be ashamed because I let them brush her teeth and stick her finger to take her blood. What possible difference can it make now? Why can't I be more of a bitch and spare her these petty annoyances?

Her skin is so dry. I take lotion out of the drawer by her bed. I put it on her shoulders, but there's still some left over, so my hands spread it lower down. I have a flash of lesbian paranoia. There is only a curtain between me and the nurse's station. What if the nurses see me fondling this woman's breasts? Then I stifle my fear. If Cynthia could drag my naked ass to parties where dozens of gay men were hanging in slings waiting to get fisted, I can damned well do this for her.

I put lotion on her breasts, her stomach, her thighs. I try not to disturb the catheter. I even put lotion on her feet. It seems to calm her down.

A few weeks ago, she was flirting with me. She wanted to get together and play. I said no, having had too much experience with the way a date with Cynthia turned into a relationship overnight. She was a sarcastic and critical bottom, and I had gotten enough bad reviews from her when I was her lover. She was living with a man who paid her rent and kept her fed and kept her company at night. They weren't having sex. She was contemptuous of him and terrified that he would leave her. I wanted to stay out of the whole fucking mess.

Besides, there wasn't much she could do. She didn't want to get beaten anymore. She had almost no energy. It was hard for her to get fisted. I have always reserved tender sex, the fantasy games about dominance and submission, for my lovers. The games I play with tricks are rougher, physically heavier, easier on the heart and head.

Do I have to tell you that I wish now I had been able to imagine an evening for her, some way to enchant and dazzle her? I doubt I would have succeeded. Real sex always disappointed Cynthia. But it would make me feel better now to know I tried.

■■

In September of 1991, a study of 379 heterosexual couples in San Francisco in which one partner was HIV-positive and the other was not found that the virus moves from men to women during sex far more easily than it moves from women to men. Unprotected heterosexual intercourse is at least seventeen times more dangerous for women than for men. Nancy Padian, lead author of the study and an assistant professor of epidemiology at the University of California at San Francisco, told the press that she was afraid some heterosexual men would interpret the results of her study to mean they could stop using condoms.

A year later, police are still busting sex workers and giving them mandatory HIV-antibody tests. Newspapers are still whipping the public up about Typhoid Mary hookers who are so irresponsible or drug-addicted that they infect their customers. Nobody busts the clients — who are, after all, the ones who have to wear the condoms if prostitutes are not going to get infected. And nobody studies johns to find out why they think it's okay to give their wives and children AIDS.

I guess the results of this study should make me feel better. It would certainly seem to indicate that it's less dangerous to have sex with an HIV-positive woman than with an HIV-positive man. But a low risk is not the same thing as no risk. If women can pass HIV on to their male partners during sex, I believe they can pass it on to me.

■■

An ex-lover in Alaska writes to me, "Everyone here tells me that you died of AIDS two years ago." Then she goes on with her news — where she's working, who she's sleeping with. I can't see the letter; I can only see red.

Last week I went to San Francisco for the International Ms. Leather contest. I had lost some weight. People noticed. I expected compliments. Instead, I got anxious phone calls. "Are you sick?" Are they really disappointed when I say no, or am I just indulging in paranoia?

■ ■

When I did research for my lesbian sex manual, *Sapphistry*, in the midseventies, none of the doctors I talked to, including lesbian physicians, thought gay women had to worry about VD. I went out on a limb and wrote the chapter on sexually transmitted diseases anyway. The publisher didn't want to include it. Today it's pretty common knowledge that women can give each other just about any STD. But there are still "experts" who claim that AIDS is not on that list. Why? Dr. Charles Schable of the Centers for Disease Control told a reporter at *Visibilities* that "Lesbians don't have much sex." Well! I'm sure we don't have much sex with *him.*

The fact is that the CDC don't know whether lesbians are at risk for AIDS or not because they don't bother to ask. They don't keep track of us. Despite the absence of any official statistics on lesbians, we've still been able to determine that at least 100 women with AIDS in the CDC's files have reported having sex with other women. Nearly 700 out of 5,000 women's sexual preferences couldn't be categorized because there wasn't enough information on the report forms. The CDC are unable to determine how 23 percent of the women with AIDS became infected. Wouldn't we be a lot more upset if one-fourth of the men who had AIDS became ill for an unknown reason?

Every lesbian health worker I've ever talked to knows or has treated dykes who have AIDS. Many of them die in the closet. Two women I once knew in New York suddenly disappeared. They stopped coming to public functions and quit seeing their friends. Years later, I heard a rumor that one of them had died of AIDS. They were afraid of anybody finding out because the sick woman thought she would lose all her medical benefits from work. The surviving partner is socially active once more, but she refuses to discuss her partner's death. I wonder if she's having safe sex with her new girlfriend.

■ ■

By my bed, I keep bottles of water-based lubricant, a box of rubber gloves, and Trojans, the brand preferred by lesbians because everybody is allergic to nonoxynol-9, and who wants to put a dildo down your throat that has a lubricated condom on it? The rule is that I will always use latex barriers with tricks. I will have unsafe sex only with my lovers, and then only if we both test HIV-negative.

In fact, I hardly ever bring people home anymore. I tell myself it's because I can't deal with the emotional complications. It's easier to keep casual sex partners separate from my lovers if I only have casual sex in public. When I do scenes with people at parties, I usually don't fuck them. I tell myself it's because I don't want them to expect the scene to turn into a relationship. So I wind up using maybe six gloves a year. And suddenly I have a lot more women in my life whom I consider my lovers.

One of my girlfriends calls me to bitch about her slave, Ricki. She just found out that Ricki has been letting her drug dealer — a man who has AIDS — screw her. They are not using condoms. "What do you care?" I say. "You've been using gloves with her, haven't you?" There's no answer. "Haven't you?" I insist.

No, they have not. My lover and I start having that old argument about whether or not you can get AIDS from putting your hand in somebody's cunt or in somebody's ass. I accuse her of not caring about me, of being indiscriminate, careless, stupid. I scream at her that she has to go get tested right away, and I hang up on her.

I should be ashamed of myself. The whole thing is stupid. An HIV-antibody test won't fix this. She hasn't done anything with Ricki that I didn't do with my other girlfriends. Do I really think romance will protect me? I'm glad I moved to Los Angeles, where there's nobody I want to have sex with anyway. I haven't written any porn for a year, and I don't care. It's not real fiction anyway. It doesn't matter. Nobody will miss it. Just like I don't miss sex.

■ ■

A year after Cynthia's death, the mixed-gender S/M organization that she founded, the Society of Janus, asked its membership to vote on whether they should require safe sex at their parties. After bitter debate, the majority voted not to "force" members to have safer sex at Janus events because AIDS isn't an issue for heterosexuals.

■ ■

A gay male friend who sees the latex stash by my bed tells me sadly, "Gee, I was really hoping that you girls were still carrying on without having to worry about bagging it. I guess I thought if the party was over for us, somebody was still having a good time." I try to tell him I'm still having a good time, but he doesn't want to hear it. The details about what I do with my pussy or anybody else's pussy make him queasy.

■ ■

When I start telling friends that my new lover has a chronic, debilitating disease of unknown origin, which her doctor will eventually label chronic fatigue immune dysfunction syndrome, many of them advise me to leave her. "Think what a negative impact it will have on the rest of your life," they say. The same friends would be absolutely scathing if two men broke up because one of them could not deal with his boyfriend's AIDS diagnosis.

There are days when my lover is in so much pain and so disoriented that she can't get out of bed and go to the bathroom by herself. We have a running joke about waiting for our Shanti volunteer and our free bag of groceries. But soon we realize that most of our gay male friends have dropped us. I think it's because we are no longer on the list of potential caretakers. The joke isn't funny anymore.

I have become progressively more angry about gay men's ignorance about women's sexuality, bodies, and health issues. I have started talking about the fact that breast cancer is an epidemic. People think I am a crazy separatist. And of course that's the very worst thing you can be — a woman who puts other women first. But I am tired of taking care of men who have no idea what I do to get off, what my other passions might be, why reproductive rights are important, or what I do when I am not picking up their laundry, giving them medicine, or cleaning up their puke.

I have stopped going to AIDS benefits unless the money is earmarked to provide services to women. I even tell one of my gay male friends that if he gets AIDS now, he has no excuse, and I am not going to take care of him. I can't tell if I'm just depressed and burned-out, or if I really mean it.

■ ■

In January of 1989, the *New England Journal of Medicine* published a letter from two doctors in Massachusetts about a sixty-year-old man, rendered impotent by diabetes, who seroconverted after having oral sex with an HIV-infected prostitute. He said he'd never had a homosexual encounter, done IV drugs, or even had a blood transfusion. He'd never gone down on her when she was bleeding.

I wonder what Sarah Schulman has to say about this case — that needles and men are lurking in the background?

■■

When I use gloves, when I keep my mouth off somebody's cunt, I feel virtuous the next day. I'm relieved. I can't quite believe I managed to behave myself. But it reminds me too much of the way I used to feel when I believed masturbation was a sin, and I managed to quit (in the middle of raging adolescent hormone storms) for a week or even ten whole days.

I can tell myself it's not the same thing. Safer sex is not a form of prudery. It's not based on hatred of the body, on aversion to bodily fluids, on a fear of sex. I tell myself and I tell myself, but my tongue does not believe what my brain believes. My hand does not believe what my brain believes. I need what lies beyond the barrier.

It took me so many years to understand that I wanted to put my tongue in between another woman's legs. Years more to learn how to do it well enough to make her want to keep me there. When I put my face between my lover's broad thighs, I am hungry for the smell and taste of lesbian desire, and I am making her a promise that what we do with each other is real, it matters, our bodies are valuable and beautiful. I am the kind of girl who prefers to swallow it. It is affirmation and salvation. Sex without that salty taste makes me lonely.

It took me years to believe that my hand working in a woman's cunt could make her come, really satisfy her; years more to be able to strap on a dildo and fuck the way men fuck with a dyke's knowledge of where the hot spots inside a woman's body lie, how the passage inside her ass curves, and how to search out her cries, her wild movements, her desperation and her fulfillment. I want that slickness between my thumb and forefinger, I want the palpable evidence of my prowess to make my hand wet to the wrist.

■■

In the Spring 1991 issue of *Lesbian Contradiction*, Beth Elliott published an article entitled "Does Lesbian Sex Transmit AIDS? G.E.T. R.E.A.L.!" The acronym stands for "Getting Empowered to Re-Educate the Anti-Lesbian." According to Elliott, being anti-lesbian means saying that lesbian sex transmits the AIDS virus. Elliott believes this is "a fable invested with an aura of fact, like the story of the poodle in the microwave." If gay men "have re-opened sex clubs, complete with glory holes, on the theory that fellatio is safe," she wants to know why AIDS activists are telling women to use dental dams during cunnilingus. She believes that "pressuring lesbians to identify with AIDS" is an attempt "to replace lesbian feminism with a forcibly-integrated community in which lesbians play the traditional female role." She adds, "Lesbians are cooperating, but getting no more respect than in the past. Whether from guilt or our upbringing as caregivers we have been uncharacteristically silent while losing our lesbian identity. To the general public, we are just like gay men in lifestyle, AIDS risk and sexuality. We are no longer lesbians: we are now Mrs. Homosexual. And our rights are at risk because the best weapon against AIDS backlash lesbians and gay men have — the reality of lesbian lives — is something gay men do not want to face."

When Risa Denenberg wrote an article in the Summer 1991 issue of *Out/Look*, "We Shoot Drugs, and We are Your Sisters," Elliott responded in a letter to the editor, "Giving IV drug users the message that their behavior and culture are welcome in a community aiming to support, empower and validate women ... is a very bad idea. ... Denenberg doesn't care one bit about lesbians and the women's community."

■■

I overhear a conversation in the hallway at work. "Daniel's HIV-positive," somebody says smugly. Just passing by.

"Well," is the tart reply, "I guess we all know what *she's* been up to now!"

There is no compassion in these voices. I happen to know that one of the men talking already has KS.

■■

Suppose it's true that sexual transmission of HIV from one woman to another is practically nonexistent. Suppose it's true that every lesbian who is HIV-positive got the virus because she had unprotected sex with men or shared needles. What should these women do now — stop having sex? Who thinks it would be safe to put her hand inside one of these women without a glove? Would you put your tongue on her? Would you do it if she was having her period?

Would it help her, do you think, to be told that she is part of a community that has historically behaved in a very faddish manner? Do you think she needs to know that a dental dam really fits into a lot of people's shame about their sexuality? Would her girlfriend be comforted by the information that dental dams have never been tested for efficacy? Do you think at that point that either of them really gives a damn how this disease entered their lives?

Queer Nation girls would hit the streets if the government started rounding up HIV-infected men and shipping them to quarantine camps. But how many of us are doing anything about the invisible quarantine that exists around the bodies of bisexual and lesbian women who have AIDS?

Maybe the handful of dykes who have AIDS are like the handful of men who had PCP in the seventies. Maybe they represent the tip of the iceberg, and ten years from now we will be sorry we didn't anticipate a deluge of lesbian AIDS cases. Maybe not. Maybe there will always be only a few women who have AIDS who want to have sex with and love other women.

There isn't enough money to go around to fight this disease. So is it okay if a dozen women a year die in isolation, and possibly infect others because they don't know any better? How about two dozen? Two hundred? A few thousand? What's an acceptable cutoff point before we divert resources to prevent this tragedy? What's the bottom line? Does it make a difference if these women don't speak English as their first language? If they are not white? What if they don't call themselves lesbians? Do they have to be in recovery? What if they have children? Maybe they want to have more children. Maybe they used to be hustlers. Maybe they still turn tricks.

It's confusing. It would be so much simpler to think about these issues if women would just be consistent, have simple identities, and stop behaving in complex ways that are affected by their culture and their need to survive. What we need is a little more monogamy and purity and all the other virtues of the white middle class. Including the money. Most of all, we could use the money.

■ ■

I have someone stretched underneath me. Her hands are tied. I have cut her back, and I suppose I could pretend that I don't intend to put my mouth on the wound I've just made. But this is not an ornamental cut — an orchid, a whip, a snake. It is utilitarian, two short lines that cross each other at right angles. It delays the clotting of blood, which wells up thick as tar, a bead of perfect scarlet. Any second now, it will break and run. It will be wasted.

I have my cock up her ass. The smell, the sounds of ass-fucking are all around me. My hands are wet with sweat and lube. I'm going to come soon, and I put my face down to her back and bite the skin around the cut so the blood spurts into my mouth.

The sight of blood makes most people sick. It means there's an injury, pain, maybe even the possibility of death. But I can smell a woman who is bleeding across a crowded room. I bleed myself every month. I'm not afraid of it. The sight of someone else's blood, my own blood, makes me shake with excitement. It is life. Shedding it and sharing it is the ultimate violation and intimacy for me.

I try to fend off the moment when I have to drink it. I will not cut anybody. Or I will just cut myself. I appreciate my own pain, enjoy the adrenaline it takes to slice my own skin, but my own blood has no taste. So I have to take this need to someone else. But I will just smear it on my skin, my face, where I can smell it, but it isn't in my mouth. If I have to drink it, I'll take it out with a syringe and squirt it into brandy to kill the virus.

But this is tonight; this is urgent. It's been too long. This is something I have to have. I drink with the intensity of a newborn child.

If I get sick tomorrow, will you feel any compassion for me?

■ ■

A friend of mine says, "Even if I can't catch AIDS from my tricks, I don't want to catch any of the little things either. There's no cure for herpes, and it's unbelievably painful. Later for that. Check the pockets of my jacket. I always carry lube and rubber."

■ ■

When I confess that my track record with safer sex is less than perfect, I'm not trying to tell everyone to throw away their condoms. I haven't thrown away my gloves. Someday I'll even try those goddamned dental dams again. Maybe it would make a difference if I used them with somebody I wasn't about to break up with. Maybe Saranwrap doesn't pull your short hairs out. At least it's transparent.

Most of us are doing the best we can, trying to scrape through this epidemic with as much of our libidos and our sanity as we can rescue. Some of us are celibate. I think of those folks as being shell-shocked by the sex wars. Some of us deliberately do stupid things — like the man I know who won't use condoms because he always pulls out before he comes, and he firmly believes there is no HIV in precome. Or the johns who won't use rubbers with prostitutes. Or the dykes who think they can keep themselves safe by avoiding women in high-risk categories. Some of us know what we should do, we do it most of the time, and sometimes we slip.

We slip because the condition of being aroused creates moisture. Hazardous footing. Melts boundaries. Makes the edges fuzzy. Creates immediate needs that overwhelm our ability to plan for the future. I know I should scold you, punish myself, there probably ought to be a law.

Think about that. No. No. There should not be a law. The desire itself is always honorable. Always. Even if it carries unwelcome microbes along with it, like a Helms amendment riding on a budget bill. Never be sorry that you know what sex tastes like. Never be sorry that you have touched another human being intimately, drawn a part of them into your body. It is worth the price.

I think we must paraphrase that saying about a hard cock having no conscience. When the sexual flesh is hard, engorged, it has no conscience. Gender is not the determining factor. Most of us know only one or two ways to get off. Most of us have a hard time finding somebody we desire who is also able and willing to get us off. There are so many barriers between us — money, time, fear, age, race, violence, shame, inhibition, ignorance. Nobody wants another barrier. It's no wonder that a piece of latex doesn't look like protection. It doesn't look like freedom from anxiety. It looks like another obstacle, another wall we have to break through if we are ever going to inhabit our bodies like free ecstatic animals.

Sex has always been a high-risk activity. I continue to struggle to make it as safe as I possibly can. But I can't lie to myself and pretend that I haven't given something up. And sometimes I just can't make myself believe that the bargain is worth it. And then I slip. When I slip, I do things that endanger my life. But I also find the hope I need to go on compromising, struggling, doing without, and getting by.

Alyson Publications publishes a wide variety of books with gay and lesbian themes. For a free catalog, or to be placed on our mailing list, please write to:
Alyson Publications
P.O. Box 4371
Los Angeles, CA 90078
Indicate whether you are interested in books for lesbians, gay men, or both.